George Jacob Holyoake

Sixty Years of an Agitator's Life

Vol. 2

George Jacob Holyoake

Sixty Years of an Agitator's Life
Vol. 2

ISBN/EAN: 9783337094768

Printed in Europe, USA, Canada, Australia, Japan

Cover: Foto ©Andreas Hilbeck / pixelio.de

More available books at **www.hansebooks.com**

SIXTY YEARS

OF AN

AGITATOR'S LIFE

BY

GEORGE JACOB HOLYOAKE

AUTHOR OF "HISTORY OF CO-OPERATION"; "SELF-HELP 100 YEARS AGO";
"TRIAL OF THEISM," ETC.

"In order to become acquainted with an age or a people we must also
know something of its second-rate and obscure men. It is in
the beliefs, sentiments, and lot of unimportant individuals
and unknown families, that the lot, the sentiments, and the beliefs of the country
are to be found."—GUIZOT

VOLUME II

SIXTH IMPRESSION

T. FISHER UNWIN

LONDON   LEIPSIC
ADELPHI TERRACE   INSELSTRASSE 20

1909

CONTENTS OF PART II.

CHAPTER LXVI.

CHAPTER LXXXVIII.

CHAPTER CX.

CHAPTER CXI.

CHAPTER CXII.

[All these 112 chapters, save three, are revised from the *Newcastle Weekly Chronicle*, 1891–2. The new chapters are "Famous Fights," "Murder Considered as a Mode of Progress," and "Reporting Speeches which Never were Made."]

CHAPTER LVIII.

UNSUSPECTED SPIES.

(1855.)

Spies are of two classes—those in the pay of despotism, and those who watch and report upon the proceedings of the enemies of the people. The vocation of the spy is at best a repulsive pursuit. Deceit, false pretences, and treachery constitute the capital of the business, and its success is the success of a traitor. In war it has its only justification. Where murder is the object of both sides, treachery does not count ; it may abridge, or prevent, worse disasters. But in peace it is doing evil that good may come, and introduces baseness into policy. In avowed war the spy of a forlorn hope of a patriotic cause is a pathetic figure. He lives under a double suspicion, and his life is in peril at the hands of foe and friend. He is killed if discovered by the enemy, and he often shares the same fate from his friends, who suspect him from observing his intercourse with the foe. Bound by his mission of secrecy and peril, he is unable to explain himself to any who may be ignorant by whose instruction he acts. And when he succeeds in what he has undertaken, he may find that those to whom he looked for defence and honour may have themselves perished in the same conflict before his dangerous undertaking is over.

The spies of which I write are the venal and baser sort. Some of them do not restrict themselves to discovering plots, but devise them and seduce men to engage in them, in order to betray them.

One of these was Edwards, the spy of Fleet Street, who was employed to prevent the publication of Thomas Paine's works, by finding out the persons engaged in their secret issue, or, failing that, to implicate Richard Carlile in some plot by which he might be got rid of. Edwards, under which name this spy went, was a clever man, who took a room opposite Carlile's shop, professing to be a sculptor, an art for which he had talent. Avowing great sympathy with Carlile's intrepid efforts for freeing the press, and not less admiration for the author of "The Rights of Man," he made a statue of Paine in proof of his sincerity, and presented it to Carlile, who made it one of the ornaments of his shop. The statue is now an ornament in one of the ancient halls of Northumberland. Edwards did not succeed with Carlile, who had such plentiful experience with Government prosecutions as to have vigilant suspicion of all overtures from strangers.

There were several spies in the pay of the Government in the Chartist agitation of 1839. They attended at the meetings of the Chartist Union, whose leaders were against physical force and sought the extension of the suffrage by moral means. These spies sent to congenial papers reports of venomous speeches which were never made, leading the public to regard the speakers as wild and dangerous insurgents. The *Morning Chronicle* was one of the papers open to these reporters. One morning a leader appeared saying—" If the ruffianly language held at the Snow Hill meeting on Friday night—language so foul, so flagitious [which was never uttered], that we reluctantly sullied our columns with expressions which reflect scandal upon an assembly of Englishmen, and are calculated to bring the privilege of free discussion itself into odium and disgrace— if such 'open and advised speaking' is to pass with impunity, then truly the law is a dead letter, and the Government deserves all the contempt with which it is assailed."

The *Morning Chronicle* described two meetings held at Farringdon Hall, Snow Hill, as "Chartist and Irish Confederate gatherings." They had been neither. They were called by the Co-operative League, a body bent more on social reform than political agitation. The meeting, on Friday night, stated to have been held at the " King's Arms " Tavern, Snow Hill, was held in Farringdon Hall, a building quite distinct from the tavern. It was stated that several of the Foot Guards were there. Only one was present, and he in undress uniform. Mr. Ewen was announced as chairman. The chairman was Mr. Youll. Mr. Walter, reported to have seconded the resolution, was Mr. Cooper ; and an indecent expression attributed to Mr. Shorter was never uttered by him. It was stated, also, that the Co-operative League was under the auspices of Douglas Jerrold and William Howitt, who were never seen or heard of in connection with the body. These facts were made known at the time, but with little effect.

About that period there was a small black man bearing the absurd name of Cuffy—a name, however derived or acquired, he foolishly retained, though continually ridiculed by adversaries because of the appellation. He was about the stature of George Odgers, who, many will remember, was once nearly elected member for Southwark. Cuffy was a victim of spy machinations, and was transported. His name contributed to convict him, yet he was an honest, well-conducted man, and much sympathy was felt for him. Mr. Cobden showed him respect by employing Mrs. Cuffy in some domestic office in his household.

The favourite and most successful device of the spies was to advise "speaking out." Their cry was, " The time has come to let the Government know what men think ! " Measured and reasonable speech, calculated to impress power without irritating it, was described " as mealy-mouthedness," and men were sent to meetings to applaud, on a secret signal, any outrage of speech by which both speaker and meeting were made to compromise the cause advocated, and justify the repression by force and prosecution, which " friends of order " were always ready to counsel. Their policy was to alarm the timid, who knew nothing of the facts, by a terror which did not exist, and who therefore gave their vote for "strong measures" for exterminating a small struggling party with right and misfortune on their side. Then there would appear among the Radicals a plausible person affecting to burn with patriotic indignation, and professing to have military and chemical knowledge which he would place at their service. By judiciously giving a subscription to their fund, which he represented as coming from persons who did not wish to be known, he acquired confidence, and created the impression that there were powerful persons in the background willing to aid, provided a blow was struck which would " prove to the Government that the people were in earnest." One of these knaves produced an explosive liquid, which he said could be poured into the sewers, and, being ignited, would blow up London from below. This satanic preparation was tried in a cellar in Judd Street, while I was taking tea in the back parlour above. I did not know at the time of the operation going on below, or it might have interfered with my satisfaction in the repast on which I was engaged.

Another person induced to join in this subterranean plot was a young enthusiast, who had impetuosity without experience, and who was afterwards the subject of many friendly attentions from a Conservative peer. The enthusiast is still living, and there is no reason to suppose that he was not an honest man. He was the type of the men, ardent without foresight, who come into this lumbering, slow-moving world, and are indignant that it does not mend its ways all at once. Their honourable but uninstructed ardour is the material upon which a treacherous spy selects to work. The two spies I next describe were of a superior class. I had personal communication with them extending over several years.

One went under the name of André, a suspicious name, for Washington hanged one of the family. This André was as fat as a Frenchman could be. He was handsome, literally smooth-faced, and mellow ; he was quite globular, and when he moved he vibrated like a locomotive jelly. His speech was as soft as his skin. He had an unaffected suavity of manner, and an accent of honesty and enthusiasm which entirely beguiled you, save for a certain vagueness of statement which warned you to wait for its interpretation in action before you entirely trusted it. He had large commercial views with an indefinite outline, a faculty for finance proposals difficult to fathom, and an instinct for the friendship of men who, possessing money, had philanthropic aspirations without business experience. He first appeared as the friend and counsellor of a group of generous-minded disciples of Professor Maurice, who became known as Christian Socialists. When they became interested in the organization and the extension of co-operation, his subtle penetration enabled him to see that a business agency might be founded in London for the supply of stores. There was then no Wholesale Buying Society such as that afterwards founded in the North, and which has attained great magnitude. Premises were taken in Charlotte Street, Fitzroy Square, which became costly by the alterations made for the transaction of wholesale business before there existed stores sufficiently numerous to support the agency created for serving them. The antecedents of André, so far as they were known, were calculated to inspire confidence in him. When a young man, he was one of the enthusiastic followers of St. Simon, in Paris, distinguished for intrepidity and devotion in their cause, and he had created a strong impression by his eloquence and propagandist fervour. It was difficult to conceive that a rotund gentleman of luxurious habits could ever have been an ardent apostle ; but, with all his soft obesity, he had the energy of Count Fosco, whom Wilkie Collins has depicted in his "Woman in White," and, like that energetic hero, was not unacquainted with secret conspiracies. When Enfantin and other leading St. Simonians sought effacement, he sought employment—without delicacy or scruple as to the nature of it. He came to England on a political mission devised by the conspirators of the Empire. He was, I believe, an agent in the purchase of the *Morning Chronicle* in the interest of the French usurper, but this was unknown to the gentlemen of the party with whom he connected himself. His business here was that of a spy of the Empire.

The better to effect this object, and to justify his secret employment, it was necessary that he could prove his acquaintance with insurgent parties in England, and his connection with so respectable a body of social agitators as the disciples of Mr. Maurice not only ensured him from suspicion, but afforded him the means of influencing popular opinion in favour of his political paymaster. He became acquainted with famous Chartist leaders, and, as I was personally acquainted with the friends of Mazzini and Garibaldi, he showed me many acts of courtesy.

At that time Christian Socialists were generously promoting
the interests of working men and desirous of establishing
co-operative workshops. As many of these existed in France,
and many were subsequently subsidised by the Emperor with a
view to making the Empire popular with working men, André,
who had been among them, had precisely that kind of knqw-
ledge useful to gentlemen who honestly thought that working
men would become more interested in Christianity if they were
better cared for, and a considerable fortune was expended by
one of the most generous of the party, Mr. E. V. Neale, in
establishing co-operative workshops. They did not sufficiently
appreciate that the elevation of the working men can only be
affected by education within, rather than from without, and
that their training is most sure when they employ and risk
their own capital. Working men may be aided in their efforts,
but they quickliest acquire prudence when they peril their own
money as well as that of others.

André inspired me with a feeling of friendliness towards him
which has never left me. He was the greatest artist in espionage of any spy I have known. He never asked me for any
information which would have awakened suspicion in me, but
he gave me opportunities of mentioning things. As, however,
my habit was to consider as their own the affairs of others in
which I was in any way concerned, I never added to André's
political knowledge, but I have no doubt he knew how to turn
his acquaintance with me to his private professional advantage,
and in ways of which I was unconscious.

As I had never seen Oxford, and had a great desire to learn
something of its interior life, André had penetration enough to
see that a visit there would be agreeable to me. He had a
personal interest in influencing the Dean of Oriel as a subscriber
to the capital of a new business project of his own, which he
called by the well-chosen title of the " Universal Purveyor."
The Dean, like many other excellent Christians, believed that
the neglect of the social condition of the people was the cause
of popular alienation from Christianity. It never occurred to
them that its evidences were defective, and that the alienation
the Christian deplored arose in most minds from difficulties it
presented to the understanding. The interest I took in any
proposal of theirs tending to infuse morality into trade, giving the

workmen participation in the profit of his industry, appeared
to them to proceed from growing reconcilement to church
tenets, especially as I openly honoured and worked willingly
with any Christian person who would render help in this direction. André knew how to colour that action with theological
hope. Accordingly, he took me down to Oxford, where I
became for awhile the guest of the Rev. Charles Marriott,
then Dean of Oriel. I then saw Oxford for the first time, and
the happy days I stayed there will always dwell in my memory.
The rooms occupied by Mr. Ward, who afterwards became a
convert to Rome, were entered through the Dean's chambers,
and when we were dining Mr. Ward would sometimes have
occasion to pass through. Only once, when he was entering,
did I catch a glimpse of his florid face and well-fed figure, so
different from Mr. Marriott, who was pallid, thin, and gentle in
speech and manners. As Mr. Ward passed through, he carried
his hat on the side of his face—a delicate consideration, so that
Mr. Marriott's guests might not be under conscious observation.
I thought it betokened a gentlemanly instinct, but it also
prevented us from observing him.

One day Mr. Marriott conducted me round several of the
colleges, showing me things he thought might interest me, and
we discoursed on the way on matters of opinion. I told him
that I did not share the confidence he had in the premises of his
faith, though desiring as much as himself to know the will
of Deity, and to do it when I did know it. I was restrained by
the difficulty I had of knowing what the Infinite Will might
be, except through the works of nature and the necessity of
justice, truth and kindness in society. I remember he paused
in his walk, and, turning to me, said : " Mr. Holyoake, I would
rather reason with a thinking atheist than with a Dissenting
minister. I find the minister has always a little infallibility of
his own which you can never reach ; while the atheist, who
proceeds upon reason, is open to reason, and there is a common
ground upon which evidence can operate."

By this time much of the wealth of the Christian Socialists had
been dissipated. André appeared alone as the projector of the
Universal Purveyor. His prospectuses were models of plausi-
bility and just sentiments, of which the only thing certain was
the expensiveness of putting them into practice. As I approved

of his professed object, he had a right to count on my aid ; but he sought it in a form for which I was unprepared. It was that I should put my name to a bill for him to negotiate in the City to meet some immediate requirement of his business. I explained to him the rule on which I acted in such cases, which was never to put my name to a bill unless I was able to pay it if the drawer did not, and was willing to pay it if he could not.

Some time afterwards he returned to Paris, and when, subsequently I inquired for him there, on grounds of friendship, I heard he was in a Government office under the Empire. When the Empire happily fell, it transpired that he was in the pay of the Emperor as Director of the Secret Bureau of Espionage, where his personal knowledge of the English parties and press rendered him a competent and useful agent. He had been a spy all the while he was in England. The last I heard of him was a report of his death, which was probable, as he was too fat to live long ; but the report may have been but a form of effacing himself peculiar, to the St. Simonian order to which he formerly belonged. It is a resort of many, no longer solicitous of personal recognition, to put in circulation a rumour of their decease.

A man of a different stamp, inasmuch as he had scruples of honour, was a certain Major W——, in whom I had more trust, because he had more ingenuousness of manner, and by reason of the company in which I found him. He professed to me to be an agent of Mazzini, to whom I believe he was really attached. He never awakened more than a transient suspicion in that penetrating Italian leader. The major often came to me to give me information, intending to enlist my confidence in his zeal. Now and then he would make me a present of a new patent pen, or some other little novelty which he thought might interest me. He was a well-built, good-looking man of about forty, possessing considerable strength. He lived at Fulham, in comfortable lodgings, and always appeared to have means. This observation led me to inquire, from his friends, whence they were derived, as at the Café d'Etoile, Windmill Street, I often found the major playing billiards with other foreigners, manifestly having time on his hands and money to spend. Occasionally he disappeared, at the time of the rising of the Italian patriots or some affair of Garibaldi's, when he would send me a small paragraph for insertion in the papers. Sometimes there would appear from other hands a paragraph in the incidental way of news, stating that Major W—— had been wounded, which probably never occurred. When the Empire fell, and the list of Napoleon's agents found at the Tuileries was published, we were all very much surprised to find, in addition to the name of André, that of the major. There was no doubt that he communicated to the enemy information of the forces and resources of the insurgents. But there was reason to believe that he made, as many other Italian spies were known to do, a resolution never to betray Mazzini, nor compromise any movement under his instructions.

A sensuous obesity had much to do with André's success. Fatness is a force in politics, though its influence is overlooked. Cassius would never have been suspected by Cæsar had he not been lean. Blatant bulk without sense goes further with a popular audience than bones with intelligence. The Tichborne Claimant would never have had so many followers had he been thin. A fat person is always graceful ; his motions are without angularity, even the inclination of the head is self-limited ; the nerves themselves are so embedded that they betray no emotion on the surface. This was shown in the Claimant, who, when his friends and the noble lord who was his supporter returned to the Claimant's chambers in Jermyn Street, all depressed and unmanned by the adverse turn affairs were taking, he was entirely unperturbed, maintaining an easy air, which shamed and reassured his dismayed friends. A peer could not have manifested more dignity, or a philosopher more calmness. It was all owing to the physical impossibility of his manifesting solicitude.

CHAPTER LIX.

UNPUBLISHED LETTERS OF WALTER SAVAGE LANDOR.

(1856–7.)

WALTER SAVAGE LANDOR, whose age at his death exceeded ninety, enjoyed for seventy years reputation as a poet. As is the case of few poets, he excelled in prose as well as verse. In all his life there was hardly any tyranny against which his brave spirit did not utter an indignant protest. In early manhood, after he had dealt with his patrimony in land with more than princely splendour, he led a troop to join the Spanish patriots who rose against Napoleon I. On every act of national heroism he lavished splendid praise. Late in life an action was brought against him by a lady in Bath, who had provoked him by acts which he regarded as implying meanness and ingratitude. Against her he wrote verses with a satiric vigour which belonged to him alone, which even Swift did not equal. Judgment was given against Landor, when he asked me to print for him a justification of himself, and desired me to transmit copies to certain persons whose names and addresses he gave me. Though he knew his publication would involve him in serious consequences if traced to him, he made no stipulation that I should keep the commission secret. Nor did I (though, as printer, I was liable in law in like manner) make any stipulation for indemnity. In applying to me, I supposed he had reason to believe that he could trust me in a matter where confidence might be of importance to him. I had Landor's manuscript copied in my own house, so that no printer should by chance see the original manuscript in the office. My brother Austin, whom in all these things I could trust as I could trust myself, set up and printed with his own hands Landor's defence, so that none save he and I ever saw the pamphlet, until the post delivered copies at their destination. A reward of £200 was offered for the discovery of the printer, without result. Twelve years later, Landor being then dead, I told Lord Houghton I was the printer of his "defence," but until this day I have mentioned it to no one else.

In his first letter to me, Landor contemplated my publishing the copies, but this idea was soon abandoned, as appears in his letters. The action against him, which had then recently been decided, had cost him more than £1,500, and another action might arise had I placed the "Defence" on sale.

The eight-paged octavo pamphlet bore the title—

MR. LANDOR'S REMARKS

on a

SUIT PREFERRED AGAINST HIM

at the

SUMMER ASSIZES IN TAUNTON, 1858,

Illustrating the

APPENDIX TO HIS HELLENICS.

Landor's first letter to me was the following :—

"FLORENCE, *March*, 22, 1859.

"SIR,—I know not whether you will think it worth your while to publish the papers I enclose. Curiosity, I am assured, will induce many to purchase it, my name being not quite unknown to the public. For my own part, I can only offer you five pounds for 100 copies—the rest will remain yours. The esteem in which I have ever held you induces me to make this proposal.—I am, sir, very obediently yours,

"W. S. LANDOR.

"No action was brought against the tradesmen for their reports, which I twice published in Bath, and the publications were bought up by Mr. H. Yescombe ; nor dared he produce them in his action against me. The action was for verses which the judge would not permit to be recited in court, where two falsifications might be pointed out, one of which (as a juryman is reported to have said), *would have altered the case,* and, of course, the verdict.   W.S.L."

Landor did not take into account that further indictable matter after the conviction would be regarded by the Court very seriously.   The " falsification " he refers to in the preceding letter is a curious instance of the value of a comma.   The appellation which the lady who brought the action against him took to herself was Caina, which is in Dante a region of hell. The judge did not remember the meaning of the name, and appears to have assumed that Landor applied it to her. Landor, using Milton's allegory of " Sin and Death," whose offspring would not be fair to look upon, alluded to a young lady whom he considered had been ill-treated by Caina, and wrote :—

> " Thou hast made her pale and thin
> As the child of Death by Sin."

" That is, begotten by Death on Sin.   But the plaintiff's lawyer," Landor said, " inserted a comma which was not to be found in his lines."   The lawyer, by placing a comma after Death, would make it appear that Caina was guilty of some horrid sin.   The jury found out too late what had been done.

After he had received a proof of his " Defence," to use his own term, he wrote :—

"Your letter has highly gratified me.   Would you kindly take the trouble to send copies to the following ?—

To Phinn, M.P. 3
Monckton Milnes, M.P.. 3
The Judge whosoever he was (It was Baron Channell)... 3
Lord Brougham 3
Mr. Hall, Highgate.. 3

And the principal periodicals, newspapers, &c., Leigh Hunt, Linton, and whoso else you please.   The rest to me at Florence."

In another letter he further directed me to send copies to other persons, and named the papers he wished to receive them — *Times, Daily News, Literary Gazette, Examiner, Edinburgh Review, Quarterly Review.* John Forster, Montague Square, 3 copies; Kossuth, Admiral Gawen, Sir W. Napier, Scinde House, Clapham Park, 3 copies; 20 to Florence; the remainder to Charles Empson, Esq., The Walks, Bath.

In a further letter he wrote, saying :—

" DEAR SIR,—I forgot, it seems to me, a few persons to whom it seems desirable a part of my hundred copies should be sent :—

3 to Mr. Carbonell, Camden Street, Camden Town.

3 to Mrs. West, Ruthen Castle, Denbighshire.

3 to some Masters in Chancery, whose sorry adversaries have tried to obtain an injunction that nothing should be paid to me or my family out of my estate.—I remain, Dear Sir, truly yours, W. S. LANDOR."

As I had become unwell from overwork, my brother Austin reported what had been done, and the following letter Landor wrote to him :—

" DEAR SIR,—I am grieved to hear of your brother's illness. I very much esteem him, and hope he may soon regain his usual health.

" Many thanks for your care in sending the copies according to my direction.

" I know nothing of the American publishers, but will inform my friends in that country that they may obtain copies from New York. My opinion is that many would be sold in that country. I am, Dear Sir, yours very truly, W. S. LANDOR.

" Mr. AUSTIN HOLYOAKE.

" Pray send 3 or 4 copies to J. Forster, Esq., Montague Square, London " (not remembering that he had mentioned them before).

His next letter was to me :—

" MY DEAR SIR,—I am as sorry to hear of your continued illness as at my failure of obtaining redress in my grievous wrongs. It may be necessary that the title page containing your name should be torn off; but surely *then* it would be quite safe to send a dozen copies to Captain Brickman, Beaufort Buildings, Bath, with my compliments. Could not the whole come out as printed at Genoa? This is suggested to me as being safe and practicable. Of what is now printed, send me a dozen, without the title page containing your name. I have promised them to friends about to leave Rome and Florence for a tour in Switzerland.—I remain, my Dear Sir, with high esteem, yours,   W. S. LANDOR."

In the letters I quote of Landor's in relation to his defence, I omit many remarks and also names which, however justifiable they were from his pen in relation to his own cause, I, who have no resentment to pursue, do not reproduce. They would be painful to others or the survivors of others. Forster in his "Life of Landor" quotes some letters which ought to have been omitted for the same reason. What is true, unless it has public interest or instruction, should have no place either in history or biography; and what is known to be untrue, and which Landor, being a man of good faith, would not persist in when it was shown to be untrue, should be precluded from repetition.

The next letter I quote in full :—

FLORENCE, *Oct.* 5.

"MY DEAR SIR.—On the tenth of last month I wrote a few lines to you enclosing a letter, in reply to a very polite one, remonstrating on mine to Emerson. A few days ago, I found my few lines intended for you in my desk. Pray let me hear, at your leisure, whether this reply ever reached you; for several of my prepared letters entrusted to a servant never arrived at their destination.—Believe me, Dear Sir, very truly and thankfully yours,   W. S. LANDOR."

Forster, in his "Life of Landor," if I remember rightly, relates that Emerson had seen some wonderful microscopes in Florence, and spoke of the uses to which they were applied; but he found that Landor despised entomology, yet in the same breath said, "The sublime was in a grain of dust": which anticipated the fine saying by Herschel about the microscope and telescope being explorers of the infinite "in both directions."

So far as I know, Landor's reply to the friend who remonstrated with him concerning his letter to Emerson has not been published. It covers four large quarto pages. Singularly, being from Landor, it was against the impending war for the extinction of negro slavery. It is a remarkable defence of the Southern side of the argument. I cite here only a few sentences in which his bright precision is visible in every one :—

" Interest is a stronger bond of concord than affinity. Beware of inculcating unintelligible doctrines. Men quarrel most fiercely about what they least understand. Laws are religion ; let these be intelligible and uncostly. It is pleasanter at all times to converse on literature than on politics. However, on neither subject are men always dispassionate and judicious. They form opinions hastily and crudely, and defend them frequently on ground ill chosen. Few scholars are critics, few critics are philosophers, and few philosophers look with equal care on both sides of a question."

One day I received the following letter :—

" 6, CLIFFORD STREET, *July* 7, 1872.
" DEAR MR. HOLYOAKE,—I remember well having a little talk with you. At what time of the day are you at home, as I should like to renew the acquaintance.—I am yours sincerely,
" HOUGHTON."

I answered Lord Houghton, saying I should appreciate the honour of his calling. Ordinarily I was at 20, Cockspur Street, where I then resided, from 5 to 9 p.m. When the House of Commons sat in the morning, I was home much earlier ; but it was an act of mercy to say that my chambers were at the top. Once there it was a pinnacle from which could be seen all the kingdom of London and the glory thereof ; but I include no other feature in the reference, remembering Lord Brougham's admonition, " Beware of Analogy."

Afterwards Lord Houghton asked me "to give him the pleasure of breakfasting with him at Clifford Street at 10.30 on Saturday next, the 20th instant."

The breakfast justified the celebrity Lord Houghton's morning repasts had obtained. Several breakfasts and dinners remain in my mind. Even the flavour as well as the charm I can recall ; but for profusion and variety of joints, birds, fish, wines, fruits, coffee, and cigars, Lord Houghton's breakfast exceeded all. I remember the astonishment he expressed to a new footman who brought in coffee half an hour before the birds and wine ended. On an easel near the table was a new portrait in oil of Landor, which was shown to every one. This led me to mention that I had several letters of Landor's, at which Lord Houghton expressed great interest, and I promised he should see some of them. I made up a parcel, with notes explaining them. Being precious in my eyes, I left them myself at his house. I heard no more of them. At times I sat behind him when he came to the Peers' Gallery in the Commons, and expected he would refer to them. At length I wrote and asked for their return. In July, 1873, he wrote from the House of Lords to say, " he was distressed to find that, acting on the supposition that I had given him the Landor MSS., he had bound some of them up with one of his books. If worth while, he would take them out again and send them." As he had never acknowledged their receipt, I did not understand how he came by the impression that I had given them to him. It was as proofs of Landor's confidence in me that I most valued them, and also as evidence of the risks I was willing to incur for him. The letters his lordship had bound up I told him " I was quite content should remain in his possession, as it would be a pleasure to think they would be preserved by him." As Lord Houghton was a valued friend of Landor's, I felt that he was a congenial custodian of relics of him. He sent me copies of the letters he retained, and others which accompanied them he returned, writing :—

" FRYSTON HALL, FERRYBRIDGE, *Nov.* 28, 1873.
" MY DEAR SIR,—I am obliged for the loan and the gift. I am afraid Landor's repute still remains in the world of men of letters, and not in that of national literature. There is no doubt that with him the thing said is less important than his manner of saying it. Every day we become less and less careful of style for its own sake.—Yours sincerely,
" HOUGHTON."

On such a subject no opinion of mine is comparable with Lord Houghton's ; nevertheless, I own I value Landor's writing for its sense as well as its style, and think that his "repute" in "national literature" is higher and more assured than Lord Houghton supposed.

Landor did me the honour to write to me many times (after the affair of his pamphlet) on Italian affairs. Some communications I sent to the *Newcastle Chronicle,* where they would be more influential than in any paper of mine ; some, relating more to social life and character than to public affairs, I inserted in the Journal I edited. Landor made scarcely a correction in his proofs. He was sure of what he wanted to say, and said it in unchangeable terms. He seldom dated his letters. In one from Scena, July 3 (during the Italian struggle), he remarks :—"If I had any photograph, I would gladly send it you. Three were sent to me from Bath, but I know not the name of the artist. Ladies have all three." He wrote with enthusiasm of Garibaldi, saying, "I hope Sicily may become independent, and that Garibaldi will condescend to be its king under the protection of Italy and England." The following sonnet he sent me ends with a fine line on Garibaldi :—

> " SICARIA.
>
> Again her brow Sicaria rears
> Above the tombs : Two thousand years
> Have smitten sore her beauteous breast,
> And war forbidden her to rest.
> Yet war at last becomes her friend,
> And shouts aloud
>   ' Thy grief shall end.
> Sicaria ! hear me ! rise again !
> *A homeless hero breaks thy chain.'* "

Walter Savage Landor I admired for his force, simplicity, directness, and the wonderful compression of his style : for his singular fearlessness, determination of thought, and his Paganism. As I was precluded from engagements on the press by reason of my name, I adopted that of "Landor Praed." Landor in his graceful way sent me his authority to use it, for reasons I may not repeat, as they existed alone in his generosity of judgment.

One night near the end of his days, after Charles Dickens

and John Forster had left him on their last visit, he wrote his own epitaph in these noble words :—

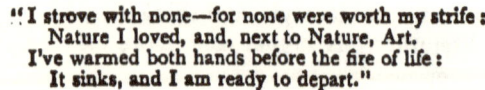

> "I strove with none—for none were worth my strife :
> Nature I loved, and, next to Nature, Art.
> I've warmed both hands before the fire of life :
> It sinks, and I am ready to depart."

He said, in his incomparable way, "Phocion conquered with few soldiers, and he convinced with few words. I know of no better description of a great captain or a great orator," which might be said of himself.

CHAPTER LX.

IN CHARGE OF BOMBSHELLS.

(1856.)

It was at Ginger's Hotel, which then stood near Westminster Bridge, that I first saw the bombs whose construction was perfected afterwards for use in Paris, in the attempt to kill the Emperor Napoleon III. The bombs were in sections then. When strangers came into the coffee-room, Dr. Bernard laid them back on the seat between him and a friend. Understanding machine work, I could judge whether they were well devised for their purpose, which was my reason for being there. At a later stage I was told that Mazzini thought they might be useful in the unequal warfare carried on in Italy, where the insurgent forces of liberty were almost armless.[1]

He who gave the order in Birmingham for their manufacture, also gave his name and address at the same time, and went down to see the maker when there was delay through doubt as to the kind of construction specified. He used no disguise or concealment of any kind. He acted just as an inventor might act who wanted a new kind of military weapon made. When two of the shells were afterwards delivered to me to make experiment with, I understood that they were a new weapon for military warfare in Italy, to be used from the house tops by insurgents, when the enemy might be in the streets

---

[1] Many persons imagine that novel deadly projectiles are a device of insurgents and are of modern date. Whereas "Infernal Machines" were used by the English at Dunkirk and St. Malo, and at Havre de Grace by the English and Dutch, under King William. The first inventor of them, or the first known to employ them, was Frederick Jambelli, an Italian engineer, at the siege of Antwerp, under the Duke of Parma, 1585.

firing into houses, as the Louis Napoleon troops did in the days of the Presidential butchery in Paris at the *coup d'état* of 1852. At the time of the meeting at Ginger's Hotel, if there was any thought of operating in Paris, the design was known only to the six persons ultimately concerned—among whom neither myself nor Mazzini was included.

When the war-balls came into my hands I had small conception of what I had undertaken in consenting to test them. The detonating powder with which they were filled had been prepared for quick explosion. "Elizabeth," a courageous young woman engaged in the household in which Orsini resided, had, well knowing the danger, superintended the drying of the powder before the kitchen fire, where, had accident happened, she had been heard of no more, and any persons above would have been made uncomfortable. Percussion caps were on the nipples of the shells (which, like porcupine quills, stuck out all round them) when I received them. Their bulk being from four to five inches in diameter, they were heavy enough to be quite a little load to carry about ; and thinking that any force used in removing the caps, which were firmly fixed, might cause an explosion, for which I was not provided, I left them on. Deeming it best to carry them apart, lest coming into collision with each other they might give me premature trouble, I put one into each of the side pockets of my coat. As I went along the street it occurred to me, that it was undesirable to fall down, as I might not be found when I wanted to get up.

When I arrived at home I packed the bombs considerably in a small, harmless-looking black brief bag ; but where to put the bag was the question. I had no closet which I was accustomed to lock, and to do it might occasion questions to be put which I did not want to answer, as the truth might create apprehension that the inscrutable things might go off of themselves, which for all I knew they might. This was, however, the only futile apprehension that occurred to me, for my wife made no trouble about the matter, and found a place of safety for the parcel. She had respect for those for whom I acted, and readily aided.

The next morning found me setting off to Sheffield, where I had an engagement to lecture, and in which town I had proposed to try this new weapon of war. The insurgent leaders of that day had no funds to spare ; and by choosing a time when I had to travel anyhow, it avoided the expense of a special journey. The selection of Sheffield was made by me as being a noisy manufacturing town, where the addition to its uproar of a bomb going off would be little noticeable. Going on the journey out to the railway station, I did not take a cab through fear the cabman or porter might snatch up the bomb-bag in which I had placed the shells, and afterwards throw it down carelessly. So I carried that bag in one hand and my portmanteau in the other. At the station I found opportunity of putting the contents of the bag into my pockets. I was afraid of the bag in the carriage : it required so much watching. A passenger might at any minute suddenly remove it to make room for some box which might strike against it, and as suddenly disperse the travellers themselves. Besides, I could never leave the train for refreshment, with the bag in it ; and the third-class journey was long in those days from London to Sheffield—the Midland Company not having set the generous example of carrying third-class passengers with swift trains. With a shell as large as a Dutch cheese in each pocket, I looked like John Gilpin when he rode with the wine kegs on either side of him. But I passed very well as one who had made ample provision for his journey. My only anxiety was that some mechanic with his carpenter's or plumber's basket might choose to sit down by my side, when a projecting hammer or chisel might be the cause of an unexpected disturbance. For the same reason I thought it wiser not to sit in the corner of the carriage, where one of my pockets oscillating against the side by sudden motion of the train might occasion difficulties there.

On arriving at Sheffield the trouble did not end. In the house where I lodged new perplexities arose. I might ask for a closet in which I might lock up my peculiar luggage, but my landlady might have a duplicate key and be just curious to see what I was so careful in securing ; and thus some accident might ensue upon the discovery. This fear deterred me from that expedient. My watchfulness kept me a prisoner in the house, and when I went below to write I took the bag and placed it on the table, keeping pens and paper in the same receptacle to divert attention from the other contents. Sunday was an entirely troublesome day with my percussioned companions, because I had to carry the bag twice to the morning and evening lecture and place it upon the table before me while I spoke. As I took my notes and papers from the bag, its presence on the table was a matter of course. It was not prudent to put it under the table, lest the toes of some excited adversary might kick against it there. Had my opponents, who were numerous at that period, had any idea of the contents of my bag, they would have been very brief in their observations. At night I was again solicitous, fearing something should occur in the house, where there were many inmates.

Monday was welcome to me when I could take one of the missives out with me and seek a place for its explosion. As I might need to move rapidly after throwing it, I concealed the one I left behind between the mattress and the bed in my room, after the bed was made for the day. Had anything happened to me to prevent my return, the next lodger sleeping in the bed had found something quite inexplicable under him. I had lived in Sheffield and knew my way about, having walked through its suburbs with Ebenezer Elliott and other rambling friends of that time. But I had never observed the roads with a view to present requirements. I walked in various directions until afternoon, before finding a sufficiently straight road, without houses upon it. It was necessary to command with my eye a long sweep of way, since I must operate in the middle thereof, and be sure that no person could enter upon it from either extreme without my seeing him. Besides, I had to examine both sides of the road to be certain there was no lane or bye-path by which unseen persons could emerge and be struck by any flying fragment about at that minute. After all my trouble, pedestrians, or vehicles, or horsemen, were continually coming into sight ; and I had to return home without making any attempt that day. And night was useless, it being more dangerous for my purpose than day. Had I had a companion to keep watch with me, we might have found an opportunity ; but it was my duty not to trust any one with a knowledge of my object. There was no knowing what alarm he might take at being in my company with the uncertain missives I bore about me.

The next day I took a different course—that of selecting a disused quarry, as that would test the quality of the bombs under the most favourable circumstances. If one would not

explode by its own momentum of descent on so hard a floor, it
would show that its construction was an entire failure. The
quarry was in an immediate suburb, not very far from the
centre of the town. There were several villas in sight of it,
with gardens that came near to the verge of it. What would be
the amount of noise I should create, or what would be the effect
of it, I could not tell. I had to trust that it might pass among
other commotions to which Sheffield was subject. Having
examined the quarry to ensure that there was no one in it, and
finding no one above, I threw the bomb from the top—from a
point where I could shelter myself in case the explosion brought
any fragments my way. The sound was very great, and rever-
berated around. Expecting people would run from their houses,
I quickly arose and sauntered away. I met a person hastening
towards the spot. "Did you hear that great noise?" he asked.
"Oh, yes!" I answered. "I think it came from the quarry,"
he replied. "Had it come from there I must have seen it," I
answered, "as I passed by it. It might be some cannon firing.
If you can show me a pathway to yonder field, we should see if
there is anything going on there." He turned and went with
me, but we found nothing there. I was desirous he should not
get to the quarry until the smoke had disappeared. Later in
the day I returned to the place, lest some portions of convexed
nippled iron should lie about, which being found might excite
curiosity; but nothing was to be seen. I posted a paper to
London, without address or signature, saying :—

"My two companions behaved as well as could be expected.
One has said nothing; perhaps through not having an opportunity. The other, being put upon his mettle, went off in high
dudgeon. He was heard of immediately after, but has not since
been seen."

Finding the deposited shell in the bed where I had left it, I
returned to town with it, when it was proposed that I should
take another shell with the one I had, and proceed to Devon,
where dwelt one who had the courage for any affair advancing
the war of liberty. For this journey I received thirty-two
shillings, as the distance was great ; and this was the cost of
the third-class fare. It was the only expense to which I put

the projectors of these wandering experiments. The object was to ascertain whether the new grenades would really explode, when thrown as high as a man could throw them, and falling on an ordinary road. The journey West was less troublesome than that to the North, as the railway carriages were less crowded, and mechanics carrying tools were much fewer. My friend lived in " The Den." This was the actual name of his residence, and not inappropriate, considering the nature of the business we had on hand, when we two issued from it. The vigilance falling to me was much diminished, as my host could take care of my " brief bag " when I needed personal liberty.

We soon found a suitable highway. My friend watched the way, and, being tall, could take a wide range of view ; but it was necessary to choose a field which had a stoné fence, where, after throwing the bomb into the air, I could at once lie down and be protected while the fierce fragments flew around. There was, however, little need of the precaution, as no explosion followed. The nipples buried themselves in the earth, and the obstinate shell remained fixed and silent. I had not foreseen this, and it was necessary to remain on the ground a while lest the thing might go off after some time. It was not possible to wait long, for a signal told me a passenger was descried. The difficulty then was to get the perverse ball out of the earth, since plucking it might occasion an abrasion of the cap, and cause it to burst while I was over it. Happily, I restored the wilful shell to my pocket and I went to meet the traveller to ask him " if he knew where there was a good place for football about "—in case he had observed the unusual movements on the way.

Having no taste for further trials on the common roads, we found opportunities of throwing the two portable thunderbolts on a really hard surface, where, with loud report, every fragment flew into untraceable space. It was not without satisfaction that I saw, or rather heard, the last of my perplexing companions. My next report to London said :—

" Leniency of treatment was quite thrown away upon our two companions. As a man makes his bed, so he must lie upon it ; still out of consideration, we wished it to be not absolutely hard. But that did just no good whatever. The harder treatment had to be tried : and I am glad to say it proved entirely successful. But nothing otherwise would do."

The result of the experiments was that the bombs in the first state in which they were perfected were proved to be inefficient ; unless thrown to a great altitude in the air they would not explode on an ordinary roadway. If the percussion caps did act, they failed to ignite the contents of the shell. Except upon a well macadamized and hardened ground, or upon flagstones, they could not be depended upon for the purposes for which they were intended. They would not answer for ordinary military operations, where the surface might be soft ground or grass land. Whether the bombs used in Paris were improved, or whether the choice of Rue Lepelletier, where the ground was firm, was determined by the experiments upon which I reported I never inquired.[1] If my report ever became known to any one concerned in that affair, it probably had some instructive result.

[1] Some time ago sections of the shells used in Paris were drawn and published. They certainly were not of bombs which passed through my hands.

CHAPTER LXI.

ORSINI THE CONSPIRATOR

(1856.)

ORSINI was an egotist, but, like Benvenuto Cellini, he had something to boast of. His love of heroic distinction helped to make him a patriot ; the passion for renown helped him to excel all other patriots in daring and in doing things of which Italian patriotism may always be proud. The escape of Baron Trenck was not more wonderful than Orsini's escape from the impregnable fortress of San Giorgio. The narrative of his astonishing adventures, published under the title of " The Austrian's Dungeon," and translated by Madame Mario, shows, in force of narration, that he was a good writer as well as an intrepid soldier. When it was ready for the press he came to me, through the instructions he had received, for suggestions as to the best mode of issuing it. I see him now as he stood in the shop in Fleet Street, the sun falling upon his dark hair, bronzed features, and glance of fire. I told him I would bring out his book gladly, but that Routledge was able to put many more thousands into the market than I was, and would no doubt give him £50 for the MS., which, though it did not amount to much, was of moment to an exile. Routledge did give him £50. The title, " The Austrian Dungeons in Italy," was one of interest at the period, but, if reprinted under the title of " The Wonderful Escape of Orsini," or some other which indicated its marvellousness, it would have interest in the literature of adventure as permanent as Silvio Pellico's story. There were heroes in Italy all about. Bystanders took Orsini, lame and stained with mud and blood, on the morning of his escape, and secreted him with a certainty of themselves suffering torture and death in the same fortress, were they discovered. The whole district was then overrun with spies. He who realises this will appreciate the courage and resource of the peasant people—only to be matched in Ireland. I know of no single book concerning Italy which more stirs the blood of indignation at Austrian subjugation than Orsini's narrative. The address appended to his book (he could give his address in England) was 2, Cambridge Terrace, Hyde Park, July 10, 1856. A year later he was headless.

Felice Orsini relates that an Austrian colonel was one day galloping through Mercato di Mezzo, followed by a large dog. A youth of sixteen was passing by with a smaller dog, which was attacked by the colonel's and almost killed. To save his dog, the youth picked up a stone and hurled it at the colonel's. By chance it struck its head, and it fell dead. By order of this colonel the youth was arrested and sentenced to 30 blows on the cavaletto, which meant 90 strokes of the bastinado—for three strokes counted as one blow. When the unfortunate youth was removed from the Cavaletto he was dead. On the following day the colonel was sitting with some of his fellow officers in the Café dei Grigioni. A man suddenly appeared in their midst, and after despatching the colonel with several stabs of his poniard, disappeared before any one could arrest him. This was the father of the boy who had died under the bastinado. That was a righteous assassination.

Orsini, by his attempt to destroy the French usurper, intended also to avenge Italy upon the false President of the Republic who sent troops to put down the heroic Republic of Rome. Orsini perilled his head to do for France what thousands wished done, and no one else attempted, with the same determination. When Cato visited the palace of a tyrant and saw the persons he put to death, and the terror of the citizens who approached him, he asked, "Why does not some one kill this man?" Orsini came forward in like case to do it. Those who engage in political assassination should have no hesitation in sacrificing themselves. If they are careful for their own welfare, they lose their lives all the same. By using bombs, Orsini imperilled the lives of others, and, being wounded by a fragment which filled his eyes with blood, was unable to complete his design.

After his execution at La Roquette, a compromising article appeared in the *Westminster Review*, upon which I addressed the following letter :—

"147, FLEET STREET, *June* 17, 1860.
"TO THE EDITOR OF THE 'WESTMINSTER REVIEW.'

"DEAR SIR,—On the part of the colleagues and friends of Orsini, I am requested to solicit your attention to the following passages in the *Review* for January, 1860. We believe we shall not appeal to you in vain to do justice to the dead. What is asked is the correction or proof of the statements questioned.

"You say—'Through a confidential agent, he (Louis Napoleon) conveyed a solemn assurance of his intentions to Orsini, who had been a member of the same Carbonaro conspiracy in 1831 with the Emperor. Orsini declared himself satisfied with this communication. He gave the persons who brought it a list of friends in Italy, whose co-operation was to be sought at the proper time, and then wrote as the testament of his dying convictions the famous letter, pointing to Napoleon III. as the coming liberator of his country, which was printed in Turin, having been sent thither by the Emperor for publication. Soon followed the interview at Plombieres with Count Cavour, and the project succeeded rapidly towards execution.'

"In connection with this statement, I submit the following facts :—

"Orsini was not born until the end of December, 1819.

"In 1831, when he is alleged to be a joint conspirator with Louis Napoleon, Orsini was a boy at school, being only eleven years of age ; and he remained at school until 1836—until he was sixteen.

"It was not until 1843 that he was a member of any secret society.

"He never was a member with the Emperor. He never was a Carbonaro at all.

"He never saw Louis Napoleon before the year 1857.

"The 'famous letter' referred to was not in Orsini's French. He did not write French well. The letter appeared in pure Florentine Italian. Orsini was educated as a Bolognese, and was by no means a master of good Italian.

" Without proof it is not to be believed that Orsini, of all
men, would 'give a list of his friends ' to the man whom he
sought to kill. He was not the man to do it to save his own
life. Was he likely to have done it when his life was not to be
saved ? Without proof, no assertion of this kind is to be
believed. It is a serious calumny upon Orsini, and to be
resented.

" Again you state that—' The Emperor learnt at Milan, from
the mouth of his own couriers. . . . and especially of that confidential one whom we have repeatedly mentioned, and who
brought to Milan the discouraging results of his interview with
Orsini's friends, whom he had found deaf to Bonapartist suggestions.'

" No doubt they were found 'deaf.' Were they ever found
at all ? No such persons have ever been visited. A confidential
agent of the Orsini party has been sent over the whole ground,
each *capi* or chief of sections has been inquired of, and the
answer of each is that no Bonapartist emissary nor any such
pretended communication has ever reached them. The ' confidential one' whom the writer 'repeatedly mentioned ' was M.
Pietri.

" The *Westminster Review* has given too many proofs of its
profound sympathy with Continental liberty, and for those who
have given their lives to promote it, for the friends of Orsini to
be under any other impression than that you have been mislead or misinformed of the facts of Felice Orsini's character and
career.—Yours faithfully,   G. J. HOLYOAKE."

With his usual fairness and promptness the editor inserted
this letter at the end of the next issue of the *Westminster
Review*, regretting that he had inserted the communication,
which he believed at the time to be trustworthy.

When in England Orsini was for many weeks the guest of a
friend in the North, whose doors were always open to exiles.
His daily habit was to ride through the country, and his fine
figure and handsome resolute face was met by passengers as he
galloped through splendid scenes and over sterile moors where
the volcanoes of industry reminded him of those of his own
brighter land.

When Madame Herwegh presented Orsini with white gloves,

he laid them aside to wear on the morning of his execution, although he was then free. He had so often been near death that he thought death always near him, and, as it was impossible for him to cease to conspire for the freedom of Italy, he regarded himself as destined to the scaffold. He had known the perils of prisons—he had mastered the language of stone walls—the language of misery—by which the last messages of the condemned are struck from cell to cell. When the last hour came and Pierri, who was with him, faltered, Orsini, not only un daunted but bright and daring as was his wont in danger, counselled Pierri to be of good courage and acquit himself as a patriot should.

CHAPTER LXII.

A FRENCH JACOBIN IN LONDON.

(1856.)

FROM 1851 to 1856 we had a real French Jacobin active in England, sprung like a Revolutionary Phœnix from the ashes of the Parisian clubs of 1793—Dr. Simon "Bernard le Clubiste," as he signed himself in his first letter to *The Times*. Dr. Bernard was born in Carcasonne in 1817. A physician by education, he, as surgeon on board a man-of-war, displayed intrepidity in two or more sea battles. He was a Phalansterist of the school of Fourier. He edited insurgent papers, and was chairman of the club of the Bazaar *Bonne Nouvelle*, where he addressed five thousand people nightly. Unintimidated when his colleagues were shot, he carried the agitation to Belgium, and was soon in prison and on his trial there. He got into trouble about Robert Blum, the publisher, who was shot by the Austrians in Vienna. Eight prosecutions had spent their rage upon him, when in 1851 he came to England, and practised as a physician at 40, Regent Circus, Piccadilly, London. Before two years were well gone he was in Newgate. His knowledge of the physiology of elocution, in which he excelled, and of the cure of the impediments of speech, would soon have brought him fame and fortune. His skill in Belgium had brought him great renown. We who knew him, liked him for his simplicity, genuineness, and courage. Becoming involved in the Orsini affair, he was tried for his life at the Old Bailey, in London, and would have been condemned had it not been for the defiant spirit of a city of London jury, who would not convict any one at the bidding of a foreign power. Louis Napoleon, the usurper, was understood to ask that Dr. Bernard should be put upon his trial, which was done.   The case lasted five days. Edwin James, an advocate politically popular in his time, defended the doctor.   I was in court, and heard with amazement his ornate appeal so materially destitute of facts.   He was unacquainted with what he was supposed to know, or might have known—and should have known.   The Attorney-General, Sir Fitzroy Kelly, who prosecuted, made it a point of horror that a letter from Orsini found in Dr. Bernard's room inquired "How about the Red and Co.," which the jury were told, with upturned eyes and uplifted hands, referred to the "Red Republic," for which the doctor and his terrific correspondent were plotting. All the while Orsini's letter merely inquired after a lady, the colour of whose hair he exaggerated because she had refused his offer to marry her.   He always afterwards referred to the committee of which the lady was a member as the "Red and Co." Mr. Edwin James had no explanation to give.   He had not inquired into the facts of the case which a question would have elicited.   The Attorney-General Kelly was he who shed tears before the jury in attesting the innocence of the Quaker, Tawell, who had confessed to Kelly that he had murdered the woman at Berkhampstead, for which Tawell was hanged.   From Sir Fitzroy, pious without scruples, Dr. Bernard had nothing to expect.   Edwin James, his counsel, trusted entirely to the hereditary spirit of English defiance of foreign dictation, and modelled his appeal to the jury on the famous reply of Mirabeau to the message of the king.   Fortunately for Dr. Bernard, this intrepid eloquence succeeded.   Spoken in a loud, strong, imperious voice, the following is the passage which won, or justified, the verdict :—

"Gentlemen, I need not remind you that it has been of the greatest advantage to this country that her free shores have been open to exiles from other lands.   The revocation of the Edict of Nantes drove to our shores the Saurins, the Romillys, and the Laboucheres, who have shed a lustre on this country. Will you, then, at the bidding of a neighbouring despot, destroy the asylum which aliens have hitherto enjoyed?   Let me urge you to let the verdict be your own, uninfluenced by the ridiculous fears of French armaments or French invasions, such as were raised in Peltier's case. You, gentlemen, will not be intimidated ; you will not pervert and wrest the law of England to please a foreign dictator ! No. Tell the prosecutor in this case that the jury-box is the sanctuary of English liberty. Tell him that on this spot your predecessors have resisted the arbitrary power of the Crown, backed by the influence of Crown-serving and time-serving judges. Tell him that under every difficulty and danger your predecessors have secured the political liberties of the people. Tell him that the verdicts of English juries are founded on the eternal and immutable principles of justice. Tell him that, panoplied in that armour, no threat of armament or invasion can awe you. Tell him that, though 600,000 French bayonets glittered before you, though the roar of French cannon thundered in your ears, you will return a verdict which your own breasts and consciences will sanctify and approve, careless whether that verdict pleases or displeases a foreign despot, or secures or shakes, and destroys for ever the throne which a tyrant has built upon the ruins of the liberty of a once free and mighty people."

Lord Campbell—one of those Whigs who apologise for their honourable sympathy with liberty by acts which Tories might covet, and then wonder why they are not popular—summed up for conviction. As the jury were about to retire, Dr. Bernard, lifting his hands and standing erect in the dock, exclaimed with great fervour, " I declare the words which have been used by the judge are not correct, and that the balls taken by Georgi to Brussels were not those which were taken to Paris. I have brought no evidence here, because I am not accustomed to compromise any person. I declare that I am not the hirer of assassins, that Rudio has declared in Paris, on his trial, that he asked himself to go to Orsini. I was not the hirer of assassins. Of the blood of the victims of the 14th of January there is nothing on my heart any more than on any one here. We want only to crush despotism and tyranny everywhere. I have con-spired—I will conspire everywhere—because it is my duty, my sacred duty, as of every one ; but never, never, will I be a murderer."

On the verdict of acquittal being given, men waved their hats, the members of the bar cheered, ladies stood on their seats and waved their handkerchiefs or their bonnets, and cheered again, and again, the crowd outside catching indications of the nature of the verdict, sent back in still louder cheers, their greetings at the result.

"At length," says *The Times* reporter, "silence was restored, and Bernard, whose eye sparkled, and whose frame quivered with intense emotion, said, in a loud voice, "I do declare that this verdict is the truth, and it proves that in England there will be always liberty to crush tyranny. All honour to an English jury!"

Thus the great Jacobin escaped being hanged. Unhappily he came to a more lamentable end. A bewitching angelic traitor was sent as a spy to beguile him, and to her, in fatal confidence, he spoke of his friends. When he found that they were seized one by one and shot, he realized his irremediable error, lost his reason, and so died.

Dr. Bernard had every virtue save prudence. I observed with apprehension that he would talk in a loud voice in the streets, of things it were best to whisper with circumspection in private. It suggested itself to me that if I conspired it would be well to watch the ways of him I conspired with. Dr. Bernard had that fervour which made him imagine all the world had come to his opinion, and took the town into his confidence. Partly it was England that misled him, he could not imagine that spies were in English streets.

Edwin James was not a man of many scruples. When he was a candidate for Marylebone he spoke one day at the usual hustings at the Regent's Park end of Portland Place. His adversary put himself forward as a "Resident Candidate," when James exclaimed, "I may be one day a happy resident—but, alas! as yet I have no wife and family." "You old incubator," exclaimed a loud-mouthed and abrupt elector, "you have three families in the borough already, and you know it!" The "gentle Edwin" was not abashed, but laughed and spoke on. The electors knew when they voted for him that he would sell them if he could get a price for them, calculating that, if he could not, he would serve them well. In which they were right. Within twenty minutes of his entering the House of Commons after being declared duly elected, I heard him take part in a debate, and offer himself to Lord John Russell. But Lord John, when the opportunity came to him, would not buy, and James remained a popular member—until Lord Yarborough gave him the choice of leaving England or being indicted here. He went to New York, where the enemies of the Republic said the bar had fewer scruples as to its associates. Edwin James found to the contrary. After many years banishment he returned to England. Re-admission at the bar being impossible, he began a new legal career, and kept terms in a solicitor's office, to come up for examination as a new candidate. I often met him walking to the city at an early hour, pale, sedate, unostentatious—his ruddiness, grossness, and pomposity gone out of him. I felt respect for his courage and perseverance. Death intervened, and he came to his end without attaining his purpose.

CHAPTER LXIII.

THE STORY OF CARLO DE RUDIO.

(1857–62.)

Rudio—" Count Carlo de Rudio " [1] he called himself, but there was little of the " Count" about him—was an Italian, and one of the shell-bearers when Orsini and Pierri made their attack on the Emperor Louis Napoleon in Paris. Rudio bore a shell, but whether he threw it is doubtful. " He could not get near enough," he said. Though deported to Guiana for his reputed share in the transaction, he escaped, it was believed by connivance of the French authorities there. In a small boat he managed to reach the English colony of Berbice, and afterwards worked his passage to England. Dr. Bernard stated on his trial at the Old Bailey that Rudio came and was not sought. Why he came, or who sent him, demanded scrutiny by those who received him before employing him, or suffering his participation. He may have been impelled to join in the enterprize by patriotism, and afterwards have shrunk from the consequences. The *Daily Telegraph* of August 30, 1861, described him as one who "betrayed his confederates," and stated that "the revelations he made were of considerable help towards the prosecution of Dr. Bernard." The allusion must be to information given at the time of Rudio's own apprehensiòn. Nothing transpired at Bernard's trial as to " revelations " made by him.

In England Rudio afterwards asked my advice and aid to bring out a Life of himself, of which some pretentious numbers

[1] I remember he traced his descent from Nosa Danus, whom the Emperor Otone the Great, in the ninth century, made Governor of Belluno.

appeared. Probably I published some numbers for him. He
went about lecturing. At some places, as the *Telegraph*
reported, he complained that he was underpaid for his expedi-
tion to Paris, and that " Dr. Bernard only gave him £14 and
his railway ticket " ; further, that " Mazzini refused to recom-
mend him to the Revolutionary Committee." Making these
statements looked like the act of a traitor. It was, as far as his
word could go, fixing on Dr. Bernard a complicity of which he
had been acquitted by a jury, and doing so in a form which no
one had attempted to prove against him. Though Rudio's
words did not affect Mazzini, who refused to recognize him,
they served to give the public the impression that Rudio had
a right to look to Mazzini as a patron. My wish was to decline
any communication with Rudio, and I would have done so but
for the request of a friend of Dr. Bernard, who, too generously
commiserating Rudio's condition, besought me and also Mazzini
to aid him.

Mazzini, always forgiving to his enemies, had pity for Rudio,
because he was an Italian who had, peradventure, entered into
conspiracy and peril for his country, and because he thought
that probably fear had led him to betray others. At that time
attempts were made in Parliament, and in the press of the
governing classes, to connect Mazzini with every act of insurgency or outrage in Europe, as was afterwards done towards Mr.
Parnell with respect to Ireland. Yet Mazzini incurred the peril
of affording a colourable pretext for this imputation against
him, as he had often done, from motives of humanity.

One of Rudio's letters to me was the following :—

" 4, FELIX PLACE, BARKER GATE, NOTTINGHAM,
" *Feb.* 16, 1861.

" DEAR SIR,—I have received a letter from your friend, ——,
which tells me that you offer yourself to help me in my publication. Of course my letter is to let you know that my publication cannot go further for the want of pecuniary means, and
I am obliged to leave off, as I have resolved to leave this town
and go elsewhere, where I hope I shall find means of subsistence for myself and my poor unhappy family. But, as I am
without the most necessary means of carrying out my views, I
will take the liberty to make you an offer ; and that would be

to sell you the copywrite of my pamphlet, leaving at your consciousness the value of it. I assure you, dear sir, that no man of my condition has more suffered than I, in this last few months especially. Many a day we have been without any thing to eat—without coal to warm us; twice some propositions very brilliant has been offered to me; but them was brilliant to those that have another heart than mine. With strength of mind I have rejected them, and preferred to suffer than become a spy. To you, then, I appeal as a man of religious and political principles equally to those that I am proud to have; no, sir, no human power shall have the chance of turning me out of that path that I have been for twelve years. Death only shall put a stop at my principles, but until I shall have a drop of blood in my veins I shall always be ready to run against the danger for the benefit of our noble cause, though I have been repayed with the blackest of ingratitude. Still I will pessever while my heart still beats within me, and the taske I have undertaken is unaccomplished. Hoping of a reply, I with my wife and child, send our best expression of gratitude, and believe me, Dear Sir, your truly and fellowman,

"C. CARLO DE RUDIO.

"P.S.—I hope you will excuse my bad styl of the English language; I have a great presentiment, 'and that is only the aliment that keeps me a life,' that I shall no longer stay without that my person will again be sacrificed for the great principle of patriotism, liberty, and honour."

This letter, creditably written for one in humble society who had taught himself, had the fault of protesting his fidelity to one who did not question it, nor believe it. Interest in the American Civil War led Rudio to wish to go to that country. By that time he had his English wife, whom he married at Nottingham, and two children. He wrote to me, January 13, 1864, saying, "Mr. Bradlaugh had promised him aid," and Rudio entreated me for more. I had sent him £6 on the second of that month (as I see from the cheque before me). The following letter to me relates to these affairs :—

" MY DEAR FRIEND,—I shall be very grateful for all that you will do with W. to help our collecting. I did most unhappily give to Rudio the £1. But if £1 shall be wanted for his going, you may reckon on another one from me. It will be economy too, for if he remains I shall have to help him often.—Evei faithfully yours, JOSEPH MAZZINL"

At length the means for a voyage were collected, and I gave Rudio a warm poncho to protect him from the cold at sea. At that time I was expecting daily apprehension for selling unstamped papers at Fleet Street, and this poncho, as I have said, was kept under the counter with biscuits and a small flask of *eau de vie*. I had had experience of apprehension, and knew the value of warmth and refreshment the first night. As Rudio was leaving me, I thought this would protect him from the Atlantic blasts. Whether he perished in the war, or on which side he fought, I never heard, nor have I heard of him since.

CHAPTER LXIV.

STABBING SPIES IN LONDON.

(1857.)

DESPOTISM is the nursing mother of murder. It employs spies to betray patriots to the scaffold. The friends of liberty have often no choice but to conspire and kill in self-defence. Sometimes these desperate feuds, originating in Naples or St. Petersburg, in Berlin or Paris, were fought out in London.

One day an announcement appeared in the London papers that a young Italian, on patriotic duty, had stabbed four foreigners in a restaurant in Panton Street, Haymarket. They were all seriously wounded by thrusts which had the vigour of assassination in them. It was a miracle none were killed. They were conveyed to an hospital, and the active assailant, who had attacked them with such invincible rapidity that they were unable to detain him, was "wanted" by the police. The question was put to me whether I would provide for him. I readily agreed to do so, as I held a house convenient for that purpose. The back rooms overlooked open-gate grounds, and I could watch the arrival of the police in that direction if they made a descent in the rear. So if they came at the back, I could let my active guest out at the front—if they came at the front, he could escape at the back. If they came both ways at once, I had an apartment at the lower end of the garden, and as soon as they had passed over him to enter the house, a signal would enable him to leap into adjacent gardens before they could be aware of the movement. I had information that my guest would probably refuse to be taken alive, and a desperate encounter would have caused alarm in my family, in which there was illness. As a guarantee against this could not be given, other arrangements were made for the determined visitor. Afterwards I much regretted having made the inquiry as to his intended resistance, as he was not brought to me, and I lost the pleasure of succouring so alert and brave a man, for whose safety I had matured preparations. The four wounded men were foreign spies supposed to be in the pay of the Emperor Napoleon, and mouchardism is a profession we did not recognise in London.

When the men in the hospital recovered, they went their way. They knew very well who their assailant was, but would never tell, nor could the police induce them to appear before the magistrates and make any charge. They had sufficing reasons for not allowing their own identity, or the nature of their business, or the name of their employer, to be known, and the fourfold attempted assassinations in Panton Street consequently passed out of the memory of London. Their intrepid assailant knew the spies very well. He had tracked them to their lair, and fallen upon them with almost superhuman fury. He kept his own counsel, and no one who knew it spoke his name. The contest had to be renewed elsewhere—at another time. The terrible silence of the perilous enterprise was never broken.

CHAPTER LXV.

PARLIAMENTARY CANDIDATURE IN THE TOWER HAMLETS.

(1857.)

It was in 1857 that I first became a Parliamentary candidate. It was in opposition to Sir William Clay, who had for twenty-four years represented the Tower Hamlets, but who was regarded as a stationary Liberal.

Eleven years later (1868)—never being impatient — I addressed the electors of my native town, Birmingham. Fifteen years afterwards, in 1884, I was a candidate at Leicester, on the retirement of Mr. P. A. Taylor. My object this time was to promote the passing of an Affirmation Bill for members of Parliament, which would open the doors of the House to all persons who found the ecclesiastical terms of the oath not in accordance with their personal belief. As I should on this ground have refused to take the oath, I might have aided the cause of affirmation had I been supported by a constituency whose self-respect lay in the same direction. But that was not to be. On addressing a public meeting at Leicester, twenty-nine questions were put to me. Nine of them were still-born, were ideal and impracticable, and never had working life in them. The other twenty I had invented myself or advocated being put to candidates years ago when in Leicester, before the questioners were out of their cradles. The answers therefore were easy to me.

My candidature in the Tower Hamlets was the first claim ever made to represent labour in Parliament ; and it was the first time Mr. Mill supported such an intention. It was at

42

my request that Mr. Mill's subscription of £10 was not made public, as I knew his generosity would do him more harm than it would do me good. Mr. Mill would have accepted the consequences, but it was not for me who profited by his friendship to impose the risk upon him. Some years later, when he sought to re-enter Parliament for Westminster, it was reported that he had, at the same time, given a subscription to support the candidature of Mr. Bradlaugh at Northampton, as little popular as myself—and it cost Mr. Mill his seat.

My Committee Room was at 4, West Street, Cambridge Heath, N.E., and Mr. Charles Bradlaugh was one of my committee. My address to the constituency was the following, which shows the questions in the minds of those regarded as "advanced" Reformers of that day :—

"GENTLEMEN,—During sixteen years in which I have been engaged in the public advocacy of Industrial and Religious Reforms, I have only been solicitous to be of service. The last prosecution in this country for the independent expression of theological opinion was sustained by me. I was the last person against whom the Queen's Exchequer Writ was issued for the part taken in securing the Repeal of the Newspaper Stamp, and but for the risks thus incurred the public might still be struggling with that question. I have constantly helped public movements, not the less when those who accepted my services thought it well not to acknowledge them—the rule of modern political life being to ignore those who do the work lest you should discourage those who never do anything. In all this I have acquiesced, because it is the first duty of a publicist to help without permitting any personal consideration to hamper the public cause.

"I should vote for Residential Suffrage ; and the Ballot, which would make it honest ; and for Triennial Parliaments, which would make it a power ; and for Equal Electoral Districts, which would make it just. A public opinion which can only make itself heard in the streets, and cannot reach the Cabinet, is impotent. In the late war the only character that stood the test was the character of the people. When aristocratic administrators failed, the people were efficient. Therefore, if English honour was safe in the hands of the common soldier in the bloody defiles of Inkermann, it may equally be trusted to the common people at the polling booth.

" First among social improvements is the measure introduced by Sir Erskine Perry for giving, under just conditions, married women an independent right to their property and earnings.

" Next is the demand that the State should establish well-devised Home Colonies upon the waste lands of the Crown, which might eventually extinguish pauperism—home colonies where the labourer in distress, instead of taking his wallet for the parish loaf, need only take his spade to dig his honest bread —home colonies which should be training schools of emigrants, who might leave England not as now so often to perish helplessly out of our sight, but as qualified to support themselves as agricultural experience alone can enable them to do.

" In this country there is a decided element of active and progressive opinion, systematically denied recognition ; and which is misjudged, because never legitimately represented. This is nowhere more evident than in the Tower Hamlets.

" There wants more than the abolition of Church Rates. All religious endowments are but a tax imposed by the strong upon the consciences of the weaker party.

" Then why should a Christian State accept the credit of the Rothschild House, and refuse Parliamentary position to a member of the family ; and where is the religious equality in a State which admits the Catholic and excludes the Jew ? Religious liberty is not in half the danger from the Chief Rabbi that it is from the Pope.

" Public justice requires that the oath, like marriage, should be a civil or religious rite, at the option of those concerned. Without a law of Affirmation in favour of those who conscientiously object to the oath as now administered, the magistrate is made a judge of religious opinion, and awards to unscrupulous consciences advantages denied to veracity.

" In this country, where the mass of the people are so hard worked, Sunday recreation is both a necessity and a mercy , and, where it can be accompanied by instruction, it is also a moral improvement. Hence I should support the opening of the Crystal Palace, the National Gallery, the British Museum, and similar places on the Sunday afternoon. Since nonconformity of creed is permitted among us, uniformity of conduct should not be enforced by Act of Parliament. The poor man who is a slave to-day and a pauper to-morrow should not be dictated to as to how he shall spend the only day which is his : whether in seeking the fresh air from which he has been six days excluded, or in affording instructive enjoyment to his family. To deny him this humble freedom is surely the worst of the insolences of opinion.

"All progress is a growth, not an invention. Legislation can do little more than enable the people to help themselves. But this help, given with a personal knowledge of their wants, and in a spirit free from the temerity which would precipitate society on an unknown future, and free from the cowardice which is afraid to advance at all, may do much.—I am, gentlemen, your obedient servant,   GEORGE JACOB HOLYOAKE.

" 147, Fleet Street, March 23, 1857."

Looking at this address with its manifold proposals so long before their day, the reader will not wonder at my not being elected.

Mr. Acton Smee Ayrton was popular in the Tower Hamlets because he promised more thoroughness in Liberalism than Sir William Clay, who was a gentleman of fine manners and fixed principles—fixed also in the sense of not moving forwards, and this made many electors wish for a member capable of progress. Mr. Ayrton's election was uncertain, my candidature could not be successful, but by persisting in it I might imperil his chances ; so I wrote to him to the effect that I would retire and advise my friends to vote for him. At midnight he wrote me a grateful letter of acknowledgment.

On the day of the declaration of the poll, I was on the platform. Mr. Ayrton was not only hoarse, but his voice had that vinous impediment of utterance that Lord Garlies manifested when addressing the House of Commons on the Disabilities of Women, or Viscount Royston's when he spoke upon the Game Laws late at night. The returning officer, seeing Mr. Ayrton's distress, with kindly consideration procured an orange, no easy thing to get on that crowded platform, and handed it to Mr. Ayrton, saying—" Here, sir, try an orange, it may relieve you." A Tower Hamlets election mob thirty years ago was not a very dainty crowd, but they had an instinct for an act of public courtesy, and cheered the returning officer who showed it. To their astonishment Mr. Ayrton tossed the orange back into the giver's face, saying, with incredible rudeness, " I want no orange ! That's what they offer people when they are going to be hanged " —accusing the returning officer of treating him as a culprit. The remark was probably meant to be a witticism, and the speaker looked to the audience as though he expected the crowd would laugh. Their astonished silence did them credit. The returning officer never offered any more oranges to distressed members elect, but left them to roar unrelieved.

At the end there was a cry among some of the electors for me to speak. The majority of the crowd refused to hear anybody speak but Mr. Ayrton, and the returning officer, who was courteous to every one, said to him, " They will hear you ; just speak to them, and procure Mr. Holyoake a hearing." Though he had so recently written to me a letter of thanks for having contributed to his success, he turned away, and refused compliance with the request. As his election was assured, nothing could harm him further. But civility was contrary to his nature, nor could the obligation of gratitude reconcile him to it. The habit of offensiveness never forsook him. When he became the Right Hon. Commissioner of Works, he was always throwing the orange in somebody's face.

Mr Ayrton came into St. James's Hall after the great Radical procession to Hyde Park, and reproached the Queen for not being present in the Mall to see it pass. Mr. Ayrton himself was not there. It was then Mr. Bright arose and made his famous defence of the Queen. The Board of Works, of which Mr. Ayrton became Commissioner, suggests familiarity with scaffold poles, excavations, and brick carts, and Mr. Ayrton's manners were in keeping. He addressed Mr. Barry, the architect of the House of Commons, as though he were a jerry builder, and he compared Sir Joseph Hooker, the great botanical professor at Kew, to a " market gardener." These uncivil outrages cost Mr. Ayrton his seat at the Tower Hamlets, and I own to feeling gratification when discomfiture befel him. His unpopularity excluded him from Parliament ever after.

Long before his death I aided in promoting his return to the House of Commons by writing words to his advantage, where they were likely to be influential (in the *Nineteenth Century*) :

because, though manners are much in politics, principle is more, and Mr. Ayrton had principles to which, in his offensive way, he was true. The interest of the public service required that the architects' accounts and the Kew Gardens accounts should be audited by the Board of Works. Mr. Ayrton was an honest minister, and he encountered hostility enough on this ground without augmenting it by ill taste. It was to his credit that he opposed every system of centralisation, aided the repeal of the taxes upon knowledge, and procured the extinction of the editorial sureties. He had the credit when in the House of being the only member who read every bill brought in. He knew all that was attempted, and if he sometimes made mischief he stopped much. I ought also to mention that it was Mr. Ayrton who, finding in the archives of his office my suggestion made to Lord John Manners to have a light on the Clock Tower, put it up.

CHAPTER LXVI.

A LONDON REVOLUTION.

(1858.)

THIRTY-THREE years have elapsed since the parcel of papers and placards relating to the "Anti-Conspiracy Bill Committee" of 1858 (which were for the first time untied February 21, 1891) were laid aside. Most of those who took part in the agitation, which overthrew Lord Palmerston at that time, are now dead. Of Parliamentary men, Bright, Byng, Baines, Cobden, Disraeli, Gibson, Gilpin, Roebuck, Lord John Russell, Sir John Shelley; of members of the Committee, Mr. Ashurst, Mr. Shaen, Col. A. B. Richards, Mr. Richardson, and Mr Mackintosh have all died.

Few persons of the general public now have any definite idea of what took place in London in the third week in February, 1858. After the attempt of Orsini to kill the Emperor of the French in Paris, it was believed the Government would be asked to, and would, give up Dr. Bernard and another London citizen, reputedly associated with him. Some French colonels who happened to be in Paris at the time made warlike and menacing speeches, expressive of their readiness to come to London and fetch Dr. Bernard to be disposed of in Paris. This was an outrage upon the Queen, as it proclaimed a hostile invasion of her capital; but the Emperor of the French did not cause to be introduced into the French Parliament any bill to deal with these belligerent and compromising colonels. On the contrary, he directed Count Walewski to bring a charge against the English Government of "sheltering assassins and actually favouring their designs." Lord Palmerston, a friend

of Louis Napoleon, who connived at and encouraged his usurpation, made no reply to this insolent despatch, but brought in a
bill to call foreigners to account who in this country conspired
against a friendly government abroad. The bill was reasonable,
but untimely. Being brought in immediately after Walewski's
despatch, it gave the people of England the impression that
we were going to alter our laws, or make laws, at the dictation of a foreign Power. To this Englishmen never consent.
Neither Radical, Whig, Tory, nor Quaker would countenance
this un-English proceeding. Then I witnessed the only per-
emptory revolution occurring in England in my time, of which
I saw the beginning and the end.

Lord Palmerston brought in his Conspiracy Bill, and the
House of Commons passed the first reading. The next day,
Mr. W. H. Ashurst, Mr. James Stansfeld, Mr. P. A. Taylor,
Sir John Bennett, and Mr. Shaen, subscribed £5 each ; Colonel
A. B. Richards, George Leverson, Alderman Healey of Roch-
dale, Mr. John Mackintosh, and Mr. Connell subscribed lesser
amounts ; and I see, on the list made at the time, the name of
C. Bradlaugh for 5s., of which he had very few in those days.

On Saturday afternoon it was resolved to call a meeting for
Monday night, in the Freemason's Hall, though the intimation
of it, owing to shortness of time, could only be given by word
of mouth to political societies. On Monday, a meeting was
held in the Secular Room at my house, 147, Fleet Street. Mr.
W. H. Ashurst, Mr. W. Shaen, Mr. J. Stansfeld, Colonel
Richards (a Conservative, and then editor of the *Morning
Advertiser*), Mr. John Mackintosh, Mr. J. B. Langley, Mr.
George Leverson, Mr. Connell, and others were present. I
was asked to take the chair, and a committee was appointed of
those present, with power to add to their number. Funds
were to be collected, and I was elected treasurer. A demonstration was projected, if it could be brought about, to be held
in Hyde Park on Sunday.

On Monday evening, when we arrived, the Freemasons' Hall
was so crowded that the conveners of the meeting were unable
to get in. Mr. Stansfeld spoke to the manager of the hall,
who conducted us through the wine cellars to a private passage
that led on to the platform. In a small gallery on the opposite
side of the hall, fronting the platform, were two French spies,

disguised as gasfitters—assumed to be placed there by the
manager in case their services should be required. They were
admitted in the interests of the French Emperor. There were
no foreigners on the platform, nor were they observable in the
meeting. It was an English meeting called to consider an
English question. The variety and excitement of the audience,
who knew not who had called them together, was metropolitan,
and we saw that the question was in the hands of the people.
It then occurred to the leaders on the platform that they might
proceed to call a public meeting in Hyde Park on the following
Sunday, where the people of London could assemble to give
their opinion on the steps taken by the Government concerning the honour and reputation of the country. We had objections to holding political meetings in Hyde Park on the Sunday
except on a great national emergency, when the voice of London
required to be heard. Owing to business pursuits, the people
in imposing numbers could be assembled on no other day. It
was thought that the occasion justified a Sunday meeting in
the Park, and I was asked to announce it. The audience in
the hall was tumultuous, and, fearing I might not speak with
sufficient loudness for every one to hear, I asked several gentlemen to make the announcement for me. They, however,
proved unwilling to take the responsibility of it. I explained
that the committee took that onus, and merely wanted to
borrow a voice. Mr. Mackintosh, who wrote as "Northum-
brian" in *Reynolds's Newspaper*, who had been a schoolmaster,
and had stentorian lungs, finally complied with my request.
For a time he demurred ; but on my saying "Use my name,
and say you give the notice at my request," he consented. The
committeé desired notice given to that meeting, as there were
not sufficient funds to make known to the whole of London
their intention.

From the way in which the announcement was received,
there was no doubt those present would extend the publicity
of it. At eleven o'clock on that Monday night it was a matter
of doubt if London could be interested in the protest against
the proposed bill. Yet on the following Friday morning all
London was in the streets. I never knew London change so
in a few days. Not one shopkeeper in a hundréd takes any
part in public affairs. Probably not one man in a thousand of

the four millions of population can be counted upon to appear
in public agitation; yet on that Friday morning the shopkeepers in Oxford Street, from Holborn to the Marble Arch,
were at their doors conversing with passers-by, and discussing
the motion of which Mr. Milner Gibson had given notice for
the rejection of Lord Palmerston's Bill. The first reading of
that bill had been carried by the enormous majority of 200.
To destroy that majority in a week was an unusual undertaking. The Government were not merely confident—they
were jubilant. Mr. Baxter Langley placed his office in 3,
Falcon Court, at our disposal for placard purposes; and the
committee, at 147, Fleet Street, issued the following circular to
known publicists, societies, and clubs in town and country, for
none of us expected that success would come so swiftly as it
did :—

"You are urgently requested to co-operate with the great
movement which has commenced with the meeting at the
Freemasons' Tavern on Monday night, for the purpose of
opposing, by all legal means, the iniquitous Act of Lord Palmerston, called the Conspiracy to Murder Bill. We shall be
happy to receive delegates from the provinces to appear at our
public meetings in London, and we beg to impress upon you
the value of haste, in order that support may be given to those
members of Parliament who have voted against the bill, and
that the supporters of Palmerston may receive a warning from
their constituencies that if their votes be repeated they will lose
their seats. We intend now to hold meeting upon meeting, as
rapidly as possible, in every quarter, in order to elicit from the
people and the press a full expression of the wide and deep
feeling of disgust which pervades the public mind in London."

We need not have been so solicitous. Resentment at foreign
interference we found to be instinctive in the English heart.
In the meantime we issued placards. The longest, which follows, was drafted by Colonel Richards :—

"THE PEOPLE OF LONDON

will meet in Hyde Park on Sunday next, the 21st February, at
3 o'clock p.m., to protest by their peaceable and orderly presence

against the new Conspiracy Bill, introduced by Lord Palmerston under the dictation of the French Emperor, Louis Napoleon.

"Think of your countryman, the Engineer Watts, driven mad at Naples.

"Think of the insults of the French colonels.

"Are Foreign Spies and Police to be allowed to act on British Soil?

"Let those who attend in Hyde Park on Sunday next
Maintain perfect order.

"By order of the Freemasons' Hall Meeting Committee."

The next two were written by me :—

"ENGLISHMEN,

"On Monday, at Bow Street, an English magistrate presided at a political trial, under the surveillance of French Police Agents. Sir Richard Mayne sat on one hand, and a French Agent on the other. Is it come to this in London?

"Keep the Peace.   Attend at Hyde Park,
"Break no Law.   On Sunday, at 3 o'clock.
"Beware of all who attempt it."

The second was as follows :—

"MEN OF LONDON,

"Lord John Russell has said that, whoever may vote for Lord Palmerston's Bill, dictated by the French Government, 'that shame and humiliation he will not share.'

"Let all who would not share it either be present in Hyde Park on Sunday, at 3 o'clock."

Another placard was a passage from *The Times*, not complimentary to Lord Palmerston. We did not know then that *The Times* attacked him in the interests of despots :—

"It is impossible to mention a spot from the Tagus to the Dardanelles, from Sicily to the North Cape, where Lord Palmerston has founded one solid tangible claim to our gratitude and confidence. We will not measure him as a Russian

Minister, or an Austrian Minister, or a French Minister, because, if we do, we must admit that he has given Russia a plea
for successful aggrandisement ; that he has helped to aggravate
and confirm the Austrian dominion in Italy, rend her influences
in Germany ; and that he may even claim a share in the honour
in making France what it is. He has played the game of our
national rivals and political antagonists, or, to borrow a sentence
from Mr. Osborne, he has merged into a tool and automaton
whose hands have been directed, and whose moves have been
made, by the will and unseen influence of a foreign prompter.
There is no constituted authority in Europe with which Lord
Palmerston has not quarrelled ; there is no insurrection that
he has not betrayed. The ardent partizans of Sicilian, Italian,
and Hungarian independence have certainly no special cause
for gratitude to a minister who gave them an abundance of
verbal encouragements and then abandoned them to their fate."
—*The Times,* June, 1850.

There was another side to Palmerston's character. He
expressed more sympathy with " struggling nationalities " than
any other foreign Minister of his day, which, from one in his
position, was an advantage to them. Foreign leaders in some
cases expected military aid to follow, and in their disappointment condemned him for not doing what he had not promised.
Lord Palmerston must have had good in him and have done
some, since every despotic government abroad, save Louis
Napoleon's, detested him. We next placarded Lord John
Russell's famous speech against the Conspiracy Bill.

"' The threat (of France) has been somewhat too barely
exposed, somewhat too loudly uttered ; it has been so uttered
that I confess if I were to vote for this bill I should feel shame
and humiliation in giving that vote. Let those who will
support the bill of the Government ; that *shame* and
humiliation I am determined not to share.' (Tuesday,
February 9, 1858.) "

We enjoined order on every placard and suspicion of all who
did not observe it. London was overrun by foreign spies, and
is, indeed, never free from them. " Ignorant men, strangers

to public affairs, accuse in general the police of itself fabricating the plots which it discovers." Thiers said this, and his word has to be taken into account, as he had had great State experience. The police are often accused in this matter wrongfully; but experience also shows that they are at times accused rightfully. They have invented plots in England, as they do in Ireland to this day. There are always "fool friends" of progress who commit the cause quite enough without police plots.

We issued smaller bills for shop windows and for hand to hand circulation.

"Will you submit to surrender your rights and liberties at the demand of a Foreign Sovereign? If not—if you have still the same spirit your fathers had—attend in Hyde Park to protest against Lord Palmerston's Conspiracy Bill dictated by the French Government."

A meeting of delegates from England and Scotland was assembled in London then. Mr. Alderman Livesey, of Rochdale (a school-fellow of John Bright), presided, and made the most British speech delivered from any platform at that time. At this meeting I moved a petition to Parliament which set forth that no foreign prince ought to have power or jurisdiction in this realm, and that the "French Colonels' Bill"—as it had become to be called—was unnecessary, impolitic, and humiliating to the British nation. On receiving the petition, Lord John Russell wrote to me from Chesham Place saying he should have pleasure in presenting it.

Our meeting at the Freemasons' Hall was held on Monday night, February 16. On Friday, in the same week, Mr. Milner Gibson moved the rejection of the bill by an amendment drawn, as the press of the day said, " with his consummate skill." Mr. Walpole spoke against the bill, and so did Mr. Byng. Mr. Gladstone, too, made a speech against it, which Mr. Byng—a very good judge—said " excelled the finest efforts of Burke or Fox." Sir Robert Peel made against it the most sustained and dramatic speech he had delivered in the House. The Government had employed a Mr. Bodkin to prosecute Dr. Bernard. The way in which Sir Robert pronounced "Lawyer

Bodkin" filled the House with laughter. That night every
Liberal speaker seemed nationalized. Though only one public
meeting had been held and one Hyde Park meeting arranged,
the excitement of the country had taken possession of the
House. I have witnessed many great debates in Parliament,
but I never saw the same vehemence and national spirit as was
displayed from eleven o'clock till twenty minutes past two
o'clock on Saturday morning. I saw the proceedings from the
Reporters' Gallery. Those who think Mr. Gladstone cannot
speak with directness, compression, and economy of words,
should have heard his speech that night. Lord Palmerston was never less happy or less relevant. His voice was
thick and halting, as though he foresaw defeat. When the
division came, the 200 majority of the Government changed
sides or vanished, and, instead, a majority of 19 was recorded
against the "Colonels' Bill." Hats were waved (an unusual
thing in the House then) when the announcement was made.
The lobbies were crowded, and Palace Yard contained a large
throng of publicists and patriots waiting to learn the decision.
They went huzzaing along the streets, and people leaned out of
their bedroom windows to learn and cheer the good tidings.

A Cabinet Council was held the next afternoon, and the
Government resigned. From an early hour we were busy
endeavouring to undo what we had been energetically doing—
namely, to prevent the meeting we had called in Hyde Park.
The Government being overthrown, and the "Colonels' Bill"
dead, we wished to save London from tumult. We therefore
issued the two following announcements :—

1. "The committee of the Freemasons' Hall meeting, who
have been making arrangements for a great open-air demonstration in Hyde Park on Sunday, have resolved on abandoning
such meeting in consequence of the defeat of Lord Palmerston's
Conspiracy Bill by the House of Commons on Friday night."

2. "This morning a deputation from the committee for
arranging the Hyde Park meeting waited upon Sir Richard
Mayne to obtain his advice as to the best means of preventing
the public inconvenience from the announced meeting."

We spent more money on the Saturday and Sunday to

prevent an assemblage in the Park than we had spent all the week. We had notices of abandonment of the meeting posted at all points indicated by the police, where they would meet the eye of the East End throngs who might set out to the Park. However, the people went all the same, and it was computed that 200,000 were present on the Sunday afternoon, who came to rejoice instead of to protest.

There were some cases of disorder before the courts the next day, when the London magistrates were offensive and brutal to the people, as they usually are when political issues arise. Some cases of pocket-picking occurred, as they do even at the Lord Mayor's Show. Mr. Beadon, the Marlborough Street magistrate, said the committee who brought the people together were " morally as guilty as the pickpockets." Calling upon the public to meet in defence of national honour is legal, and it was the duty of the magistrate to aid the committee on asserting that right, and to punish and denounce only those who abuse a public right. But London magistrates acted otherwise. The police authorities well knew that the committee kept on legal lines. We had nothing to conceal. I sent to Sir Richard Mayne and the Home Secretary copies of all placards and circulars the moment they were issued. We had no idea that a vast meeting would result from any appeal we could make. It was well for us the bill was defeated, or London in still greater numbers would have been in the Park, and the excitement would have been beyond our control. But for that the Government alone would have been " morally " responsible.

The most memorable contribution to the agitation was the following brilliant answer to Louis Napoleon by Walter Savage Landor. The French Government described England as " a den of assassins." The poet published in the *Daily News* this " Reply from the ' Den ' " :—

" We encourage assassins ! Sir ! Have no fear,
No hold has the murderer or sympathies here:
England loathes an assassin, and loathes him no less
Whether shameful by failure or great by success—
Whether hiding from sight, or set high on a throne—
Whether killer of thousands, or killer of one—
Whether bribe or revenge, or the hope of a name,
Or the dream of a ' Destiny ' ' damn him to fame.'
Whatever the prompting, whatever the end,
Has he slaughtered a people he swore to defend :

Has he banded with ruffians, like him, to strike
At a brother assassin—we loathe him alike !

E'en where, Cain-like, by Providence guarded from ill,
With a mark set upon him that no man may kill ;
Where prosperity seems all his projects to crown,
We've no faith in his Favour—no fear of his Frown :
Undismayed by his Fortunes—unawed by his Fate,
We smile at his ' Destiny '—WATCH him and WAIT."

People did so—and saw the dynasty of the Usurper go down
under the sword of Germany and the assegai of a Zulu.

CHAPTER LXVII.

MURDER AS A MODE OF PROGRESS.

(1859.)

My experience at one time made me a connoisseur in assassination—a question often defended but seldom discussed in a practical way. Unconsidered applause on one hand and uninstructive reprobation on the other, are all that meet the public ear. Professor Tyndall made a notable contribution to physical science, entitled " Heat a Mode of Motion." It is not less useful in political science to consider the question of " Murder as a Mode of Progress." If the theory of political murder were understood, it would not command many followers. Yet, in consequence of its being treated as a suppressed question, it has for many persons the enchantment which belongs to the " forbidden."

Intelligence may be revolutionary, but ignorance, especially if it be hungry, always is. Its impulse is change by force—its reason a sense of unendurable wrong. It has no plan—its future is only a day or a week, yet retaliation as a remedy is far from being the doctrine of the ferocious. I have known persons of real tenderness and sympathy, and for whose humanity I could unhesitatingly answer, who yet have had a reserve of sanguinary principles for advancing political progress. Those who look to see not what they expect to see, but what is to be seen, will find that a Government which upholds its authority by the discriminate killing of adversaries, accepts itself the principle of progress by murder. Seeing this, persons of strong purpose whom I have known come to think that the oppressed may use the same means. Despotism being mere force, wielded

-3

by irresponsible will, tyrant killing, undertaken for public ends, with a view to temper or suppress despotism, is *not* regarded by moralists as murder. It is apparently a necessity of progress *there* and at that stage only, and is only defensible when done under such circumstances that armed resistance cannot be reasonably attempted. Where the justification of irremediable oppression does not exist, tyrant-killing is a mistake.

It is admitted now that the old theory of kingship is worn out. Formerly a man was regarded as a lawful ruler who reigned by what he called " divine right." Since representative government began, a king is regarded as a despot unless he reigns by Parliamentary right. A ruler may be good or bad, but he is still a despot if he rules by his own authority, or prevents any one else ruling by public appointment. If he be a good ruler, he is called " Paternal "—if bad, he is called a " Tyrant." But in both characters he is a despot. Force used without public consent officially expressed, is tyranny, and he who employs it is a tyrant, whether his purpose be good or evil. Mankind are prone to be enslaved, and are generally content so long as they are enslaved pleasantly. If a succession of good kings could be secured, paternal government would be eternal. The indolence of mankind would never attempt the honourable trouble of self-government. Therefore the good tyrants are seldom attacked. Yet they render manliness and progress impossible. Every man who seeks self-government himself, or seeks it for his countrymen, is a judge and adversary of him who renders it impossible. Nevertheless the good despot who rules justly cannot be usefully killed, since one cannot be sure that an untried government, introduced by force, could rule better than he. Self-government is justified as offering greater security for peace and wider progress, and cannot consistently be begun by blood. But the base ruler, whose power is personal and regulated by his own will for his own ends, and not by public law for the public good, is the enemy of an intelligent people : and if he withstand by force the advocacy of liberty, the law of progress exposes him, like a beast of prey, to be destroyed when met. Despotic rulers know this well.

The doctrine of tyrant killing is not a doctrine of the people merely : it has been accepted by kings as well as peoples.

Silas Titus was accorded a colonelcy under Charles II., because he had published a pamphlet of deadly purport against the chief ruler—the Lord Protector Cromwell. The English Tories favoured the assassination of Napoleon I., and he in his turn pensioned a man who meditated the assassination of the Duke of Wellington. Charlotte Corday's knife was applauded by the monarchs of France. Royalist assassins always abound. Lord Beaconsfield in a famous triplet—" Blessed the hand that wields the regicidal steel." Mr. Froude shows that Catholics and Protestants have alike approved tyrannicide and used it. The doctrine is not confined to the class of "agitators." Governments hold the doctrine and act upon it. They often cause persons to be put to death on principle. They have often held it to be good policy to kill a few popular leaders in order to strike terror into their followers. Carlyle favoured this policy, Governor Eyre put it in practice in Jamaica, and he found Canon Kingsley (just minded as he was in most things) and men more eminent than he came forward to approve it.

Four things seem necessary in him who assumes to act by his single hand as the agent of a nation :

1. That the tyrannicide must have intelligence sufficient to understand the responsibility of setting himself up as the redresser of a nation. If set upon the work by others he is a tool, or secondhand operator—an instrument in the hands of others ; a bravo rather than a self-determined patriot.

2. He who proposes to take a life for the good of the people must at least be prepared to give his own if necessary—both as atonement for taking upon himself the office of public avenger and to secure that his example shall not generate other than equally disinterested imitators. The many failures of tyrannicidal attempts have been mainly owing to the precaution taken by the actors for their own safety, and who end by bestowing upon the tyrant the reputation of " bearing a charmed life," when retaliatory oppression is brought upon others. Colonel Titus, the royalist pamphleteer who wrote "Killing no Murder," which advised that some one should put Cromwell to death, was without pretension to the dignity of a tyrannicide, since he was a mere inciter of assassination which somebody else was to take the risk of committing.

3. The adversary of the despot must not be weak, vacillating,

or likely to lose his head in unforeseen circumstances, nor be deficient in the knowledge and skill needful for his purpose. Without these qualities he should keep clear of an undertaking where failure will prove dangerous to those he professes to free.

4. He should have good knowledge that the result intended is likely to come to pass afterwards. History tells us how many noble men have been sacrificed ; how many a holy cause has been put back for years, or for centuries even, by untimely self-sacrifice. Curtius would have been an idiot if he had leaped into the gulph before he was well-assured that doing so would close it.

If tyrannicide is to be approved as a policy the business of the despot-ender should be an art, and praise should be given under conditions. The public avenger is one who aspires to the foremost place which patriotism can occupy. He, by his single hand, is the deliverer of a nation from an overshadowing terror and danger. He voluntarily accepts supreme peril that his country may escape it. More disinterested than the hero who perishes in battle, where he has chances of escape, he ranks with the martyr who gives up his life for the freedom of others. For him we change the dread epithet of " murderer " and call him by the proud name of " Avenger of the People." He should be no mean man for whom we do this.

In days when men were wanted for forlorn hopes, I received letters from persons whom I knew and could trust, offering to engage in any work involving death which I might commend. I could not advise where I took no risk. The decision I left to them when they knew the circumstances of the occasion : and the higher the ideal of duty and peril in their minds the less likely they were to act heedlessly or needlessly.

Once I was asked to meet a number of ladies, two or three were wives of members of Parliament. Politics interested them, and they had capacity for public affairs. They asked my opinion upon tyrant killing, which they favoured, and there were else-where many ready to act upon their sanction. I answered that " at the time preceding the French Revolution many ladies held the same opinion, and if these English ladies spread the doctrine with the same fervour and had the same influence, they would assuredly share the same fate. For myself, I had not made up my mind that murder was a mode of progress."

I saw that character of the doctrine had not occurred to them, nor that it was a doctrine that may have unpleasant adherents. " Disciples," I said, " might arise of more advanced views than their own, and who might, in the interests of public progress, apply the doctrine to them."

It was because death by private hands begets death that it came to be limited by law. The French revolutionists of 1793 were insurgents created by oppression, who, having no experience of the limitations of freedom, contrived to make Liberty a greater terror than despotism. They killed on suspicion. Tyrannicide became a profession, and thousands followed the calling. Mrs. Francis Pulzsky once said to me at her own table, " Mr. Holyoake, when we had power we gave our influence to prevent any throat being cut. But no sooner were our enemies secure, whom we had saved, than they cut the throats of our party. When we get power again," said the brilliant little lady, " we will cut theirs without mercy." I said " I hoped not, for the forbearance she regretted was the noblest example democracy ever set." Leniency may fail for a time, but in politics it is a noble error. Acts of kindness will fail in private life, but kindness in the long run proves the first of virtues. She was speaking not of her own country, but of the policy of the Continental defenders of liberty, among whom were the Hungarian patriots, who suffered everywhere when the " Saviours of society " again got the upper hand.

In a free country " tyrannicide " is a worn-out theory. Under representative Government, the ballot-box, penny newspapers, and the right of public meeting, those who cannot extend the bounds of freedom do not understand their business. The printing press has made opinion a force in politics. If all those who depend upon the knife for improvement were to display half the amount of self-sacrifice which they have to make in their perilous method of extermination, they would see accomplished what they wish earlier and more surely.

CHAPTER LXVIII.

DEFENDING A POLE.

(1858.)

WHEN a publisher in London, I had my business to consider, but so often as a public question arose I found myself under some unprofitable impulse to take part in it, when others with a more prudent sense of personal interest abstained. Louis Napoleon, in one of his disquieting and menacing New Year Day addresses, had announced that—"The Empire seeks a strong power capable of overcoming the obstacles which might stop its advance." "I do not," he said, "fear to declare to you to-day that the danger, no matter what is said to the contrary, does not exist in the excessive prerogatives of power, but in the *absence of repressive laws.*" This is exactly what has often been said of Ireland.

The President of the Senate, addressing the Emperor in reply, said—"Sire, your glorious House sits as firmly as the throne of England. The revolutionary spirit has been driven from France. [The Emperor having made the bloodiest revolution on record.] It is from foreign strongholds, situated in the centre of Europe [meaning England] that hired assassins are sent. Foreign Governments and people *do not take measures to give a legitimate support to the cause of order.*"

Mr. William Carpenter, the author of the best " Political Text Book " of the time, was chairman of the Discussion Forum, which the French Government described as "a coffee-house near Temple Bar," and he had to write to the Emperor informing him that "the members were for the most part substantial tradesmen and men of business, who discussed the question ' Is

Regicide Justifiable ? ' without reference to existing governments or politics." The Emperor replied that he was satisfied
with the explanation, which he well might be, as he knew all
about it, and had hung about the Fleet Street Forum himself.

At this time (1858), Felix Pyat, M. Besson, and A. Talandier
published a " Letter " in French, entitled " Parliament and the
Press." Proceedings were taken against a Pole, Stanislaus
Tchorzewski, for publishing the letter here. I thought that
the ground of the prosecution, and the manner of it, were alike
objectionable and unnecessary. The English could not read
the letter in French, and the few Frenchmen likely to see it
in this country were not likely to be influenced by it, as it told
them nothing they did not already know. I asked Professor
Newman for his opinion upon it, as one far more competent
than myself to judge it. He answered (*Reasoner*, No. 615) that
" the outline of thought in the pamphlet was judicial and its
conclusion breathed no spirit of blood-thirsty revenge. It
reminded us that Louis Napoleon was deposed and condemned
for high treason by a lawful court, and that after this, being no
longer a lawful officer, he had slaughtered citizens for doing
that which the law commanded them to do—namely, to uphold
the Constitution against him ; and that by such lawless violence
he had seized and kept supreme power." There could be little
danger from the Pyat Letter since it took Lord Derby, who
was then in power, three weeks to make up his mind whether
it ought to be prosecuted. The proceedings against the Polish
publisher were believed to have been taken at foreign instiga-
tion, and amounted to denial of freedom of speech for the exiles
among us—exiles who, being friendless, were entitled to our
sympathy, and who, being residents in England, were entitled
to equality ; who, being our guests, were entitled to our protection. I objected to the policy of prosecuting the publisher of
Felix Pyat's " Letter," because it in no way endangered the
life of Louis Napoleon. The conspirators who are to be feared
are, as a rule, not those who are weak enough to proclaim their
wishes, or suicidal enough to publish their intentions. By doing
so they invite observation to themselves and fix suspicion upon
their friends. Conspirators who publish their plans usually give
hostages to the police that they shall never succeed.

The prosecution of Tchorzewski was a purely French prosecution, conducted with a political indecency alien to English sentiment. On the left hand of Mr. Jardine, at Bow Street, there sat, during the investigations, Sir Richard Mayne, the chief of the Metropolitan police, and on the right, agents of the French police ; and we saw an English magistrate so unmindful of British dignity as to sit under their surveillance and act like a French official, and, forgetting his character as an English gentleman and his duty as an English magistrate, deliver himself of sentiments which we could only suppose were dictated to him. When Mr. Sleigh, speaking as a British barrister should, in the presence of the British people, uttered a few words which found their way to the heart of some poor exiles in court (who, glad to believe that a foreign servility was not tainting every English tongue, gave utterance to their feelings), Mr. Bodkin made offensive remarks upon Mr. Sleigh, who deemed it necessary to apologise for his own manliness. Mr. Bodkin (Sir Robert Peel's Bodkin), the prosecuting counsel, all the while spoke himself to that interfering Tuileries public whom, instead of his own countrymen, he represented. No demagogue in London, nor all the pamphlets published by exiles, had produced so much ill-blood between the two nations as the proceedings in Mr. Jardine's court. We cheer the demagogue and forget his speech. We invite the violent exile to dinner, and neglect his exhortation ; but we remember as an abiding degradation when the English magistrate insults us in the eyes of the foreigner, and that too in London, where the countryman comes with wonder, the artizan with pride, and the provincial gentleman to watch our highest public manners. I was in Sheffield when I read the account of these proceedings against Tchorzewski. I consulted no one. My own sense of duty dictated the step I took, and I telegraphed to London to instruct my brother Austin to procure a translation and put it in the press.

The newspapers soon acquainted the Government that one result of their prosecuting an unknown Polish bookseller in Rupert Street, for having issued a French pamphlet, which few would ever see, was that a publisher in the city of London had issued an English edition which everybody could read. As I had no wish to be Bodkinized or Jardinized, I begged the Attorney-General to distinguish between this act of public defence and one of defiance. In the preface I wrote to the English edition I issued at Fleet Street, I stated that it was not my interest to incur imprisonment, that I knew what it was and was not covetous to renew that experience, and that I neither wanted notoriety nor martyrdom. Therefore, I prayed the Government not to honour me with their perilous attentions. I sent the first copy of the Tchorzewski pamphlet in English to Lord Derby, who was then Premier, saying—

"MY LORD,—Permit to me the liberty of enclosing to you a pamphlet which I deem a public duty to publish. I do not send it to each member of the Cabinet—that might appear a defiance. Not to send it to any one would be a discourtesy ; I therefore send it to your lordship as one who, in the opinion of the people, views all political questions in an unprejudiced English spirit."

In the silence of abject submission which reigned in France, we heard only the chains of the slave and the voice of the informer. That state of things concerned us. Despotism so near cast its shadow over England. To extend liberty here was a reproach to our ally ; every discussion upon it in London made Paris uneasy. Every plea for it here was an indirect reflection upon the ruler there. Still England did not desist. For myself I sought shelter under no technicality. I invited no consequences, nor did I evade them. I did but justify an English act by English reasons.

The pamphlet published by Stanislaus Tchorzewski was signed by the " Committee of the Revolutionary Commune— Felix Pyat, Besson, A. Tallandier." Tchorzewski I never saw ; Pyat I did not know, nor Besson. Tallandier was a friend of mine. He was the first who translated my "History of the Rochdale Pioneers" into the French language ; but no personal reason induced me to publish the manifesto of the Commune in English. My object was to vindicate the liberty of the English press. In my note to the English edition I said, " I regretted the inopportune appearance of the Letter. Being issued while the fate of Orsini was undecided, it was calculated to ensure his execution. It was so illtimed that the Emperor might have been suspected of instigating its appearance." But at the request of Tallandier I omitted these words. Mazzini wrote me a letter approving of the Tchorzewski publication in English, as calculated to convince the Government of the futility of these prosecutions. Upon re-reading the prosecuted letter of Pyat, many years later, I thought its style neither so good, nor its sentiments so bad, as they were both believed to be then.

At the same time I commenced editing a series of " Tyrannicide Literature," and began with a cheap edition of " Killing no Murder," by Colonel Titus, to show Englishmen what the Royalist doctrine of assassination was. I also published a remarkable poem entitled, " The Peace of Napoleon," by my friend, the late Mr. Percy Greg, and signed with the name under which he usually wrote for me—Lionel H. Holdreth. The poem was more indictable than anything which the Government honoured by prosecution. I quote a few prophetic verses :—

> " Peace ! Hark, the voices of despairing men
> Pining in exile, squalor, solitude,
> Cry from the deadly swamps of far Cayenne—
>   ' God ! give us blood for blood !'
>
> Since that sad morning when December's sky
> Scowled on the brave who fruitlessly withstood
> The Perjurer's arms, the stones of Paris cry
>   ' God ! give us blood for blood !'
>
> And thou, fair partner of the Perjurer's throne,
> Recreant to virtue, truth, and womanhood !
> Think, if perchance he should not fall alone,
>   'Twill but be blood for blood !
>
> I pray thou may'st be scathless—spared in scorn—
> Husband, child, empire gone, till thou hast rued
> In bitter tears the hour that thou wert born
>   When God sends blood for blood !
>
> Blood shall have blood ere long, if One on high
> The prayer of earth hath heard and understood ;
> To whom the nations ceaselessly do cry—
>   ' God ! give us blood for blood !' "

Notwithstanding, no proceedings were taken against me. By what reason the Government were actuated I know not— probably it was the City that saved me. I was a freeman of the city of London, which always sets itself against prosecutions of the press. My friend, Edward Truelove, at that time published a pamphlet entitled "Tyrannicide," and his house being west of Temple Bar, he was arrested and taken to Bow Street. My house being in the City, I must have been taken to the Mansion House. It was impossible to prosecute the Pole for his French publication, and I be left unmolested. In the end the prosecution of Tchorzewski was dropped, and that against Mr. Truelove was compromised. Miss Harriet Martineau, Mr. William Coningham, M.P. for Brighton, Mr. John Stuart Mill, and Professor F. W. Newman publicly subscribed to a fund for Mr. Truelove's defence, names which may have induced the Government to desist from the prosecution they had commenced against him.

When the Government ceased to prosecute, the tyrannicide literature ceased also. The object was not persistence in it, but to vindicate the liberty of the press. Just resistance is of public advantage even when not successful in its aim, as in the case here related it appeared to be. Thiers said of Orsini's bombs —" They missed the Emperor, but they killed the Empire."

CHAPTER LXIX.

A LOST WILL.

(1858.)

MR. FLETCHER, a gentleman of Kennington, often came to the Fleet Street House. One day he proposed to make me a loan of £250 in the form of a bill for three years, which I was to get discounted. I offered it to W. Devonshire Saul, who dealt in bills and wine, and who knew Mr. Fletcher. Without giving reasons, he declined it. To put it in circulation I must sacrifice a large proportion of the amount. As I felt bound to repay Mr. Fletcher, a large discount would render me unable to do it. All the while he intended to give the sum to me, but did not say so. Eventually I returned the bill, lest I incurred an obligation beyond my power to meet. This act no doubt wounded his commercial pride, and also gave him a deplorable impression of my business ability. Had I been a "smart" man, I should have got what I could for the bill, and have left him to take it up. Had I had business wit, I should have kept the bill and had it presented by a confederate, when matured, and thus have profited. It was the feeling of being bound in honour to repay the money if I received it which prevented my retaining it. Herein scrupulousness was a disadvantage.

Mr. Fletcher showed no resentment, and made his will in my favour. At that time he estimated his fortune at £30,000. Having fair expectation of life, he invested a large portion in purchasing an annuity of £2,000 a year, expecting that in due course the proceeds of the annuity would make him still richer. The will he handed to me in a sealed parcel, which my brother Austin kept for me. At the end of two years he asked for the parcel again. One day he invited Robert Cooper and me to tea, and afterwards in my presence handed him the will. Mr. Fletcher had acquired a prejudice against me, being told by the chief person in my employ that fair play had not been given at Fleet Street to Mr. Cooper's works — he being an author and lecturer like myself. This was entirely untrue. Had I been aware of what had been told to Mr. Fletcher, it would have been easy to disabuse his mind. If my conduct had been what he believed, he would have been justified in resenting it. Mr. Cooper was editing the *Investigator*. He considered himself a rival to me, and his paper frequently contained attacks upon me, not conceived with the intention of being pleasing. But I published his paper all the same, never caring what anybody said. Never did any one, save Lloyd Garrison, of America, publish more articles against himself than I did.   In the *Reasoner* similar articles were constantly published, nothing being omitted save dishonouring imputations upon others. My chief clerk at Fleet Street was formerly a local preacher, who seemed trustworthy. Finding that he owed his last employer £20, I lent him the money to pay it, as I declined to take an indebted man into my service. This person ultimately appropriated to his own uses upwards of £100 of my money. For reasons of his own he told Mr. Fletcher that I kept back Mr. Cooper's books, although I had enjoined him that Mr. Cooper's publications should be kept prominently in sight—and they were so kept—that he might have no cause for jealousy.

No doubt in due time Mr. Fletcher would have found that he had been misinformed and would have restored his will to me, but in a few months he unexpectedly died. Being penurious, though rich, he was insufficiently clothed in inclement weather, and, being overtaken by a storm, the effects were fatal to him in a few days. Mr. Cooper received the remainder of his fortune, which, however, did not do him much good, as he went into a banking business and lost it. For three days only after Mr. Fletcher's death the sense of my loss was a sharp discomfort, but it passed away then. During the time the will was in my possession, I was constantly away debating with adversaries in distant parts of England and Scotland, and seldom had time to see Mr. Fletcher, or I should have found out what influence he was under. Thus absorption in public work was against me.

When the local preacher referred to ceased to be in my employ, he owed me £112. He then sought an engagement as minister among the Unitarians. The Rev. Samuel Martin, hearing of this, told Mr. Kendrick, in whose hands the appointment rested, that he "had better see Mr. Holyoake before he made it." How Mr. Martin came to know of the indebtedness to me I was never aware, though I was indebted to Mr. Martin's consideration. Mr. Kendrick came to me and asked my opinion of the candidate. My reply was that "he had zeal and doubtless good intention, but was wanting in self-control, but under clear and strong direction he might make a useful preacher." As I had once trusted him, I was unwilling by any word of mine to stand in the way of his future.

Mr. Kendrick then asked me for what sum, if any less than that owing, the candidate's indebtedness could be condoned, as they could not receive him into their communion unabsolved. My answer was that, as "I had once told him, if he repaid me the half of that which he owed me, I would acquit him, I would do so still." That sum was sent me, and I owed that sum to Mr. Kendrick's Unitarian sense of honour. I wrote a letter at Mr. Kendrick's request, which enabled the appointment to be made. No acknowledgment was ever sent me by the person concerned for the consideration shown him, nor any return made for the half amount in equity due to me, when it became possible to him to make it.

CHAPTER LXX.

MR. SECRETARY WALPOLE AND THE JACOBIN'S FRIEND.

(1858.)

A GOVERNMENT ought to be more scrupulously just and more considerately generous than private individuals, for they have unlimited powers of damage, annoyance, and penal revenge in their hands. They can strike at the innocent and guilty alike, and that passes for commendable vigilance in them which in individuals would be seen to be rank spite. The Dr. Bernard trouble did not end with his acquittal. One not a Frenchman, but because he was a friend of Dr. Bernard, became a person of so much interest or anxiety to the English Government that they offered £200 for his head. They did not put it in that plain way, but their object was to try him for his life. He was known as a man of noble friendships and generous courage, or he had not permitted himself to be regarded as Dr. Bernard's personal acquaintance.

His high spirit, his disinterestedness, his philosophic mind and personal intrepidity, were a constant cause of inspiration to all who knew him. He became, as I have said, the subject of solicitude on the part of the Government, who thought they had international reason for hanging him. They had no just cause for such belief, but made a show of assiduity in the matter, to gratify the susceptibility of the Emperor of the French, who was then considered our " good ally." The friend whose death was sought Dr. Bernard and I sometimes met at the White Swan Hotel, Covent Garden, and at Ginger's Hotel, which, as I have said, then stood near Palace Yard, Westminster Bridge Road.

After the Lepelletier affair, the Government were induced to offer a reward of £200 for the discovery of my friend, who, having means of knowing what was in their minds, was nowhere apparent in the British dominions. For two years he was an exile. The reward for his apprehension being still in force at the end of that period, I and Mr. Baxter Langley waited upon the Home Secretary, who in those days was Mr. Spencer Walpole. We presented ourselves to him as persons who had a friend to sell, provided we were sure of payment. We were not so lost to self-respect as not to put a price upon our virtue. We were prepared to be perfidious for £200. On our being guaranteed the reward, the gentleman the Government desired to see would appear. He had no objections to being hanged if that was thought right, but, being accustomed to outdoor life, he objected to be imprisoned, but would (he instructed us to say) present himself on the day appointed for trial. We stated that the reward offered for his appearance, which we applied for, was to defray the cost of his defence, as it was not reasonable that any one void of offence should be put to expense to prove it. Though aided by gratuitous services on many hands, Dr. Bernard's defence cost him £850. He, with no means but his earnings, had many lectures, lessons, and prescriptions to give before he paid that serious bill. All we asked further was that when our exiled friend appeared within British precincts, the police who might become aware of it should not have a right of reward as against us, who brought him within their range. The Government took time to consider the proposition. The sagacious Home Secretary surmised some plot, and Mr. H. Waddington, writing from "Whitehall, June 18, 1858," told us that "he was desired by Mr. Secretary Walpole to inform us that the reward of two hundred pounds offered by the Government in the case referred to by us had not been withdrawn." This was so far assuring—the money was to be had if we could induce Mr. Walpole to sign a cheque for it.

My friend the "Man in the Street" (the writing name in the *Morning Star* of Mr. Langley) took steps in his way, and I in mine, to cause Mr. Walpole to know that the object of the application made to him was simply the return home of the political wanderer in whom the Government had taken such complimentary but mistaken interest. Mr. Milner Gibson put one of his skilful questions in the House of Commons. Mr. William Coningham, M.P. for Brighton, always for justice, spoke with Mr. Walpole. In twenty-four days Mr. Waddington wrote a much more intelligent and satisfactory letter, thus :—

"WHITEHALL, *July* 12, 1858.

"GENTLEMEN,—I am directed by Mr. Secretary Walpole to inform you that, since the date of my answer to your application, the law officers of the Crown have been consulted and have expressed the opinion that it is not advisable to take any further steps in the prosecution in question. The Government have consequently determined to put an end to the proceedings against that gentleman and to withdraw the offer of a reward of £200 for his apprehension.—I remain, Gentlemen, your obedient servant,   H. WADDINGTON.

"Mr. G. J. Holyoake—Mr. J. B. Langley."

This letter was a charter of freedom. Mr. Walpole, in his gentlemanly way, so intended it. It was explicit and complete. We have had Home Secretaries and Irish Secretaries who would have gone so far as to say that the reward was withdrawn, and have kept silence as to whether other " proceedings " might or might not take place at the discretion of the Government. The terms of our letter of inquiry as to the reward would have been answered and no more. All the requirements of cold, contemptuous, red-tape courtesy would have been fulfilled, and we could have made no complaint. Besides, Mr. Walpole was under no necessity of showing civility to one reputed to be a friend of Orsini and Dr. Bernard, however distinguished his social position might be. In the opinion of Mr. Walpole's class, insolence would not only have been condoned, it would have been applauded, as we have since seen with Irish gentlemen. Silence as to future proceedings would have been thought politic. The Emperor of the French had his views of the affair ; and silence as to whether " further steps were put an end to " would have amounted to an unexpressed ticket-of-leave, without incurring the odium of formally issuing it, although no trial had been held and no verdict of guilty given. Dr. Bernard's friend, as a gentleman of independent spirit, would have still remained under accusation and must have stayed abroad.

But this was not Mr. Walpole's way. He did not agree with us on any question of opinion or politics, but he was a man of honour—an adversary of generous instinct—and his letter was a charter of acquittal. Withdrawing the reward, he withdrew the charge. And the exile returned to England, and dwelt many years in the land with honour.

CHAPTER LXXI.

LORD PALMERSTON AND FEARGUS O'CONNOR'S SISTER.

(1858-64.)

LORD PALMERSTON was a Minister for whom I had respect without sympathy. He was without prejudice, and without enthusiasm. Mr. Cobden said of him he was absolutely impartial, having no bias, not even towards the truth. This was not a general estimate of him, but provoked by an incident as to what Mr. David Urquhart called the "falsification of the Burnes despatches." Personally Lord Palmerston was capable of generous things, but in politics he was a Minister of the stationaries, and for years was kept in office by Whig and Tory, because he could be trusted not to do anything. He never said he was the enemy of reform, but he never "felt like" promoting it.

The author of no great measure, the advocate of no great cause ; like the singer, the dancer, and the actor, Lord Palmerston's genius was personal, and died with him. His power of waiting was something like Talleyrand's. He became great simply by living long and keeping his eyes open. His length of days was an advantage to him in diplomacy, as he knew all the tricks of two generations of intriguers all over the world, and had Palmerston any passion for the service of the people he had opportunities to do them good. His face was wrinkled with treaties. If pricked, he would have bled despatches.

The best thing ever said of him was that foreign tyrants hated him. It was not clear in his day why they did. The reason being he was seldom ready to befriend them. He caused the recognition of Louis Napoleon's usurpation which disgraced England

76

and set France against us. Yet Palmerston had merits which those whose aspirations he opposed were unable to estimate, or Mr. Gladstone would not have esteemed him so highly as he did. It was brought against him by Liberal leaders abroad, that he held out to them hopes of assistance, but rendered none when the time for it came. Still it was to his credit that he had diplomatic sympathy with their aims. It was seldom they found that in an English Foreign Minister. Any foreign leaders whom I knew, who spoke to me on the subject, I warned against expecting anything more than sympathy (and they might be glad if they got that), as the Foreign Office was quite independent of the people, and very often a generous Minister could not, under dynastic restraints, do what he wished.

About 1838 I was asked to join a political society which met at Mr. Jenkinson's (No. 6, Church Street, Birmingham), a bookseller and politician. It proved to be a Foreign Affairs Committee, established by David Urquhart. The object of the society I found to be to cut off Lord Palmerston's head. Things were bad among workmen in those days, and I had no doubt somebody's head ought to be cut off, and I hoped they had hit upon the right one. The secretary was a Chartist leader named Warden, who ended by cutting his own head off instead, which showed confusion of ideas by which Lord Palmerston profited. Poor Warden cut his own throat. He was a man of ability, and had a studious mind. He gave me a volume of the speeches of Demosthenes, which he often read. It bore his name written in a neat hand. Lord Palmerston was not to be assassinated, but " impeached " in a constitutional way, and the block at the Tower was to be looked up, and the too long disused axe was to be furbished and sharpened for the occasion. This was my first introduction to practical politics.

Lord Palmerston always had an airy indifference of manner —*Punch* drew him with a straw in his mouth, as though he regarded politics from a sporting point of view. Buoyancy was his characteristic. Shortly before his death, when he was more than 80, I watched him crossing Palace Yard, one summer evening, when the House was up early. Cabs were running about wildly, but he dodged them with agility, and went on foot to Cambridge House, in Piccadilly, where he resided.

This notice of Lord Palmerston is, of course, confined to
matters of personal knowledge, or of the influence he exercised
on agitations in which I was concerned or interested. Cobden
warned all reformers anxious for an extension of the franchise
that nothing would be done while Lord Palmerston lived.
There was no hope until heaven called him away. When at
length he died, I wrote that "the political atmosphere was
fresher, if not sweeter." The Reform Club draped itself in
black as his remains passed by its doors. The Carlton Club
might have done this consistently. The Princess of Wales sat
at the window of St. James's Palace, next her own house, to see
the Premier's funeral pass., How they bury public men in
Denmark I know not. She could not be favourably impressed
with the English way. A dreary, ugly hearse, with horses
carrying on their ribs a tinfoil, gingerbread-painted plate of
the Palmerston arms, was the tinsel centre of the pageant—
not inappropriate considering the noble lord's career as far as
the people were concerned.

He learnt from Lord Melbourne the art of doing nothing.
Melbourne valued most those advisers who could show him
how a public question could be let alone. Palmerston had the
merit in his turn of impressing Disraeli with the advantage of
gaiety in politics. The rich were glad to have reform put back
with a jest, but working men had not the same reason for
satisfaction.

Towards the end of his life, Lord Palmerston was invited to
Bradford to lay the foundation-stone of the new Exchange. On
that occasion, the working men were desirous of presenting an
address to him, upon their wish for an extension of the franchise. Mr. Ripley, chairman of the Exchange Committee,
utterly ignorant of Lord Palmerston's nature, refused to permit
any approach to him. The worst enemy of Lord Palmerston
could not have done him a worse service. Nothing would have
pleased him better than to have met a working-class deputation. His personal heartiness, his invincible temper, his
humour and ready wit would have captivated the working men,
and sent them away enthusiastic, although without anything to
be enthusiastic about.

At that time, 1864, I was editing the *English Leader*, read
by many working-class leaders in Bradford. What I could do

by articles and lectures in the town to encourage them to maintain public silence on Lord Palmerston's visit I did. They put
out an address in which they told the people that more was
involved in the visit than the ceremony of laying a foundation
stone.

"The principal actor," they said, "being no less a personage
than the Prime Minister of England, the working classes
will be expected, by the promoters of the visit, to assemble
in thousands, and give his lordship welcome—receiving him
with plaudits without a thought as to whether the object of
their homage is a friend or foe to their just rights and privi-
leges. But will it be wise on your part—who are as yet
unenfranchised, and mainly so through the influence of this
Minister's antagonistic policy—to greet him with demonstra-
tions of gladness? What has he ever done to merit it?
Nothing. Then reserve your enthusiastic cheers for such
men as have with talent and influence—on the platform and
by the pen—advocated your social and political advancement
in society as a class. Working men, would it not be more
manly and becoming to exhibit, in some measure, your disappointment at the manner in which your claims have been
received—not by hisses and groans—but by a dignified and
significant abstinence from all cheering, or other noisy demon-
strations of joy?"

This was a remarkable address. I urged adherence to this
policy, saying, "The middle-class cannot cheer like the people.
Gentlemen never do it well; they don't think it respectable.
It is contemptuously said that the working class will cheer
anybody, and Lord Palmerston is just the man to make an
argument against the people, if they run after him. He is
sure to say that 'they receive him with acclamations as they
do Mr. Gladstone; that their voices go for nothing, for they
have not the self-respect to keep their mouths shut, or sense to
tell a friend who would give them a right from one who will
give them nothing.'"

Bradford men did act on the advice given them. There
were said to be 30,000 in the streets. The Exchange Committee, and friends of their way of thinking, did set up a cheer
for Lord Palmerston, but, not being taken up by the people, it
had a faint-hearted effect, and soon ceased. Lord Palmerston,

as Mr. W. E. Forster afterwards told me, was "touched and pained" at standing as it were alone in that vast and voiceless crowd. No hissing or groans would have produced such an effect. Hooting would have called forth counter-cheers, which would have been magnified in the press into effective applause. Silence could not be misrepresented.

Lord Palmerston, apart from Liberalism, had popular qualities. He had boldness and common sense. No Minister save himself had ever told the Scotch elders that it was useless to proclaim a public fast to arrest the cholera until they had cleaned the city. He thought more of scavengers' shovels than bishops' prayers.

In anything I wrote of him it was always owned that he had generous personal qualities which adversaries might trust. On one occasion I wrote to him, informing him " there was a Miss O'Connor living, a sister of Feargus O'Connor, and the only survivor of the family. She had more eloquence than her brother, but the poor lady was in very straitened circumstances ; and although Feargus O'Connor often denounced his lordship, I believed he would not remember that against his sister in her day of need. It would be regarded as a very generous thing by the Chartists if his lordship would advise her Majesty to accord some slender pension to Miss O'Connor."

She had written to me at times, by which means I became incidentally aware of her necessitous condition. My friend Mr. Thornton Hunt conveyed my letter to Lord Palmerston, who kindly sent me word that "though it was not in his power at that time (the appointments of the Civil List being made for the year) to propose a pension, yet if the gift of £100 would be acceptable to Miss O'Connor, that sum should be at her disposal."

I sent her the letters, which otherwise I should quote here. I never heard further from her. The poor lady often changed her address. Whether the letters ever reached her—whether she died in the meantime—whether she accepted the offer and informed Lord Palmerston privately of it as I advised her, I never heard. But Lord Palmerston's generosity is a matter I record in his honour.

It was on Thornton Hunt's representation that Lord Palmerston agreed to procure me a seat in Parliament. He said "he knew Mr. Holyoake would often vote against him, but at the same time he should find in him a fair adversary." Lord Palmerston's object was to show that a working-class representative could be brought into Parliament, and therefore there was no necessity for a Reform Bill for that purpose. Lord Palmerston's death prevented him carrying his intention into execution. Therefore I had reasons personally to respect Lord Palmerston. But respect does not imply coincidence of opinion, and it was on public grounds of political policy alone that I ever wrote dissenting words concerning him. He had secular views which I could well agree with. When Sir James Graham spoke in the China debate of the approval of conscience and the ratification of a Higher Power, Lord Palmerston declared that for his own part he did not look so far, and was content with the support of that House. This was the real Palmerston. The approval of conscience was always to be regarded, but he took a just view when he suggested that peace or war was better determined in Parliament by human than by ecclesiastical considerations.

CHAPTER LXXII

THOMAS SCOTT—THE FRIEND OF BISHOP COLENSO.

(1858.)

ONE morning, at the Reception Room we kept at 147, Fleet Street, a gentleman was announced who wished to see me. He was a tall man, of military bearing, with a long grey beard, abundant hair, and a voice of explosive power. It was Mr. Thomas Scott, then of Ramsgate, well known among scholars for his attainments in Hebrew literature. After some conversation on means of circulating works of theological criticism he was issuing, he said, with a pleasant frankness which I afterwards knew to be characteristic, "I had a great repugnance to meeting you, but I have come at the suggestion of Bishop Colenso. I was making in his presence some remarks against you, when the bishop said, 'You go and see Holyoake ; you will find the devil is not so black as he is painted.'" In those days I was commonly thought of under some Satanic similitude, and Bishop Colenso was the first ecclesiastic who suggested an abatement in the colour. I suppose I fulfilled the bishop's forecast in point of hue, as Mr. Scott's acquaintance passed into friendship which only ended with his death ; and many were the happy days I spent when his guest at his home in Ramsgate and Norwood, which Mrs. Scott made enchanting to all visitors.

Mr. Scott, I understood, had been employed in some military capacity among North American Indians. He told me he had camped out for two years at a time, without sleeping in a house. The son of a Scotch professor of great learning, he had Hebrew in his blood, and when he came home he was a Tory

in politics and a Liberal in religion. Dr. Colenso had so much
confidence in his critical erudition that he submitted the proofs
of his celebrated works to him. Mr. Scott presented to me a
bound volume of proof sheets which he had corrected or revised
for the bishop.

When Bishop Colenso went down to Claybrook, in Leicester-
shire, to preach, the then Bishop of Peterborough (the pre-
decessor of Dr. Magee) sent an inhibition. Mr. Scott, who was
skilled in things ecclesiastical, was waiting in the churchyard
the arrival of the inhibition. The bishop's messenger did not
appear until Sunday morning, shortly before the service would
commence. Mr. Scott met him and demanded the inhibition
from him. Whether, from Mr. Scott's magisterial manner or
authoritative voice—for he had the appearance of one of the
Sanhedrim—the messenger thought he was Bishop Colenso, or
an official representative thereof, was never known, but he at
once handed the inhibition to Mr. Scott, who dismissed him
and put the document in his pocket. As Bishop Colenso found
the inhibition never came, he preached in due course. The
inhibition would have been respected had it been delivered ;
but as it was not, the Bishop of Peterborough could do nothing
against Dr. Colenso. All the bishop could learn was that his
messenger had delivered his inhibition to a gentleman whom
he supposed to be authorised to receive it, and who neglected
to deliver it to Dr. Colenso until after the sermon had been
delivered. Dr. Colenso knew nothing of it until after, and was
no party to its being intercepted.

Mrs. Scott, who was in earlier years a ward of Mr. Scott, was
a lady of singularly bright ways—and the aptest, most inde-
fatigable post parcel maker in the world. The innumerable
pamphlets issued from their house were mostly made up by her.
No committee could have conducted the remarkable propagandist bureau Mr. Scott administered. He being a gentleman,
writers with a secret as to their authorship could trust him,
when a committee, however honourable, could not command
the confidence which was accorded unhesitatingly to one.
He was an institute in himself. Ecclesiastics (Bishop Hinde was
one) professors, and others to whom it was not convenient to
give their names to the public, wrote for him. His house was
a theological pamphlet manufactory. Ladies were among his

contributors. In some cases atheists wrote, whose names it would not have been prudent in Mr. Scott to print, as their arguments on independent subjects would have been misjudged. Mr. Scott himself was an ardent, unswerving Theist. His own works were as remarkable as any he published from the pens of others. He issued more than two hundred separate works to my knowledge—none of them mean or unimportant. The whole constituted a pamphlet library of controversy never equalled.

Mr. Scott died, and no successor has appeared. As the wise adviser and intrepid friend of Bishop Colenso, he will long live in the memory of all who knew how great his services were. To others, the old warrior devoting his years to scholastic research and criticism, with the enthusiasm of a young professor, will be a singular figure. He was the greatest propagandist by pamphlets of his own origination ever known to me, in reading or experience.

CHAPTER LXXIII.

HOW BISHOP COLENSO BECAME CONVERTED.

(1860.)

ON one or two occasions I met Bishop Colenso. His earnest, alert, inquiring demeanour, his frankness and tolerance would suggest to any one that he was for truth first and faith afterwards.

One Sunday night I was lecturing at the Hall of Science, City Road. At the conclusion notice was given out that it was expected Bishop Colenso would speak in that place next Sunday. He had been invited to lay his views before the audience assembling there. Simple as a child in matters of duty, he was ready to vindicate his views before any whom he supposed to be earnest inquirers. He never counted the risks; he never thought of them. Though he rejected the literary and arithmetical errors of the Scriptures, he was deeply Christian, while the audience he would have met were not so. I at once said it would be unfortunate for the bishop's cause if he came there, and I wrote and told him so. The Hall of Science had an atheistic reputation, and his enemies, who were then very fierce against him, would never dissociate his appearance at the Hall of Science from sympathy with the far-reaching heresy promulgated in it. It would have been a distinction to the side to which I belonged that the bishop should appear among us, but it would not have been generous in us to have permitted it at his peril. The audience, I was glad to see, thought so too.

The bishop sent me a brief note of thanks, and did not appear there. He may have had this incident in his mind when he told Mr. Scott that I was a paler sort of Satan than I was usually represented to be.

Or Bishop Colenso may have had in memory an earlier incident. When he was appointed to the See of Natal, he selected (I forget how it came to pass) an intelligent Secular carpenter and frequent correspondent of the *Reasoner* —Robert Ryder— to go out and build his church and school-house. Mr. Ryder, when I first knew him, was employed at New Leeds, near Bradford. He afterwards came to London, and kept a small inn off Gray's Inn Road, which he gave up to go to Natal. As Ryder had never been abroad, he asked my advice as to going, and I encouraged him to accept the Natal engagement. He had become acquainted through the *Reasoner* with Herbert Spencer's writings, and was his earliest disciple whom I knew. His fascination was the first edition of "Social Statics." It was to him as a new Gospel. He had a copy with him wherever he went. Its contents had coloured his mind, and he took the book with him to Natal. He was in the bishop's employ several years, and sent me photographs which he had taken of the actual Zulus who were said to have converted the bishop, long before any such conversion was heard of in England. This English carpenter and builder was an agnostic, an enthusiast, and a ready disputant. Zulus were workers under him, and the bishop saw them daily and conversed with them as to their religious views, so far as they had any. They were very shrewd and good at argument, as the bishop admits in one of his works. My friend told me that the Zulus used to remark upon the fact that the bishop had a room built in the rear of the church, in which he stored an eighteen-pounder. They knew what that cannon was for, and they thought that the bishop, fair-spoken as he was, did not place his ultimate reliance on the "Good Father" in whom he told them to trust.

Afterwards the bishop's builder came to consider that his contract was not fairly fulfilled by the bishop, and sent me particulars for publication in the *Reasoner*. I endeavoured to dissuade him from an action at law which he contemplated. Being a mathematician, the bishop was more likely to be right in matters of charge than he. Besides, the bishop was a gentleman as well as a Christian, and therefore to be trusted. Further, it would be a scandal for a Secularist to go to law with a good bishop, who had incurred the enmity of his order by his splendid tolerance. It came to pass that Mr. Ryder had to sue the bishop, when occurred the only instance in which the bishop displayed the prejudice and injustice too often the characteristics of his profession.

It was years before Bishop Colenso's criticisms of the Old Testament were "noised abroad," when my friend Robert Ryder became his mechanical manager of works in the diocese of Natal. Mr. Ryder, in a letter which I published in the *Reasoner* in June, 1858, said :—

"I am the same R. R. I was when you knew me in England. I have laboured for the last three years to prove that it is possible for an atheist (so-called), holding extreme speculative views, to work with a party, for a secular object, whose views are diametrically opposed to mine. I endeavour to prove in my own person that duty, faithfulness, and honesty are moral qualities independent of creed. I have risen to the highest honour and confidence my employer can bestow upon me—not for what I believe, but for what I have done, and the manner in which I have served the mission in general. The bishop is quite familiar with my views, but he is one of those noble men who adorn Christianity by his consideration, his kindness, his life, and his freedom from all intolerance. He often comes to get one of your works out of my library. I have my esteemed employer's certificate that I have served the cause well, and faithfully discharged my duties for three years, and am going on for two more years. I have been entrusted with thousands of pounds. I have built three churches, three schools, a corn-mill, a 20-feet water wheel fitted up with lathes and smithy, potter's wheel, and simple machines ; also an industrial training school for the natives, one hundred of whom we have in training, chiefly young boys. We do not attend much to the old ones. I brought a brick and tile machine from England, with which we have made about a million bricks. The natives have made a great number by hand, a thing they never did before. I am now building the Bishop's Palace, 120 feet frontage, with two wings of 80 feet each, in the Elizabethan style of architecture."

This passage is interesting as showing how early and to how great an extent the bishop provided, not only for the spiritual.

but for the material comfort and education of the Zulus. In publishing Mr. Ryder's letter, I divested it of all names and allusions by which any readers in England could connect it with the Natal Mission. A letter from Brazil and one from Mexico, equally divested of personal references, had brought my correspondents trouble. Therefore no mention was made of any place in Africa, and, as there was no reason to suppose that the *Reasoner* circulated there, it was concluded that any person referred to was sufficiently protected. However, the Rev. Calvert Spensley, being in England, called at the *Reasoner* office and purchased some numbers, one of them containing the letter in question. He recognized that the scene of Mr. Ryder's work was at Ekukanyeni, and sent the letter in the *Reasoner* to the editor of the *Natal Mercury*, who reprinted it under the imaginative title of " Atheistic Socialism in Natal." Mr. Ryder had been before described by the editor of the *Mercury* as "the bishop's very liberal-minded, shrewd, and independent agent." All that could be brought against Mr. Ryder was that in 1848 he had been on a deputation to Paris to congratulate the Government on the establishment of the " Republic Democratic and Social." The bishop was now assailed for employing such an agent, and charged with disseminating " Atheistic Socialism." Not a thought was given nor a word of consideration said that Mr. Ryder had, in spite of his convictions, generously devoted himself to aiding the mission work and in increasing its reputation and influence by building the churches and schools, all the while keeping silence on his own opinions that the bishop and his work might not be compromised.

The Rev. C. Spensley was engaged upon a rival Dissenting Mission, and his party naturally took pleasure in disparaging the Church Mission ; but it was not justifiable to do it by untrue and venomous accusation.

Mr. Ryder defended himself in a clear, manly letter in the *Natal Star*. He said : " I have never made a profession of atheism. I engaged to the Bishop of Natal as mechanical manager to the Mission. My labours have been perfectly secular, having nothing whatever to do with either Theism or Atheism. Neither have I taken any part in matters political or religious, private or public, or sought to obtrude any views of mine on those subjects since I came to this colony."

He accounted for the hostility of the *Natal Mercury*, the organ of the Dissenting Mission, by stating that the editor had made overtures to join the Church, and "offered himself to the bishop body, soul, and paper," which being refused, the editor was resentful.

The rival mission succeeded in doing the Church Mission some harm. As soon as Mr. Ryder's letter to the *Reasoner* appeared in the colony—in which letter Mr. Ryder had said "the Zulus had intelligence, truth, probity, and chastity, all the virtues of the Christian nations without their vices, and he did not see what Christianity could do for them"—the bishop discharged him, lest the Church Mission should suffer ; and Mr. Ryder was obliged to appeal to the law to recover the claim he had against the bishop. The decision was given in Mr. Ryder's favour. The bishop then appealed against it and lost. The judges confirmed the decision in favour of his late agent. An attempt was made to disqualify Mr. Ryder's evidence by reason of his opinions, but his word was believed against the bishop. The judge who gave the judgment of the court said : " If I followed feeling and class prejudice, I should decide in favour of the educated man of my own class, rather than for the uneducated man Ryder. But justice stands in the way." Ryder had no written engagement, but his character went with his word.

It is singular that the bishop, whose characteristic was just-mindedness, should have been unfair to one who was not a Theist. He was prejudiced against heresy when he was ignorantly described as having sympathy with it. He afterwards saw, when Christian persecution befel him, that truth and fairness often co-existed in persons who did not hold his theistical belief—from which belief he never departed himself.

Mr. Ryder had seen frequent accounts and quotations in the *Reasoner* of Lieut. Lecount's "Hunt after the Devil," and probably had the book in his library. There was nothing about the "Devil" in Lecount's three volumes, which were filled with calculations of the dimensions of the ark, with reference to its required capacity. The chief statements of the Old Testament which could be tested by figures, Lecount, being a great mathematician, had presented with an originality and vividness not before shown. If the bishop had not seen the book, it was a remarkable coincidence that he should go over the same ground in the same way, applying the same methods, and arriving at similar results.

Any reader of this chapter will see the bishop had ample means of becoming acquainted with the intellectual difficulties of heretics. Being himself an accomplished arithmetician, the investigation by which he became distinguished was natural to him, and it was quite out of the line of any Zulu to suggest it. The Zulus were strongest concerning the difficulties of Theism ; but the bishop was never in any degree moved by their arguments, except so far as their intelligence and earnestness may have inspired him with tolerance and respect for extreme difference of belief. The Zulus had a quick sense of moral preception, of the discrepancies between profession and practice, but these were points upon which the bishop did not deal in his Pentateuchal criticisms. He dwelt mainly with intellectual and scientific objections.

When his first volume on the Pentateuch came out it was said of him—

> " To Natal, where savage men so
>   Err in faith and badly live,
> Forth from England went Colenso,
>   To the heathen light to give.
>
> But, behold the issue awful !
>   Christian, vanquished by Zulu,
> Says polygamy is lawful,
>   And the Bible isn't true ! "

The bishop had not said this, but it was quite as near to the truth as clerical criticism usually gets on its first effort. Dr. Cumming was one of his adversaries. He was an ingenious prophet who predicted the end of the world in a certain year, and at the same time negotiated a lease of his house for a much longer period, whereby he obtained a reduction of rent to which he was not morally entitled. He issued some frenzied pamphlets entitled " Moses right, Colenso wrong," which I answered by another series entitled " Cumming wrong, Colenso Right ; by a London Zulu." Bishop Colenso certainly showed that an educated Christian gentleman, who had sympathy for the people and a genial toleration of the pagan conscience, could do much for their elevation in the arts of life.

The bishop took his beautiful electrical apparatus and delivered lectures with experiments in Natal to the great delight of the Zulus, who in their grateful and appreciative way called him Sokululeka, Sobantu, " Father of raising up " —" Father of the People." No Zulu heart would apply such honouring words towards Dr. Cumming, whose divinity was a snarl and his orthodoxy a sneer. One day I sent the bishop a set of the pamphlets I had written in reply to his adversary. Here in his answer dated from Pendyffryn, Conway, July 25, 1863 :—

" DEAR SIR,—I am much obliged by your note. I enclose a letter from Professor Kuenen, of Leyden, which you may like to see. He ranks not merely *among* the first—but, I believe, 'as *the* first—of living Biblical critics, and treats my book rather differently from Dr. Cumming and Co.—Faithfully yours,   J W. NATAL."

The bishop also sent me the third part of his " Examination of the Pentateuch " on its publication.

Next to Huc and Gabet's Travels in Tartary, Bishop Colenso's " Ten Weeks in Natal " is the most alluring missionary book I ever read. Had ecclesiastical appointments gone by merit in Colenso's time, he would have been made Archbishop of Canterbury, as he had more learning and more Christianity, in the best sense of the term, than any contemporary prelate. With noble self-sacrifice he ended his days among the Zulu people. He was the friend of their kings—he was ceaseless in pleading for justice to Cetewayo. He was the only bishop for centuries who won the love of a barbarian nation.

Mr. Ruskin, whose regard is praise, presented his large diamond to the Natural History Museum on the condition that the following words should always appear on the label descriptive of the specimen :—" The Colenso diamond, presented in 1887 by John Ruskin in honour of his friend, the loyal and patiently adamantine first Bishop of Natal."

CHAPTER LXXIV.

LORD COLERIDGE AND THOMAS HENRY BUCKLE.

(1859.)

MR. JUSTICE ERSKINE, in his address to me, said in 1841, that "the arm of the law was not stretched out to protect the character of the Almighty. The law did not assume to be a protector of God." But he used it so all the same. His words, however, admitted that blasphemy, as respects Deity, is not a crime which the law takes cognizance of. Blasphemy is only a secular concern, a crime that affects the peace and taste of society.

Blasphemy is an erminic creation. In the eyes of a Theistical moralist, orthodox Christianity is blasphemy of a bad kind. Yet a judge seldom considers that the conscience of an atheist is outraged by ordinary Christian language. Usually the judge protects Christians alone, and, according as he is bigoted or tolerant himself, his definition of blasphemy is malignant or generous. In cases of opinion judges make the law, and when a Lord Chief Justice is tolerant it is fortunate, since his judgment becomes a precedent which minor judges respect. Lord Coleridge, in giving judgment on certain publications two or more years ago alleged to be blasphemous, said to the jury :—

" If the law as I laid it down to you is correct—and I believe it has always been so ; [1] if the decencies of controversy are ob served, even the *fundamentals of religion may be attacked*, without a person being guilty of blasphemous libel. There are many great and grave writers who have attacked the

[1] If so, it has been disregarded by most judges.

foundations of Christianity. Mr. Mill undoubtedly did so ; some great writers now alive have done so too ; but no one can read their writings without seeing a difference between them and the incriminated publications, which I am obliged to say is a difference *not of degree, but of kind.* There is a grave, an earnest, a reverent, I am almost tempted to say a religious tone in the very attacks on Christianity itself, which shows that what is aimed at is not insult to the opinions of the majority of Christians, but a real, quiet, honest pursuit of .truth. If the truth at which these writers have arrived is not the truth we have been taught, and which, if we had not been taught it, we might have discovered, yet, because these conclusions differ from ours, they are not to be exposed to a criminal indictment. With regard to these persons, therefore, I should say, *they are within the protection of the law* as I understand it."

This judgment gives protection against Christian penalties to such writers as Buckle, Carlyle, Harriet Martineau, Huxley, Tyndall, Morley, and Spencer. It is the amplest Charter of Free Discussion yet promulgated on high authority in any nation or in any country.

One day Mr. William Coningham, then M.P. for Brighton, took me to call on Thomas Henry Buckle, who was residing with his mother in Sussex Square in that town. Mr. Coningham had often spoken to me of Mr. Buckle as one who had long been engaged on a great work which would make an impression upon the age. It proved to be the "History of Civilization," which was afterwards published. It was Sunday morning when our visit was made. Mr. Buckle wore a light dress ; he had a fresh complexion, a welcoming manner, and appeared to me as a country squire with unusual ease and readiness in conversation. He did not give me the impression that he was a philosopher, a man of ideas, of studious and immense research ; but I knew all this when I subsequently read his review in *Fraser's Magazine* for May, 1859, of John Stuart Mill's famous treatise on " Liberty." After thirty years I have read the review again with equal wonder and admiration. We have no such reviews in these days. We have writers whose sentences of light and music linger in the ear of the mind, but we have none who have Buckle's passionate

eloquence and generous eagerness in defence of unfriended
heretics.

It was in that review that he animadverted on the trial of
Thomas Pooley before Mr. Justice Coleridge, at Bodmin, in 1857,
and on the part taken by Mr. John Duke Coleridge (now Lord
Chief Justice Coleridge), who was the prosecuting counsel pleading before his father. I had written a narrative of the career and
trial of Pooley, having been down to Cornwall, at the instance
of the Secularists of that day, to report upon Pooley's case.
Mr. J. D. Coleridge replied to Mr. Buckle in defence of his
father, Sir John Coleridge, and himself, and stated, in his remarks in *Fraser's Magazine*, for June, 1859, "that every fact
mentioned by Mr. Buckle is to be found in the aforesaid report,
and often nearly in the language of Mr. Holyoake." It was so.
Mr. Mill had mentioned my name in "Liberty," and that of
Pooley, which led Mr. Buckle to inquire of me what the facts
of the case were. I sent him my published narrative. Though
I had been long before, and was at the time, exposed to a storm
of clerical persecution, no resentment colours that story.
There is no publication of mine which I would more willingly
see reprinted, and by which I would consent to be judged as a
controversialist narrator, than by that. But in any such reprint
I should withdraw the phrases in which I represent that Mr. J.
D. Coleridge "concealed facts from the jury," or was otherwise
consciously unfair ; nor should I use the same accusatory words
I did in speaking of Sir John Coleridge, the judge. Afterwards, when the remission of Pooley's sentence was sought,
and the Judge consulted upon it, he wrote to say that "he saw
no reason why Pooley should not receive a free pardon under
the circumstances stated." At the same time he remarked that
he did not suspect Pooley's insanity, that "there was not the
slightest suggestion made to him" thereunto, nor had he been
led to inquire into it, and "he should have been very glad " to
arrive at the conclusion he was insane and have "directed his
acquittal on that ground." Mr. J. D. Coleridge on his own
part said in his reply to Mr. Buckle :—" I took pains to open
the case in a tone of studied moderation. I carefully explained to the jury that the prosecution was not a prosecution
of opinion in any sense. I mentioned, and I beg their pardon
for here repeating, the names of Mr. Newman, Mr. Carlyle,

and Miss Martineau, as persons who maintained what I and others might think erroneous opinions, but who maintained them gravely, with serious argument and with a sense of responsibility, and whom no one would dream of interfering with. I said that the time was long gone by for persecution, which I thought as foolish as it was wicked ; but that as liberty of opinion was to be protected, so was society to be protected from outrage and indecency." This is not only entirely fair ; it is a generous interpretation of freedom of speech, and is consistent with what Mr. Coleridge, as Lord Chief Justice, avowed in yet · more remarkable language twenty-six years later. There was no report of the trial. No one whom I could meet in Cornwall was aware of what had been said to the jury, and the strange severity of the sentence hid from my mind the probability of its being said. The letter of the judge and the speech of the counsel I have quoted show that I was wrong in saying that there was a " concealment " of facts, or " shameful reticence " on his part, or in suggesting conscious unfairness on his father's part. As I am the only person remaining on Pooley's side, conversant with the facts of the trial as they subsequently transpired, it is a duty in me to make the correction.

Pooley had no counsel, no friend, and his side was not put before the court. The *Spectator*, which in those days was always well informed on these cases, had the only report which appeared in the London press ; the writer, probably a barrister present, was struck with the signs of insanity in Pooley. He remarks, however, that " Mr. Coleridge was quite correct in his statement of the law as it stood."

My own opinion of the clergy of Liskeard, of public opinion there and in Bodmin, of the extraordinary indictment, of the lack of discernment in the jury, and of the strange extent of the sentence pronounced, remain the same. At the same time, it must be owned that Pooley's manner of acting, with which, as my narrative shows, I did not sympathize and did not conceal, must have set all uninquiring, unsuspecting persons against him.

Had what I learned of Pooley's life been known to the counsel and judge, their trial of Pooley would have ended differently. Had I known what limited knowledge of facts the court had of Pooley's history, I should have written differently of those who conducted the trial and decided his fate. It did not seem to me to be possible that the pathetic facts of Pooley's life, for fifteen years known to his family, neighbours, and employers, could be unknown to gentlemen in the same town. It was not then known to me that Truth is more lame-stepping than Justice, and is very dilatory in making known what she knows. It was not then known to me that the rich know no more of the lives of the poor than persons on land know or care to know of the ways of fish in the sea. It was not known to me that theological prejudice may so close the eyes and ears of the mind that it neither sees nor hears outside itself. It was not known to me then, as it has been since, that in political warfare educated gentlemen on one side do not believe in the integrity of equally educated gentlemen on the other side, and not only put on their acts a construction never thought of by the actors, but will report as true the falsest charges after they have been publicly and often confuted. So I did think, without misgiving, that the pagan insensibility of Pooley had excited the indignation of counsel and judge, and led them to ignore the facts which I supposed them to know. Mr. Buckle, I doubt not, were he living to revise the statement he made, would cancel all imputations upon the personal honour or conscious unfairness of judge or counsel in this case, for Mr. Buckle himself invited all readers of his to peruse the defence of Mr. J. D. Coleridge, and he reprinted and circulated the most vehement passages against himself, and they were hardly less fierce than his own. Mr. Buckle always had fairness in his mind, and his publishing and circulating the strongest passages in reply to himself which his adversary had penned, is a proof of it. Only a candid man who cared more for the truth than for himself would do it.

That such a prosecution could take place and such a sentence as that upon Pooley could be pronounced excited Buckle's generous indignation. His brilliant defence of the poor, crazed, but intrepid well-sinker of Cornwall, is the only example in this generation or this century of a gentleman coming forward in that personal way, to vindicate the right of Free Thought in the friendless and obscure. Mr. Mill would give money, which was a great thing, or use his influence, which was more, to protect them, but Mr. Buckle descended personally into the arena to defend and deliver them.

CHAPTER LXXV.

BEQUEST OF A SUICIDE.

(1860.)

IT is the common experience of those who advocate liberty in some new direction to receive an unforeseen and undesirable adhesion of all the "cranks," religious, social, and political, extant in the innovator's day. I mean by a "crank" one who mistakes his impressions for ideas, or, having ideas resting on proof only perceived by himself, insists, in season and out of season, on attention being given to them. He is a crank, whatever his "views" may be, who persistently claims notice for them before he has thought them out to their consequences and described the grounds on which they rest, so that others can discern and test them. The number of "cranks" are much larger in most parties than are supposed.

An innovator who knows his business presents his case as that of reasoned truth. The "crank," not knowing the justification and conditions of innovation, rushes at you from all directions to carry his fad forward. But discrimination is necessary, lest you repel a thinker who seeks direction or confirmation, which your experience may afford him. Sometimes a well-convinced but too ardent pioneer has fallen into evil environments from which he cannot see his way out. Among these was Bombardier Thomas B. Scott, 7th Battery, 8th Brigade, Royal Artillery, Cove Common, Aldershot. Having the making of a good soldier in him, he enlisted in the Royal Artillery, on being assured by the recruiting officer that he should have the rank and pay of a bombardier from the date of his entering the service. On this condition he entered, but he soon found, as Mr. Bradlaugh found, that faith is not kept with recruits in the army. Scott found the condition was ignored, and when he complained, he was told it was un-authorised and used merely as an inducement for him to enlist. He concluded, therefore, that as his enlistment was false and a fraud, it was illegal, and he wrote to Mr. Sydney Herbert, who did not deny the fraud, but did not redress it. The reply of the Secretary of War was sent to me, which I returned or I would quote it. It seems strange that a man of Sydney Herbert's high character for honour neither accorded censure nor redress for admitted deceit. Scott's personal character was good, but the position assigned him was that of a gunner merely. He was employed as schoolmaster, and received certificates of competency from the General Inspector of Army Schools, from two head normal schoolmasters, and from his colonel, captain, and officers. He was requested to stand exami-nation as a candidate for a studentcy in the Military Asylum at Chelsea. He did so, and passed. He might have risen from the ranks, as was his ambition, had it not been for his specula-tive opinions and his untimely zeal. He had in camp some works I had written, and others, "Volney's Ruins of Empires" among them. This becoming known, he was arraigned before his colonel and officers on the charge of being an "atheist," though Volney was a Theist. A soldier enlists for the purpose of being killed, as the exigence or convenience of war may warrant. Scott did not object to this, and it does not appear what these officers had to do with a gunner's opinions on out-side questions, entirely apart from his duty ; and his trial for the purely ecclesiastical offence was irrelevant.

Scott made the mistake of considering it his duty to do as the apostles did (which is only counted meritorious in them) of standing by his opinions. For doing this he was sent back to do his duty as a gunner, was denied the privilege of entering the Normal School, and his prospects of military advancement were cut off. This made him despondent.

In December the same year (1860) Scott had written to me to advise him as to some mode of obtaining his discharge ; but as I had no means of procuring funds for that purpose then, I counselled him to observe circumspection as to his opinions until he could be bought off. He then, through his captain, sought to speak to his colonel on the subject of Mr. Sydney Herbert's letter. He was received in a very forbidding way. The colonel denounced him for his opinions, and told him that if he would abandon them, he would do something for him, and further told him that, until he did, he should not allow him to hold any rank or appointment in the Royal Artillery. Scott replied that his convictions were involuntary, which he could not change until stronger evidence appeared before him ; that, if the colonel believed him to be in error, it was his duty, as a Christian, to convince him rather than coerce him. Where-upon the colonel sent for the sergeant-major and ordered him to confine Scott in the guardroom, and the charge of insubor-dination to be entered against him. After two days' imprison-ment, Sunday occurred, and he was marched under guard to church. Scott, therefore, desired a communication to be made to the officer in charge to the effect that he did not wish to enter the church, as his habit was to attend the Wesleyan Chapel, which he frequented, as all soldiers are obliged to attend some place of worship. Scott did not refuse to go, but expressed his wish not to go to church, and claimed liberty of conscience, as he did not agree with what he should hear in church. Being offensively addressed by the officer, he refused to go. He was then sent back into confinement, and an additional charge of "insubordination" was entered against him. Eventually he was taken before a court martial. Twelve hours prior to his trial, a copy of the charges against him was given to him, and he was told to frame his defence, but was denied writing material. He sent me a very dramatic account, on eight foolscap pages, of the whole affair. Around a large table in the mess-room sat three lieutenants, two captains, one major, and one colonel. On the table lay the Articles of War, a large Bible, and Jamison's Code. The officers seized the Bible, and, placing finger and thumb upon it, each kissed it, like cabmen, and swore to give justice on all sides, which they could not intend to do, being a military court without ecclesiastical func-tions or competence.

Scott found the court martial a mere department of the Church. Every scrap of evidence was made the most of against him ; but when he attempted to correct the misstatements of his judges, he was put down. He stood up manfully for his principles, which was considered a new offence. He said he was ready to render the best service in his power to her Majesty, and give his life in discharge of his duty, but his conscience was his honour, and he could not change. They might drive him to suicide, but he would not deny his conviction. They did drive him to suicide, which was discreditable in gentlemen. Scott, on his own showing, spoke very plainly, and the court resented his contumaciousness; but they should have remembered that they had got him into their power by fraud, and after knowing it, they kept him there. Being an intelligent, logical-minded man, this injustice preyed upon him. How long he was imprisoned I never heard. His health was broken, and he became an inmate of the hospital. There he had been two months when I next heard of him. He was daily harassed about his opinions. The doctor, the chaplain, the lieutenant, a captain's wife, and others assailed him from time to time. He stated to a Roman Catholic comrade, who had great regard for him, that he would give four years' service to any one who would get him bought out, as I learned afterwards. His own family were unable to do it. He had religious connections better able ; but his opinions prevented his being aided in that quarter. Solicitous always and to the end that no discredit should come through him to the cause he espoused, he provided that all his few debts should be paid. His prospects in the army ended, friendless and assailed, he died by his own hand. A faithful comrade of his, having occasion to write to me in 1862, informed me, in answer to my inquiry after Scott, that he had long been dead, of which no notice was sent me, although he had bequeathed what little property he had to me. I wrote to the colonel of his troop, and otherwise obtained information of his bequest. On learning that his family had need of anything he had, I transferred all his possessions to them, valuing all the same this proof of the dying regard of which he intended to assure me. Thus closed the career of the brave suicide, who will have no record save this.

In the Indian mutiny of 1857 the Mahometans would save any one who would consent to profess himself a Moslem. Those who would not were knocked on the head. Only one half-caste saved his life by denying his faith. Mr. A. C. Lyall, an eminent Indian official, wrote lines of noble praise of their heroic honesty. One of those who thus died held the same opinions as poor Scott. In Mr. Lyall's poem he tells of the honest soldier's convictions and fate :—

> " A bullock's death, and at thirty years !
>   Just one phrase, and a man gets off it.
> Look at that mongrel clerk in his tears,
>   Whining aloud the name of the prophet !
> Only a formula easy to patter,
> And, God Almighty, what *can* it matter ?
>
> I must be gone to the crowd untold
>   Of men by the cause which they served unknown,
> Who moulder in myriad graves of old,
>   Never a story and never a stone
> Tell of the martyrs who die like me,
> Just for the pride of the old countree.
>
> Aye, but the word, if I could have said it,
>   I by no terrors of hell perplext—
> Hard to be silent and get no credit
>   From man in this world, or reward in the next.
> None to bear witness and reckon the cost,
> Of the name that is saved by the life that is lost."

These lines may fitly serve as Scott's epitaph. The conscientious heroism of the heretic is as noble as that of the Christian.

Other soldiers have written to me at times, who had found that volunteering to fight for the liberty of others did not include freedom for themselves—not even of their own minds.

CHAPTER LXXVI.

VISIT TO A STRANGE TREASURER OF GARIBALDI.

(1861.)

In the year 1860 I was acting secretary to the London "Garibaldi Fund Committee." In many towns money was generously given for "the General," as Garibaldi was popularly and affectionately called. In some cases money so subscribed was sent to Garibaldi; in others taken to him, to prevent misadventure. Some local treasurers neither sent it nor took it. Thus some sums were lost, and others held back by persons who did not know where to send them to; and in some cases a treasurer would refuse to part with the funds in his hands until he was personally and specially certain of its reaching the General. For the convenience and satisfaction of all who held funds given for him, Garibaldi appointed Mr. W. H. Ashurst, his personal friend, as his treasurer. Mr. Ashurst was known in America as well as England for patriotic services and high character.

In an important town—not Newcastle-on-Tyne and not Birmingham—it was known that a banker held upwards of £400, which the General needed, but which never came to hand. I do not mention the name of the banker, because he was much and justly esteemed for his personal honour and interest in public affairs. In this narrative I therefore speak of him as Mr. Marvell, itself an honourable name in history. Mr. Ashurst wrote to him from 6, Old Jewry, London, E.C. (April 15, 1861), saying :—

" DEAR SIR,—I received on Saturday a despatch from General

Garibaldi, from which I beg to forward you the following extract :—

" 'I have already by my last letter requested you to act as treasurer, or collector-general, in your country, of all monies raised in aid of the cause of Italy, and subject to my order, and this position I request you still to hold—advising me as before of the amount in hand, as to the disposal of which you shall from time to time receive instructions from me.

" 'I now urgently call upon you to let it be known to the various committees and friends of Italy throughout Great Britain, that funds are greatly needed to complete the good work of aiding in the emancipation of those parts of our country which are still subject to priestly misrule and foreign oppression, and the liberation of which will require all the efforts of the patriots of Italy.'

" I have the pleasure of bringing this instruction under your notice, and request that you will forward to me the balance remaining in your hands on the General Garibaldi account.—I am, dear sir, yours respectfully,

" To D. M., Esq.   W. H. Ashurst."

To this friendly letter the following singular reply was sent, April 17, 1861 :—

" Dear Sir,—We have peculiar notions on some subjects, and do not sympathise in all the views set forth in your favour of the 13th inst.

" We decline to send any contributions to London, as we prefer to act independently, and shall take our own course when the proper time arrives,—I am, dear sir, yours faithfully,
" D. M."

It had been known for some time that this gentleman was unwilling to pay over the money in his hands to the General's treasurer. At length the London Committee of the "Garibaldi Fund" instructed Captain de Rohan, the General's aide-de-camp, to ask him for a special authorisation to be shown for the fuller satisfaction of hesitating and "independent" persons. Mr. Ashurst, on April 25, 1861, wrote again to the banker in question :—

" DEAR SIR,—I received your letter of the 17th inst., and communicated its contents to the committee. I found that they had already communicated with General Garibaldi in order to obtain from him some authority which should satisfy you as to the mode in which you should apply the money in your hands collected for him ; and it is now my duty to enclose to you the original authority from General Garibaldi, received by me this day, to send to me, as his treasurer, the money you have in hand. I have kept a copy of the authority and of the translation.

"In yours of the 17th, acknowledging mine of the 15th, you say that you 'do not sympathise in all the views set forth' in mine of that date. On reference to my letter you will find I set forth no views, but simply enclosed you the translation of a letter from General Garibaldi, and requested you to act upon it.

" To me personally it is of course indifferent what you do with the money the various contributors have confided to you for the Garibaldi Fund ; my duty is simply to follow out the instructions of General Garibaldi.

"I request the favour of your prompt acknowledgment of this letter, stating the course you intend to pursue, and remain, dear sir, yours faithfully, W. H. ASHURST."

To this Mr. Ashurst received no reply.

Time went on and needs increased, for Garibaldi was still in the field—but the money came not. Mr. E. H. J. Craufurd, M.P. for the Ayr Burgh, being the Chairman of the Garibaldi Fund Committee, then wrote to the banker resenting the distrust and non-compliance of the request the general treasurer made in the name of the committee. No notice was taken of this communication, and there was no prospect, therefore, of obtaining the money. There was no legal remedy, and, had there been, the committee would not have felt justified in expending any funds to obtain it. I therefore proposed to the committee that they should give me 30s., which would be the third-class fare to and fro, to go to the town where the money lay (I paying my personal expenses myself), and I would collect the money for them. No one thought I should succeed, but, as they were unable to obtain the money themselves, leave was given me to try.

On arriving in the town I went to a society of working men, some of whom had been subscribers to the local fund, and informed them that the money intrusted to their treasurer had never been paid over, although a request to do so had reached him from Garibaldi. Then I asked them to make that fact known to other subscribers. Knowing members of the congregation where Mr. Marvell worshipped, I asked them whether it was possible that he could not be a man of good faith, or that he could have any object in withholding the Italian fund which had been intrusted to him from the uses for which it had been subscribed. We could not understand in London why he should disregard the written request of the General which had been sent him to forward the money to his treasurer. My calculation was that Mr. Marvell would very shortly have inquiries addressed to him by persons whose opinions he would not be likely to disregard. He being mayor of the town, I next communicated the information to such members of the Town Council as were known to me, who were promoters of the subscription. They were astonished to learn that the money was still in Mr. Marvell's hands. I remarked that we understood him to be a man of unquestionable honour, which they said was the case. I asked whether it was common in that town for a banker to withhold money contrary to the wishes of the subscribers ; besides, it was not respectful to Garibaldi (to whom it was due), whose friend he professed to be.

When I thought that news of these remarks made in the town by me, as acting secretary of the Garibaldi Committee, who must know what he was speaking of, had had time to reach the bank, I called there myself, and asked for an interview with Mr. Marvell, on business of personal importance. I was told that he was absent at his home, through indisposition, and I was asked whether it was business the manager could transact for him. I said I would explain my business to him, and he might himself judge. I said we understood in London that Mr. Marvell was a man of honour—that he not only kept public faith, but as a magistrate was bound to vindicate it. The manager said that was so, and wished to know on what ground any question to the contrary could be raised. I answered that he was aware that his principal was treasurer to the Garibaldi Fund, and that subscribers in that town entrusted their money to him in the implicit belief that it would, in reasonable time, be paid over for the use of the General. But that was not the case, as several hundred pounds were still detained at that bank.

He admitted that the money was detained there, but said there were reasons why it had not been paid over. I answered that I knew that, but I had come down to inquire what those reasons were. Had not Mr. Marvell received communications from the General authorising and requesting him to pay all money in his hands for the General's use to his treasurer in London, Mr. Ashurst? The manager admitted Mr. Marvell had received them, but he was not satisfied with them. "That means," I said, "that Mr. Marvell doubts their authenticity. If they were genuine, he had no choice but to comply with them ; and if he thought they were not genuine, how came it to pass that he had taken no steps in consequence? If they were not genuine, they were forgeries, and it was an attempt, being practised upon him, to obtain by forged documents money in his possession. Yet he had taken no steps to expose the forgery, or warn the subscribers or the public that he held proofs of so infamous a proceeding in his hands. The manager looked a little confused at that aspect of the question. I therefore added—"You are well aware who the persons are who have sent these fraudulent communications from the General. One is Mr. W. H. Ashurst, the Solicitor of her Majesty's Post Office, and the other is Mr. E. H. J. Craufurd, a member of Parliament, and counsel for the Mint. If they have taken to forgery, and have acquired such confidence in their success that they can venture to practise upon a banker and a magistrate, so distinguished for sagacity and public spirit as Mr. Marvell, that is a very serious thing, which ought not to be concealed from the public. The law ought to have been set in motion long ago. The Attorney-General should have been informed of the proceedings of the Solicitor of the Post Office, and the Speaker should have been made acquainted with this conduct of a member of Parliament and counsel for the Mint. If Mr. Marvell doubted the authenticity of Garibaldi's communication, he could have sent it to Count Corti, or the Marquis D'Azeglio, the Italian Minister in London, who knew the General's handwriting well, and in twenty-four hours Mr. Marvell could have taken proceedings ; but he had, now for two months or more, concealed or condoned this extraordinary and scandalous forgery. If he would give me Mr. Marvell's address, I would at once proceed there, and speak to him upon the subject."

Upon being informed of his residence, I took a cab and drove straight to his house in the suburbs, where I was received by Mrs. Marvell, who informed me that her husband was unwell, and unable to see visitors. I said in that case I would await his recovery, although the matter upon which I wished to see him was serious and of public importance. Upon her remarking that if it were a matter which I could communicate to her she might, at a convenient opportunity, mention it to him, I told her precisely what I had told the manager of the bank, which she appeared to hear with some consternation. I learned by post shortly after that Mr. Ashurst had received £411 from Mr. Marvell, the amount of all the subscriptions received by him.

I knew all the while why this banker wished to retain the money in his hands, until he had opportunity of sending it to the General himself. It was because he thought Garibaldi might direct its employment by Mazzini, who was doing everything in his power to send reinforcements into the field to aid the General. It was Mazzini who inspired the men who shed their blood under Garibaldi's standard, and not one sixpence of the money would have been used except in Garibaldi's service. It was not the province of any treasurer to dictate how money should be applied which was subscribed for services in Italy, of which he was merely the custodian, and every hour he withheld it he was in danger of imperilling Garibaldi's interest and his fortunes in the field.

CHAPTER LXXVII.

FAMOUS FIGHTS.

(1863.)

ARE science and courage a match for overwhelming strength? Can a man skilled in the art of hand-fighting overcome an antagonist immensely his superior in stature and power? I saw this done at Wadhurst in 1863.

After the fight between Sayers and Heenan it became a question whether Heenan could be beaten. He certainly was not beaten by Sayers. In his contest with Heenan, Sayers made a high name for English pluck. Seldom had a short-built David of pugilism undertaken to fight such a ponderous Goliath of Heenan's altitude. A single blow disabled Sayers,s left arm. Heenan struck like a battering-ram. It implied no mean skill and pluck in Sayers to parry and return the blows of such a tremendous assailant for many rounds, in that disabled condition. Had not the ring been broken by the crowd, Heenan would have killed his adversary. A subscription was made for Sayers at the House of Commons, Lord Palmerston subscribing the first guinea. Exhaustive training, excitement of victory and subsequent excess, have death in them, and soon laid Sayers low. No contests or feats of great danger ought to be encouraged. All whose presence incites them are morally participants in self-murder, disguised as a spectacle in which the actor kills himself for renown.

Heenan having a name of international repute, I reported the last of his battles—which was with Tom King—for the *Newcastle Daily Chronicle*. Washington Wilks, a journalist whom you could always trust for chivalry, represented the *Morning Star* and we agreed to go together. I knew Mr. Feist, editor of the *Sporting Life*, whose office was next to mine in Fleet Street, and by his invitation we joined him. From him I obtained a railway ticket to the fight for £2 10s. At that time I was publishing in the *English Leader* Dr. Shorthouse's articles on the "Biology and Pedigree of Racing Horses." The Doctor afterwards continued them under the title of *The Sporting Times*. He understood his subject so well that one year he predicted the winner of the Derby, which no one else foresaw. Dr. Shorthouse, knowing I had to write an account of the fight while it was progressing, suggested that I should have a "nurse." On consulting Feist, he named Johnny Broome as my "nurse," who in consideration of a guinea, undertook to protect me from molestation probable in that belligerent society of which I was not a recognised member. The duty of a "nurse" is to secure you a good place close to the ring and to "punch anybody's head" who interferes with you. Johnny was himself a pugilist of renown. Some time later he killed himself, for which I was sorry, for he was a good fellow according to his calling. He rode with us to the fight. Feist wore a dark fur cap, which well became him, and moreover was of excellent service in a blast or a rush. When, some years later, Sir John Sinclair, M.P., sent me £5 to buy something I ·liked, I bought a sealskin cap like Feist's, and had it on when run over by an omnibus at Charing Cross. It kept well on my head ; had I worn a hat that day it would have fallen off, and getting under the horses' feet embarrassed them in their friendly efforts not to tread upon me, in which they succeeded.

It was midnight early in December, 1863, when the fighting party assembled at the London Bridge railway station. There we hung about the waiting-rooms until word was given to take the train, which had glided noiselessly into the station. None of us knew where we were going. About five o'clock we alighted in Sussex, at a place thought convenient for the business in hand. A mounted policeman being observed by the scouts sent out, it was conjectured he might ride for aid and interfere, so we were recalled to the train and proceeded to Wadhurst, where we again alighted and started about two miles or more to the interior. Rain had fallen during the night, and the run over fences, ditches, and stiles was more diverting than agreeable. We were a rough, strong-footed gang. The wet, clayey mounds were as slippery as hillocks of soap, and one or two noblemen, as well as others, were soon on their knees. A field was chosen and the stakes set. Tom King, though nearly as tall as Heenan, was but a handsome stripling compared with him. Both were pallid, and their lips were pale and bloodless. Experts said they were overtrained. Their flesh seemed concreted as though no blow could indent it. Heenan won the toss both for the higher ground and for the shade, and King had to take the declivity of the field with the sun in his eyes. I had a seat on the ground next the ring, in the circle of those who had paid for near places. As the excitement of the fight grew, surrounding spectators pressed down, and would have trampled on me had not the vigilant eyes of Johnny Broome been upon them, who passed the word that he was "nursing" me. That was sufficient to the wise, who knew they would have to answer to him on the spot if they incommoded me. And those who were not wise soon became so when they were subjected to a volley of Johnny's threats, expressed in the minatory language of the Prize Ring. Otherwise I could not have maintained my place when the fury of the fight became contagious. At first King merely sparred at his great antagonist, dancing round him, alluring him to parts of the ring in shadow. This lasted some minutes. At last King struck Heenan a series of blows on mouth and face with a rapidity the like of which I had never seen. Heenan was not dazed, but amazed. Before he could get his elephantine arms into play he was again and again subjected to a rain of blows, resembling the Chinese punishment with the flat bamboo, in which short, rapid strokes produce intensity of effect. These King delivered in showers, and leaped back like a kangaroo, and Heenan was never able to retaliate effectually. The monster could have knocked his assailant over the ropes into the adjoining field could he have got a fair blow at him. But the nimble King took care this chance should not occur. Never was a more majestic figure than Heenan beheld in the ring ; such splendour of strength I have never seen since in combat. As he stood up, his broad chest and massive arms were defiant, and more so his mien, as, raising erect his colossal frame, he planted his spiked boots well in the grass

and strode down like a buffalo to his adversary, with conscious
pride of power and contempt for his foe. Up till the seventh
round he smiled as he met King ; but it was observed then
that his smile was a squirm, as his mouth was so swollen that
the laughing-lip was no more in use ; but his savage courage
kept him from knowing it. After this Heenan commenced
his native mode of fighting. After the battle with Sayers he
said he would never again be fettered by English rules, in
which his prairie prowess could not express itself. His policy
was to seize his opponent, crush like a boa constrictor the
strength out of him, throw him down, and fall upon him with
his elbow on his neck. He did this. No doubt he could
kill any single antagonist who was unable to evade his strong
grip. He rushed on King, and compressed him under his arm.
King was entirely helpless. He fibbed away with one arm at
Heenan's back in a feeble, ineffectual way. He was thrown down
and fallen on. When he was picked up his face was black.
Heenan had beaten him. King could not be brought up to
time. But "time" was not called according to rule. He was
given more. The barbaric restoratives of the ring were
applied, when he reappeared before his foe alert as a fox.
Before long Heenan became blinded by King's incessant blows.
By the sixteenth round we were all excited. We of the inner
circle sat on the ground that the outer crowd might the better
see. But the fury of the battle took possession of us. We all
arose. When the combatants were on my side of the ring it
seemed as though they would fall over the ropes upon us.
Both fighters were raging, especially King, probably from spirit
given him, but more from the madness of battle. His eagerness to get at his opponent was such that his feet were on the
knees of his second and he sat upon his shoulder. Instead of
being behind, he was now ready before his time. Cans of
water were thrown in their faces to refresh Heenan's eyes and
enable him to see King. By this time Heenan fought wildly.
His senses were going under the fierce unparried blows of
King. The Jupiter of the Prize Ring was beaten : overwhelming strength was defeated by science which waited for
its chance and knew how to profit by it.

By that time some policemen were on the ground, more
anxious to witness the fight than to prevent it. They were

too few to stop it, and they were told it would all be over before they could collect aid, which they were quite willing to believe, and made no attempt to do so. Subsequently the combatants were tried at the Lewes Sessions, but no evidence was forthcoming and they were acquitted. Yet there was no doubt of the fight. Heenan was led by his seconds to the train. Besides being unable to see his way, his strength had been so reduced that his arms were supported on the shoulders of his guides. Tom King, with scarcely a mark upon him, came gaily round the carriage windows to collect, as is the custom, a present for the loser of the battle. We made up about £25.

Accustomed to write on the railway, in boats, in cabs, and crowds, making on occasion notes on a short man's hat, whom I allowed to stand on my toes in order to raise himself higher, I had no difficulty in getting my account of the fight (two thousand words) ready for the telegraphist when I got to town. It was calculated that two thousand words were all we could then get over the wires in time for the afternoon edition. I was the first person at the telegraph office with a report of the fight. The chief of the department on seeing it, came to me to ask whether I could allow him to delay sending it on to Newcastle that he might send it to Windsor, as the Prince of Wales wished to see the first account of the fight. I answered the report was the property of the paper I represented ; I had no right in its disposal, but had no doubt Mr. Cowen would himself assent to such an act of courtesy to His Royal Highness ; but I must ask that no other account should be sent anywhere over the wires until the *Chronicle* report was despatched. My condition was assented to, and the Prince first received the description of the fight, which was at least unlike any other common in that day, or since. There was no slang of the ring in it, no technicalities of experts which confuse the general reader. My object was to give a brief, vivid account of what took place which a gentle-man might peruse, and which would tell the readers of the *Chronicle* what actually took place. Prize-fighting is not necessary for the cultivation of public courage ; but the last fight of Heenan, in which science was matched against strength, was not without instruction, and not without national pride in the victory of skill.

To this day I look back with satisfaction to the Titan fight on that December morning—it was the 10th—on the plateau at Wadhurst. The passion of Newcastle-on-Tyne is for the oar, the naval sceptre of the Norse kings, but one cannot carry an oar about for inland defence—hence the Wadhurst fight had interest on the Tyne. Its purpose, its swiftness, its pluck were unexampled in my experience. Passion, pride and power struggled on both sides for mastery ; the grand gleam of disdain and conscious strength which shone in the eyes of the American Ajax during the earlier rounds was a sight not seen more than once in a generation. For fighting as Englishmen fight, King was the regal type. Sayers was King's chief second, who astonished the boxers present by appearing in a yellow shirt. English prejudice against anything new at once burst out. The colour was too glaring, but some distinctive colour was the right thing. But it was jeered down, and Sayers who never gave in at a blow was beaten by a laugh, and put on a coat over his yellow shirt. Why should not seconds be distinguished from the umpire? Were jockies to ride in their daily attire, the race for the Derby would be as dull as a run of mounted costermongers. Sayers deserved credit for the sense and courage of his picturesque device. Sayers died a year or two later, and his colossal dog lay on his master's rug on his car and was chief mourner at his grave. King died not long ago, well regarded for his character and accomplishments. Heenan is no more now, and Ada Isaacs Menken, the dreamy-eyed, spiritualistic poetess, whom we knew at the exhibition of the Davenport Brothers, and as " Mazeppa " at Astley's—who was as lovely as she was dreamy—was personally attached to the Benicia athlete—is also dead : so is Feist ; and Dr. Short-house, for whom I had great regard. He was a lineal descendant of Dr. Johnson's wife, who was a Shorthouse. He became an LL.D. as well as an M.D. because he was proud of his descent, and he wilfully resembled the Doctor in a rough frankness of manner ; but though he had the bear in his speech, he had an angel in his heart. He practised, when I knew him, at Car-shalton, and every poor creature for miles round could command his services and his medicines, although they were never able to pay him. Once, when I was unwell, I was a guest six weeks in his house, and I saw what took place among his poor patients, who had no other friend in their sickness. At my request Dr. Shorthouse visited many publicists who needed the skill of the physician. Though his speech was not encouraging or attractive, his kindly acts won every heart. The only time I ever engaged in sporting was when he asked me to join a sweepstake. I took two tickets, and forgot all about them. Some time after he remarked to my brother Austin that he had £50 due to some claimant who had never appeared ; and one day my brother Austin, who remembered I had tickets, looked among my papers and found that one of them was the ticket wanted, and the £50 was paid to me. Alas ! the excitement of the turf was too much for Dr. Shorthouse, and he died all too soon for those who had affection for him.

In my youth I had barbaric taste enough to look with favour on fighting, and had some ambition that way. Once I went out on that business. A tendon of one wrist had been cut when a boy, which lamed me for life, and otherwise I found that prize fighting was not my vocation. The war spirit, engendered by Napoleonic battles, had not abated in my youth. Shaw, the famous Life Guardsman at Waterloo, was a prize fighter. The Ring was popular in Birmingham in my time, and would be again did invasion threaten us. Phil Sampson was a local hero and, had Hammer Lane been successful in his amour, I should have been nearly related to him. The first fight I witnessed was between two women. It took place on the Old Parsonage ground, which was then open previous to its being built over. The combatants were two lusty women, between thirty and forty years old, as far as I judged. They had come from courts adjoining the open ground. Having quarrelled, they challenged each other to fight. In their neighbourhood fighting would be common, their husbands might be boxers. There were few persons about, and the women fought because they were enraged. Each was so far stripped that their bosoms and arms were bare. They had full breasts, and the strangeness of their appearance caused me to stop and look at them. They sparred in the usual way, but after a few blows they closed, and then seized each other by the hair. Some women who had become aware of the fight rushed up and parted them. There was only one round. That was the first fight I saw. I have given an account of the last.

CHAPTER LXXVIII.

THE LAST LESSONS OF THE HANGMAN.

(1864.)

FOR fourteen years I wrote against the hangman, intending to abolish him so far as any influence I had might go—and if not abolish him repress him as a public teacher. Had I not been myself a teacher in Glasgow, and found that pupils never seemed eager to come up for instruction, I should never have felt jealousy of my successful rival, Jack Ketch, who in those days was put forward with great parade and circumstance as the chief moral teacher of the Government. I had some knowledge of murderers besides that acquired by connection with the press, through being ordered to report public executions. In the days of the *Leader* newspaper, I was required to supply an account of the hanging of a man and woman in Jail Square, Glasgow. It was then (1853) I first became envious of the success of the Professor of the Gallows in drawing crowds of scholars to his classes.

The most eminent teachers lament the indocility of mankind to receive moral impressions. They exhaust all the arts of blandishment and persuasion, and win but scant pupils and reluctant learners. All the while the Government were in possession of a secret which genius, earnestness, and solicitude had failed to discover. Exchange the blackboard of the teacher for the black cap of the judge, the desk for the gallows, and the scholars rush up in crowds ; every student is eager : you cannot count their numbers ; you require strong and far-extended barriers to restrain their impatience for instruction.

In Jail Square at an early hour of a Glasgow summer morning I found the Trongate impassable. At every angle perspiring mobs of dirty men and tattered women came down like an avalanche. Hans Smith Macfarlane and Helen Blackwood were out in Jail Square, and the operation of strangling them was about to commence. The Salt Market was wedged full of raw depravity. You could take the dimension of villainy by the square inch. The cubic measure of Scotch scoundrelism in the city of Glasgow could be ascertained that morning.

A fog hung over the city, and the approaching spectator could only discern the edge of the struggling mass in Glasgow Green. Its thick murmur resounded like the coming of the cholera cloud, said to be heard by its first victims. The vast span of the bridge adjoining Jail Square was covered with human heads, gilded by beams from the bursting sun. All beyond and before that living arch was an undefined sea of glaring life. The huge city appeared to have lined its square and streets to welcome home some national hero. The city welcomed no victor—it was regaling its villains. The Lord Provost had bestowed on the public another moralising and deterring spectacle of a public strangling ; the policeman and the gaoler profitted—and thus civilisation was advanced.

Eleven years later (in 1864) I had to report for the *Morning Star* the " public killing " (as Douglas Jerrold called hanging) of Franz Muller. That morning was devoted by the Government to public instruction by the hangman. His subject was a German murderer.

In London professional debauchery and well-fed brutality transcend in quantity that of Glasgow. Calcraft, the teacher, had announced that he should give a lesson at Newgate. A surging throng attended his summons. Housetops, windows, and streets were crowded with pupils though a heavy rain was falling. What a commonplace, contracted, unsightly, uncomfortable, hideous area is the popular schoolroom of the Old Bailey ! Well may the murderous teacher exult in the punctuality of his pupils. No Pestalozzi, no Fellenburg, no Arnold, no Key, no Temple, no De Morgan was ever able to command the painful, prompt, and spontaneous allegiance of so many scholars. Neither Cambridge nor Oxford can compare with the University of Newgate. Ratcliffe Highway, Shoreditch, Houndsditch, and every other ditch that harbours a thief; Billingsgate, the Seven Dials, and the Brill of Somers Town sent their choicest representatives. The knave and the burglar had run and raced from every purlieu of the metropolis in order not to miss their Newgate lecture. The pickpocket was there. The ticket-of-leave man was present. The drunkard and the wife-beater found means to profit by this great State opportunity. The sickly, the consumptive were among the throng—defying the cold, which must be misery, and the damp, which may kill. Eager for the instruction the gallows imparts, the most vicious business is suspended. The garotter lets his intended victim pass ; the burglar leaves the shutter half splintered, and hastens on when the hangman is teaching. An influence stronger than lust, more alluring than vice, more tempting than plunder, is exercised by this seductive instructor. The condemned has been kept a fortnight within hearing of the very footstep of Death, daily coming nearer and nearer to him. He is brought out upon the scaffold. Twenty thousand strange eyes glare upon him, with hungry terror-striking warning. He is shown to the excited mob before his face is covered. The spectators see the last spark of hope die out of his soul. No reprieve has come ; no horseman rushes up to the throng ; no shout of pardon is heard ; no possible rescue, which always lingers in the mind of the doomed, occurs. The wretch stands face to face with inevitable, pitiless, pre-meditated Death, and the crowd know that he knows it. They see the frame quiver and the blood rush to the neck. A thrill passes through the congregated scoundrels whom the Government has thus undertaken to entertain. If Godfrey Kneller said he never looked upon a bad picture but he carried away a dirty tint, we may be sure that no eye looks upon the scaffold but it takes or transmits a tint of murder.

I was not much before my time in urging these arguments upon public consideration. Two days after my last letter upon the subject appeared in the *Star* (November 16, 1864), news-papers wrote against the spectacle which had never so written before. No doubt the distrust of public killing had crept into many minds. *The Times* had a leader which might be taken as a summary of my statements (so closely was it analogous to them), and admitted that public executions were disastrous in

London ; but arguing that the hangman's lessons told on those who were absent, treating the gallows as a school where only those pupils profit who do not attend ! The *Standard* afterwards published a poem strenuously deploring the effect upon the public of the appearance at the gallows of two teachers together—the Clergyman and the Strangler, the one preaching mercy and the other murder. Soon after the Grand Jury at Manchester protested against executions in that city, and advised that they should " take place within the precincts of the gaol for the hundred of Salford." This the law eventually conformed to, and public instruction by the hangman ended.

CHAPTER LXXIX.

AN ADVENTURE WITH GARIBALDI.

(1864.)

INCIDENTS when Garibaldi was at Brooke House in 1864, are worth relating. I was, by instruction, in attendance upon him. I had been since he was received at Southampton. The *Ripon*, which brought him there, was stormed by crowds of deputations and persons who, in his day of insurgency and unpopularity, never showed him friendship or sympathy, but were even among his defamers. They were all anxious now to show themselves as his friends. The only persons who displayed dignity, self-respect and knowledge of the situation were Mr. Joseph Cowen—the general's old friend in adversity—and the Duke of Sutherland. The Duke simply greeted Garibaldi, and, neither officious nor persistent, gave him an invitation to his house in London when it suited him to come, and then went away. Mr. Cowen (Garibaldi's eyes brightened as he greeted him) explained to Garibaldi the English situation, and what course would be best for Italy for him to pursue, and left him.

After I had been a week at the Isle of Wight—often seeing Garibaldi, once dining with him, and sometimes joining him in his morning walk in the gardens of Brooke House—all Mr. Seely's guests returned to England in the *Medina*. It was stated by members of Parliament on board that 100,000 men intended to file before the General at Nine Elms. As it was desirable to save him the fatigue of standing five hours while this was done, a wish was expressed that a different arrangement should be acted upon, but no one was willing to take the

responsibility of suggesting it. Mr. W. E. Forster, M.P.,
therefore, said to me, "Holyoake, you do it."

Not being able to understand why Mr. Forster or any one
should hesitate about doing a right thing, I drew up and
telegraphed to London to personal friends at the head of the
proposed procession, as follows :—

"ON BOARD THE 'MEDINA,'

"10 o'clock, *Monday.*

"If the 100,000 persons, as reported here, are to file before the
General at Nine Elms, he will have to stand five hours. He
will be weary ; his entry into London will be delayed till dusk.
If practicable, let the General go first, and the procession follow
and defile before him at Stafford House. Nobody else here will
take the responsibility of saying this, although every one wishes
it said."

There was also in the train a vain Italian tradesman who put
himself forward as representing the Italians in the metropolis.
All the years while the English friends of Italy had been working and subscribing to promote Italian freedom, the name of
this person was never heard ; nor was he ever seen at any of
their meetings. He had no colour except that of an enemy of
Mazzini. He had met me in the Isle of Wight, and knowing
me to be in communication with Mazzini, had conceived against
me hostility on that account. With the wit which small
enmity sometimes has, he discerned that Mr. Seely might be
acted upon. He went to him, and, speaking English, which
the General and Menotti (Garibaldi's son) had but limited
knowledge of, obtained from Mr. Seely authority, even using
Mazzini's name, to remove me from the train on the pretence
that my presence in it, on arriving at London, might compromise the General. He then informed the stationmaster,
one Mr. Godson, who (an exception to railway officers) was a
discourteous person, that he had Mr. Seely's authority for my
removal from the train at the Micheldever Station.

As I was the representative of the *Newcastle Daily Chronicle*
and the *Morning Star*, I had a seat in the press carriage.
Menotti was with his father. Mr. Charles Seely, M.P. for
Lincoln, whose guest Garibaldi had been at Brooke House, was

with them. When we arrived at the station my removal was attempted. My colleagues on the press, representing *The Star*, *Times*, *Standard*, *Daily News*, *Telegraph* and *Morning Post*, were in the same compartment with me. When Mr. Godson demanded that I should leave, not one of them resented this proceeding, though two of them had depended on me daily for information—which I alone could give them—for their journals. For one of them I had myself, at a cost of fifteen shillings, driven across the island to telegraph for his paper news in my possession which he desired to have sent ; and I had lent him thirty shillings to pay his hotel bill, when he fell short of money. Neither of these sums were ever repaid. I refused to leave the train, and told Mr. Godson it was an outrage on a member of the English press.

Seeing on the platform my friend Mr. Forster, whose guest I had twice been, and who the night before had obtained from me private information of what had taken place concerning Garibaldi during the week he had spent in the Isle of Wight, I felt sure of friendly interference. Stepping out of the carriage, I told him what was being done, and said, " Please speak to Mr. Godson, and tell him that an English member of the press cannot be removed from a public train at the instiga-tion of a foreigner. A word from you, a member of Parliament, will prevent this." He turned away, however, saying, " he could not interfere." I saw then that he knew all about it, and was a party to it.

The stationmaster, seeing Mr. Forster turn away, prevented me from returning to the carriage. Baffled thus, I would have opened the General's carriage door, and leaped in. I well knew he would never allow me to be removed, as I was the represen-tative of the paper of Mr. Cowen, his earliest and greatest English friend. But this would have caused a scene. It would have got into the papers, and been taken advantage of by the enemies of the Italian cause. So I said to Mr. Godson that, " as the objection was to my entering London in the train of the General, I would give my word that I would leave the train at Nine Elms." I was then allowed to return to my carriage.

When we arrived at Nine Elms, I did what I could to fulfil my promise ; first waiting until the General and all other persons had passed out.   Then I found the station in possession of the police, who informed me they had orders to prevent any one going out save through the station exit.   In a minute I was nearly under horses' feet in the midst of the mighty throng. Here I found a number of carriages waiting.   I was invited by the Garibaldi Committee to take a seat with them, but I preferred the private carriage of a friend, having first procured a seat for Basso, who was in attendance upon Garibaldi.   I had met Basso in company with Menotti.   Not knowing a word of English, he was hopelessly lost amid the half million of people who lined the streets between Nine Elms and Pall Mall.

Without perceiving it, the carriage I had chosen was next to the General's, and thus, without any intention of my own, I rode right before Garibaldi, in the centre of the mighty throng which lined the road all the way to the Duke of Sutherland's.

The conduct of the eccentric Italian was all the more preposterous, since I was elected at a large meeting of the London Tavern on the same reception committee as himself, and I had as much right to prevent him appearing in the General's train as he had to prevent me.   Yet this man, who never rendered assistance nor made sacrifice in any of those enterprises which had built up Garibaldi's reputation, now thrust himself forward, even to the exclusion of Menotti from his father's carriage, taking his seat himself.

Mr. Washington Wilks, who was in the train on the part of the *Morning Star*, was the only gentleman among the reporters of the press present.   His chivalry towards me I have never forgotten.   He expressed his contempt for my press colleagues in the carriage, because of their cowardly silence when I was attacked in their company.   Afterwards, when some of them went abroad for their papers in the Franco-German war, and met with outrage in a country in which they were foreigners, at the hands of the inhabitants who had a right to object to them, they had reason to remember their own conduct in tolerating and conniving at an outrage instigated by a foreigner in their own country.   When it came to their turn, they sent home shrieks to the Foreign Office for protection.

Mr. Wilks went down to the House of Commons the same night.   Mr. Forster told me that he attacked him with fury in the lobby, and Mr. Seely also.   Mr. Forster assumed not to know what the occasion of his resentment was. The proprietor of the *Newcastle Daily Chronicle*, with his customary public spirit, at once made known the personal indignation with which he regarded this interference with its representative. The *Morning Star*, as might be expected from its independence, held the same tone. The editor of the *Daily News* was prompt to animadvert upon the proceeding in its columns, not knowing that its own reporter, to whom I had twice supplied information, connived at it.

When Mazzini heard that his name had been used for a pretext for the proceeding recounted, he at once sent me the following letter :—

"*April* 22, 1864.

"My DEAR FRIEND,—It is with a deep regret and sense of humiliation for Italy that I have heard of the uncourteous, ungentlemanly, ungrateful conduct of an Italian towards you. I have written to him [Negretti] that he has offended me, too, through the unwarranted use of my name. Let me apologise for him to you. If he was different from what he is, I might proceed further, and insist on his apologising to you. But he is, in intellect, tendencies, and manners, belonging to that class of men whom I call ' irresponsible.' Forget him, and be contented with knowing that I and we all are, not only esteeming and loving you, but grateful for your efforts in our cause.— Ever faithfully yours, JOSEPH MAZZINI."

In justice to the Italian nation, it ought to be said that every public man who became acquainted with the facts volunteered his personal regret. Guerzoni, Major Woolf, and others were foremost. On the day that his illustrious father visited the House of Commons, Menotti stepped across the lobby, from the side of the Earl of Shaftesbury, with whom he was conversing, to stand by me and show by that act his disapprobation of the occurrence. It is due to Italians to say that the outrage Menotti resented was the act of a single " irresponsible " Italian.

The outrage was aimed at Mazzini (whose name had been treacherously used), who could not be reached, and in whose place it was an honour to stand. But the professional conse quences were a very different affair. A newspaper proprietor would have on important occasions to despatch another representative to accompany me, to take my place when under arrest, which would not conduce to engagements.

When Garibaldi learned what had occurred, his indignation was unmeasured. My friend Mr. James Stansfeld, to whom meanness or cowardice of any kind was instinctively abhorrent, did not conceal from Mr. Forster or Mr. Seely his opinion of their conduct at Micheldever.

Mr. Seely was really a generous, kind-hearted man, but without strength of intellectual conviction. I have seen him come out of the House of Commons, and finding in the lobby two Chartist agitators without means necessary for their work, give a £5 note to each. He joined with Mr. Forster and Mr. Mundella in providing permanent means of comfort in his declining years for another Chartist, Thomas Cooper, whose honesty and ability they knew ; and Colonel Seely, with the same honourable kindness, continued the payment after his father's death. I wrote to Mr. Seely to ask for an explanation, whether he had given authority for my removal from the train. Mr. Seely gave no denial, but drove over to my house and left word with my son, I being out, that he wished me to call on him and talk the matter over. This I declined, as "no private word was a compensation for a public affront." I wrote to him saying :—

"Either you were a party to the outrage upon me or you were not. If you were, why should you hesitate to say so ? Mr. ——, whom you authorise to write to me, fixes upon you as the authority under which he acted. I always understood that an English gentleman neither did a wrong nor suffered the imputation of sanctioning it ; his pride dictated, if his honour did not, instant reparation. Had not you and your confederate calculated that my independent opinions would prevent me having friends to publicly take my part, you had not ventured to treat me thus—neither he by his act, nor you by your silence."

Shortly afterwards Mr. Forster again met me at the House of Commons, when he mentioned Mr. Wilks's vehemence to him, and said he had no power to interfere with the arrangement of the train. I answered, "That was not it, Mr. Forster ; you did not want to know me in public. I did not ask you to know me—I did not appeal to you as a friend. I addressed you as I would any other member of Parliament whom I knew to be such. I claimed, as a stranger might, your political protection of my civil right, and you refused it. Had it been Mr. Newdegate who, though Tory and Churchman, was passing as you were, and I had claimed his interference, he would have stopped twenty trains before he would have permitted an Englishman to be seized and detained at the instigation of a foreigner." Mr. Forster spoke some general words of regret, and hoped I would dismiss the subject from my mind. On leaving me, he offered me his hand, which I took, because I had memory of his former courtesy, and had been his guest ; but I addressed him no more for twenty years.

At the end of his Irish Secretaryship, and when he had volunteered to go back after the murder of Mr. Burke and Lord F. Cavendish, notwithstanding the many perils of assassination through which he had himself passed, I again conceived a great admiration of his courage and noble spirit of duty. I was proud that an Englishman should show these qualities. For when intimidation or murder is attempted, it is not English to submit to it, and not English to give in, and I forgot and forgave everything. One night at the House of Commons, as I was standing in the lobby, Mr. Forster came by. I assured him I had honour for his courage, and was glad that adversaries he had tried to serve had not succeeded in killing him. He said "They certainly did their best." He asked kindly after Mr. Thomas Cooper and the comforts of his home, of which I gave him an account. We parted friends again, and remained so all his days, and he saw many proofs in the press of my regard for him.

In accepting the office of Irish Secretary in succession to Lord Cavendish, Mr. George Otto Trevelyan was in one sense yet more to be honoured. Mr. Forster was naturally indifferent to danger, and rather liked it. Mr. Trevelyan was less adventurous by nature. His was the courage of duty ; he was intrepid by force of will. One night when I spoke to him of the manner in which he had undertaken the Irish Secretaryship he appeared gratified, and added lightly, " They do not particularly wish to kill me, but to make a protest against English rule." " Yes," I rejoined ; " but it is not particularly pleasant to be the subject of the protest "—at which he went away laughing.

CHAPTER LXXX.

UNPUBLISHED INCIDENTS IN THE CAREER OF W. E. FORSTER.

(1864.)

MR. FORSTER has been described mainly by those who happened to agree with him in the respects in which he was wrong, saving Mr. Justin McCarthy, who, differing from him discerningly, gave, in an article in the *Contemporary* for August, 1888, a true impression of him.

Mr. Forster was ambitious, and without recognising that there is no understanding him. Ambition was stronger in him than any other sentiment. Humanity and liberal principles were, to the end of his days, characteristic of him, and he preferred advancing his personal ascendency by these means ; but they had not the personal dominion over him that ambition had.

When I first knew him he gave me this impression. He did not profess to share my opinions, but he had an inquiring mind, and wished to know what the opinions of others were, and on what they were founded. Had he not been of a liberal and just mind himself, he would not have cared to know such views as I held. His choice would have been not to know them. He would have judged them without knowing them. Because Mr. Forster was friendly to me, I never assumed that he agreed with me. I never assume this of any one, unless he tells me so. It would make friendship impossible with independent thinkers, if it were held to imply coincidence of ideas.

Mr. Forster told me at that time the nature of his opinions on education. Had he likewise told his friends in Bradford, and they had understood him as I did, they would not have been disappointed in their reliance on his educational policy, as they would never have had any expectation of his going in the direction they wished.

What he said to me was—" Those who stand at the head of society and argue that the minds of the people must be left alone or they will break loose from the religious ties which are supposed to bind them, and drift away no one knows whither, must take a new course, as the people are already free from those ties; and they who mean to guide them must guide them speedily, or some one else will do it for them."

Mr. Forster had been present at lectures and discussions in which I took part. He was surprised very much to see that the majority of large meetings were entirely in sympathy with what were then regarded as the heretical views submitted to them. He was then quite resolved, should he attain power, that the authority of the State Church should be the agent of national religious instruction. My impression was that his marriage with Dr. Arnold's daughter further excited his ambition to serve the ends of the Church.

In my time I have seen many men treat every principle in which they were interested as subordinate to ambition. Also, I have seen opponents who, disliking the ambition, shut their eyes to every other quality the ambitious man had, and over-look the services he might render to right principles when they did not interfere with his personal ends. I have known many men promote movements they did not much care for, their object being to obtain influence in them in favour of some view of their own. Thus the recruiting sergeant will have honest admiration of a straight, well-made man, because he has the qualities of a soldier in him. The sergeant will be civil to such a man, will praise him, will take an interest in him, and even desire his welfare from a professional point of view; but his main object all the while is to enlist him.

Thus the Rev. Frederick Denison Maurice took interest in co-operation, not because he cared for it for its own sake. As he said himself, " His great wish was to Christianise Socialism, not Christian-socialise the universe." So far as co-operation infused morality into trade Mr. Maurice did care for it, and his sympathy was of great service to it. I have known many

Christians, whose ability and good feeling commanded regard, take part in social and political efforts, without caring intrinsically for them ; but, as Comtists do in like cases, they sympathised to what extent they can from quite a different motive from that which inspires those whom they serve.   It would, however, be most unjust to many not of my way of thinking to conceal my knowledge that they do often promote the interests of others without any considerations of their own. For myself, I never cared one jot whether the persons whose movements I promoted adopted my views or not.   I never, with a view to their adopting my views, treated Christians with fairness and respect, or spoke with courtesy to them.   I acted so solely because courtesy, fairness, justice, and discernment of the good qualities of others were right principles in themselves, and should for their own sake be observed towards all persons, whether adversaries or friends.

A fortnight before his marriage Mr. Forster had driven me over to Burley for a night's conversation.   We did not set out until after my lecture that night in Bradford.   Burley was ten or more miles away.   We had a fine high-stepping horse ; the night was dark, and the roads were steep.   Never before nor since have I ridden with any one who drove so furiously as Mr. Forster.   I fully expected to be found next morning distributed on the wayside banks between Bradford and Burley.   The anecdote of Mr. Forster's dare-devil driving which Mr. Wemyss Reid relates in his " Life " of Mr. Forster accords with my experience.

Shortly after his marriage, I was again a guest at Burley. Mrs. Forster appeared to me a pretty and gentle lady—in every way a contrast to her tall and energetic husband.   She lent me the travels of Huc and Gabet in Tartary, which has seemed to me, ever since, one of the brightest of all books of missionary adventures.   She walked by my side as we went down to dinner.   Being a stranger, and diffident, I did not offer her my arm, doubtful whether it might not be presuming. Afterwards I asked Miss Martineau what I was free to do under such circumstances.   With that ready condescension and instructiveness, always a conspicuous grace in her, she wrote me a letter of great interest, telling me that, being a guest, I was for the time being an equal, and might have complied with the opportunities of the hour with propriety. Some time previous to Mr. Forster's death I mentioned the letter to him, and he asked me to let him see it, but some person who admired it had retained it.

In a town of influence where the question of education was much discussed, Mr. Forster one day sought an interview with the leaders whose influence might facilitate his entrance to the Cabinet. He had a communication to make of importance, it was said. Those interested in hearing it were present in assembly. Mr. Forster suggested that it would be better not to have reporters present, as what he wanted to say might, in the hands of adversaries, produce obstacles. The communication was made, and filled the little assembly with enthusiasm for the ascendency of one so likely to carry their wishes into legislation. When Mr. Forster obtained the position in which he could give effect to what he was understood to have in his mind, his proposal and his speeches did not correspond with the expectations entertained by his hearers. They thought they might have misunderstood him, and were about to refer to some independent record of what he did say, when they remembered his objection to reporters being present. The impression they had, therefore, was that they had been out-witted ; and they certainly thought that what appeared reasonable diplomatic precaution was a trick. Whether they ever wrote to Mr. Forster to ask him what he did say, I know not. They probably distrusted him then so much that they thought the proceeding futile. Mr. Forster was a man of truth, and would probably have answered frankly, as he was not lacking in courage to stand by what he had thought proper to do. Judging of Mr. Forster by his antecedents, they might have interpreted his words through his character and Nonconformist predilections, while his actual words might have admitted of the interpretation he put upon them. But the indignation with which the narrative was related to me by one who was present showed that the impression was strong that they had been deceived, and that they had used influence they never would have exercised had they understood what was afterwards to happen.

I was in the House when Mr. Forster made his declaration that " he had Puritan blood in his veins." He held out his

arm as he spoke, as though he would bare it that the House
might see the blood throbbing. I said at the time, to a
member who was speaking to me, that if Mr. Forster would
put a drop of that Puritan blood into his bill, his adversaries
would all be satisfied. Afterwards I asked Professor Huxley
or Professor Tyndal to get a drop of that Puritan fluid and
analyse it, to see if some adulteration were not present.

Soon after, at a large deputation of Nonconformist ministers
at Downing Street, Mr. Forster put to them the plain question
whether, as the character of religious education to be given in
Board Schools seemed to present irreconcilable difficulties, they
were prepared to give education without the Bible. There
was an immediate and general response "without." Mr.
Forster in the House described this deputation of three hundred
Nonconformist ministers as though they were three hundred
infidels ; though any one of them had stronger religious
convictions than Mr. Forster, who said at the same time that
"there was no Church which satisfied him to which he could
attach himself." It was this rancorous tone on the part of Mr.
Forster, unbecoming in a Minister and unseemly in him, which
embittered the controversy. He might have said that it was a
question between no national education at all and the conces-
sions he made to the ascendency of the Church ; and that he
would have done better if he could, but he thought so much
of national education that we had better have it, and leave the
Church to manipulate it, than to be without it. This would
have justified Mr. Forster. Such a policy might have been
the necessity of statesmanship. Nonconformists might have
thought Mr. Forster wanting in judgment in not better interpreting the temper or liberalism of the nation, but there would
have been no abiding anger, and he would never have forfeited
the personal respect of his adversaries of another way of
thinking. Mr. Forster did not do this. He said he would not
do other than he did if he could. He spoke in Parliament in
terms which seemed intended to elicit the applause of the ancient
enemies of Nonconformists, and at times spoke of Nonconformists as unpleasantly as ever they did of him. They spoke in
defence of their traditional principle, and he spoke in defence
of his departure from it. This came from his early Quaker
training, which made resentment in him more determined and

persistent than in other Christians, for reasons which I explain elsewhere in the chapter on Mr. Bright.

To give ascendency to the Church as against the Nonconformists, and say he " would not do better if he could," took all his neighbours and supporters by surprise. Their familiar friend, whom they had placed where he was, was henceforth to them a man of almost unknown principles.

When the election came again he refused to trust those who had trusted him, and appealed to the Tories whose interest he had served, and who had done their best to keep him out of Parliament. This was neither chivalry nor gratitude, nor cordiality to those who had been his friends when other friends he had none. If they were less enthusiastic for him than heretofore, it was not he who could reproach them. Mr. Forster had his reasons, and they the disappointment. A man cannot command trust and not reciprocate it. One bold, frank, generous speech such as Mr. Forster at other times was capable of, would have bound his old constituents to him all his days.

Towards the close of his career, he made a speech, or gave some vote, the effect of which was hostile to Mr. Gladstone, or was so interpreted by the Tories. I was given to understand by a confidential friend of his that Mr. Forster regretted this. This was like his real self, whose instincts were liberal. One of his last speeches in Bradford was too plaintive, and made too much of the " anxieties " of statesmanship. He went to Ireland, he said, with a " heavy heart," and he had more reason for disquietude than we know. Yet it is the commonplace experience of statesmanship to find difficulties. To have a " heavy heart" about it is entirely a waste of time. Unpleasantnesses fall to every statesman who does his duty. One half of his friends will complain of him not going far enough ; the other half for going too far ; and his adversaries will denounce him whichever way he goes, and not less if he stands still. However, Mr. Forster made it clear that, while Liberal Irish advocates were denouncing him for considering landlord interests, the landlords denounced him because he was utterly neglecting them. They were right ; Mr. Forster in his heart was always with the people.

I was myself of Mr. Forster's opinion that a law should be

enforced against crime that was clearly crime. It seemed to me that Irish Americans were attempting to run secession in Ireland, as they had tried to do in America—out of spite to England, and not unnaturally, so long as Nationalist aspiration was regarded as a form of crime. The more a Minister exerted himself and conferred upon them local benefits to divert their minds from nationality, amelioration seemed hateful to them. The Chartists in England manifested precisely the same spirit when they were offered ameliorative measures to divert their minds from enfranchisement. When the Irish were generally enfranchised, and they sent eighty-six members to represent the national demand for self-government, and Mr. Gladstone showed that that was possible without separation, the Irish people became our friends, and no longer desired separation. The offer of substantial independence cancelled the hatred and distrust of seven centuries.

One day, when the agitation for a real Reform Bill in England was in progress, a conference was held in Leeds to promote it. A gentleman entered the room who had spent more money than any man in England to bring it to pass. His mode of attire was far from fashionable. He despised fashion —but he cared for service. Seeing Mr. Forster, whose political interests he had strenuously promoted, he went up to him first to greet him. Whether it was that Mr. Forster thought a further acquaintance unimportant, or whether he did not care to identify himself with a man of the determined views his friend was known to entertain, Mr. Forster took no notice of him. Mr. Bright at once rose to greet the unimportant looking delegate. Then Mr. Forster went over and offered his hand, which the repulsed delegate in his turn declined to take, long afterwards entertaining contempt for Mr. Forster. Many years later, when both were members of Parliament, I was with the delegate at Wimbledon Station when Mr. Forster stood there in volunteer uniform waiting for a train ; but my friend kept me in conversation, walking up and down the platform lest Mr. Forster, to whom he would not speak, should accost him. For some reason I never knew, my friend afterwards became reconciled to him. Something inexplicable had been explained.

When I was in frequent communication with Mr. Forster, he passed me by without notice when I stood by accident in his way. When I came to know that Mr. Forster was short-sighted, I thought this explained much ; men engrossed in thought will often pass by persons without seeing them, and, if short-sighted, may do this without knowing it. Many persons are indignant at being slighted when no slight is intended. If we only knew everything, many men would be acquitted who are now condemned.

In 1875, when an annuity was given me, there appeared in the list, " An Old Friend," £20. I asked who that was, but was told I was not to know. After Mr. Forster's death Major Bell told me the " Old Friend " was Mr. Forster. I never experienced any act more delicate and generous than this. It was during our feud when he sent the subscription which he suspected I should refuse if I knew who gave it ; or he might think that if I knew I might regard it as intended to mitigate my anger against him. He was too manly to incur that suspicion. But he wished to serve me, and took a way of doing it which I could neither resent nor acknowledge. When I learned this I was glad we had become friends, and that I had done him some service in his later years, which he acknowledged in a letter he sent me from Torquay shortly before his death.

CHAPTER LXXXI.

NAPOLEON III. IN LONDON.

(1865.)

LANDOR's injunction—"Watch him and wait"—was followed both by the Government and the people. Every year Louis Napoleon was on the throne of France it cost us millions a year to watch him, since no Bonaparte was to be trusted. Palmerston, though a comrade of the false President, never trusted him. The people waited, and they saw him twice— once a visitor and then a fugitive. Had a bill been passed for giving up Dr. Bernard, no Royal exile had any more found peace on these shores.

When the Queen went to Paris on a visit to the Emperor, I was instructed by the *Leader* to proceed there and report the features of the Royal journey. I then saw the Emperor for the first time. He was smoking a cigar on a verandah in Boulogne. His 70,000 troops were massed for review below, awaiting the arrival of the Queen. The Emperor was then in the prime of his usurpation. The next time I saw him it was before my door in Fleet Street, where he stopped some time and read some placards which interested him, and which met his inquiring eye.

It came about in this wise. He was then on a visit to the Queen in London. Great preparations had been made for his safety, as he had not many friends in the metropolis, and the natural anxiety of the Court was that nothing unpleasant should happen to him on that occasion. In those days Daniel Whittle Harvey was Commissioner of Police in the City of London, and things were always pleasant between the City police and the people. The City police always treated the working class as citizens, and as such entitled to protection in their political processions; whereas Sir Richard Mayne, as all Metropolitan Commissioners do, treated the working class as a criminal class, and more frequently attacked them than assisted them. Commissioner Harvey, therefore, knew he could count upon the good-will of the people in any regulation he wished observed. Sir Richard Mayne had no such ground of confidence; and, on the night before the arrival of the Emperor, he and Commissioner Harvey met together on horseback in Fleet Street before my publishing house, to consult as to what they should do with regard to it. They suspected that some unpleasant persons might be within who had good reasons not to be amiable towards the Emperor. Police agents had been to me several times, making inquiries, which I answered in a manner calculated to satisfy them that they need be under no apprehension on my account. I said I regarded the French Emperor as the guest of the nation, and should oppose any discourtesy being shown to him while he appeared in that character. At that time Mazzini and Professor Francis William Newman were both contributors to the *Reasoner*, and, with the "courage of conviction" characteristic of them, permitted me to make the announcement. It happened that their names appeared in large red letters on a placard which stretched across the fanlight of my door. The question discussed by the two Commissioners when they met, was whether I should be asked to take that placard down, lest it might meet the eye of the Emperor and produce disquietude in his mind. Mazzini had addressed an eloquent and indignant "Letter to Louis Napoleon" which had not contributed to his peace of mind. The Commissioners came to the conclusion that they had no right to ask me to take down a business placard, and, next, they did not think I should do it if they did. Commissioner Harvey respected City independence.

The next day the Emperor duly came by, accompanied by guards, and seated in a carriage said to be lined with plates of steel, lest a stray shot from some Fieschi might strike the panel. There was a great throng in the street, and every house had its windows let to curious and other spectators. I gave orders that my house should be closed as on Sundays, and that no persons employed in it should appear at the windows. I would show the unwelcome visitor no active disrespect, neither would I show him any attention, and least of all any jubilation. It happened that at that time Mr. Samuel Bright, brother of John Bright, was at the office of *Diogenes*, with which he was connected. It had a window in Fleet Street, but he did not wish to appear there, and he came over with his pretty wife, to whom he had not long been married, to ask me if I would allow them to see the Emperor from my window. This was contrary to the rule I had laid down ; but as I had been his guest at Spotland, I could not refuse him. He had just returned from the Continent. He had a dark flowing beard, and wore a high Hungarian hat, and might be mistaken for a brigand or for the heir-at-law of William Tell. As he sat on the window-sill he certainly looked a suspicious person. The Emperor could not fail to see him as he glanced up the street. The moment he arrived opposite Mr. Bright, his horses reared and the carriage suddenly stopped. The air was filled with thousands of pieces of white paper, like a heavy snowstorm. This sudden descent of floating, flickering flakes had frightened the horses. Not knowing what could be the matter, the Emperor looked for a moment out of the carriage at the house, and then his eye met the name of Mazzini in red letters, which was not reassuring. In a minute the horses were calmed, and the procession passed on.

The next house to mine was the office of the *Sporting Life*, then a new journal. Mr. Feist had printed 50,000 small bills announcing the paper, and the printers were out on the house-top showering them down on the procession. It was this that caused the procession to stop. It was odd that it should have occurred before my door.

There were many patriots very indignant at the Queen for kissing the Emperor on his arrrival, and they said so in the newspapers. It might be a regal ceremony, but it was not pleasant to think of. It was bad enough to have such a visitor, but to kiss "false, fleeting, perjured Clarence" was worse. It made people think that Royalty was unfortunate, or was not fastidious.

CHAPTER LXXXII.

VISITS FROM A MURDERER.

(1865.)

WHEN I had chambers in Cockspur Street, London, a man called upon me several times who stated himself to be "Ernest W. Southey." His real name was Stephen Forward. I suppose, from what I afterwards knew of his character, that he had taken the name of "Southey" as more imposing, and as suggesting that he was a possible relative of the poet; but his proper name, Forward, much better suited his disposition. He was a somewhat handsome man, with a glistening, feverish eye. He had a grievance which he represented was against Lord Dudley. So far as my visitor was known to have an occupation, it was that of a billiard-marker at some hotel in Brighton. His story was that Lord Dudley, being there, had sometimes played with him (which he might have done for practice when he found no one else at hand, Forward being an intelligent person). His account was that Lord Dudley played him a match for £1,000, and of course lost it. He refused to pay it. If Forward had lost, it is quite clear he could never have paid it ; and it is not supposable that his lordship would play a match for such a sum with a billiard-marker who had no money. His primary grievance was the claim for this debt of honour. Afterwards he went down to Witley Court, Worcestershire, Lord Dudley's country seat, with a person professing to be his wife, and demanded of Lord Dudley the billiard money. In the end, a charge was brought against Lord Dudley of accosting the woman in the Court grounds and making some improper overtures to her. The case was heard

137

at the local police court, and, being without any foundation, was dismissed. As "Southey" pressed his tale of distress upon me, I procured him some aid from friends, and sometimes met him in the lobby of the House of Commons. He had written to Mr. Gladstone and Lord Russell, representing he was in distress and should commit some dreadful crime unless he had assistance. Earl Russell gave him five pounds. One day, after a protracted visit, he told me that, since he could not get his £1,000 from Lord Dudley, he should murder his wife and children. I told him that "it was very absurd to kill them because of the fault of another. The logical thing was to go and kill Lord Dudley!" My impression was that a man who talked of killing people was not at all likely to do it. Great was my astonishment when, a few days later, I found from the newspapers that he had killed seven persons—his wife and six children. Five children of his by another person he took to a coffee-house off Holborn, and poisoned the whole of them in one night. Then he went down to Ramsgate, and killed his wife, who resided there, and one of two children whom she provided for. The other child fortunately escaped.

His object was to make a great sensation by a great crime. Tropmann in France had obtained notoriety even in the English press in this way. "Southey" coveted this sort of attention. He knew that any one who perpetrated a murderous atrocity could depend upon having his statements and remarks published in the newspapers. He knew that ladies, who forgot that their sympathies were due to the unhappy victims or their unhappy relatives, sent delicacies to the cells of famous murderers. Clergymen were assiduous in their attentions to them, and promised them certain and early admission to Paradise. This notoriety and distinguished attention induced Forward to qualify himself for them. I thought it impossible, until I knew him, that any man would sacrifice his life for this brief and perilous applause. I remembered afterwards that he had said that he thought it would be "a fine thing to call attention to the injustice of society," which neglected persons in his condition—meaning the hard-heartedness of gentlemen who would not give money to an intelligent man who was not willing to work. I understood too late that killing his wife and children was the "fine thing" he had in his mind.

After he had committed the crime, he wrote to me from Sandwich Gaol inviting me, as "a leader of enlightened opinion, and connected with the press," to come down and see him early, as I might thereby "serve my own interests by striking a blow at the hypocrisies and superstitions of the country." He informed me that "he was aiding, as far as he could, in the work in which I was engaged"—that was, any one would think, murdering innocent persons wholesale! His desire was, he said, "to obtain respect for the class of opinions we mutually hold." This monstrous letter I knew would be read by the governor of the gaol before he despatched it to me. I read it with indignation, as the governor must have regarded me as a confederate abroad, engaged in the atrocious propagation of opinion by blood. The following are copies of his letter, and the reply which I returned to it :—

"PRISON HOUSE, SANDWICH,
"*Sunday, August* 13, 1865.

"SIR,—As a leader of enlightened opinions, as an advocate of the abolition of capital punishment, as a man connected with the press and publishing houses, if you would run down here and see me at an early opportunity, I assure you you might find such an opportunity of serving your own interests, as well as an opportunity of striking a great blow against the hypocrisies, superstitions, and ignorance of the country, such as you could not estimate. I ask you to send me a line, for I am aiding so far as I can in the work you are also engaged in, and with help I may be enabled to assist in obtaining respect for that class of opinion we mutually hold, and which I should be sorry to be the means of bringing into disrepute.—I am, dear sir, yours faithfully,   ERNEST W. SOUTHEY."

"20, COCKSPUR STREET, LONDON, S.W.,
"*August* 14, 1865.
"MR. STEPHEN FORWARD.
"SIR,—I am reluctant to kick a man when he is down, even though he be a murderer ; but the letter you send me strongly inclines me to do it. I am sorry to give you pain, unless I could increase the deep remorse which I trust you are beginning to feel for the frightful guilt you have incurrea. I can have

no 'interest' to serve by seeing you. Were you innocent, I would not try to make anything out of your misfortunes, and I scorn to do it out of your crimes. I know not what you mean by 'opinions' we mutually hold. I knew you had a grievance, and I was sorry to hear you say your family were suffering. You came to me a stranger. I never saw you but four times. I treated you kindly, because I thought your mind unhinged. When I last saw you at the House of Commons I counselled you to dismiss the idea of suicide from your mind, and with your busy intelligence not to be afraid of honest work to extricate yourself. Don't write to me any more. Your prate about justice must end, now you have imbrued your hands in blood. I can only feel sorrow for you if you show contrition.   G. J. HOLYOAKE."

The vain scoundrel did not attempt to kill the mother of the five children whom he put to death, probably because she was inaccessible, being out at work earning means to feed the poor things. The wife who was keeping, by her own industry, her two deserted children he did kill, and one of the little ones. The knave had religious belief, and carried a Bible in his pocket. It may be that he pretended to be a Christian, as he pretended to be of my opinions, with a view to obtain money and notice.

Afterwards I reflected that, had he acted on my preferential suggestion, and killed Lord Dudley, and said that I had advised it, it had been unpleasant for me. He murdered for publicity. It was a frightful taste, but it was his. Madame Tussaud put the scoundrel in her Chamber of Horrors. It was his grim ambition to figure there.

On the last Sunday before his execution, he arose in the chapel, and addressed his fellow-criminals there assembled. No murderer before had thought of this expedient for obtaining notice in the press. There is no doubt "Southey" would make a speech in the infernal regions if they would condescend to hear him there, and he thought the Satanic reporters would publish it. When on the scaffold he had the impudence to stop the chaplain in the prayer he was reading, and request him to say only what he would dictate, which the compliant chaplain did. It was imprudent in the chaplain to consent, for "Southey" might have said something which it would be unbecoming in a clergyman to repeat, and an altercation with a man with a noose round his neck would not have been edifying. He had the effrontery to make the chaplain "commend him, his brother, to God who had redeemed him." Not even the gallows could repress his lust of notoriety.

Wherever I could I called attention in the press to the evil effects of publicity at that time accorded to murderers; as I had previously written against hanging in sight of a crowd of ruffians, who were afforded the gratification of "assisting" at murder without responsibility. Forward's trial was but briefly mentioned in the newspapers, and less distinction has since been accorded to murderers.

A writer, signing himself "H. B. Dudley," wrote to the *Newcastle Chronicle*, apparently with authority, to explain that the gentleman who played with "Southey" was a "relative" of Lord Dudley, whom Southey understood to be Lord Dudley. I wrote to "H. B. Dudley," who professed to have written "without consulting any member of the late lord's family," for such authentication as would warrant me in making corrections due to the late lord. But no answer came. Nor did Lord Dudley himself question my statement, which I sent to him at the time.

CHAPTER LXXXIII.

AMONG THE FISHERMEN OF CROMER.

(1867.)

IT is at once incredible and amusing to contemplate the primeval spiritual subjugation which parts of this little island are still under. I was wandering in 1867 on the stormy coast of Cromer. The boisterous sea visible there was once covered by cliff and forest. Druidical temples, Aryan altars, villages and churches had all been beaten down by the fierce waters which now roll over their sites. The noble church of lofty arches and majestic towers which now stands in Cromer would have been swept away ere now had not a stout sea wall protected it. The great ocean, being free, had no doubt suggested to the inhabitants round about that thought ought to be free also. I had never been in the place, but on the morning of my arrival it was noised abroad that I was the guest of a Quaker of repute thereabout. On Sunday I attended church. In a new town I take the first opportunity of hearing the most distinguished preacher in it. Preachers of different denominations often utter noble sentiments in a noble way, and hearing them enables one better to appreciate the eclecticism of piety. The preacher at the church was a greyheaded, dignified ecclesiastic in the maturity of his powers. He was a dean who preached. He said that there was a class of persons of high character, of perfect intellectual probity, who had that living morality which bound society together. Yet they professed not the Christian name. Nevertheless, it must be observed that, while morality bound man to the world, it was spiritual life which bound man to God. The sentences were clearly cut, as though chiselled by the hand of Woolner. Nor were the sentiments taken back

again in any part of the discourse, as is often the case with
some preachers. One often hears a fine concession at the
beginning of a sermon which is explained away at the conclusion.

The next day it was represented to me that many inhabitants
of the town, and especially the fishermen, would like to hear
from me a lecture on the " Orators of the English Parliament."
A messenger was sent miles away to the nearest printing press,
and early next morning, as I went down to the beach, I found
neat little placards in every shop window announcing my
lecture for the evening. In some windows which faced the
town two ways, placards were exhibited on each, announcing
that I would speak in the evening. Outside the Bible Society's
Depôt one of the bills appeared. So amicable was everything, I
thought I had alighted in an unfrequented corner of the
Millennium ! The fishermen's room was readily granted by
two of them who had authority over it. It was in that room
that an eminent member of Parliament, Charles Buxton, used
to deliver annual summaries of Parliamentary proceedings,
which ranked among the classics of political criticism. He was
dead then ; and a memorial window of great beauty of colour
and design, which I was told cost a thousand guineas, had been
put up in Cromer Church to his memory. The clouded and
chastened light which passed through the window recalled
those fine sentiments he used to express, in which philosophy
had softened and variegated the fierce light of the controversies
of his day.

Before noon a great change had come over Cromer ; there
was consternation in the place. Muffled whisperings were
heard behind every counter. The vicar had been in the town.
The bill on the Bible Society's door had attracted his attention.
He did not know me, but he knew I was not one of the apostles.
Though my name is partly Biblical, the vicar had the announcement bearing it removed. He went to the shopkeepers and
requested them to take the bills from their windows, and not to
go to the lecture. He admitted my subject was not in itself
objectionable, but then I might say something else in speaking
upon it. He was told that I regarded it as a breach of faith to
announce one subject, and, after inciting people to come to
hear that, to speak upon another. Whether the vicar was con-

vinced, I know not ; but, as he did not call again at the places
he visited to reverse his request, the bills were not replaced,
and by the afternoon not a single copy was to be seen anywhere
in the town.   Had Mr. Buxton, whose guest I had been, been
living at hand, things would have been different.

In the meantime I composed, in case the fishermen had a
choir, a variation of one of Byron's Hebrew Melodies—beginning, as they say in chapel, at the second verse :—

> " Like the leaves of the forest when summer is green,
> Placards in the windows at sunrise were seen ;
> Like the leaves of the forest when autumn has blown,
> The placards at sunset lay withered and strown.
>
> The vicar of Cromer came in with the blast,
> And spoke at the door of each shop as he past ;
> And the hearts of the keepers waxed deadly and chill ;
> Their souls but once heaved and thenceforward grew still."

When I returned from a tour of inspection, I sent word to
the fishermen who had let their rooms to me, that if they
thought anything would happen to their families through their
act, they were quite at liberty to recall it.   I thought it likely
that the vicar might be the almoner of many kind-hearted and
wealthy families in the neighbourhood, and the people might
fear being passed over when they wanted help in the hard
seasons that befell them.   " Tell the men," I said, " that I am
no pedlar of opinions ; I do not hawk my principles about the
country ; and if Cromer would rather I should not speak in the
town, I had no wish to speak to unwilling ears."

The stout fishermen probably reflected that they earned
their bread in the tempest, by day and by night, holding
their lives in their own hands, while the vicar passed his days
secure from harm, and that they would get through my lecture
as they had through other storms.   Hence they answered " they
should light their best candles for Mr. Holyoake, and make
their room as bright and cheerful as they could, if he chooses to
come."   When nightfall arrived, I marched through the village
with my host (whose Quaker blood was a little stirred) to
lecture.   Not a soul was moving in Cromer.   Nearing the
rooms, we observed a solitary man emerging from a cottage in
the direction of the Lecture Room.   His back was made visible
by a penny candle in the window.   " There does not appear,"
I said to my friend, " any great stampede to the lecture, but I

shall deliver it to you, and our friend, whose back we have seen, should he arrive there."

On entering the room I was astounded by an immense shout of welcome. The fishermen were there in force. A respectable inhabitant of the place was voted to the chair, and a gracious little speech of introduction was made by the gentleman, Mr. Kemp, whose guest I was.

I delivered my lecture. As I explained the difference between oratory and mere public speaking, and the characteristics of Bright, Gladstone, Disraeli, Lowe, Bernal Osborne, Buxton, Sir Wilfred Lawson, Stansfeld, and others, and pointed out the gradations of that art by which men climb on phrases to power, signs of discernment arose sufficient to satisfy any speaker. A reverend visitor, Mr. Valpy, whose father was a great classic authority, made a neat little speech at the end.

We said not a word about the vicar. I made no allusion to him, direct or indirect. It is a long time since those little peculiarities of the ecclesiastical mind, which he had displayed, affected or concerned me ; and the audience imagined I did not notice what he had done. I doubt not he was a kind-hearted gentleman to whom many have been indebted for words of counsel and acts of humanity. He was, perhaps, a little apt to forget that the people of Cromer were citizens as well as Christians, and had a right to know what affected them as Englishmen—that they needed to understand the secular merits of those great men who influence their destinies and make the English name distinguished on the earth. The Cromer men had no doubt reasons for respecting the vicar in removing the placards which were distasteful to him, and respected themselves by giving a courteous hearing to what a stranger had to say to them.

In any other town in England it is necessary to advertise a lecture two or three days ; but in Cromer it is sufficient to advertise a lecture for three hours, and this may have been the reason why they took the placards out of the windows at midday. However, to the inexperienced visitor, it seemed that Church courtesy in Cromer had contracted the qualities of the East wind, and dictation of the Romish type, which many thought obsolete in England, was still in force in that remote corner of East Anglia.

CHAPTER LXXXIV.

STORY OF THE LIMELIGHT ON THE CLOCK TOWER.

(1868.)

DURING several pleasant years I was secretary to a member of Parliament. His residence being at a considerable distance from the House of Commons, he had no means of knowing when " the House was up." Some days there would be an early " count out." Most members daily leave the House during what is termed " dinner hours " to dine, but it sometimes happened that the House would be counted out in the dinner-time. Then the return journey to the House was needless. A member in constant attendance at committees and Parliament would be glad to absent himself until later in the evening, when a division in which he was interested might be taken. But though the House might adjourn before the usual time ; there was no means of discovering this until he drove into sight of Palace Yard.

At that time the limelight was coming into use, and I thought it might be made available to prevent this inconvenience to members. The present Duke of Rutland was then at the Board of Works, and I addressed to him a letter on the subject which remained some years in the archives of the Board of Works, and is probably there now. I have no copy of the letter, but I well remember its purport. It was to this effect :—

" Being secretary of a member of Parliament, I have observed that considerable inconvenience arises by members having no means of knowing when the House is up, at times when they are unable to foresee it. There are no means by which a member can know it, unless he provides some one to send him a telegram to an address which he would have to renew every night, according to the place where he expected to be after leaving the House sitting. If he dined at one of the great clubs, he would learn when the House was up there, by members coming in who had recently left the House, or from the arrival of the hourly report of the proceedings in Parliament. But he might be dining four or five miles away, and must drive to one of the clubs to get the information. It is true that in Palace Yard gas lights, which have three arms, have only the centre one left burning—to indicate to persons arriving there that the House is up. But any one must drive to the bottom of Parliament Street before the single light can be discerned. It is a probable calculation that many members in the course of a session drive five hundred miles before they can reach Palace Yard to learn that the House is up. Reporters and others who have business with members at the House at night are subject to similar inconvenience. All this might be prevented if a limelight were placed at the summit of the Clock Tower. It could be seen six or seven miles in most directions, and members could learn at will whether the House was sitting or not."

This letter was longer than would seem necessary ; but it was needful to explain in detail the inconvenience to which members were subjected which might be so simply obviated. It was necessary to show that all the existing means of information were taken into account by the writer, for if any one had been omitted the suggestion might be thought based upon insufficient information—the official mind being always quick to show that there is no necessity for doing what it does not want to do.

Lord John Manners, the name by which the Duke of Rutland was then known, acknowledged the receipt of the communication, but without indicating whether it would be considered. Nothing came of it until Mr. Ayrton became Commissioner of the Board of Works. Though he excelled all Ministers in making himself unpleasant in debate, he also excelled in being the most vigilant of servants of the public in Parliament, being tireless in his attendance and reading more Parliamentary papers than any four members. He found my letter in the pigeon-holes of the Board of Works, and put up the limelight on the Clock Tower, which has made the House of Parliament as it were a beacon light visible all over London during the night sittings. An article upon it in *The Times*, after Mr. Ayrton had ceased to be Commissioner, giving a description of this Tower light, began by the remark that "a former Commissioner of Works found the suggestion in the office." The article was evidently written by a well-informed but reticent writer. It implied that the Commissioner who put up the light did not originate it, but it was not said how the suggestion came into the office, or who sent it there.

CHAPTER LXXXV.

PARLIAMENTARY CANDIDATURE IN BIRMINGHAM

(1868.)

My second candidature was in Birmingham. It was constantly said that the working class had no reasonable measures to propose which the middle class would not pass. This was not, and is not, true ; for the master class no more feels as the workmen feel than the old aristocratical class before 1830 felt, or as the middle class proved they did, when afterwards they came into power. And if it were true that the middle class would now do all the working men want, it is better that the working men should do it for themselves. For these reasons I sought the opportunity of addressing my own townsmen, to whom I could naturally speak with most freedom, upon the conditions and consequences of working-class representation.

In my address delivered in the Town Hall I said—

" More than thirty years ago I was a member of your Political Union, and since that time there has been no combination (sometimes called " conspiracy ") in this country to bring general enfranchisement about, which I have not, by speech and pen, advocated without intermission. Now we have a considerable extension of the suffrage, there are things of evil to cancel, and conditions of progress to create.

" We have, though limited, a ' political commonwealth ' at last, and one result is that working men will, sooner or later, find their way into Parliament. Venturous of it myself, it is my townsmen whom I address. My ancestors lie here ; I know most of, and naturally care much for, Birmingham. In all my writings I have looked on public affairs in the light of the workshop. A Democracy is a great trouble. Everybody has to be consulted. The Conservative is enraged to have this necessity put upon him ; the Whigs never meant it to come to this ; and I am not sure that many of the Radicals like it.

" Several things will happen now. 1. The Irish Church will go. Well I remember the horror with which the news was received in the workshops of this town of the massacre of Rathcormac, when a clergyman of the Irish Protestant Church had the sons of the poor Widow Ryan shot before her eyes for the non-payment of tithes. The middle class mother cannot feel resentment as a poor woman can ; she can afford to pay tithes, and no dragoon shoots her children down. But Widow Ryan's sons were labourers—they belonged to us. The shriek of the mother reached us. We in England could do nothing to avert or avenge their murder. But let us not have the baseness to forget it. Now that slow, tardy, long-lingering retribution has put the Irish Church in the noose, let *us* hope it will be allowed a good drop.

" 2. We shall have compulsory education. There is no ascendency for the people without sense. We live in a world where the battle of life can no longer be fought by fools ; and the child who is turned out into it ignorant is bound, hand and foot, in the conflict. We shall put away with contempt that pitiful, fitful, partial, mendicant instruction with which voluntaryism has cheated and degraded us so long.

" 3. Pauperism will be put down as the infamy of industry. A million paupers—a vast standing army of mendicants—in the midst of the working class, depending for support upon the middle class, is a reproach to every workman now. Every law which deprives Industry of a fair chance must be attacked ; whatever facilitates the accumulation of immense fortunes and tends to check the natural distribution of property must be stopped.

" 4. We shall have the ballot. Open voting is merely an insolent device for getting at those electors who do their duty. The poll-book is a penal list, first made publishable by those who intended to act upon it—and it is acted upon by all who are enraged at defeat."

It does good to create a popular belief that the day of progress has arrived ; that men need no longer despair of improvement, or seek to obtain it by conflict of arms, as they were formerly justified in doing under the hopelessness of obtaining it by reason. In my address I ventured to say that the Irish Church would go ; that we should have compulsory education ; that pauperism would be regarded as the infamy of industry ; that elections would be decided by ballot. I had heard the four things I had spoken of, hoped for, agitated for, and they seemed no nearer, and were believed to be no nearer, than the right of women to sit in Parliament is now. Yet each of these things, then regarded as words of Utopian enthusiasm, have come to pass.

The object of my being a candidate at Birmingham was to test and advocate the question of working-class representation. At that time there was no strong feeling on the part of the working class in favour of the representation of their order. Had I sought I could have obtained a sufficient support from Conservatives to have embarrassed the prospects of Mr. Bright or his colleague, and the Conservatives would have obtained the credit of supporting a principle for which they did not care and would disown when their own end was served. I might have obtained some publicity useful to a candidate by such an alliance, but it never seemed to me to be any more right in politics than in morals to do evil that good may come. For thirty-six years the representation of Birmingham had been in the hands of the middle class, and though the working class were twenty times more numerous than they, it had never occurred to the middle class that the industrious majority were entitled to any personal representation. Certainly they never offered or facilitated it.

CHAPTER LXXXVI.

A DANGEROUS VISITOR.

(1868.)

A FEW years ago, London was startled by the discovery of a murder in Whitechapel which recalled the Red Barn murder of Maria Martin, by William Corder, half a century before. A woman was shot in the rear of some business premises in Whitechapel and buried there, and her murderer, one Wainwright, was caught in the streets twelve months later, conveying the body to another hiding-place.

Some time previously a public writer, for whom I had much regard, became unwell. One day a lady came to me at Cockspur Street saying that he was very ill, that she was his wife and needed aid for his succour. She met my offer to visit him by assuring me that he had a malignant fever, and I had better not call. This was to deter me from calling, but I did not suspect it. Soon after she came again in deep mourning, in the character of his widow. She was a handsome, voluptuous woman, with great dramatic talent. Her speech, tears, and gestures were very eloquent, and I promised to ask for subscriptions for her. This entertaining applicant gave me to understand that she had been upon the stage in earlier years, and certainly she showed qualifications for acting which warranted what she said. I knew that my lost friend, who was really dead, had at one time £30,000 in a public company, which yielded 10 to 12 per cent., when he lived opulently in a house in Piccadilly. Afterwards his income fell to zero. In his prosperous days he had given eighty guineas for a jewelled watch, and presented it to Samuel Bailey, of Sheffield, in testimony of appreciation of his philosophical writings.

In the end I fulfilled my promise to the distressed lady in black, and published the substance of the story told to me by her. The eventual result was some £40 or £50. The first and second £5 I remitted to her. The lady paid me a further visit of thanks, and asked me to call upon her and take breakfast at a suburban cottage, at which she resided with a female friend, as it would save my time in writing, and I could bring any further subscription which might be to hand. Not wishing any personal acquaintance, which might raise expectations of aid beyond my means of procuring, I asked my brother Austin to make a call at his convenience, and leave further remittances for her ; and sometimes a clerk in my employ was sent. I never went myself.

It was fortunate I did not. On the apprehension of Wainwright, I saw in the papers accounts that his brother—who was afterwards transported for his complicity in the murder—was supporting a mistress, and was frequently at the very house to which I had been invited. Had I accepted the invitation to breakfast, I might have been found there by the police officers who went to the place in search of the brother. As the murderer was a lecturer at institutes of the kind I had prcmoted and been present at myself, my intimacy with him would have been inferred. Had my name been mentioned as that of a visitor at Rosamond Cottage when the address with other interesting particulars were published, I should have found it difficult to persuade everybody of the disinterested nature of my visits, especially as I could only have explained that my business there was to take money to a lady who had invited me there. My brother had simply called and left the sums I gave him, and neither of us suspected that she was not the wife of my friend.

Before the Whitechapel affair transpired, the enterprising pretender had written to several public persons on her own account. As it was my practice always to print in the paper I edited all sums for whatever purpose sent, the " widow " could see who were the friends who had answered my appeal, and she wrote to them and others whom she thought had knowledge of her alleged husband, enclosing what I had written upon him on her behalf. She was what the Scots would call an "ingenious body." All her letters to me bore a deep mourning border. Several members of Parliament wrote to me to ask whether they were warranted in giving money. In my replies I said I had no knowledge of the new applications made to them, nor was there any public claim on them, though I under‧ stood there was need of help. Several cheques were sent to me for her. When I found that I had been misled, I gave notice to all who afterwards wrote to me, and publicly cancelled my appeal and informed the applicant to that effect.

The judge at the trial of Wainwright was Lord Chief Justice Cockburn. The summing-up of some judges is often so learnedly elaborate, involved, dreary, and inartistic, that it is a species of penal infliction on the jury and only merciful to the doomed, upon whom it acts as the drugs given to the Suttee, which stupefies and makes insensible to the fatal fire. Sir John Holker, as Attorney-General, conducted the prosecu‧ tion. Sir John was a Conservative. It was frequently said there was a good deal in him, but it did not come out on this occasion. Mr. Moody made the speech for the defence, in which he said nothing wrong and nothing strong. There was no glamour of light, or pathos, or ingenuity in any one.

But when Lord Cockburn rose, the hand of the master appeared. The ornateness which he sometimes showed in speeches out of court was chastened down. His sentences were expressed with pure nervous force. Nothing was repeated, no phrase nor even idea recurred. The story of the evidence was clear, direct, vivid, brief, complete, and conclusive. The first sentences of the summing-up against Wainwright had death in them. The jury could see, as in a panorama, the per‧ petration of a foul murder, the source of the blow, and the ghastly procedure of successive concealments, as plainly as Hamlet displayed the process of the death of his father to his mother and the king. In sleuth-hound sentences the stealthy steps of the brutal, calculating murderer were tracked. Wain‧ wright must have seen the noose in every passage. Lord Cockburn's address to the jury was an unequalled piece of forensic reasoning, so far as any charge of the kind has come within my knowledge. Its coherence was not only evident to the jury—it was never out of sight. It had picturesque terms which had colour in them. The crisp, penetrating voice of Cockburn suited the finished structure of his address. Juries charged by him were instructed ; the prisoner at the bar, who had taste, was afterwards proud to have been condemned with such classic art, and the sentiment of the Court was raised above the level of crime by the genius of the judge.

CHAPTER LXXXVII.

REPORTING SPEECHES WHICH NEVER WERE MADE.

A GOOD deal of reporting has fallen to me in my time, chiefly of the descriptive kind. During several years that I had opportunity of hearing nightly the speeches made in Parliament, I found that all the new ideas expressed there could easily be taken down in long hand, since they occurred seldom and were far between. A newspaper, not having space to report everything said, might entertain and much instruct its readers by giving merely the new ideas of the debates, or remarkable ways of presenting a familiar case. Once a Cabinet Minister, who was going into the provinces to make a speech, he wished to see reproduced in London papers, asked me what he should do to secure that what he said should not be open to misinterpretation. I answered that, if he was sure of saying exactly what he intended, he might ask the editor of the leading local paper to send a reporter to take down his speech exactly as he made it. Good stenographers so abound that he would get what he wanted. But were he doubtful of being quoted at full length in the London press, he had better take a summary reporter with him, since a verbatim reporter, by his habit of literalness, would lack the faculty of bringing into focus the genius of a speech. To produce a telling summary the reporter need not be able to make the speech, but he must be able to measure the mind and discern the purpose of the speaker.

When in America in 1879, I found in some parts a class of Reversible Reporters. After an interview I found next day in the paper sentiments put down to me the very reverse of what I had expressed. Once I tried the experiment of saying the opposite of what I meant, and next day it came out all right. It was not perversity nor incapacity which misrepresented me, it was owing to professional confidence in young reporters that they knew better than any speaker did what he ought to say.

Once a friend of mine, a Jew, who knew this world as well as the Talmud, was the proprietor of a newspaper in a country town, within an hour's ride from London, asked me to come down and give an account of laying the foundation stone of a new town building and report the speeches at the banquet which was to follow at night. Some members of Parliament came down with whose ways of thought I was familiar, and I made summaries of their speeches which I knew they would be willing to circulate among their constituents. If the object is to promote the circulation of the paper, the effective portion of what a speaker says must be brought out, or there will be no orders for copies sent to the office. A reporter may make a clever report of a speech and prefix it with the remark that "the meeting was small." There are no copies of that paper bought by the speaker or his friends for circulation. If the hall is crowded it is well to say so. But no public persons care to circulate information that few care to listen to them. If the object is to discredit a speaker the question is one of policy not circulation.

Now, there was a rival paper in the town to which I went. The proprietor of the paper I represented wished his paper to excel that, which was not difficult, as it was sleepy and un-enterprising. So I wrote a leader upon the speeches at the stone-laying. A speaker who has ability is pleased to see it discerned and handsomely acknowledged. A man who acquits himself well may without vanity be pleased with the credit he has fairly earned ; and he who does not excel in expression may have merit of character and purpose to which it is the interest of the public to accord recognition.

The banquet in the evening was prolonged and boisterous. No reporter was present from the rival paper and I was instructed to report the speeches. On seeing the composition of the guests, I consulted with my Jewish friend, who, like all his race, was shrewd and foreseeing. We examined the toast list and then I inquired the characteristics of the speakers, their manner of mind, peculiarity of expression and antecedents of family, public service, and other particulars. One old farmer was reputed to represent a generation of predecessors who had held the same land from the Norman Conquest. By the time the toasts began the whole company was more hilarious than coherent. Some never could speak in public, and little was expected from them. A few when they began to speak were unable to stop. Some had forgotten what they intended to say, and others had nothing to forget. Some could speak better before the banquet began than after, and some acquired boldness in consequence of it, and made up by audacity what they lacked in relevance. By eleven o'clock I had sent out speeches for them all, and by midnight their orations were all in type, and the paper was out in the early morning. The town was astonished at the enterprise to which it was unaccustomed. The principal orator had a speech of some brightness to read at his breakfast, of which he was unconscious when he retired to rest. My friend the proprietor of the paper had misgivings when he read the report. He said the town would be surprised that such speeches were made. I answered, "the town was not present. The guests who did not speak were not in a condition to know what was said, and, take my word for it, no speaker will disown what he is reported to have said." And no one did. As a leader upon the proceedings of the day confirmed and illustrated the report by descriptive characteristics of the speakers, which the town knew to be true, my friend received many congratulations on the variety and vivacity of that issue of his *Gazette.* The office was not rich, and for all the writing from midday till midnight my remuneration was but thirty shillings, but I served my friend and increased for that week the reputation of his paper and its commercial value when he transferred it, as it was his intention shortly after to do.

"Reporting speeches which never were made" is a title open to the objection of being incomplete. The speeches were made, but not in the manner which met the public eye. Two or three of the festive orators had sagacity and brightness, though, on that occasion, not of the consecutive kind. Every provincial assembly of speakers furnishes instances of native wit or idiomatic humour. If these points are preserved in the report of the proceedings, an interesting monograph of the meeting is the result. Every night in Parliament occur notable relevant passages, occasional flashes of common sense, sometimes overlaid with words, and sometimes insufficiently expressed, of which an epitome would be good reading. Every day the Parliamentary reports of speeches presents them in a more effective form than the hearer was sensible of during the delivery. When *The Times* sought to destroy the popularity of Orator Hunt of a former day, it reported his speeches verbatim. There are many speakers in Parliament who would suffer in public estimation if their repetitions and eccentricities of expression were recorded. On one memorable occasion the *Morning Star* reported a passage from a speech of Mr. Disraeli's, with all its bibulous aspirates set forth, which few forgot who read it. It was on the night of his famous financial speech when Lord John Manners carried into the House five glasses of brandy and water to refresh him— which got at last into his articulation. The late Sir John Trelawny told me that he had preserved notes of speeches made after midnight in the House of Commons over a period of twelve years. At late sittings scarcely a reporter remains, and the necessity of going to the press with some account of the proceedings obliges the editor to give but a brief summary in which the speeches are not only divested of flesh and blood, but are almost boneless. Yet things are said at those times which the public would read with amazement both for their instruction and their boldness. Sir John said he did not intend his notes to be published until after his death. It will be a remarkable volume when it appears.

A London daily paper of age and pretension, often describes speeches of note which are never found in the report in its columns. Sometimes it quotes sentences of distinction which nowhere appear in the speech in its pages. Only one paper gives a full Parliamentary report. Once five papers did it. On the great debate when the Taxes on Knowledge was the question before the House, five daily papers gave full reports. So marvellously accurate were they, that there was scarcely a variation of a word in them. I heard all the speeches and compared the reports the next day. Competition in reporting produced a perfection which exists in London no longer.

CHAPTER LXXXVIII.

AN UNTOLD STORY OF THE FLEET STREET HOUSE.

(1868.)

THIS chapter illustrates the wisdom of the proverb that zeal without experience is as fire without light.

It was an early ambition of mine to have a publishing house in Fleet Street. There Richard Carlile had established the right of heretical opinion to publicity. I was for continuing it there. The Duke of Wellington headed a society to drive Carlile from the street. He did not intimidate him, nor was the society able to remove him except by procuring his further imprisonment. Resentment at this incited me to succeed him. Fleet Street was one of the highways of the world. A million curious people pass through it every year, of every travelling nationality under the sun.

We had won the right to say what we pleased, and the question arose, What did we please to say, and how were we going to say it? In the combat for the right to speak, very picturesque invective had been used. In the use of that weapon our adversaries much excelled us; but, we being the party of the minority, the blame of employing it fell upon us. When we had won the field we could hold it only by fairness of speech, the " outward and visible sign " of just intention and just principles.

William and Robert Chambers had established a secular publishing house in the High Street of Edinburgh. I proposed to my brother Austin that we should do the same thing for Freethought, in Fleet Street, London. The printing business was to be his—the publishing and its risks mine. The responsibility of capital, trade salaries, rent, and taxes remained with me. My name alone was on every bond.

Mr. James Watson had been, since the days of Julian Hibbert, the publisher of Carlile's works, taking like peril. As the new house in Fleet Street would necessarily affect his business, which was his only means of subsistence, I asked him what would compensate him for loss of trade thus caused. He said £350, which, with what he had, would provide for him in the future. According to the accepted morality of trade, I was under no obligation to consider his interests. A man sets up in business next door to one in the same line, doing what he can to lure away his neighbour's custom, and it is not counted dishonourable. It seemed baseness to me, and I promised Mr. Watson the money. This proved an unfortunate thing for me. When he came to know the indispensable business expenses of the new house were £300 a year, he did not see how I was to meet them, apart from fulfilling my promise to him, and, being of an apprehensive nature, he could not conceal his misgivings; and as he knew the chief country agents upon whom I depended, his fears transpired in personal communications with them and to my chief friends whom he knew, they having as much regard for him as for me. The effect of this was disastrous on a young business. My solicitor, who had advanced me purchase money of the lease, asked me what I was to have for the money to be paid to Mr. Watson. He thought me imprudent. I had nothing to produce, save the right of selling his books, which never yielded £50. Nevertheless I kept my promise. My brother Austin was as solicitous as I was to do it. Seeing Mr. Watson on the opposite side of the street, looking in his wistful way at the house, I sent my brother with the only £60 in hand to go over and pay him the final instalment, which he did. The transaction was in every way unfortunate to me, but I never regretted it. Nor do I now. The curious thing was that no one respected me for it, or believed it, and no one ever made any acknowledgment of it, not even Mr. Watson. Mr. W. J. Linton in his " Life of Watson " omits it, although it made the end of Watson's days pleasant. It was treated as incredible, and for the first time I came to understand the sagacious maxim of the Italians,

"Beware of being too good." I had known few persons in danger of transgressing the rule, and did not suspect I was one.

A valued colleague, Charles Southwell, took a very different view from Mr. Watson as to the profits obtainable in Fleet Street, and thought I was making riches there, as many others thought, so what was loss to me was envy to others. Southwell published pamphlets on my prosperity. One day I sent for him, showed him the bonds I had signed, and that I owed all the money he thought had been given me. His exclamation was a full acquittal—"Jacob, you are a damned fool !" I asked him to publish it. "No, I won't own I was wrong ; but I will no more say what I have said," was all I could get. The financial part of the story may end here. The £250 given me after the Cowper Street debate, £650 given me subsequently, a gift of £250 and all I could earn by lectures and writing— over the needs of my household—were all lost.

Propagandism is not, as some suppose, a "trade," because nobody will follow a "trade" at which you may work with the industry of a slave and die with the reputation of a mendicant. The motives of any persons to pursue such a profession must be different from those of trade, deeper than pride, and stronger than interest.

Afterwards there came mischief of another kind, which I had bespoken without knowing it. As a co-operator I was an advocate for profit-sharing, and I made this arrangement with those I employed. As the law then stood, this made them my partners, and gave them an equal claim with me to the property. One who had some knowledge of law, and was hostile to me, incited two servants to act on their "rights." They might have carted the stock away, and could only be prevented by force, which I had reason to avoid. An assault case would then have come on at the Mansion House which would have had an effect bad for the secular cause. The addresses of my friends were copied from my books, and letters sent to them, which cost me for many years many valued friendships, for reasons I could not answer—not knowing them. The manager of the newsagents' department was instructed that he might take away the business books, and did it. It was two years before I could recover them by process of law. Then I had to keep outside the court because, were I called upon to give evidence, I could not take the oath, and that fact would have set the court against me. The judge said that had I come into court he would have given the man twelve months' imprisonment.[1] This affair put me to £200 expense—besides losses through having no proof to adduce of the balances of newsagents due to me. Had the law which, later, Mr. Wm. Scholefield, M.P. for Birmingham, caused to be passed, been in force then, I should not have been at the mercy of enemies. Now-a-days, an employer giving profits to servants does not constitute them partners.

Just then, when my fortunes were least to my mind, Mr. Ross, at that time an optician of repute, learning that I was being unfairly used, came down and gave me a cheque for £250. That was a bright, unparalleled morning which I shall never forget until remembrance of all things fades.

Despite all difficulties, " 147, Fleet Street " was kept in force from 1853 to 1861. Its objects were—

1. Promoting the solution of public questions, on secular grounds, apart from theology.

2. Obtaining equal civil rights for all excluded from them by conscientious opinion not recognised by the State.

3. Maintaining a publishing organisation which should influence public affairs.

4. Maintaining a centre of personal communication open to publicists at home and from abroad.

5. Stimulating the free search for truth, without which it is unattainable—the free utterance of the result, without which search is useless—the free criticism of it, without which truth must remain uncertain—the fair action of conviction, without which public improvement is impossible.

6. Maintaining an organ which should be open to all writers, without regard to coincidence of opinion, provided there was general relevance and freedom from odious personalities.

The shop was made bright, and, by removal of partitions, spacious. All new books of progress were on sale, and

[1] He was a Wesleyan and of good integrity, until seduced by prospect held out to him of setting up himself with my business.

advertised in papers of the house without cost to the authors. A large room was fitted up for meetings and for the use of visitors. In each panel hung a portrait of some eminent writer. Visitors from every part of the world interested in New Thought came and found information respecting all lecture halls and places they wished to see. We published a catalogue of all the chief works of advanced thinkers (giving the prices and the names of the publishers to promote their sales), by whomsoever issued. No other house ever printed a catalogue like it. The house was an Institute. There have been other houses in Fleet Street since with similar objects, but none like it—none having the same features. The main object was the advancement of new opinion : business was an appendage to be well attended to ; but it stood in the second place.

When the peace of 1856 was proclaimed—though the great nations of the Continent were left still enslaved—we illuminated in front of the house those nobly reproachful words of Elizabeth Barrett Browning, which said :—

> " It is no peace.
> Annihilated Poland, stifled Rome,
> Dazed Naples, Hungary fainting 'neath the throng,
> And Austria wearing a smooth olive leaf
> On her brute forehead, while her troops outpress
> The life from Italy."

These words were read by a quarter of a million of people. Every newspaper in London agreed that this was the sole illumination which expressed the political truth of the hour. These things could never have been done save in a house standing in one of the highways of the world, where those must pass whose eyes it was worth while engaging, and where nothing can well be ignored which was done. On other public occasions Garibaldian and Italian flags greeted memorable processions.

In 1857 there was the Day of Humiliation proclaimed on account of the Indian Mutiny. Instead of joining in it, a placard appeared in our windows which attracted crowds of readers. It was entitled, " Objections to the Humiliation."

" 1. It is an ineffective proceeding, seeing that temporal deliverance is not to be obtained by intercession of Heaven.

2. It is offensive, as imputing to the judicial act of God the blunders of the East India Company.

3. It is impolitic, if we have enemies in India, to give them the satisfaction of thinking that they have brought Great Britain to confess ' humiliation.' "

Without a publishing house we could not have rendered the service in the Repeal of the Taxes upon Knowledge mentioned in a previous chapter. In the affair of the opposition to the Conspiracy Bill, the committee met in the Fleet Street house, as did the Garibaldi Committee at the time when the British Legion were sent out to Italy. Then, for several days, a committee of soldiers sat in the visitors' room, and the shop was constantly crowded with Garibaldians who volunteered to join the Legion. My brother was as much occupied as I was. This was international service, but it was not business.

We published works for Mazzini, Robert Owen, Kossuth, Louis Blanc, Professor Newman, Dr. Arnold Rouge, January Searle, Major Evans Bell, William Maccall, W. J. Birch, and many others.

I had a bust of Kossuth made by a Hungarian sculptor, and one of Mazzini by Bizzi. The original of Mazzini was purchased by Mr. Ashurst. The mould, which cost me £7, was never returned to me by the bust maker. It was said it had been broken. A few years later I saw several busts in a window cast in my mould, which I judge still exists.

We printed and published also the "Manifesto of the Republican Party," by Kossuth, Ledru Rollin, and Mazzini. Though written by Mazzini, he modestly, as was his wont, put his name last. All the publications I issued bore my imprint as printer as well as publisher, for the law makes the printer responsible. Were there no printing of books, there could be no publishing of books. The publisher may be a nominal person, of residential address unknown ; but the printer is real, and commonly has a plant of type which may be confiscated, while he himself can readily be found and incarcerated. The law aims mostly to intimidate the printer. I, therefore, took the responsibility of the printer as well as publisher.

Julian Hibbert gave Carlile £1,000 with which to furnish his shop when he opened it, and he had like sums from him on other occasions for publishing purposes. Notwithstanding the vicissitudes which befell us, we should have succeeded in a "business point of view" had we had money sufficient to continue when hostilities were surmounted. As it was, we did enough to justify the expectation of usefulness which induced so many to support the undertaking.

When we opened this house the voice of the Socialist was silent in the land and the watch-fires of the Chartist were extinct. As far as we were able, we intended to maintain the claim of Socialists and Chartists and some other causes for which they cared not. We cared for political freedom at home and abroad, for unless it prevails abroad it can never be secure at home. There is an aristocracy of sex quite as offensive as an aristocracy of peers. Manhood suffrage was popular with the Chartists, but they cared nothing for women's enfranchisement.

In a passage which I quote from a manifesto of Kossuth, Rollin, and Mazzini, which did but express our ambition :—

"A great movement must have an arm to raise the flag, a voice to cry aloud—*The hour has come !* We are that arm and that voice. . . . Advanced Guard of the Revolution, we shall disappear amid the ranks on the day of the awakening of the peoples. . . . We are not the future ; we are its precursors. We are not the democracy ; we are an army bound to clear the way for democracy."

It was my intention to "disappear in the ranks." As soon as I had extinguished all the liabilities I had incurred, I volunteered to hand over the place to the promoters. I thought if others had the profit which might accrue they would continue the work without direction. This was my mistake. To me it was of no consequence who had the advantage if the house was maintained. But nobody believed this.

Freethought is of the nature of intellectual Republicanism. All are equal who think, and the only distinction is in the capacity of thinking. I never set up as a chief. I never talked of loyalty to me, but of loyalty to principle alone. In freethought there is no leadership save the leadership of ideas. I went into this undertaking with this conviction, and as I went in I came out.

CHAPTER LXXXIX.

LORD CLARENDON'S CONCESSION

(1869–72.)

THIS chapter describes another instance of work which, my being of the Secularistic persuasion, I was incited to attempt. In my Christian days I had been taught that the safety of my own soul was the supreme object I should keep before me ; but experience showed me that the human welfare of others was a more honourable solicitude, and more profitable to them.

It has been the custom of the Government, since 1858, to instruct her Majesty's Secretaries of Embassy and Legation to prepare "Reports on the State of Manufactures and Commerce Abroad." It seemed to me that the same persons might collect information of not less importance to working men. At times, during several years, I made attempts to get this done. Through Mr. Milner Gibson, I obtained a copy of the original circular of instruction for the preparation of the manufacturers' reports on commerce, as I intended to base on them a plea for reports on labour.

At length, in April, 1869, Lord Clarendon being Foreign Minister, whose generous sympathy with those who live by industry was known, I concluded he might, on due representation, make this concession. It was then I wrote to Mr. Bright, whose attention was always given to proposals which could be shown to be reasonable, useful, and practical ; for that which is reasonable may not be useful, and that which is useful may not be practical, while a project which is at once relevant, beneficial, and possible, is self-commended. Seeing me next midnight at the House of Commons, he called me to him, saying, "Tell me now what you want." On hearing it, he answered,

" Write me a letter with your reasons in it, and I will give it to Lord Clarendon." By the courtesy of Mr. William White, chief doorkeeper of the House, I wrote in his room the letter the same night, and posted it in the Lobby before two o'clock. The next day (April 19, 1869), Mr. H. G. Calcraft (Mr. Bright's secretary, he being then a Minister) wrote to say, " Mr. Bright would ask Lord Clarendon to take into consideration my suggestions." On April 21st following, Mr. Calcraft again wrote, " by Mr. Bright's request, to say that Lord. Clarendon thought my proposal an admirable one, and that he had given instructions that the information may be obtained from the several Legations." My letter upon which Lord Clarendon acted set forth that workmen needed information of the condition of labour markets abroad as much as their employers. Strikes against reduction of wages take place, which reduction is often owing to competition abroad, but is not believed, owing to the knowledge upon which the employer acts being unknown to the men. Authentic information accessible to trade unionists would be instructive and useful. Emigration is promoted by Government. Some who go out suffer great disappointment from want of knowledge of the right places to which to go. This becoming known, many are deterred from emigrating, and thus miss good opportunities of advantage through ignorance of where the right labour markets in other countries lie. In Turkey 6,000 stone-masons were suddenly wanted for one of the Sultan's new palaces, while masons were emigrating to countries where stones were not used in buildings. I enumerated certain kinds of information secretaries of Embassy and Legation could furnish from the countries in which they were stationed.

Questions to which I asked answers were :—

1. What was the state of the labour market ? What openings were there, if any ? And what kind of workmen were wanted ?

2. How would English workmen be hired and housed ? What kind of dwellings would they find ? What wages would they be offered ? What rent would they have to pay ? In what quarters would they have to dwell, in healthy or unhealthy places ? Would they find tenements available— ventilated. drained, and free from air poisoning ?

3. What was the purchasing power of money in other countries? All prices should be reduced to English values. A workman at home earning £2 a week, on hearing he could earn £6 a week abroad, would resolve to go out ; whereas the cost of food, clothing, and rent might be thrice as high as in England, and his £6 in a new country might go no farther than £2 at home.

4. What is the dietary and habits to which an Englishman must conform in another country, as respects health-preserving power. Should a workman live in some places abroad as he lived in England, he would be dead in twelve months. Workmen who have overcome every industrial disadvantage and have raised themselves to competence abroad, yet rush down the inclined plane of excess, the bottom of which is social perdition. A report which afterwards came from Egypt said— " Spirits must be avoided. Temperate workmen keep their health well. The intemperate die." The report from Réunion said "Rum is rank poison to the European. None who contract the habit of drinking it can remain in this country and live." These are torpedo sentences which arrest the attention of the unthinking transgressor. In the mining districts of Alabama night air is deadly.

5. School questions need also to be asked. If an emigrant took out a family, what education could he get for his children ?

6. What is the standard of skill among native artizans with whom the Englishman would have to compete ? Do they put their character into their work, or are they without artizan pride ? Would they make a stand against doing bad work as they would against bad wages ? In what degree would good quality in work have effect in raising wages ? A workman might deteriorate among new comrades if they were shabby, bungling, careless workmen.

All these questions were not contained in my first letter. They were increased by permission of Lord Clarendon, as mentioned hereafter. The additions incorporated were three —(a) those relating to health-preserving power abroad, (b) to means of education of children, (c) to the quality of artizan skill.

A few days after these suggestions were made (April 26), Sir Arthur (then Mr.) Otway informed me that "he was to state that Lord Clarendon, who fully shared my views as to the interest and importance of such information, had received my suggestions with much pleasure, and that it was his lordship's intention to instruct her Majesty's Secretaries of Legation to furnish reports on this subject, which Lord Clarendon proposed eventually to present to Parliament in a collective form, which he hoped might meet the objects indicated in my letter." When the first volume of these " Reports upon the Condition of the Working Classes Abroad " appeared, they received from the *New York Tribune* the name of the "People's Blue Book," given, I believe, by Mr. G. W. Smalley. The volume was found to be of unexpected interest, and abounding in curious information. Some Secretaries of Embassy excelled in brightness, variety, and relevance. As each volume appeared, I wrote a letter in *The Times* describing it. On April 13, 1870, and on September 26, 1871, leaders in *The Times* were written, illustrating the value of the reports, concurring also in my representations of their usefulness. Lord Clarendon was pleased to express the satisfaction with which he read my first letter to *The Times*. His death unfortunately occurred soon after.

In Lord Clarendon's instruction to the Secretaries of Legation, I observed that he had changed my phrase "*purchasing* power of money" into "the *purchase* power of money." " Purchasing power " was a phrase new to the Foreign Office, nor was I aware that it had been used in this financial sense before I employed it. It seemed a fair form of the participle. The term afterwards came into general use, and is quite common now.

Occasionally a consul of an inquiring mind, who happened to be in England when the instructions were first issued, had doubts as to their purport. Lord Clarendon sent him to me, at Cockspur Street, where I then had chambers, and I had the honour of explaining the nature of the information sought.

In due course, Mr. Robert Coningsby, a young working engineer, known at that period as the author of letters on social questions having a Tory tinge, wrote to *The Times*, saying, " It was all very well for Mr. Holyoake to connect his name with these Blue Books. The Society of Arts is entitled to the credit of bringing the subject before the Government, and the credit of bringing the subject to the notice of that society belonged to him." The Society of Arts did not corroborate Mr. Coningsby, nor did he know how early had been my efforts in this matter. Nor did he pretend that he conceived or defined the scope of the questions, or method of obtaining the information required. The Foreign Office frankly accorded me permission to cite the communication received from them. I therefore explained in *The Times* that Lord Clarendon sent me the minute he had forwarded to the Embassies beginning with the words—" Mr. Holyoake has made a valuable suggestion as to the steps to be taken to ascertain the facts as regards the position of the artizan and industrial classes in foreign States." This minute was also sent to me for my consideration with the intimation " that Lord Clarendon would be happy to consider any suggestions I might have to offer, as to any other matters connected with foreign countries in which the industrial classes in this country take an interest, on which the Secretaries of her Majesty's Legations might be instructed to report." This I did, as the reader has seen, in the enumeration already given of questions to be answered. Sir Arthur Otway, with the spontaneous courtesy usual with him, wrote to me, saying that " these reports which were found so useful and interesting were mainly due to my suggestions, and that the late Lord Clarendon, as also the late Mr. Spring Rice, spoke to him more than once of my services in this matter in terms which would be very gratifying to me." After these facts appeared in *The Times*, Mr. Coningsby made no more claim of being the originator of these People's Blue Books. Three volumes of reports, of nearly 1,000 pages, were issued. Had the trades unions subscribed £20,000 and sent out commissioners, they could not in five years have collected and published the same amount of accurate, verified, and trustworthy information contained in these volumes thus supplied without cost to them by the Foreign Office. It was believed that these reports would be furnished at intervals of five or ten years. Twenty have elapsed since the last was issued. Changes in artizans' condition, interests, and aims have occurred since then, and new reports would now have new uses and new influence. Before the People's Blue Books appeared, the information necessary for industrial advancement abroad depended mainly on chance and charity, and as Madame de

Staël said of M. de Calonne, whether he meant mischief or service, "he did not do it with ability"—for want of knowledge.

Men learn patience if not contentment by a comparison of their condition with that of others, which may be no better or worse than their own. They may be encouraged by examples of success attained under discouraging circumstances. A workman can appreciate industrial causes in operation apart from himself, which he fails to discern or estimate through familiarity and prejudice, while he is in contact with his own condition. Principles true in our own streets are discerned more vividly when their operations are traced in the destiny of strange and distant communities. Artizans gain expansion of knowledge, like that which travel gives, when they are brought into the presence of international facts, and are inclined to respect a Government which, instead of lecturing them or coercing them, gathers the experience of nations into a page, and bids them read it for themselves.

CHAPTER XC.

ASSASSINATION BY A JOURNALIST.

(1870.)

ABOUT the time of the sixth volume of the *Reasoner* (that is not an accepted calender of events, though it enables me to fix the date of many) two young Irishmen came to London seeking their fortune in literature, and to them I was able to be of some service. Both made acknowledgments of it in after years, which I did not often experience in other instances. One of them, Mr. Gerald Supple, came from Dublin ; for him I had regard because, out of his slender earnings, he always sent a portion for the support of his mother and two sisters. He had seen patriotic service in 1848, having been concerned in an insurrection planned in Meath. He wrote for me in the *Reasoner* on secular subjects. Afterwards he wrote in the *Empire* and *Morning Star*, to which I introduced him. At length he went to Australia, studied law, and became a barrister. As is the case with the best Irishmen, his sympathies were with liberty and freedom everywhere, and he never forgot the claims of his country. He had many friends at the bar, and no one who knew him could fail to be impressed by the generous qualities in his character. In 1848, he had been a contributor to the *Nation*, then at its best, and several national ballads written by him are to be found in Hayes's collection, to which good judges assigned great merit. Mr. Ebenezer Syme said in the *Argus* that Mr. Supple " always wrote with extreme moderation and good taste, never permitting his private predilections or animosities to influence his public writings. On several subjects outside the newspaper sphere, he had a fulness of knowledge, and wrote upon them with a judgment that was admirable. He wrote on Irish genealogies and antiquities in a manner no other Australian journalist could approach."

In 1870 news came that he was under sentence of death in Melbourne. Newspaper controversialists, as is common in new colonies, are addicted to primitive forms of invective. Melbourne resembled then the amenities of journalism which prevailed in Canada, a much older settlement, until Mr. Goldwin Smith infused refinement in it ; and my friend in Melbourne believed that no reformation in certain quarters there was possible except by the pistol. He therefore resolved to shoot an imputative adversary, one George Paton Smith, at sight—and did it, the shot taking effect in his arm. Mr. John Walshe, a retired police officer, hearing shooting about, with the instinct of his profession, rushed forward to defend the man assailed. Mr. Supple, being near-sighted, mistook the ex-officer for his enemy, shot and killed him. It was his near-sightedness which caused him to entertain unfounded resentment against many persons whom he thought showed him public disrespect by passing him without notice, who had no unfriendly intentions towards him ; he was simply unable to observe their recognition. His brother barristers considered that he had suffered in his professional career by loss of briefs through his infirmity of sight, and he had become moody and unhinged in mind. They therefore set up a plea of insanity to save him. This Mr. Supple repudiated in court, stating that he knew perfectly well what he was doing, and that he intended to kill Mr. Smith, but did not intend to kill Mr. Walshe.

Many persons who commit brutal outrages, or even commit murder in a brutal manner, when it comes to their turn to suffer, squeal and whine to be saved from that which they have inflicted upon others. It was not so with Mr. Supple. In his speech to the Court, before sentence was pronounced, he declared " his purpose was to teach certain persons in Melbourne a lesson in manners. He well knew the consequences of what he had undertaken, and did not object to be hanged." Mr. Supple continued :—" Some years ago I quarrelled with G. P. Smith because of his scurrilous abuse of the people of my country, written by his pen and published in the newspaper he edited. I was the only Irishman on that paper, and I resented it. He who will not stand up for his country is a paltry person. From that time Mr. Smith slandered me. In this colony there is no check on slander. An action for libel does not arrest it. The duel does not exist here. If any man sent a challenge he would be handed over to the police, and his challenge treated as a farce, as a piece of swagger or bravado. In England public opinion acts as a check on slander. There is nothing of the sort here. I have done this colony good service in reviving something of old-fashioned honour, in the middle of this coarse and wholly material civilization—this mean and sordid thing, in which little seems to be valued higher than the dinner or the bank account. The time will come, and my act will hasten it, when the community will cease to tolerate the assassin of character. As for me, I hope to give my life very cheerfully in this cause. Hanging cannot disgrace me. The gallows cannot disgrace me—I shall confer honour upon it. I shall be glad to get away from this colony, and I can leave it no other way than by the gate of death."

This manly speech could not but inspire respect for the prisoner, however much one must feel that society would be impossible if everybody should resent slander in the deadly way he had adopted. Mr. Supple was sentenced to death. But his counsel appealed against it, on the ground that it was not justifiable to hang a man for an act he never intended to commit. A plea good in morals, but not in law. Mr. E. J. Williams, who was in the Gallery of the House of Commons, and who knew of my early friendship for Mr. Supple, having intimation of the appeal, asked me to aid in saving him from execution. To this end I made the following affidavit, which Sir Wilfrid Lawson did me the favour of attesting for me :—

" I, George Jacob Holyoake, of 20, Cockspur Street, London, County of Middlesex, do truly and solemnly make declaration that I knew well Mr. Gerald H. Supple, now imprisoned, as I am informed, in Melbourne, Australia, on charge of murder. When he was in England he was employed by me in journalistic work : I assisted in procuring him engagements. I had and still have great respect for him as an honourable man ; but I observed a moodiness in his manner, varying from impulsive generosity of speech to inexplicable reticence. His shortness of sight was greatly against him. He seemed a despairing man at times, and I used to consider him a person whom some great calamity would one day overtake. From the difficulty his manner put in the way of his friends serving, or indeed being sure when they were serving him, I feared great suffering would befall him. Though very intimate with me, and as I believed having personal regard for me, he went away without saying such was his intention, and never communicated with me at the time,[1] nor mentioned me in writing to friends of mine who had served him at my instigation. I doubt not he had acquired some distrust of me, utterly without reason. No doubt he was liable to dangerous delusions.

"GEORGE JACOB HOLYOAKE.

"Signed in the presence of WILFRID LAWSON, Justice of the Peace for the County of Cumberland."

Having rendered political service to Lord Enfield in his Middlesex candidature, I asked him if he could do me the favour of enclosing my affidavit in the Foreign Office bag, he being then in that department. The transmission would then be surer and probably swifter. Lord Kimberley, who became aware of my request, directed (Aug. 4, 1870) me to be informed (which I was by Mr. J. Rogers) that my "affidavit would be forwarded by the next mail to the Governor of Victoria." But Lord Kimberley did much more than this, as I afterwards learned. Seeing that a man's life was at stake, his lordship, from motives of humanity and kindness, directed that the substance of my affidavit be telegraphed to the Governor or Ceylon with instructions to transmit it to Lord Canterbury at Victoria. By good fortune, which ought always to attend on so generous an act, the telegram was received in Melbourne on the very day before the appeal, and, being delivered by the Foreign Office messenger, it was a welcome surprise to Mr. Supple's counsel, and gave the Court the impression that the Government at home were desirous that the prisoner should have the advantage of whatever evidence existed on his behalf. The result was that, instead of the sentence of death being con-

---

[1] Afterwards he did, and I was of service to him by sending him letters of introduction.

firmed, Mr. Supple was granted a new trial on the ground of his mental condition.

Four months later a letter arrived from Lord Canterbury upon the subject. Lord Kimberley, still remembering my interest in the fate of my friend, desired Mr. H. T. Holland to transmit to me a copy of the following despatch from the Governor of Victoria :—

" LORD CANTERBURY TO THE EARL OF KIMBERLEY.

"GOVERNMENT OFFICES, MELBOURNE,
Sept. 7, 1870.

" My LORD,—I have the honour to acknowledge the receipt oɪ your lordship's telegram forwarded to me through the Governor of Ceylon, relative to the mental state of health of G. H. Supple (now under sentence of death), and stating that a despatch and affidavit would be forwarded by the next mail.

"I lost no time in forwarding this telegram to the Law Officers of the Crown. I may mention that a point of law was reserved at Supple's trial which comes on for argument before the full court to-morrow.—I have the honour to be, &c.,

" CANTERBURY."

It is clear from this despatch that but for Lord Kimberley's calculating promptitude my affidavit had been all too late.

The next communication I received was dated Melbourne Gaol, October 4, 1870, from the prisoner, saying :—

" MY DEAR MR. HOLYOAKE,—How can I thank you for your friendship and kindness in stepping in so promptly to my help ! That telegram must have been an expensive one—I understand from £15 to £18. My friends only ascertained from the Government the day before the last English mail left that it is you who thus came forward for me.

"I have been thirteen years in this country now. Ebenezer Syme was my very good friend, thanks to the favourable things you said of me in your letter of introduction to him.

"I calculated upon getting into trouble for what I did, but I cheerfully accept the consequence as a smaller evil than endurance. The medical commission found I was no lunatic. I was to be hanged last month, when, two days before the morning fixed, leading members of the bar picked flaws in the legal proceedings, the public was stirred with interest, and the Government granted a reprieve and an appeal to the Privy Council. I was notified of a new trial—the same case under another aspect. My legal friends insisted on the plea of insanity. I would have no more of it, and defended myself. The jury were half for acquittal and half for conviction. I may not be hanged for some time yet.

"I often think of those days in London in '50 and '51, and again in '56, when you and Mrs. Holyoake made me feel as if I were at home.—Ever yours sincerely and gratefully,

"GERALD H. SUPPLE."

In the end he was sentenced to imprisonment during her Majesty's pleasure. A year later (Aug. 11, 1871), he wrote again from his gaol, saying :—

"I am unable to express what I feel, and how grateful I am, for what you have done for me, so kindly and ably in such various ways, at a time " when a friend is twice a friend." Your articles in the press, your telegram, and Lord Kimberley's kind interference, thanks to you, have each and all had a great effect in my favour on public opinion here. Your article in the *Reasoner*, which I saw (as well as that in the *Birmingham Post*, which you enclosed to me), was put into one of the papers here, the *Herald*, and has done me much service. The public in Australia are much influenced in all social matters by opinion at home, and your word goes a long way here as well as in England, even among people who may differ from you in politics and theology. After the appearance of that article I had an unusual number of visiting strangers, including three or four members of the Legislature, cordially promising me their good offices at opportunity."

How difficult Mr. Supple was to serve was shown by Sir Charles Gavan Duffy. When he was in office at Melbourne, Supple, at that time a law student and journalist, asked him for permanent Government employment. Several months afterwards, he offered him a post with a salary of £400, which had been previously held by another journalist, one of Supple's friends.   Supple had a short time previously been called to the bar.   He indignantly resented the offer, which made Sir Gavan think his mind was affected.   He was a singular being, but his courage, disinterestedness, and noble scruples, were honourable singularities.   He had done that for which, as a lawyer, he knew he deserved hanging, and felt bound in honour as a gentleman not to shrink from nor evade the penalty.   Eight years' imprisonment in Melbourne Gaol elicited from him no murmur.   He wrote articles with his dim eyes, and continued his support of sisters who needed aid.   Mr. Eaton, of the Treasury Department in Melbourne, was a valued friend of Supple's.   On his visit to England we consulted how Supple's imprisonment might one day be changed into banishment, and ultimately the Government considerately permitted him to reside in New Zealand, where he followed pursuits of literature to the advantage of himself and his connections, and he had ever a grateful word for whoever had served him.

CHAPTER XCI.

THE STORY OF THE BALLOT.

(1868–71.)

HAVING been foremost, or at least publicly persistent, in main-taining that the secular duties of this life had precedence in time and importance over ecclesiastical considerations, it became incumbent on me to follow my own precepts, and, as far as in my power lay, to improve the opportunities of daily life. Being a member of the Council of the London Reform League in 1868, I undertook to vindicate the claim for the Ballot by a " New Defence " of it, of which 10,000 were circulated. Mr. Henry F. Berkeley, M.P., who succeeded Mr. George Grote as the advocate of the Ballot in Parliament, wrote a letter to the press asking attention to my " Defence." He had previously written to me, saying "a greater than I has arisen"—not meaning that I was great and he less than before, but merely that the argument for the Ballot was not exhausted, as the House of Commons supposed, and that I, a young man, might continue an advocacy which the nearness of death to him would soon compel him to abandon. Mr. Bright also was of opinion that the reasons for the Ballot had all been gathered in, and he wrote to me, saying "yours is the only original argument I have seen," which implied no more than that all advocacy of it had proceeded from the points of view of the party politician and the electioneering agent. No one had treated it from the point of view of the working-class voter, which constituted the distinction, whatever it amounted to, of my argument.

Mr. John Stuart Mill, notwithstanding the long championship of the Ballot by his friend Mr. Grote, declared that " it ought to form no part of a measure for reforming the representation of the people. He thought it unmanly that men should not resent intimidation and defy it. It did not occur to him that it was unmanly on the part of Liberal politicians to allow the means of intimidation to exist. Like Mr. Herbert Spencer, Mill was for individuality and self-help—not thinking that self-help has its limits. To help yourself as much as you can, and as far as you can, is a condition every man must fulfil before he has a claim for the aid of others where his own strength is insufficient. There is no sense in telling a man whose legs are broken he ought to walk unassisted. Under open voting none who depend upon others for employment can be independent without ruin, and it is not practical politics to expect from the people impracticable virtue. Liberals in my time were overwhelmed with the prestige of mad manliness, and used to apologise for the Ballot by saying they " wished the people were strong enough to do without it." Whereas the Ballot was no crutch : it was protection. It was a device which destroyed intimidation by rendering it impossible. Mr. Mill, who, like Jeremy Bentham, was a master of what an American would call " ironclad " phrases, said that the Ballot meant " secret suffrage "—that was the merit of it. Secret suffrage is free suffrage — it means an impenetrable, an impassable, a defiant suffrage ; since intimidation could not touch it in the case of those who could trust to the secrecy of the ballot box. There is a base secrecy which men employ in mean, furtive, or criminal acts, but there is a manly secrecy when a man locks his door against impertinent and intrusive people meddling with his affairs without consent. Privacy in what concerns a man vitally—concerns him alone—is manly and justifiable. My argument was that of the following paragraph :—

The old doctrine was that voting was a duty the elector owed to his country. Then it was the duty of the country to take care that he did discharge it. Voting, therefore, should be made compulsory, and intimidation impossible in the discharge of a public duty. The voter is a known person : he is selected by the State—his qualifications are approved : he has recognised interests at stake. He has assigned to him a duty to his country and to his conscience. It is only by a secret suffrage that he can without "let or hindrance" discharge it. I am said to be an "independent" elector, I am told it is my duty to be independent. Then why should any one want to know the facts of my vote? It is no affair of my neighbour *how* I vote, or for *whom* I vote, or *why* I vote, since I exercise no power nor use any freedom which he does not equally possess. I am not called upon to consult my neighbour as to what I shall do. If I am obliged to consult him, *he is my master.* But he has no business with a knowledge of my affairs; and if he wants it, he is impertinent—if he insists upon it, he is offensive, and means me mischief if I decline to do his bidding. The theory of Representative Government calls upon me to delegate my power to another for a given time. Once in seven years I am master of the situation; afterwards I am at the mercy of the member of Parliament I elect. He may tax me, he may compel the country into unjust and costly wars; he may be a party to base treaties; he may limit my liberty; he may degrade me as an Englishman, but I am bound by his acts. From election to election, he is my master. I must obey the laws he helps to make, or he will suspend the Habeas Corpus Act, and put a sword to my throat, or fire upon me with the latest improved rifle he has made me pay for in the estimates. I may howl, but I cannot alter anything. My only security is that a time will come when I shall be master again without fear from my neighbour, or customer, or employer, or creditor, or banker, or landlord, or priest. I shall taste of power for one supreme minute when I shall stand by the ballot box. Then I can vote to displace the member who has betrayed me, and choose another representative in his stead. Representative Government confers upon the English citizen *one minute of liberty every seven years.* It is not much to ask. It is little to be content with. It is a wondrous proof of the people's docility that they yield obedience on such terms. The State ought to keep faith with the elector one minute in every three millions of minutes which elapse on the average between one General Election and another.

The enemies of the Ballot thought fit to oppose this slender concession. Sydney Smith derided it. Lord Palmerston held that it was un-English. According to this reasoning, the use of armour-plates is cowardly, and it is un-English for a gunner to fire from a casemate. It is madness, not manliness, in a man who opposes his single head to twenty swords. His foolhardiness will merely deter others, and the reputation for courage he will acquire will not outlive the coroner's inquest upon him. There might be more individuality of character than there is if every man rejected the enervating equality of the law, which protects the weak against the strong. Then even the coward must fight and the weak must struggle or perish. But it is insanity of individuality which wantonly enters upon unequal conflicts ; and open voting is of that nature. Secret suffrage is the needle-gun which places the proletariat and the proprietor upon an equality in the electoral combat.

Whittier understood this when he wrote :

> " We have a weapon firmer set,
> And better than the bayonet ;
> A weapon that comes down as still
> As snowflakes fall upon the sod,
> Yet executes a freeman's will,
> As lightning does the will of God,
> And from its force no bolts or locks
> Can shield you—'tis the ballot-box."

Much more to the same end was in " The New Defence of the Ballot," which it was said at the time did. something in determining the minds of many members of Parliament when they came to vote for the bill who had never looked upon the Ballot from the working class point of view.

After being before the House of Commons for forty years, the Ballot Bill went up to the Lords—a body of gentlemen endowed with legal power to maim or stifle any live measure of progress which they may deem premature. To allay the fear of change which constitutionally agitates them, I said, wherever I had the opportunity of being heard, that the first effect of the Ballot would be to give us a Tory Government for ten years. I wrote to *The Times*, *Daily News*, and *Echo*, urging—

" The two great fears of the Ballot are these. One is that electors will vote so differently under it as to disturb the balance of parties in many boroughs. The other and greater fear is that such numbers will vote under the Ballot who never

voted before, that nobody will know what will happen anywhere. For three centuries the political vote in England has
been a trust, under the condition that the elector used it under
the cognizance and in accordance with the views of *somebody
else*. Tory and Whig, employer and squire, Radical and
Quaker, have all done their best to enforce this doctrine of
trust. Relieve the electors of this hereditary pressure, and
after allowing for much that habit will do, and less for the
action of intelligence, we come down to what the late Lord
Derby needlessly dreaded—the dark, unknown land of ignorance, prejudice, passion, of honest but blind hope. The
Liberals do not quite like that risk, the Conservatives shudder
at any change, and the Radicals think of the cost of providing
for the neglected political education of the people, *which must
then be attended to* if they are to hold their own. [The rise of
Liberal Clubs, never before heard of, soon proved this.] The
Conservatives who collect the suffrage of stolidity will be the
first to profit by the Ballot. In an uneducated nation the
'stupid' are always the majority, and the Tories have so often
profited by the fact, that they will be the 'stupid party' themselves if they throw away the mighty chance now before them.

"The working class accept the Ballot, not because it will very
early benefit their order, but because it is an indispensable
condition to their being able to benefit themselves. Therefore,
let no one be apprehensive of the change which will approach
with the Ballot. In politics nothing approaches; everything
has to be fetched.

"The fear of the Ballot is as old as England. It is the fear
lest another should take his own way, and not take yours. It
is in religion as well as in politics, and not easily eradicated.
Error (it was an early maxim of mine) is like a serpent alive at
both ends; if severed, it may still sting; while it wriggles, it
lives, and those who mean to end it must chop at it."

It would be futile to recite now this prediction concerning
the Ballot, if the reader could not turn to the *Echo*, August
5, 1871, and read it there. The first election after the Ballot
gave us a Tory Government, and old London Reformers
bewailed to me that, after having laboured for fifty years to
give the working class the power to be their own friends, they

used it to vote for those who always opposed their having a vote. The nature of a nation does not change all at once with power. All history gives examples which seem to be unobserved. The French Revolutionists did but do as they had been done by. It may be regretted that they did not do better. To pour on the Revolutionists the censure of Europe, and conceal that the censure belongs to those who made them what they were—is ignorant criticism. Liberty does not take care of people. It is intended to enable them to take care of themselves, and it generally takes them a long time to learn how to do it.

The story of the Ballot illustrates the characteristics of the English political mind in the last generation

CHAPTER XCII.

ADVENTURES AT THE HOME OFFICE.

(1870.)

It is good advice that a man should guard himself from misconception. But, do what he will, misconceptions will come to him. Then all he can do is to explain—stand to the truth and never mind.

At the time of the Reform League agitation in 1866, being a member of the executive, I was one of a deputation to the Home Office, to confer with Mr. Walpole concerning a meeting the League intended to hold in Hyde Park. The Government was then Tory, and the Tories are always against public meetings, as being unnecessary and inconvenient. Then (1866) they said : " We had Trafalgar Square to go to, and what better place could we have ? Hyde Park was impossible." In 1888, twenty-two years later, they said " we could not have a better place than Hyde Park, and that Trafalgar Square was impossible."

Mr. Walpole showed an honourable anxiety to prevent collision between the police and the people, for fear of " bloodshed," which Mr. J. S. Mill said in Parliament, the next night, " the League firmly believed would result." Mr. Walpole stood in the recess of a window at the Home Office, and our small deputation stood near him.

Mr. Beales stated that our object was " not to censure the Government, but to declare the public sentiment on the franchise," and therefore we demanded permission to hold a public meeting in the park on Monday. Mr. Walpole (deprecatingly) : " Don't ask me that." After consulting with Lord

186

J. Manners, Mr. Walpole said, "Well, put your request in writing to me. I will consult my colleagues, and, that there may be no mistake, I will send an answer in writing." It was, however, agreed that we might occupy a platform that night in Hyde Park to dissuade people from assembling further.

Afterwards, being at the House of Commons, I told all this to many members who inquired what had occurred at the Home Office. Later, I went to Hyde Park to attend the dispersion meeting, and, being on the platform, I heard Mr. Beales announce that we had permission to hold a meeting on Monday night. Whereupon I asked him whether Mr. Walpole had since given him permission to do so, as I did not so understand him at our interview. The next morning a letter appeared from Mr. Walpole in *The Times*, stating that Mr. Beales's letter had been received, but no answer had been given. The same morning placards appeared, issued by the League, stating that a public meeting would be held in the park by Mr. Walpole's permission.

That morning, Mr. George Howell, secretary of the League, sent me by hand to Waterloo Chambers, Cockspur Street, a summons to attend another deputation to Mr. Walpole at 2 o'clock. At that hour I went there, but, seeing none of my colleagues, I supposed they had already arrived, and were in some room awaiting the interview. I asked to be shown to the deputation to Mr. Walpole, and I was told "there was no deputation ; and Mr. Walpole himself was not at the Home Office." I said that was incredible, as I had been summoned to attend a deputation to him at 2 o'clock. Seeing that I was unconvinced, an officer said, I "had better see Mr. Walpole's secretary and satisfy myself." Accordingly I did so, and was told that "Mr. Walpole really had declined to receive any deputation." I answered that, "as the League had sent me notice to attend the interview, they should have sent me word it was not to be. I understood we were to see Mr. Walpole respecting his letter to *The Times*, and that I intended to say I for one thought Mr. Walpole right in his letter. The placard assumed that the meeting was agreed to, which was not my impression."

The secretary asked whether he might state that to Mr. Walpole. I answered "certainly." I went at once to the

Reform League, and explained to Mr. T. Bayley Potter, M.P., and other friends of the League present, what I had said at the Home Office, and learned then, for the first time, that Mr. Beales was decidedly under a different impression. Mr. P. A. Taylor asked me at the House of Commons the same day to put in writing what took place with Mr. Walpole, which I did, and placed it in the hands of Mr. John Stuart Mill, who, I knew, was always for the truth.

In the meantime Lord Derby in the House of Lords, speaking in defence of the Home Secretary, accused by his party of indecision, said : " Mr. Holyoake, one of the members of the deputation to Mr. Walpole, having seen the placard, *came* this morning to repudiate in the strongest terms Mr. Beales's proclamation. He spoke to many Liberal members last night at the House of Commons, informing them that Mr. Walpole had not given his consent to the meeting announced."

Mr. Walpole, on his part, stated in the House of Commons that, " in justice to a member of the Reform League, who is known to many members in this House, and who was present with the deputation—I mean Mr. Holyoake—he, in a manner which reflects infinite credit on him, *volunteered* to come to my office to-day. I was so busily engaged I could not see him, but he saw my private secretary, who came into my room immediately afterwards, and told me what had passed between them. I (Mr. Walpole) said, ' The words which you say were used by Mr. Holyoake are so important, let me, while they are fresh in your recollection, take them down.' The words taken down are these : ' He *came* to repudiate in the strongest terms Mr. Beales's proclamation.   He perfectly understood Mr. Walpole to decline to sanction any meeting in the park, and to ask that an application for that should be made in writing.   He spoke to many Liberal members last night, and also to Mr. Beales, *when the proclamation was being posted.*' "

Reciting these incidents serves to show by authentic instances how difficult it is to get at the truth of history, and how the simplest facts become transformed into what Carlyle would have called "curiously the reverse of truth."   Even when the facts are fresh—not even an hour old—variations of them occur even while passing through the minds of educated official persons.   Neither Lord Derby, Mr. Walpole, nor his secretary, could have any intention of perverting the truth, and yet the perversion transpired on the part of each of them. Mr. Walpole said that I " volunteered to come to his office." I did not " volunteer " to go to the Home Office. It never entered into my mind to go—I certainly never should have gone on any notion of my own. My going was solely through the instruction sent me by the secretary of the Reform League. It was quite unforeseen by me that I should enter the secretary's room. It was purely incidental that I was asked by an official to do so. It was to account for my acquiescence in seeing the secretary that I mentioned the subject of the placard. The officer in the corridor of the Home Office told me " Mr. Walpole was not in the building." Yet Mr. Walpole said " he was busily engaged there." My words as related by the private secretary, and as taken down by Mr. Walpole, were that " I came to repudiate in the strongest terms Mr. Beales's proclamation." I did not go for any such purpose. The words taken down represent me as saying " I spoke to Mr. Beales when the proclamation was being posted." I never saw Mr. Beales at that time. I was not present when the proclamation was posted. My words were : " I spoke to him the same night at Hyde Park." That was before the placards were printed.

The *Express*, the evening issue of the *Daily News*, remarked that the Tory papers commended me, the *Standard* describing me as " a man of high honour and probity, whose opinions, however offensive to the general feeling of society, had not prevented him from commanding the respect of all who knew his reverence for truth, and his thorough loyalty in all dealings with friend or foe."

It is not a matter of suspicion when any one is commended by his adversaries, unless it appears that he has abandoned his professed principles to win their praise.

Notwithstanding my explanations, the Reform League regarded me as a traitor who had gone down to the Home Office privately, and made a communication against them. A great meeting was held, within a few days of these events, at the Agricultural Hall. Mr. Mill asked me to accompany him from the House of Commons to the hall, and afterwards I returned with him to the House. It was well I was in his company, as my colleagues of the Reform League were wrathful

with me.   Had I done what they supposed, their indignation
would have been justified.   Certainly the version of the affair
given by Ministers was calculated to confirm their impressions.

Mr. Walpole for a time fared no better at the hands of his
colleagues than I did with mine.   They accused him of weak-
ness in giving way to the League Radicals.   They even said
he wept before the deputation.   Lord John Manners could
have contradicted that, as he was present, but he made no sign.
Had it not been for my accidental testimony, which, being that
of a political opponent, satisfied both Houses, it was said that
Mr. Walpole must have resigned.   On the following Sunday
he sent me a handsome letter of acknowledgment.   At no time
did I ever speak to Mr. Walpole, nor did he ever speak to me.
My action with regard to him was public and not personal.

Afterwards some Radicals enclosed bread pills in small
bottles, labelled them "Walpole's tears," and sold them at
Reform League meetings, which was ill treatment of a Minister
who had shown honourable scruples against firing upon them.

Mr. Walpole was the first Home Secretary who, so far as we
knew, ever showed consideration for the people at his own
peril.

On the day when the Hyde Park railings fell, the Reform
League went in procession to the gates.   As I was one of the
executive, I accompanied my colleagues.   Mr. Beales was to
attempt to enter the gates, when, the police opposing him, a
question of assault was to be raised, and legal opinion taken as
to the legality of closing the gates against the people.   The
throng was dense about the entrance.   A man in a rough cap
and round jacket—in appearance like an ostler—thrust a watch
in my vest pocket, saying, "Take care of that the next time."
I thought he might be a thief who, being followed, was
planting a watch he had stolen on me to get rid of it.   But on
taking out the watch I saw it was my own.   I had no time to
thank the man, who darted through the crowd to keep the real
thief in sight.   The man was a detective, who had seen the
theft of my watch, had taken it from the man, and restored it
to me.

Thus ended my adventures on the Hyde Park question.

CHAPTER XCIII.

STORY OF A LOST LETTER.

(1870.)

IN 1870 I had expressed, in some journal or speech, the opinion that Lord Palmerston's wilful and hasty recognition (1851) of the Government of the usurper, Louis Napoleon, was discreditable to the Crown and injurious to the English nation, as openly sanctioning the massacre of thousands of French citizens, of the imprisonment of its Parliament and expatriation of many eminent men, who withstood the illegality of the false President. It was a great affront to the majority of Frenchmen, who would be incensed at England giving official countenance to Bonapartist treachery and assassination. In what way this opinion came under the notice of Mr. Gladstone I now forget, but he was kind enough and considerate enough to write me a letter, in which he explained the facts of that affair.

On February 3, 1852, Lord John Russell explained that Lord Palmerston had sent an approval to Lord Normanby, our ambassador at Paris, of the usurpation of Louis Napoleon. Lord Palmerston said " it was a misrepresentation of the fact to say that he had given instructions to Lord Normanby inconsistent with the relations of general intercourse between England and France.

What Lord Palmerston did was this. He wrote to the British ambassador at Paris (Lord Normanby), December 5, 1851, saying that he had been commanded by her Majesty to instruct him not to make any change in his relations with the French Government. " It is her Majesty's desire that nothing should be done which would even wear the appearance of an interference of any kind in the internal affairs of France." At the same time M. Turgot said he had heard from M. Walewski (the French ambassador in London) that Lord Palmerston had expressed to him his entire approbation of the act of the President, and his conviction that he (Louis Napoleon) could not have acted otherwise than he had done. Lord Normanby complained that this "placed him in an awkward position for misrepresentation and suspicion." Lord Palmerston replied next day that if "Lord Normanby wishes to know my own opinion on the change which has taken place in France, it is that such a state of antagonism had arisen between the President and the Assembly that it was becoming every day more clear that their co-existence would not be of long duration ; and it seemed to me better for the interests of France, and through them for the interest of the rest of Europe, that the power of the President should prevail."

The representative of the French nation naturally regarded this as the opinion of the Government, being given by a Minister of the Crown at the Foreign Office, and it was cited by the confederates of the usurper as proof that Liberal Parliamentary England was in favour of a murderous despotism being imposed by arms on the French people.

On February 17, 1852, Lord John Russell advised the dismissal of Lord Palmerston from the office of Foreign Secretary on the ground that "he had, first, in a conversation with the French ambassador, and next, in a despatch to Lord Normanby, expressed officially his approval of the recent proceedings of Louis Napoleon," contrary to the following instructions, laid down by her Majesty in 1850, for the guidance of her Secretary :—

"The Queen requires, first, that Lord Palmerston will distinctly state what he proposes, in a given case, in order that the Queen may know as distinctly to what she is giving her royal sanction. Secondly, having once given her Royal sanction to a measure, that it be not arbitrarily altered or modified by the Minister. Such an act she must consider as failing in sincerity towards the Crown, and justly to be visited by the exercise of her constitutional right of dismissing that Minister. She expects to be kept informed of what passes between him and the foreign Ministers before important decisions are taken based upon that intercourse ; to receive the foreign despatches in good time, and to have the drafts for her approval sent to her in sufficient time to make herself acquainted with their contents before they must be sent off."

Lord Palmerston was dismissed, and was succeeded at the Foreign Office by Earl Granville.

From this instruction it appears that Lord Palmerston two years previously had sent instructions to foreign Courts without the knowledge of her Majesty, and had in other cases changed the purport of what had been submitted to her. The Queen's note is also instructive to those foolish, misleading or uninformed politicians who continually assure the people that the English monarchy is practically a democracy, and that the interfering power of the Crown is ideal. The Crown has the power of vetoing any international instruction the Demcroacy may wish to give through its representatives. The Foreign Minister is simply the mouthpiece of the Crown. The Crown has a voice—and the people are dumb.

Mr. Gladstone, with a brevity beyond my power, explained to me that the Crown did in the case of Lord Palmerston's conduct what the people would have done. The Queen deserves very high credit for her action in dismissing him, reassuring the French people that England was neutral, intended no interference in their affairs, and lent no encouragement or sanction to the usurpation imposed upon them.

After receiving (1870) the letter of Mr. Gladstone, in which he explained all this, I placed it in the *Edinburgh Review* of that date and left it in a cab. After fruitless efforts to recover the lost articles, they were advertised for in *The Times*, in one of the numbers of that journal which was photographed for circulation in Paris during the siege. The photographed copies of *The Times* were dropped over Paris from balloons, and the contents were magnified and well scanned, but as my lost letter was never heard of, I concluded that it had probably got into the hands of some intelligent and covetous reader, and I have sometimes attended sales of autograph letters expecting to find it.

CHAPTER XCIV.

THE SCOTT-RUSSELL PLOT.

(1871.)

A FEW years ago, the Liberal world in London and at large—so far as the outer world took notice of metropolitan affairs—were surprised by an announcement that eminent peers, not before known for Radical partisanship, were about to place themselves at the head of a new movement, which was to do great things. The working classes were to be taken from pestiferous dwellings in crowded towns and put, as Lord Hampton said, out " in the open," and other advantages, never dreamt of by the unenterprising Liberals who had hitherto been looked up to by the people, were to be bestowed upon them. Mr. Scott-Russell, a naval enthusiast, who had built the *Great Eastern* ship, was the constructor of this new political vessel for carrying Tory Democratic passengers into the Conservative haven.

Certain working class leaders [1] were invited to form a committee or syndicate of popular sponsors of the new project. All were known to be on the Liberal side, but some, like the teetotal cabmen, were not bigoted ; they preferred fishing in Liberal waters provided fish were to be caught, but, if not, they had no invincible repugnance to trying another stream. They called this " being above the narrowness of party " ; sometimes they represented it as " taking an independent view " of things—phrases honestly used by men of conscientious conception of principle, but whose scruples these patriots,

---

[1] The best known were Robert Applegarth, George Howell, H. Broadhurst, Lloyd Jones, George Potter, Daniel Guile, P. Barry.

with principles turning on a universal pivot, burlesqued. There were others among them, men of consistency, who were curious to find out what these unexpected friends of the people (whom Mr. Scott-Russell assumed to represent) really intended. They asked time to consider the project to which they were to be committed. Their meetings were held at a pleasant restaurant near King Lud's in Ludgate Hill, and, as good dinners were provided to assist their deliberations, they were not impatient to come to a decision. Like men having responsible business on hand, they felt precipitation unbecoming ; they took time and dinners, too. They made suggestions, and adjourned until Mr. Scott-Russell had considered them. Then it became necessary to dine again to receive his opinion. When adjournments were played out, they, with show of reason, intimated that it was desirable that they should know who the noblemen were who were at the head of the project which they were to commend to the working class, whom these leaders were supposed to influence. A further dinner was necessary for receiving and weighing this information. It was conceded by the constructor of the *Great Eastern* that this committee should see a list of the names, which, however, were not to be divulged.

If there really were persons of eminence desirous of rendering some new service to the people, the intention was to be respected. There was one member of the committee, Mr. Robert Applegarth, who never thought there was anything in the scheme, and there were others who did not feel any sure ground under their feet. Thus the inspection of the list of peers who had popular ideas ready to put in force, was interesting. That the names were to be held secret did not inspire confidence. How could honest leaders of the people command a project of which they could not disclose the authority which alone could inspire trust. Mr. Applegarth prudently suggested to his colleagues that, since they were not to possess or copy the list, and might not remember all the names upon it, it would be well that one of them should fix in his memory the first two names, another should notice the second two, and so on through the list. Afterwards, when they met, they could verify the whole list of names appended to a document which was to be published without the names. It was observed that the names were all in the same handwriting as the text of the address prepared for their issue.

In a way never explained to the public, the list of the names—which, in the way described, came into the hands of the committee—met the sharp journalistic eyes of Mr. Stephen Girard, of the *New York Herald*, and were by him made known, much to the chagrin of Mr. Scott-Russell and to the astonishment of the peers, who instantly became subjects of comment. Each of them immediately wrote to the papers disavowing any knowledge of the affair or complicity in it. Thus it happened that the political Leviathan ship for carrying Democratic passengers into the sea of Conservatism never set sail.

Knowing all the members of the Scott-Russell Committee, their proceedings interested me, and I wrote in the public press reasons for regarding the project as suspicious in origin and tendency.

Mr. Scott-Russell had genius in his own walk. His conception of a great ship, so ponderous that the waves should not vibrate beneath it, so powerful that the storm should not retard it, showed naval daring; but the sea of politics was unknown to him, and the craft he put upon it was of antiquated build.

Every aspirant for power, who has ambition for personal ascendency, every despot who understands his business, holds out promises of what excellent things he will do if he be only secured a position whereby he may be able to act. When the power is once put into his hands, he is able to defy those who dare to claim the fulfilment of their expectations, as did Louis Napoleon, who promised great things to the working classes, and shot them when they asked for them. In the meantime the policy of holding out great hopes of this kind has its success. Like the " confidence trick," it finds a succession of credulous persons ready made. There are always a number of people ready to have something done for them, and very unwilling to be put to the trouble of doing it for themselves.

My reason for opposing the Scott-Russell plot was that Liberal working men could not join in it without foregoing their principles. A man is free to change his principles without reproach when his honest view of duty dictates it. But he should know what he is doing, and not go on pretending to be on one side when he has gone over to another. If working men calling themselves Liberals accept Tory leadership, they have left their party. If they accepted this Tory-peer scheme, in the belief that the Tory party would carry it out, they must at elections canvass for and vote for Tory candidates. It were vain to adopt a programme and not provide a majority in Parliament to give effect to it. He who chooses new leaders proclaims his distrust of his old ones, and has changed sides whether he knows it or not. Not thinking it to the credit of the working classes to be under illusions, I publicly explained the nature of the Tory democratical scheme.

If Conservatives come to profess, as they sometimes do, to be in favour of a Liberal measure, respect such concession, and give them, so far as such measure extends, aid and credit for it. But that is a different thing from changing sides and undertaking to sustain a party opposed to the main principles you profess to hold.

The names of the peers who were alleged to be the " high contracting parties " in this plot were Lord Salisbury, Lord Derby, Mr. Disraeli, the Earls of Carnarvon and Lichfield, Lord Henry Lennox, Lord John Manners, Sir John Pakington, Sir Stafford Northcote, Mr. Gathorne Hardy, and the Duke of Richmond. Mr. P. Barry wrote to *The Times* saying that " Mr. Scott-Russell had the signatures of the lords," which they naturally repudiated in successive letters to the newspapers. The Seven-Leagued programme to which these noble Socialistic Democrats were alleged to have given their assent, is not without historic interest to-day. Its planks were as follows :—

1. Something like the United States Homestead Law, with modern improvements, is to be enacted, by which " the families of our workmen " may be removed from the crowded quarters of the towns, and given detached homesteads in the suburbs.

2. The Commune is to be established so far as to confer upon all counties, towns, and villages, a perfect organisation for self-government, with powers for the acquisition and disposal of lands for the common good.

3. Eight hours of honest and skilled work shall constitute a day's labour.

4. Schools for technical instruction shall be established at the expense of the State, in the midst of the homesteads of the proletariat.

5. Public markets shall be erected in every town, at the public expense, for the sale of goods of the best quality, in small quantities at wholesale prices.

6. There shall be established, as parts of the public service, places of public recreation, knowledge, and refinement.

7. The railways shall be purchased and conducted at the public expense and for the common good, as the post-office service is now conducted

CHAPTER XCV.

RETICENCE OF THE BISHOP OF PETERBOROUGH.

(1872.)

THE Bishop of Peterborough was a prelate remarkable alike for timidity and boldness. The public were often amazed at his ecclesiastical candour. But he had apprehensive intervals, as this chapter will show. In 1871 he and the Dean of Norwich announced their intention to deliver controversial discourses in that city.

Wet, half-melted snow covered the ground, the sky above was dark and disturbed, a cold haze made chill and damp the crowd which stood in the silent cathedral yard on Tuesday night (December 12, 1871) waiting for the cathedral doors to open. No city in England has been so fortunate as Norwich in its bishops. It has had no bad bishop in our time. The memory of man runneth not back to the contrary. The preacher, however, whom we waited to hear was not the Bishop of Norwich, but the Bishop of Peterborough. In the pulpit this bishop appeared somewhat short, stoutly built, and had the look of a man who ate more than his spiritual profession required. Nevertheless the bishop's discourse was admirable. It had the chief qualities of an oration. It was delivered with elasticity : the action, though not always graceful, was pleasantly vehement, and there was a manly energy in the preacher's tones.

Dr. Goulburn, the Dean, was a very pleasant gentleman to see. He was one of those radiant divines who diffuse a sense of satisfaction around them, looking on life with a dignity that appears never to have been distressed. You saw at once that his " lines had fallen unto him in pleasant places, and that he had a goodly heritage." Yet, notwithstanding Dr. Meyrick Goulburn's sunbeam aspect, he threw out some venomous little epithets at his supposed adversaries which need not be recounted here.

The Bishop's alluring subject was the " Demonstration of the Spirit." Who could expect the future Archbishop of York, whose revenue would be princely, whose palace looked down on the lotus waters of the Ouse, whose earthly home an angel might envy, to be appreciative of the humble ethical philosophy which knew none of these things ? To the Bishop of·Peterborough whose worldly welfare was provided for by a happy destiny and a powerful patron, Christianity must seem " demonstrably " true. Mean, poor, and even wicked must seem the scruples of those who find themselves condemned to perplexity and patience ; while to others, who mean no better and strive less to realise human good, opulence and honour fall. To the prelates of that day, the efforts of obscure moralists, who, with penurious means, unaided and contemned, struggled to multiply secular comfort, to cheer the unfortunate with the consolations of duty, and kindle the fire of reason in cold and abandoned minds, must seem pitiful, and to be sufficiently recognised by being scolded into grace.

In the cathedral city of Norwich, where prelatical doctrine had the advantage of State splendour and official advocacy, it might be expected that civil equity would prevail under its supreme influence. Yet the ratepayers there had no right to the use of the public halls for which they paid. To obtain one in which to reply to the Bishop of Peterborough was impossible.

A Dissenter in Norwich, who was proprietor of a hall eligible for the proposed review of the " Cathedral Discourses," said he would let it for the purpose if he knew that it would not be displeasing to the Lord Bishop of Peterborough. I thereupon wrote to the bishop upon the subject. My chambers were then at 20, Cockspur Street, Trafalgar Square, London. The Bishop was at the Athenæum Club, Pall Mall, and our correspondence was conducted hardly a hundred yards apart.

Several letters passed between us. I did not ask that the Bishop should advise the cathedral authorities to use their influence in favour of controversial equity, or that he should interfere in the affairs of a diocese in which he had no authority, but simply to say on his own part whether it was distasteful to him that a hall should be conceded in which his Discourses should be reviewed on the part of those whose attention and concurrence he had challenged.

In his first discourse, the Bishop urged that it was "the duty of the Christian to manifest the truth in love " ; but he declined to manifest it at all. He told us how the first apostles went to Christ, saying, " Master, tell us." But the Bishop was not of his Master's mind, and would tell us nothing.

In the end I did deliver a review of the Bishop's polemical orations ; but it was owing to the independence of Mr. R. A. Cooper, who lent a large room in his Albion Mills for the purpose.

Why should the Bishop show such timidity in giving an opinion asked of him ? He had nothing to fear. No one in Norwich could harm him. A bishop is set high above clergy and deans that he may be independent and discharge even Christian duty fearlessly.

Had he spoken the one word which would cost him nothing, he had taught a lesson of toleration to a city which wanted it much, and have won for Christianity a respect on the part of adversaries which the most brilliant clerical argument would fail to create.

A curious circumstance occurred while Dr. Magee was in Norwich. Mr. R. A. Cooper, before mentioned, the largest sugar baker in East Anglia, had a place of business opposite the cathedral. During a successful career in Cincinnatti he had acquired American ways of vivid speech, and as Dean Goulburn was an adversary of ponderous orthodoxy, Mr. Cooper offered to take the cathedral as a sugar bakery, it being little used and he in want of larger premises. The Bishop being the Dean's guest at the time was told this bit of American irreverent humour, when the clever Bishop went elsewhere and declared that the Liberation Society of the Nonconformists had "shown itself willing to turn churches into drinking saloons or shoe factories "—though the Nonconformists had no knowledge of Mr. Cooper's isolated saying, had no more to do with it, or sympathy with it, than Dr. Goulburn himself.

The Nonconformists resented the wanton imputation upon them, without knowing how it originated.

CHAPTER XCVI.

GENEROSITY OF THE BISHOP OF OXFORD.

(1872.)

In two instances I had personal opportunity of forming an opinion of Dr. Samuel Wilberforce, Bishop of Oxford, and in both he displayed more fairness and candour than I expected from a bishop. Perhaps my limited acquaintance with prelates obliged me to judge them from a narrow standpoint. The Bishop of Exeter had not given me a favourable impression of the clerical bench. I knew of no case among my friends in which a reference to them in the case of injustice or intolerance had been favourably entertained, and we all knew that in the House of Lords the votes of the prelates were mostly given against the people.

Oddfellows as well as the co-operators were liable before 1852 to be robbed by their officers without redress in law. A secretary had appropriated £4,000 of the money belonging to widows and orphans of the Manchester Unity. When placed in the dock in that city, he was dismissed, as the law then gave no protection to such societies. When the Friendly Societies Bill in 1852 came before the House of Lords, the Bishop of Oxford raised objections to the legalisation of the Manchester Unity, on the ground that I had written their Prize Lectures, which he therefore concluded must be atheistic.

The Grand Master of that day, Mr. W. B. Smith, hearing this objection, asked, " Has your lordship ever read them ? " The Bishop said very frankly he had not. " Does not your lordship think," rejoined the Grand Master, " that you ought to do so before pronouncing a deterrent judgment on them ? " " Well," said the Bishop, " perhaps I ought. Send me a copy

and I will do so." At the next interview, the Bishop said candidly that, " after reading them, he must admit that they were
not irreligious—neither were they religious."

The Grand Master replied : " We have a quarter of a million
of members in our Order, and among them are included some
of every religious persuasion in the land. How could the
Lectures be ' religious ' in your lordship's sense without leading
to dissent and theological controversy in all our lodges—which
would be an evil, and inconsistent with that concord and
brotherhood our Order is designed to promote ? "

The Bishop admitted the force of this representation, and
withdrew his opposition to the Friendly Societies Act, which
was afterwards passed.

Some years later when, acting as Commissioner of the
Morning Star, I was writing upon " Rural Life in Bucks," I
became acquainted with the condition of the labourers of
Gawcott, who had, as they believed, a grievance. A commodious schoolhouse in which their little children were
educated had been taken from them, and the school was held
in a cottage quite inadequate for the purpose. The parents
believed that the schoolhouse was given to them by the kindness of the wife of a former vicar. For years the poor people
had been lamenting their deprivation of the schoolroom. No
one was able to help them. I said to a friend who sympathised
with them, " Why do they not put their case before the Duke
of Buckingham, who lives within four miles of them ? If there
be an injustice, what is the advantage of ducal influence, of
which we hear so much, if it be not exercised for redress in
such a case as this ? " The answer was, " No one had trust or
hope in the Duke, and the poor people are rather afraid of
him." " Then why not apply to the bishop of their diocese ? "
I answered. " These poor people, who mostly attend the
church, have claims upon him, and surely he is not afraid of
the Duke ? " That remedy was thought to be more hopeless
still.

Upon hearing this, though I was not exactly the person to
put their case before the Bishop with advantage, I offered to do
so, and accordingly I wrote to the Bishop of Oxford. Since they
were hopeless, no harm could come of it. Things could not be
worse if no redress resulted. My letter was as follows :—

"My Lord,—Standing without the pale of your lordship's communion, I have no personal claim upon your attention, but I unhesitatingly assume that this circumstance will not disincline you to give ear to a demand if commended by fitness and humanity.

"It is this. At Gawcott, in Bucks, is a commodious village school erected by the active charity of the wife of the then incumbent—to be held and used in trust for the benefit of the Gawcott poor. This school, the villagers say, has been appropriated to the purposes of a Middle Class School by the Rev. Mr. Whitehead. For twelve years the infant poor of Gawcott have been displaced, ill-trained, and personally ill-treated— suffering in health and morals. Their situation is a public scandal. Herewith I beg to enclose your lordship certain public letters written by myself after personal inspection of the place. In fairness I add others defensive of the incumbent. The Rev. Mr. Whitehead, the reputed appropriator, is now leaving Gawcott, if I am correctly informed, and is about to sell the schoolhouse, which, if suffered, will complicate or compromise the claim of the poor to its use. There may be a remedy for this wrong in equity, but these poor villagers can never invoke it. The Rev. Mr. Whitehead is undoubtedly a kind-hearted gentleman, who has done much in his way for the Gawcott poor. The villagers speak affectionately of him in many respects, but nevertheless say ' he has defrauded us of our school.'

"My lord, whether these poor people are acting under a painful delusion, or suffering, as I believe, a great wrong, they are equally entitled to your all-powerful consideration, which I am told is never refused to the humblest person in your diocese who really deserves it. If these villagers are under a wrong impression, let an inquiry dispel it ; let the Trust Deed be published. They will be instructed, they will be satisfied : and, if they are in error, the Rev. Mr. Whitehead will be vindicated. If, however, the reverend gentleman has acted wrongfully, none but your lordship can do these poor villagers justice. You can prohibit the sale of the school, and restore to these poor children that education which a merciful lady of your Church once provided for them. The people of Gawcott are poor, are timid, are despairing. They pray for a powerful friend. They hoped and ought to have found one in the Mayor of Buckingham. He, however, is silent, fearing the ducal influence he would confront. The Duke does not—as it would be graceful and noble to do—volunteer them protection. These poor villagers should be able to obtain redress from their own clergyman, but he is the alleged offender. You, their bishop, high in holy and independent authority, may not hesitate to act where mayors fear and dukes neglect, and for the sake of these friendless villagers I entreat your lordship's interference.—I am, your lordship's obedient servant,

"GEORGE JACOB HOLYOAKE."

The Bishop sent a courteous reply, and said that he would request the Rural Dean to inquire into the case, and when he received the report he would send it to me.

The cottage room in Gawcott, in which the poor children received their humble instruction, was as unsatisfactory as any school I ever entered. From fifty to sixty children occupied raised seats, as in a theatre. The young woman who acted as teacher stood in their midst, without room to move among them. Indeed, they were so crowded that any of them could be reached with the cane. Without other ventilation in the room than the fireplace, the air was unbreathable, and the pallid, consumptive look of the teacher showed that she found it so. The parents complained that if one child caught the measles all the children had it, and then the school was closed for a time. The description of the state of things as I found them, which I published in the *Morning Star*, I enclosed in my letter.

The Bishop was as good as his word, and in due time sent me the report of the Rural Dean and a copy of the Trust Deed, asking my opinion upon them, whereupon I wrote to the Bishop as follows, from which the reader will gather what the Rural Dean's report was :—

"My Lord,—I am under obligation for the courtesy and consideration with which you have made inquiries respecting the allegations of my letter of February 1st, and sent for my perusal the replies you have received. These enable me to present to the villagers a clearer and more definite view of the

case than I was able to put before.   There is clearly an end of
the alarm that the Rev. Mr. Whitehead is about to sell the
school.   That gentleman's denial is conclusive.   I dismiss this
point.   The grievance of the villagers is substantially this :—

"They say the schoolhouse was built for the benefit of the
infant poor of Gawcott ; that the instruction given was to be
under the direction of the incumbent is not in question.

"They say that the object of the benevolent foundress of the
school, the wife of the incumbent of that day, was to provide
a place where the infant children of the poor wives of the
village could be sent during the day.

"They say that this was the meaning of the words in the
Trust Deed 'to permit and suffer the said schoolhouse to be
used and enjoyed in such manner for the religious instruction
of the poor children of the said hamlet.'   They say that the
schoolhouse was used in this way for the eight years previous
to the Rev. Mr. Whitehead's coming to the hamlet, when
he turned the poor children out of the school.

"They say that the poor children, 70 in number, were crowded
for years into a small room unfit and unhealthy, where it was
a sin to put them and a scandal to keep them.

"It is never difficult anywhere to find middle-class subscribers
who, lured by the offer of a superior education for their sons,
will not be of opinion that their own interests include the
rights of others usurped by them.

"The Trust Deed shows that Mr. Whitehead had a right to
use the place as he saw fit, but for 'the instruction of the *poor
children*.'   But the use to which he put it was not that, but
was for the benefit of the middle-class children.   The benefits
he offers do not meet the want of an infant school and were
not so intended, as he has kept up a cruel sort of child-pen,
under the name of an infant school, in the village.   Is the rural
dean aware that Mr. Whitehead's offer of instruction is at an
age when the children begin to go to work and cannot use it ?
It is a good, but comes too late.   Mr. Whitehead's Middle
School is entirely praiseworthy and needed in Gawcott, and,
had these middle-class parents built a school for themselves,
there would have been but one unmixed feeling of gratitude
towards the reverend founder.

"Mr. Whitehead's evidence shows that he found the schoolhouse occupied as an infant school. Only three children under eight are now in the school. There were eighty under that age before Mr. Whitehead's time.

"Mr. Whitehead admits that he found the room in the occupation of an infant school. He does not deny that it had been so occupied for the eight years during which it had been built. He states that he called together the subscribers of the school. But he does not say whether these were the parties to the Trust Deed, and who subscribed to build the school. Should he not have called together the parents of the poor children who were to be turned out to make way for the children of these subscribers? Had these parents consented, Mr. Whitehead's case would be made out.

"Apart from any truth or relevance there may be in these representations—which do not affect the right to dispose of the school for other uses than those which the villagers desire— power to redress the evil which exists is, I believe, nevertheless, in your lordship's hands. Were you to express an opinion that you think, under the circumstances, the farmers, whose children are now educated in the schoolhouse, should build a new school for their own use, they would, under the encouragement of your lordship's opinion, do it. They are well able to do it, and I have ascertained from personal inquiries that many would be disposed to take that course, if commended to them by your lordship. I have the honour to be, your lordship's faithful servant,

"GEORGE JACOB HOLYOAKE."

Before making these representations I visited Gawcott again, called upon the officers of the church and several of the farmers, and suggested the erection of a schoolhouse for themselves, which would be honourable to them and insure the gratitude and good feeling of the villagers. The Bishop very generously did express his opinion and advised them to build for themselves. A new schoolhouse was built, and the old one restored to the villagers, which they enjoy to this day.

Considering how unlikely, and I fear how unacceptable, a person I was to interfere in the matter, the willing and courteous attention given to my representations impressed me, as it did all the people in the district who knew or heard of the correspondence, with grateful admiration of the impartial generosity of the Bishop of Oxford.

The Bishop was not my adversary. He had not, as the Bishop of Peterborough had done, delivered lectures against views I held, and in a manner challenged my answer. I was not a resident in Bishop Wilberforce's diocese, and had no right, except on purely public grounds, to interfere in its affairs. It showed an intrinsic love of justice on his part that he should give heed to what he might rightfully regard as alien representations.

When the Bishop died some years after, from a fall from his horse, one night in the House of Lords I listened to various encomiums on his character. Speaker after speaker pronounced eulogiums on his zeal, his eloquence, and his various attainments —no one gave any instance which impressed the public mind as to the qualities of his heart and mind ; and, though I was not the person qualified to lay a chaplet on the Bishop's grave, I wrote to *The Times* citing his conduct at Gawcott in illustration of his character.

CHAPTER XCVII.

FLIGHT OF THE EMPEROR NAPOLEON FROM BRIGHTON.

(1872.)

THOSE who otherwise followed Landor's advice and "waited," next saw Napoleon III. a fugitive and an exile. In 1872, he was at Brighton at the time of the meeting of the British Association. There arrived also a Frenchman of repute both as a politician (who had fought at the barricades) and as a man of science— Wilfrid de Fonvielle. He and his brother Ulric were my oldest friends in Paris. I had been their guest. Ulric, a man of accomplishments and courage, had had trouble with the Bonapartes. It was he who accompanied Victor Noir on his visit to Prince Pierre Napoleon. But he was not an amiable person to call upon, for he shot Victor Noir dead without provocation, and fired three times at his friend Ulric de Fonvielle, but without killing him. The Emperor had saved the Prince from being hanged as he ought to have been. If the reader bears this in mind, he will understand the perturbation of the Emperor on having to confront Wilfrid de Fonvielle, who was not indisposed to avenge the attempt to shoot his brother Ulric, as I have to relate.

It was with Wilfrid that I was most intimate. On arriving in Brighton he came to consult with me about lodgings, as the list at the Reception Room was exhausted. His intention was to join his friend and co-balloonist, Mr. Glaisher, who had taken rooms at Cannon Place, in the rear of the Grand Hotel. As Mr. Glaisher had not arrived, I induced the landlady to allow M. de Fonvielle, his friend, to occupy his chambers until he came. Thus he resided within a few yards of the apartments of the Empress, and from her window she could see his house. But he neither intended, nor sought, nor wished that situation.

The Napoleonic fête day immediately preceded the meeting of the British Association, and many Frenchmen, who were then in Brighton, had congregated a good deal about the hotel. Thinking the sound of the "Marseillaise" might remind the Emperor that liberty was still living in France, some Frenchmen paid a band to play it under the Emperor's window ; but M. de Fonvielle very properly stepped into the hotel to inquire if there were any objection to it on the part of the proprietors, who were responsible for the convenience of their guests. Not obtaining the information, he descended the steps. The band-master, seeing him come from the hotel, thought he was one of the Emperor's suite, and one of them asked whether it was right to play. On being told by Fonvielle that "he did not know," the bandsman said, "Do you not belong to the hotel? Seeing you come out, I thought you belonged to the Emperor's party." It would have been easy to mislead the band and get the terrible "Marseillaise" played, but the answer was that of a gentleman—"No, I do not belong to the hotel ; I am not of the Emperor's party." It ended in no music being played. The band offered to go to Cannon Place, and play the "Marseillaise" to De Fonvielle.

On the night of the address of the President (Dr. W. B. Carpenter) in the Dome, I was standing near him, and De Fonvielle next to me. All at once the audience on the platform and floor of the Dome rose, we knew not why. Looking round, I said to de Fonvielle, "Here is the Emperor," who was walking, with the aid of a stick, towards us. M. de Fonvielle, not remembering where he was, was disgusted to see such deference paid to the expelled adventurer who had brought such misery on the people of France. De Fonvielle and other Frenchmen cried out, "Shame!" "Shame!" "Don't do that!" I said ; "remember you are on English ground, and that the Emperor is an exile here. As such, he is the guest of the nation. We receive him as we would a Republican or a Communistic exile. Tyrant and patriot stand here on neutral ground." My friend at once desisted, but his excitement was pardonable.

The quick eye of the Emperor knew De Fonvielle, and they steadily looked at each other. The brilliant audience in the Dome settled down, and Dr. Carpenter was proceeding with his address, when a local agitation was observed opposite the ex-Emperor, between the small, compact, quick de Fonvielle and a large, diffusive, rather phlegmatic clergyman of the Church of England (Dr. Griffiths), one of the secretaries of the local committee. Rapid and subdued words, a sharp flash of the eyes on the part of the French aeronaut, a sort of aquarium look on the part of the divine, and a hasty seizing of a small parcel by the Gaul, were all that could be made out. Immediately de Fonvielle arose with a shrug of excitement. Doubling his marine cap under his arm, and raising himself erect, he marched in front of the Emperor straight out of the Dome, merely stopping as he passed me to say, " I shall see you again."

Not all the practised sagacity of the Emperor could make out that series of movements, of ambiguous meaning. Doubt soon reached the point of perturbation, for the dark-headed, square-shouldered, gleaming-eyed Frenchman returned, and striding in front of the Emperor, who might well feel relieved when he had passed him, De Fonvielle was next seen in fierce altercation with Dr. Griffiths, to whom he presented some oval packet not much unlike a small Orsini shell (as the Emperor might think who had remembrances of those missives), and then withdraw it, thrusting it into his own pocket. Immediately the clerical gentleman began an excited speech, whereupon the Frenchman threw the packet to him. The Doctor opened it, and said something to De Fonvielle which appeared to appease him. Meanwhile Dr. Carpenter, knowing nothing of the bye-play under his reading desk, went on quoting Pope until the end.

The imperial visitor must have given the Empress that evening a curious account of the mysterious proceedings in which, to his astonishment, a respectable clergyman of the Church of England appeared to take a conscious part. The mystery was never explained to his Majesty ; but it was all comedy, not tragedy. Dr. Griffiths, amid his many labours as local secretary, had acquired a sore throat, and it occurred to him that while the President was speaking he might find time to try a lozenge as a remedy. Seeing De Fonvielle in aeronaut marine dress, he took him for one of the assistants provided by the forethought of Mr. Alderman Hallett, and said to him, "I should be glad if you would take a parcel for me to Mr. Glaisher." "Mr. Glaisher, do you say?" "Yes, Mr. Glaisher," replied Dr. Griffiths. "Then I will go with pleasure. I have been all over Brighton looking for my friend Mr. Glaisher. Please put his address on the parcel, and I will go and inquire for him." And accordingly he left the Dome as I have related. Mr. Glaisher and De Fonvielle were joint editors of a work on ballooning. De Fonvielle was the first man who took a balloon out of Paris during the siege, over the German lines, and he was most anxious to meet Mr. Glaisher. It was one of his objects in coming to Brighton, and for the hope of meeting him early he was willing to forego the pleasure of hearing the presidential address. In his eagerness to meet his friend, De Fonvielle had forgotten all about the Emperor, and passed before him without even seeing him.

When, however, he reached Mr. Glaisher's, he was discomfited and astounded. It was a chemist's shop. "Mon Dieu," exclaimed the curious Frenchman, "is my friend Glaisher a chemist and in business in Brighton, and he never to say a word about it? How reticent these English are! You must live among them to understand them." And he plunged into the shop.

"I want to see Mr. Glaisher, I have a message for him from a gentleman—a priest, I think—now at the Dome meeting. Tell him M. de Fonvielle wishes to see him." "I am Mr. Glaisher," said the chemist. "I have not the pleasure of knowing you. But what can I serve you with?" "Then what is this?" exclaimed the indignant balloonist, presenting his packet. "Why, it is a note from Dr. Griffiths, inclosing a shilling, saying he has a bad cold, and asking for a box of throat lozenges." "Mon Dieu! And has he sent me on this infernal errand? And I have lost the President's address, to buy lozenges for a person I don't know; and you are not my friend Glaisher, but a chemist?" And he darted from the shop, leaving the paper and the shilling. But soon reflecting that as a gentleman he was bound to account for the money he had received, he stepped back and consented to take the box.

Returning to the Dome he again marched up the reporters'

gangway, passing again before the Emperor, but no more regarding him in his new indignation at Dr. Griffiths, of whom he demanded whom he had taken him for, and why he had sent him to buy his lozenges. "You shall not have them," exclaimed the irate Gaul, after displaying them, and he thrust them back into his pocket. "You sent me to a chemist, sir, and not to my friend Glaisher." Dr. Griffiths, understanding at last what a mistake he had made, apologised ; his indignant messenger relented, and, handing the Rev. Doctor the box, peace was made. But the mystery of it was unintelligible to the Emperor and to the audience, who observed these Gallic movements. They certainly seemed ominous to me until De Fonvielle came and explained them.

It was known that the Empress did not regard the matter with the equanimity of her Imperial husband. The lady actually had fears of some attempt at assassination, which were not allayed by learning that De Fonvielle was actually living in Cannon Place, within a few yards of her own apartments in the Grand Hotel. He did not intend being there ; it was too far from the sections. This, however, was not known, or the Mayor, Mr. Cordy Burrows, who was rightly and assiduously solicitous for the comfort of the Empress, would have explained the matter to her. Mr. J. E. Mayall, the famous photographer, and chairman of the hotel company, gave orders that no French gentleman not of the Emperor's suite should be permitted to have apartments or to enter the hotel, and, at inconvenience to himself, acted as a guard of etiquette and peace while the Imperial visitors remained at the Grand Hotel.

But for the Empress, the Emperor would have remained in Brighton. He liked the gaiety of the New Pier, and the brightness of the scene from the Grand Hotel windows. The perilous journey the poor lady made to this country, after the affair of Sedan, and the affairs in Paris subsequently, had not been of a nature to reassure her. The Empress went over Hove Place House (the property of Mr. Mayall), which the Emperor contemplated taking. It seemed admirably suited to him—enclosed grounds, a handsome house, near the pier, yet out of the way of the town, and overlooking the open country Dykewards, where he could drive for days unobserved. But nothing could reconcile the illustrious lady to stay in the town.

There were other French gentlemen in Brighton besides M. de Fonvielle, but they were all engaged in scientific inquiry, and had no intention of diverting their attention from those pursuits. They were desirous, nevertheless, of showing the Emperor that they still maintained their political hostility towards him. When an Englishman has triumphed over his political adversary, he will be civil to him, and even pay him honour. The Emperor might have remained in Brighton with perfect security. The Scriptures say that certain people flee when no man pursueth. In a few days the novelty of the Imperial visit would have subsided. The Association would be gone ; the Frenchmen, too, would have departed to their homes. They were all philosophers engaged on ideas, and that never means other than limited resources to them. They remain poor that society, which disregards them while they live, may grow rich when they are dead.

Most lovers of the good fame of England have noticed how Court journalists and Court officials continually gave to the ex-Emperor and family their full reigning titles, ignoring the French people and the Republican Government who had expelled them in the public interest. This was international offensiveness. It was done at Brighton. M. de Fonvielle, being deputed by the French Government to report upon the laws of storms, resented the description of the late Emperor as " His Imperial Majesty the Emperor of the French," and wrote to Mr. Griffith (not Dr. the Griffiths whose name has occurred in this narrative, but the Assistant-General Secretary) saying :—

" DEAR SIR,—I find that M. Louis Bonaparte and family are styled in a manner which is disregardful of the whole present state of things in France. I have no objection to meet the ex-Emperor in a scientific forum, but I should not be willingly a party in an Association which could be considered as giving some assistance to any demonstration against the French Government ; and I should protest energetically, humble as may be my individual position, against such a perversion of science for promoting the ends of hostile factions. Consequently I think I am justified in asking on what authority the Association has done this ?

" (Signed)   W. DE FONVIELLE."

Mr. Griffith replied, saying—

"DEAR SIR,—It is to be regretted that you have felt it necessary to give a political significance to a matter which has in no way a political bearing. [This was not true.] It is as a foreigner who has always taken a prominent interest in science that the ticket has been given to the late Emperor of the French. By this course the Association has not intended to express any opinion on the position of the late Emperor of the French as either *de facto* or *de jure* ruler of France. [But it did it.] " (Signed) G. GRIFFITH."

The action of Mr. Griffith was better than his explanation. The next day a new list of foreigners attending the meeting was issued, in which " His Imperial Majesty the Emperor of the French " was changed into " His Imperial Majesty Napoleon III." Whether the ex-Emperor inquired why his title was changed I never heard.

The next time I saw the Emperor he was dead. I saw him twice at Chislehurst after his decease. Death had lent dignity to his face which it lacked when living. When he resided here as a libertine, when he returned as an Emperor, and again as an exile, the expression of his face was always that of an adventurer. Seeing his end in exile without honour, it was impossible not to feel that this world is not so bad as it is painted. Napoleon I. might have continued to sit on the throne of the Cæsars could his word have been depended upon, and the dead Usurper renewed and confirmed the impression of the world that no Bonaparte could be believed on his word nor trusted on his oath. When Napoleon III. made a triumphal entry into Bordeaux soon after the Coup d'Etat, it was arranged that from an arch of flowers, under which he was to pass, an imperial crown should hang, surmounted by the words, " He well deserves it." But the wind blew away the crown, and when the Emperor passed under the arch only a rope with a noose at the end of it dangled there, with " He well deserves it " standing out in bold relief above it. The noose still hangs over him in history, and the legend also.

CHAPTER XCVIII.

ORIGIN OF THE JINGOES.

(1873.)

ONE Sunday afternoon, in March, 1878, a meeting was held in Hyde Park in support of Mr. Gladstone's policy on the Eastern Question. The two principal persons taking part in it were the Honourable Auberon Herbert and Mr. Bradlaugh. The chief supporters of the Conservative Government of the day were the music-hall politicians, a class of persons little distinguished for sober discernment in public affairs or for patriotic service. A wild and vain glorious ditty, calculated to excite the contempt of foreigners, was sung with ostentatious applause in their convivial halls. Its best known lines were—

> "We don't want to fight,
>   But by Jingo if we do,
>   We have the ships, we have the men,
>   And have the money too."

A certain Lieutenant Armitt, not much heard of previously in war or politics, assembled these jocund politicians in the park, and a conflict ensued. It was reported in the papers that Mr. Herbert was chased and had his clothes torn, and that Mr. Bradlaugh drew a new truncheon from his pocket, which he fortunately did not use—probably because those who knew him thought it undesirable to incite him to do it, as he was not a man to be intimidated in maintaining the right of public meeting. Afterwards a portion of the assembly set out to Harley Street, and broke Mr. Gladstone's windows. The poet of the music-hall patriots received a Royal letter of approval of

216

his production, and those vinous politicians thought themselves
called upon to give some public proof of their quality. It was
not advisable that truncheons should be produced at a Sunday
meeting by any party. As I was an advocate of the freer use
of Sunday than was customary, I thought fighting on that day
would compromise the claim, and that a belligerent meeting
was better held on the Saturday, since the Sunday succeeding
would give the humbler combatants time to recover before their
workshop duties on Monday commenced. I, therefore, said
the leaders of the Jingoes were better left to their own devices
on church day. I entitled my letter to the *Daily News* " The
Jingoes in the Park." This was the origin of the term
" Jingoes," and was the first time it was used. The public
reading it in the *Daily News* on the morning of March 13,
1878, the term was taken up generally, and it was added to the
nomenclature of political literature. We had then a Music
Hall majority in the House of Commons, and the patriotism of
the singing saloons and the spread-eagleism of Lord Cranbrook,
would produce a bad impression of England on the public
opinion of Europe if no one openly expressed dissent.

Mr. Justin McCarthy, in the first edition (and probably in
others) of his " History of Our Own Times," said " The origin
of the term was ascribed to Mr. Holyoake." The editor of the
World subsequently remarked, " It is a common belief that the
term Jingo was first applied to a certain political party by Mr.
G. J. Holyoake," to whom I answered (November 27, 1878)
that it was so, as I had certainly intended to mark, by a convenient name, a new species of patriots who, often found in the
germ state in their native haunts, had propagated in the
bibulous atmosphere of a Tory Government, had begun to
infest public meetings, and were unrecognised and unclassified.
Their characteristic was a war-urging pretentiousness which
discredited the silent, resolute, self-defensiveness of the British
people. Sir Hardinge Giffard, the Solicitor-General of the day,
in a speech at Salford, reported in the *Standard*, deprecated the
application of the term to the Conservative Government,
saying the " phrase was presented to the Liberal party" by Mr.
George Jacob Holyoake, who, he (the speaker) thought,
" might claim better than the accredited leader in the House
to be the leader of the Liberal party in the country, as he found

brains for them." Of course he did not mean this. His object was to disparage his political antagonists in Parliament. A term to obtain currency must be brief, relevant to the time, and easily spoken. The qualities I did not invent. I had no merit save that of discerning them in the new political pretensions of the Music Hall party and their Jingo song.

The *Irish World* (March 30, 1878), of New York, gave a cartoon, in which the British Lion, with a knife and pistol in his belt, a revolver in one hand, and a waving Union Jack in the other, is calling upon the Jingoes in the park to follow him to demolish Mr. Gladstone's house. The scene had a special application in the New York paper, as a Jingo riot had broken out in Toronto. The central figure in the cartoon is the first of the Jingoes, upon whom volumes have since been written.

In controversy which arose on this subject, Mr. G. J. Harney cited St. Gingoulph as the origin of the term Jingo who may be taken as a patron saint. The *World* newspaper is in favour of an origin more German—that of the *Salisburia* or *gingko-tree* (mentioned by Mr. A. R. Wallace in the *Fortnightly Review*, 1878)—" a pine with a foliage like that of a gigantic maidenhair fern." The *World* says the Jingo tree received the name of *Salisburia* from Smith so long ago as 1796. If this be true, it had not outgrown its name in 1878. The Ranger might plant a Salisburia in the Park. Then we should have a Jingo tree as well as a " Reformers' tree." There is an abuse of the term when applied to politicians of intelligence and sober thought who are for the consolidation of the empire or for imperial policy. The Jingoes are mainly the *habitués* of the turf, the tap-room, and the low music halls, whose inspiration is beer, whose politics are swagger, and whose policy is insult to foreign nations.

CHAPTER XCIX.

STORY OF THE ANTI-CORN LAW LEAGUE.

(1839–1874.)

IN 1874, the projectors of "Johnson's American Cyclopædia" desired to include in it an article on the Anti-Corn Law League. It came to pass that, on the advice of Mr. Smalley, I was asked to write it. I remember well that when I delivered it to the European agent of the "Cyclopædia," a poet known as "Hans Breitman, "he asked me what he should pay me. I had not thought of that, thinking there was a tariff already fixed which I should be paid per column, as is usual in these cases. Three pounds seemed to me a probable sum. I answered : "As I had to go to Basingstoke to see Mr. Paulton, I would add £1 on that account," and named £4. Producing a handful of sovereigns, Mr. Leland said, "You had better take seven." As I had expended time in research and correspondence upon the paper, and as there was nothing in my circumstances that made £7 inconvenient to me, I took it. The incident is still in my memory, as that form of payment was new to me. It was freedom of payment consistently applied to an article on freedom of trade.

Before writing it I asked Mr. Leland if he had any suggestions to make as to the character of the article. His reply was sensible and characteristic. He answered : "It would be useless. I would say, however, that I find a great disposition (and it is very creditable) among English writers for American publications to write so as to please Americans. It is a very hazardous experiment, and frequently fails." I was not likely to run this risk. My wilfulness in writing would preserve me from it. My policy is simply to tell the reader the truth relevant to the subject, so far as I know it, without implying that the reader is a fool if he takes a different view, for I never forget that the readers who differ from me may be better informed than myself. No reader is displeased who is treated with candour and respect.

In the days of the *Morning Star* there appeared a short letter from Mr. Bright to a correspondent in which the case of Free Trade was stated with a completeness I had never seen equalled. I wrote to Mr. Bright to ask if it remained in his mind, and if there were any special sources of information I ought to consult—provided " his leisure, or health, or opportunity, or wishfulness permitted him to answer." He kindly replied as follows :—

"ROCHDALE, *Sept.* 23, 1874.

" DEAR MR. HOLYOAKE,—I am glad you are to write the article on the League, but I do not know how I can help you. The doings of the League are written in detail in the 'Anti-Bread-Tax Circular' and in the League newspaper, and some copies of these exist. From them, by research and study, everything connected with the movement may be learned.

"To write much is to me burdensome, and my correspondence, diminished as it is, is still burdensome ; so I cannot sit down to tell you anything, and indeed I do not feel as if I had anything special to tell you. If I were in London, and could spend an evening with you, perhaps something might be said that would assist you. My friend Mr. Paulton is a great authority on League matters. He was its private and confidential secretary, and a great personal friend of Mr. Cobden and myself. He is living at Boughton Hall, near Woking ; but he is in poor health, and I doubt if he would be able to enter into the matter at all or not.

" I do not remember anything about the letter in the *Star* to which you refer.

" A good article on the League might do great good in America, and I hope you will be able to write it so as to please yourself. I feel sure you will do justice to your subject.

"If there is any special point on which you think I can give you an opinion, I shall be glad to hear from you again.—Yours very truly,   " JOHN BRIGHT.

"Geo. J. Holyoake, Esq., 22, Essex Street, London "

Mr. Thomas Thomasson, of Bolton, who better understood the political economy of trade than any other manufacturer of those days, and whom both Cobden and Bright consulted when they were young men, sent me, with his usual friendliness, information respecting all the works accessible of Prentice, Dunckley, and others, as did Mr. W. E. A. Axon also. Afterwards I had the pleasure of visiting Mr. Paulton, of Boughton Hall. He reminded me of Charles Reece Pemberton. Still retaining the contagious enthusiasm of his youth, he might be described as having an electric animation of manner. One thing he said I remember, because it was similar in sentiment to one Francis Place once expressed to me :—" I do not do what I can for men because I have hope of men as they are, but because of what they may be." It surprised me that two men so dissimilar as Place, the solid-minded, and Paulton, the mercurial, should have the same despair of the present and confidence in the future. Another remark Mr. Paulton made has been made elsewhere, and must occur to many observers and actors in agitations—namely, " There would be no rogues were there no fools."

I was a member of the League, and my impressions of its career, principles, and orators may, therefore, have interest for readers of this generation. The notes Mr. Bright made on my narrative when shown to him I indicate in brackets in this and the next chapter.

Anti-Corn Law League was a name taken by a famous association of Manchester manufacturers [and others], founded in 1839, for abolishing all fiscal imposts on corn. The first Manchester election of members of Parliament, which took place in 1832, carried Free Trade candidates, that electoral issue being then raised for the first time in England. In 1834, the first meeting of the Manchester merchants was called to consider the question of Corn Law repeal. In 1836, a miscellaneous Anti-Corn Law Society was formed in London which included twenty-two members of Parliament. Among the names of the adherents were those of George Grote, the historian ; Joseph Hume, the economist ; Sir William Molesworth, editor of the works of Hobbes ; John Arthur Roebuck, historian of the Whigs; Ebenezer Elliot, the Corn Law rhymer; W. H. Ashurst, a leading promoter of the Penny Postage System; Francis Place, the chief of working-class agitators [Place was not a working man in the common use of the term. He was a tailor at Charing Cross in good circumstances and of gentlemanly education.—J. B.]; and William Weir, subsequently editor of the *Daily News;* Gen. Perronet Thompson, the great exponent of Free Trade. But no intellect, however eminent and various in its force, could avail against monopoly without money and popular opinion; and of these forces the precursor was W. A. Paulton, a young surgeon of bright, incessant enthusiasm, with a genius for agitation.

In 1838, a Dr. Birnie had announced at the theatre, Bolton, Lancashire, a "Lecture on the Corn Laws." The doctor was laden with notes, in which he got so entangled that he could not tell what he had to say. Mr. Thomas Thomasson, afterwards the executor of Cobden, a man of striking energy of character and commercial sagacity, being among the auditors, said to Paulton, who was near him, "You can speak; go down on the stage and deliver the doctor." The spontaneity and capacity which Paulton showed on that occasion led to his being invited to lecture himself, and ultimately he delivered three hundred lectures against the Corn Laws throughout Great Britain. He became the private and confidential secretary of the future League, which his eloquence and thoroughness mainly instigated. At a dinner given to him at Bolton, Mr. Bright made the first public speech delivered out of his native town, Rochdale. Later in the same year Dr. Bowring, then of Free Trade repute, being entertained to dinner in Manchester, Mr. James Howie cried out, on Mr. Paulton's health being drunk, "Why could not we have a Free Trade Association?" A week later one was formed, consisting of seven persons, of which the chief was Mr. Archibald Prentice, founder of the *Manchester Examiner*, who had himself, as early as 1828, advised the foundation of such a society. A subscription of five shillings each was adopted; £5,000 each was wanted before Corn Law repeal was carried. Some members paid that amount, and Mr. Thomasson much more.

In 1838, Mr. Cobden first became prominent in the Manchester Chamber of Commerce for resistance to the restrictive commercial policy of the manufacturing trade of the country. In 1839, delegates from the manufacturing districts were appointed to proceed to London to press their opinions upon the Legislature. Mr. Charles Pelham Villiers, who ten years later became President of the Poor Law Board, undertook to represent the Free Trade question in the House of Commons. On February 19th, 1839, Mr. Villiers moved that certain manufacturers be heard by counsel, before the bar of the House of Commons, against the Corn Laws, as injurious to their private interests. The motion was rejected by an overwhelming majority. On March 12th following, the day on which the Anti-Corn Law League originated, Mr. Villiers again moved "that the House resolve itself into a committee of inquiry on the Corn Laws," when only 195 members could be found to vote for inquiry [I doubt whether so many voted so.—J. B.], while 342 voted against it.

Discouraged and dismayed, the partisans of inquiry, who had come up from Manchester to await the result of the motion, rushed over to Herbert's Hotel, then standing in Palace Yard, opposite the House of Parliament, to consider what could be done. It was in that crowded room that Cobden, leaping on a chair, reminded the delegates of the victorious effects of the Hanseatic League, which, three centuries previously, had freed the trade of Hans Towns from the imposts of German princes. "Let us," cried Cobden, "have an Anti-Corn Law League, which shall free corn and trade also." It was then and there that the League originated. Cobden proposed that a fund of £50,000 be raised, and a considerable portion of that sum was subscribed in the room. The chief Manchester commercial houses followed with subscriptions of £50 and £100 each.

The English Corn Laws, which had for their object the restriction of the trade in grain, date as far back as 1360. At that time the prohibition was against exportation. It was not until 1462 that an Act was passed prohibiting its free importation. The object of the Anti-Corn Law League of 1839 was stated by the chairman (Mr. J. B. Smith) on the occasion of Paulton's first lecture, in the Manchester Corn Exchange, " to be the same righteous object as that of the Anti-Slavery Society,

which sought to obtain for the negro the right to dispose of
himself; and the object of the League was to obtain for the
people the right to dispose of their labour for as much food as
could be got for it, in whatever market the exchange could be
made." The Leaguers little foresaw at the time the formidable
work they had undertaken, and only gradually learned themselves, as the great agitation proceeded, the principles they had
to establish. What they discovered was that monopoly always
had advocates ready made, who, sharing in its exclusive advantages, had reasons for being enthusiastic in its defence.
Any tradesman would profit could he exclude from the market
rival articles of those in which he dealt. His profits would
increase at the expense of the purchaser. The monopolist
dealer considers this protection, but the public, who are
customers of the market, find it to be but protection on one
side—the protection of the seller, while he has his hands in the
pocket of the buyer. What the public want is free purchase in
a free market, the power to procure what they want from
whomsoever has it to offer. Free buying—that is protection
to the customer. The doctrine of the purchaser is as much
food as a man can buy, for as much wages as a man can earn,
for as much work as a man can do ; and is the natural and
ought to be inalienable birthright of every man who has the
strength to labour and the will to work.

In other things besides corn, protection was always on the
side of the seller, until the Anti-Corn Law League freed all
English industry from restrictive imposts. These " Free
Traders," as the Leaguers were styled, were opposed by an
organised party, who took the title " Protectionist," and
maintained—

(1) That Protection was necessary to keep certain lands in
cultivation ; (2) that it was desirable to cultivate as much land
as possible, in order to improve the country ; (3) that if
improvement by that means were to cease, there must be
dependence on the foreigner for a large portion of the food of
the people : (4) that such dependence would be fraught with
immense danger. In the event of war, supplies might be
stopped, for the ports might be blockaded, the result being
famine, disease, and civil war. (5) That the advantage gained
by Protection enabled landed proprietors and their tenants to

encourage manufactures and trade ; so much so that, were the Corn Laws abolished, half the country shopkeepers would be ruined. That would be followed by the stoppage of many mills and factories ; large numbers of the working classes would be thrown idle, disturbances would ensue, capital would be withdrawn, and no one would venture to say what would be the final consequences.

By this formidable enumeration, it was made to appear that the end of England was certainly at hand if the corn monopoly was disturbed. No country in the world can hope to put on record a more appalling set of consequences if protection is menaced. In England they exercised a commanding influence, even over the working people, who were induced to believe that it was for their interest that bread was made dear. The learned as well as the ignorant, the aristocracy as well as the small shopkeeper, were under the same uninstructed terror. Even Sir James Graham declared in Parliament, when a fixed duty on corn instead of a fluctuating one was proposed by Lord John Russell, that "it would not be the destruction of one particular class in the State alone, but of the State itself." Sir Robert Peel at first met the effort of the League by a sliding scale, varying with the price of wheat. This was a thoroughly English device, worthy of the genius of a people who never precipitate themselves even into the truth. Had Moses been an English premier, instead of making the Commandments absolute he would have proclaimed a sliding scale of violation.

CHAPTER C.

THE ORATORS OF THE ANTI-CORN-LAW LEAGUE.

(1839-1874.)

THE Anti-Corn-Law League instructed the people, its organisation enabled the people to express their opinion, but it was the platform orators who inspired the opinion. The struggle of the League lasted seven years, and cost half a million of money. In the fourth year of its activity, Mr. Paulton stated that the League employed upward of 300 persons in making up electoral packets of tracts, and 500 other persons in distributing them among the constituencies. In England and Scotland alone they distributed to electors 5,000,000 tracts and stamped publications, while to non-electors of the working class they distributed 3,600,000 publications. In addition, the League had stitched up in monthly magazines and other periodicals 426,000 tracts. The entire number of tracts and stamped publications issued by the League in the single year 1843, was 9,026,000, weighing upwards of 100 tons.

Such were the business features of this famous association. But its success came from its inspiration, and its inspiration, as I have said, came from its remarkable leaders. Ebenezer Elliott wrote fiery rhymes for it ; Gen. Thompson wrote its Catechism ; George Wilson, the chairman of the League, admittedly the most efficient chairman in England during his day [organised its popular action] ; James Acland, a vigorous speaker, acquainted with the people, was a sort of outrider to the League, going into market towns on market days on a white horse, perhaps as a pacific emblem, but partly as a means of drawing attention. He took the fighting among the belligerent farmers, so that when Bright and Cobden came [here Mr. Bright changed the order of names and put Cobden first] the strength of the enemy was known, and the local stock of turbulence being expended, the peripatetic orators obtained a hearing. Cobden mainly addressed himself to the villagers. He foresaw the great jam industry, and predicted to mothers cheap sugar and abundant fruit preserves. Oxfordshire cottagers tell to this day of the happy tidings their mothers brought home after listening to the League orators in the Market Place. Bright dealt more with the landlords and farmers, into whose cold understanding he poured the hot shot of League logic.

The League was the first body of agitators who introduced method into public meetings. In the hour ot argument in the Covent Garden Theatre, Mr. Villiers' mastery of the question was heard, his high character lending influence to the cause. Mr. Milner Gibson, another Parliamentary voice, had a graceful and cogent eloquence which always commanded attention. Mr. W. J. Fox, a Unitarian minister, and subsequently M.P. for Oldham, surpassed all the orators of the League of that day in brilliance of speech. Shorter and more rotund than Charles James Fox, he, notwithstanding, produced effects of rhetoric transcending those of his great namesake. The term " brilliant " does not entirely describe them. You no more thought of his appearance while he was speaking than you did of Thiers's insignificant stature. His low, clear, lute-like voice penetrated over the pit and gallery of Covent Garden Theatre. " You saw in the papers yesterday," he would begin, " the case of a poacher who was seized, indignantly treated, summarily tried, and sentenced to a serious term of degrading imprisonment. If this," he exclaimed, " be the rightful treatment of the poor man who steals the rich man's bird, what ought to be done to the rich man who steals the poor man's bread ? " In words to this effect he spoke. Men remember that argument to this day. It constituted the first words of his speech. He began with it. No first words of any speech in my time ever produced the same effect upon an audience.

The public and the press were allured by the great names of Cobden and Bright. Mr. Cobden, " the palefaced manufacturer," whom the landowners believed, and the farmers were persuaded to believe, was a Manchester enemy of agriculture, and a paid emissary of the Socialist insurgents of the Continent, was himself the son of a Sussex farmer, whose ambition was to die one of that class, and did so die, seeking and accepting no other distinction than that which his genius cast around his name. He was the logician of the League. As a master of lucid statement on the platform or in Parliament, he left no equal at his death. When he had made a statement, he looked at it and around it, as though he saw it in the air before him. What was deficient he supplied, what was redundant he withdrew, by putting the question in another way, in which he omitted any mischievous word, or qualified any phrase he had used which might mislead, so that he could not be misunderstood by accident, nor his meaning perverted by design. This contributed to give the League great ascendency, since all its adherents could quote without fear of contradiction what he said, and his speeches of one day became the authority of the next.

Mr. Bright's was a grander, more imposing and impassioned order of eloquence. Cobden presented the facts. Bright put fire into them. With the finest voice of any European orator, he displayed a measured vehemence on the platform which gave the impression of unknown power. He was the Vulcan of the movement ; he forged at red heat, and hurled the burning bolts which finally set Protection on fire.

Finally there came the collection maker of the League, R. R. R. Moore, with a voice that fell on a meeting like the bursting of a reservoir. It was not what he said, so much as the sound he made, that produced the effect. The maddest clamour was not hushed—it was overwhelmed by the new roar, which was always reserved to the end of the meeting. His function was to appeal for subscriptions, and he exactly answered that end, for when his astounding voice fell upon the meeting no one seemed to have the power of going away. I do but describe my impressions ; but here Mr. Bright remarks : ["His speeches were often logical and very good. The description of his voice is greatly exaggerated. He worked hard and was of great service to the League.—J. B."]

These were the great propagandists of Free Trade Economy, who made conquest of the Premier, Sir Robert Peel, who won for himself an imperishable name, by repealing in 1846 the

Corn Laws ; thus "giving the people bread no longer leavened," as he proudly said, "by a sense of injustice." Never was there such a wreck of political reputations as took place within a few years of the abolition of Protection in Corn. Nothing happened which had been predicted by the prognosticators of disaster. Poor lands were more cultivated than before ; no stoppage of imports by war occurred ; manufacturers and shopkeepers throve beyond their forefathers' dreams of prosperity ; instead of rents of land falling, the aristocracy, the chief owners of it, grew rich while they slept—as they do still ; and farmers found "ruin" a very pleasant thing to them. The working classes became better instead of worse employed, and their wages in some places excite the jealousy of curates, while the agricultural labourers are at last able to insist upon improved provision for themselves. A stimulus, inconceivable before, was given to trade ; fluctuations in the price of corn decreased ; apprehensions of insufficient harvests no longer excited dread, and the British race became physically one-half larger in bulk and one-half heavier in weight than in the days before Cobden and Bright arose. The victory of the Anti-Corn-Law League was the greatest ever won by reason in the history of human agitations. Neither in piety, nor morals, nor trade are men for trusting one another. Everybody is for protecting his neighbour from benefiting himself. Nobody is for leaving freedom free. The principle of progress in commerce and social life is not to limit liberty, but to limit injury. It was the establishment of this principle in trade that caused this League to be regarded as one of the historic forces of British civilisation.

Mr. Cobden told me one night at the House of Commons that, despite all the expenditure in public instruction, "the League would not have carried the repeal of the Corn Laws when they did, had it not been for the Irish famine and the circumstance that we had a Minister who thought more of the lives of the people than his own continuance in power."

George Wilson was a great chairman. In a short, strong speech he explained the position of the question (to be considered) out of doors, and the case to be submitted to the meeting. But in conducting the meetings he was despotic. There was no code for their regulation then in England nor now, and despotism alone brought them to an end.

During a thousand years the theory of public meetings in England has not been revised.   In Saxon times, we are told, the wise men of the commune assembled under a tree and took counsel together. If public meetings were limited to "wise men" in these days they would seldom be crowded. Saxon public meetings were not so numerous but that every one could give his opinion who had an opinion to give, and the theory of the Saxon public meeting was that every one present had a right to be heard.   Upon this theory meetings to-day are held when they amount to ten thousand persons, or, as at Bingley Hall, Birmingham, when Mr. Gladstone was there, to thirty thousand. In the days of Thomas Attwood a Newhall Hill meeting in Birmingham was held, when Daniel O'Connell spoke, at which two hundred thousand persons were present. Had each person " stood upon his right to be heard," the meeting would have lasted a year. Whenever disorder is intended, persons are put forward to "demand" a hearing. The friends of the impossible "right" yell for it, and the friends of order yell against it. The chairman all the while is as helpless as a windmill. When Mr. Jesse Collings, M.P., was Mayor of Birmingham, he was insulted by Tories for two hours. They stopped the meeting over which he presided. They had made a large drawing of the head of an ass, and suspended it from the gallery in front of Mr. Collings, loudly calling his attention to it. At last he ordered the police to remove the asinine rioters, who indicted him for assault, which a Tory magistrate (Mr. Kynersley) sustained. At Brighton, during the Tory Government of Mr. Disraeli, no Liberal meeting could be held for five years, because the Liberals were unwilling to physically fight the Tories who were ready with a contingent of ruffians for that kind of disturbance. In Rochdale, when Mr. T. B. Potter was first elected, men were sent into the town, armed with sticks, to break up the meeting. I therefore advised that thick-headed Liberals should be put in the front, and they proved to be the most valuable members of the party of order, since they could best resist the arguments of insurgent sticks. Patriots of cranial tenuity were of no use.

It is singular and absurd that the right of public meeting should be a boasted English institution, at which no chairman can lawfully preserve order, and the proceedings can only be regulated by riot, or by the *clôture* of clamour, as in the House of Commons. The organisation of democracy is a long way off, and Liberalism is deliberate enough to reassure the most alarmed and apprehensive Toryism in the kingdom not to have established, one hundred years ago, the right of order at public meetings, and promulgated a code of procedure suitable to the conditions of modern days. The resolutions to be proposed should be described by the Chair. They should be few, the speakers few, and the time of each allotted and time for amendments provided and limited, and the authority of the Chair as to order should be made legal.[1]

[1] In this and the previous chapter I have used annotations by Mr. Bright. He then and always deprecated any words of praise applied to himself, but I did not wholly leave them out on that account.

CHAPTER CI.

CAREER OF A BOHEMIAN ARTIST.

(1847–1877.)

About 1847, two young men came to London from Oxford, not so much to seek their fortunes as to find occupation more genial than that they followed. Still they both had the instinct of distinction in them. One was George Hooper, who afterwards wrote, in the *Reasoner*, some articles under the signature of "Eugene." He brought some knowledge of Latin to town, and continued to read the classics in his leisure, which was much to his credit. I spoke of him to Mr. Thornton Hunt, and when the *Leader* was started he was assigned a place upon it. He pursued journalism and authorship, and made himself a name in military literature. His companion, Henry Merritt, came to reside in my house, where he continued nearly eighteen years, employing himself in picture restoration, in which he ultimately acquired skill and repute.

His life had been one of vicissitude. His social condition as a youth in Oxford was below hope, save by self-help. He had been in a charity school, an errand boy about the colleges, had filled various humble and precarious situations. In London he had been a Bohemian with art-love in his mind, honesty in his heart, and nothing in his pocket; with no patrons save a watchmaker in a passage off Drury Lane and a Jew coffee-house keeper in the Strand, both "good fellows" in their way.

When about Graves's shop (the printseller's) in Oxford, he had become acquainted with Mr. Delamotte, who, seeing the youth's taste, kindly gave him encouragement; and what was more valuable, he gave him instruction in art, for which

232

Merritt was grateful all his days. He dedicated his first book, " Dirt and Pictures Separated," thus :—

To
WILLIAM ALFRED DELAMOTTE, ESQ.,
Who, when I was a boy—a stranger,
Unknown to him even by name,
Carefully and gratuitously instructed me
In the rudiments of art,
I inscribe this little Volume
With long-cherished feelings of respect.[1]

As he resided with me, I had opportunities of introducing him to my friends, and at times he shared invitations with me. He occupied two rooms in my house (one being his studio), and had the use of the dining-room. He paid seven or eight shillings then. Sometimes he was in arrears several pounds, as I see from his account-book of that time. When money came to hand he paid up arrears, for he was as honest in his dealings as in his work.

When I removed to a lodge near Regent's Park, Merritt went with me by his own desire. There he worked for two years upon the oldest picture in England, Richard II., brought there from the Chapter House of Westminster Abbey, and entrusted to him by Dean Stanley, Mr. Richmond the elder superintending its restoration. Mr. Dennison, the Speaker of the House of Commons, and other eminent persons, oft came to witness the progress of the work. It was a delight to me to see this picture day by day, and see the king revealed whose face no eye had seen for 150 years. In the last century the House of Commons appointed one Captain Broome to brighten up the portrait, who knew no more of restoration than a house painter. He put upon the panel a new portrait in which the king was lost, and a staring, treacle-faced young man appeared in his place, with a sceptre as short and stumpy as a policeman's staff. Underneath Broome's paint was found the true present-ment of the pensive, timorous king whom Shakespeare drew,

---

[1] Merritt never heard of his friend more. Yet all the while he was pursuing his art in Brighton and executed some works for Joseph Ellis, who told me he had much regard for Delamotte.

holding a graceful sceptre in his hand.   Broome had forgotten
that the tails of the king's ermine pointed down, and had
painted them up.   The reader may see the real Richard II. in
the Jerusalem Chamber now.

As remarkable in its way is the ponderous panel on which
the life-sized king was painted.   It is more than an inch thick,
and is composed of three planks of oak, not only as sound as
when they were sawn five hundred years ago, but as unwarped
as a plane of steel.   Mr. Hans Holbein, who believed himself a
descendant of his famous namesake, could not by a microscope
discover the suture where the clever carpenter who made it had
joined the panel.

At the Lodge the ground rent exceeded £23, and house
charges were considerable.   Merritt occupied four rooms ; the
two chief having folding doors, made him a spacious studio.
He took up the whole time of a servant, and the Lodge grounds
were yielded to him for recreation.   Here he paid £1 a week.
Like most persons born and reared in indigence, he was
alarmed at any new expense, even when he could well bear it.
He was distressed and apprehensive even at this charge, and
never paid more to the end of his tenancy.   But I had other
interest than profit in continuing it.   It was partly friendship
—partly liking, and partly the love of seeing pictures, curious
or choice, about my rooms—a pleasure otherwise unattainable
by me.   It was diverting in another way to see, in the earlier
years, the straits of impecuniousness in artist life.   Well I
remember when at Woburn Buildings, Mr. Parrington, a friend
of mine, called with a picture for Merritt to test or restore.   It
happened he had no solvent of any kind by him, by which he
could clean the surface or remove encrustations of varnish.
Then Mrs. Holyoake secretly sent out for what he wanted, so
that the visitor might not be aware of its scarcity ; for a patron
with a valuable picture would be loathe to leave it if he suspected the need of the artist might lead him to pledge it.   Then
when the solvents came it was found that there was no linen
with which to apply or absorb them at the critical moment,
when the household collection had to be drawn upon, and sent
into the studio—as from a store-room where he was supposed
to keep his rolls of old soft linen.

Besides the interest of these episodes, Merritt was ordinarily

excellent company to talk to, or contradict. As Hartley
Coleridge said of one of his friends :—

" Fine wit he had—and knew not it was wit
And native thoughts before he dreamed of thinking ;
Odd sayings, too, for each occasion fit,
To oldest sights the newest fancies linking.

What I most honoured my friend for was his honesty in art.
By falsifying pictures, making new ones look old, and finding
the signature of the master under the paint where it had never
been put, inventing for a picture a pedigree and a character,
he might have made money as others did, but he preferred
poverty to deceit.   After many years he had his reward.   He
could be trusted.   He was known to know his art ; his word
could be believed, and his opinion was worth money.   Connoisseurs so eminent as Mr. Gladstone in Merritt's later years
consulted him.

My brother William, Curator of the Art Schools of the Royal
Academy, was useful to Merritt, as he was to others in his
way ; but Merritt could not paint, and therefore hé could be
trusted to restore.   He had colour in his blood.   He had the
patience of Gerard Dow (whom Merritt was fond of citing),
who was said to spend days in painting a broom.   I have seen
Merritt spend days over a few inches of injured canvas, until, by
careful stipling, he matched the colours, and replaced the lost
tints, so that no ordinary eye could tell where the effacing
fingers of neglect or decay had wrought mischief.   No one who
could paint could be depended upon to take this trouble, when
he could in an hour paint in the defective parts ; whether such
a one could do it better or worse, or as well, he would not
represent the genius of the master nor restore *his* work.

When we lived at No. 1, Woburn Buildings, a window overlooked the grounds of Charles Dickens, who resided then at
Tavistock Place, made Merritt's working-room the best room,
because it looked on trees.   On Sundays Dickens would have
a friend or two in the garden, and a tray of bottled stout,
"churchwardens," and tobacco would be brought from the
house. We were told that this was Dickens's protest against the
doleful way of keeping Sunday then thought becoming.   Tavistock House was the one formerly occupied by " Perry of the

Morning Chronicle," as he used to be described, but in my time
it was divided into two houses. One was occupied by Frank
Stone the elder, who died there—a very genial person to know.
The other was occupied by Sidney Milnes Hawkes, afterwards
by Mr. James Stansfield. Mazzini was frequently there in those
times. One morning, when Dickens resided there, a person
purporting to be Mazzini called, and solicited aid. Dickens
sent down a servant, who presented a sovereign on a silver
tray. The visitor took the gift with thanks. When this came
to be known to Mazzini's friends they were filled with amazement at Dickens's thoughtlessness, to say the least. How
could he imagine that a gentleman whom he had met in society,
as a man of reputation for honour and self-respect, would come
to his door soliciting alms, like an adventurer or an impostor ?
And, if he believed the applicant to be Mazzini, some inquiry,
some commiseration and identification was necessary to make
sure that one so eminent was suddenly in distress so abject.
Mazzini had a hundred friends who would have aided him
before he need have been a suppliant at Dickens's door.

Though he hardly knew it, Merritt had the ambition of
authorship in him, but he cost me infinite trouble to make him
believe it. He began by writing for me in the *Reasoner* under
the signature of " Christopher." Sometimes I suggested the
subjects, and revised what he wrote. At length I urged him
to write about his own profession, as nothing distinctive or
readable existed upon it. At last he wrote some chapters
on the Art of Restoration. At that time Mr. Hans Holbein,
then stationmaster at Euston, was frequently at my house.
His passion was to collect all the engravings of Holbein he
could afford to purchase. He induced Merritt to call his little
treatise " Dirt and Pictures Separated "—a purely technical
title which could interest nobody but connoisseurs. I added
the line " in the Works of the Old Masters " to render the title
more human. At that time Merritt was not apt with his pen,
but there was originality and fervour in him which showed
he had literary taste. He had read no books save odd
volumes of the letters of Pope, Defoe, or an old dramatist
or two, which he had picked up on second-hand bookstalls.
He had had no education save the Charity School sort—
Church Catechism chiefly, which leaves a youth helpless and

abject in the battle of life. But he had the education of the streets—an excellent school for those who have sense enough to learn in it. He knew that an acquaintance of mine who made a name as a tragedian had learned grammar from a book I had written, which he had read when he resided in the house of my sister Caroline. I had put on the title-page of the book the words :—" No department of knowledge is like grammar. A person may conceal his ignorance of any other art ; but every time he speaks he publishes his ignorance of this. There can be no greater imputation on the intelligence of any man than that he should talk from the cradle to the tomb, and never talk well."

These words incited Merritt, who had the instinct of a simple and manly style in him. Like every person of taste, he was dissatisfied with his first efforts, not only dissatisfied but dismayed and despairing, and threw his chapters on Restoration six or seven times into the fire, where they would have perished had not my wife rescued them until a more hopeful mood came to him. Again and again they were enlarged and improved, and again thrown on the fire. To encourage him, I induced the editor of the *Leader* newspaper, by my accounts of their intrinsic excellence, to publish them in the " Portfolio " of that journal, where the chief chapters first appeared.

To this end I invented reasons to prove their insertion would be relevant, and wrote the introduction to the chapters in the *Leader*, and also a handbill about them, which was sent out to artisan readers in all the towns where I was in the habit of speaking. What I said was this :—

" The interesting discussion which several times has arisen respecting the preservation of the pictures in the National Gallery renders it necessary that every man having regard to the credit of the nation in this respect should be able to form an intelligent opinion upon pictures.

"Hitherto this has not been practicable to the mass of the people, because nearly all works on the subject of painting are written from the professional point of view, and abound in technicalities unintelligible to the general reader.

"Newspaper criticisms are usually written for the initiated

alone. The editor of the *Leader*, therefore, has thought it
useful to insert a series of

PAPERS ON THE PAINTINGS OF THE OLD MASTERS.

which are written in popular language, and by explaining the
artistic processes employed in creating a great painting, and in
restoring it when unhappily damaged by accident, time, or
neglect, shall enable the general reader to understand pictures
and learn to appreciate them, and take part in the discussions
which relate to them.

"A great painter sheds renown on his country, and refinement
on all people who have the good fortune to gaze on his work.
Taste for the fine arts is a proof of the civilisation of a nation.
English artisans would not be behind those of any on the Continent, if knowledge of the right kind was submitted to them.
The names of poets and philosophers are become household
words in our land—why should not the painters become equal
favourites ? They would if equally well known. If political
economists and politicians attain popularity, surely the day of
the great artists is come. Raphael sounds as well as Ricardo,
Titian may stand by Torrens, the canvas of Correggio is as
attractive as Cobbett's Paper against Gold."

Had the *Leader* not possessed that heroic sentimentality in
favour of usefulness which practical men despise, Merritt's
papers had never appeared. He was paid, as I considered,
liberally, but such was his nature that he was dissatisfied,
although it was the first money he received for any writing,
save such limited compensation as I was able to make him for
his papers in the *Reasoner*.

The name of the errand boy of Oxford appearing in the
Portfolio of a famous journal, with those of George Eliot,
Herbert Spencer, Harriet Martineau, and George Henry Lewes,
was reputation. Merritt had not the money to purchase the
distinction, and could not have bought it if he had. Yet it was
not until I threatened to abandon him that he gave up his
purpose of writing to the office a letter of discontent at his
payment. He was as difficult to befriend as Rousseau. Yet his
papers in the *Leader* were the beginning of his fortune. He
became known to connoisseurs who otherwise had never heard

of him.   Mr. Boxall (afterwards Sir William) could then afford
to know his Bohemian townsman.

The chapters would have ended with the *Leader* had I not
induced him to complete them and make a little book of them,
which I printed in the "Cabinet of Reason" series, although
the subject was not suited thereto.   The preface was wholly
mine, and the table of the painters named in the work.   In
concert with its purpose, I added here and there in the book
remarks to enlist the interest of outside readers in a subject
which would strike them as being alien.   The publication
brought him picture clients from the provinces.   The book
had a new kind of genius, and the genius was all his own.   It
showed knowledge, devotion, and enthusiasm, qualities Merritt
alone put into the book.

CHAPTER CII.

THE PICTURE RESTORER FURTHER DELINEATED.

(1847–1877.)

HENRY MERRITT had some delightful qualities, but he was the most timid, the most irritable and inconsistent of all the children of genius whom I have known. He now possessed the status the *Leader* had given him. Next opportunity occurred of introducing him to the *Empire*, set up by Mr. Livesey, the founder of Teetotalism. The editor was John Hamilton, who had the passion of a prophet in him, and with whom I had public discussion, and for whom I had great regard. Hamilton became editor of the *Morning Star*, and Merritt came to write on art in both papers. Through the *Star*, he contributed for a time to the *Manchester Examiner*, and he went to Manchester on the occasion of an exhibition of pictures in that city. Then I was able to give him an introduction to Mr. Stephen Pettitt of Merchants' Hotel, where he made friends and had pleasant days. It was a pleasure to me to be useful to him.

An intimate friend of mine on the staff of the *Standard*, Mr. Percy Greg, was a constant visitor at my house, and I enlisted his influence to obtain the appointment of Merritt as its art critic. When he came home in Gallery days he was sometimes unable to write out his notes in time for the *Standard* the same night. Then it fell to me to write them out for him, which involved many hours of close work. Sometimes this occurred two or three times in a week. For no week, even when I spent the day at the Gallery, did I receive more than £1 for work for which he received £6. Nor should I have taken what I did had not this work prevented me from doing my own. He would have been as ready to help me in like case.

When, in a season of illness, he was unable to attend the Galleries, he would ask me to go and make notes for him. Devoid of his critical knowledge of pictures, long familiarity with them enabled me to describe their features and the story the artist had told by his pencil. Merritt found from the art notices in other newspapers, which he subsequently perused, that my reports were to be trusted. He knew the kind of work produced by each artist who habitually exhibited. His notices sent to the *Standard*, written upon my report, were confined to descriptions of the subjects and the general characteristics of the painters, reserving technical criticisms until he was able to run down to the Galleries and see for himself. On the occasions when I went for him some droll experience befell me, such as recalled Boswell in a forgotten passage, preserved by Hazlitt in his "Memoirs of Thomas Holcroft." The comedian, who knew Boswell, records in his diary that one morning Boswell, calling on Johnson, found him writing a letter for a Mr. Lowe. On Lowe leaving, Boswell followed him, and with insinuating professions began : "How do you do, Mr. Lowe? I hope you are very well, Mr. Lowe. Pardon my freedom, Mr. Lowe, but I think I saw my dear friend Dr. Johnson writing a letter for you." "Yes, sir." "I hope you will not think me rude, but if it would not be too great a favour you would infinitely oblige me if you would just let me have a sight of it. Everything from that hand is so inestimable." "It is on my own private affairs." "I would not pry into any person's affairs, my dear Mr. Lowe, by any means. I am sure you would not accuse me of such a thing, only if it were no particular secret." "Sir, you are welcome to read the letter." I thank you, my dear Mr. Lowe ; you are very obliging. I take it exceedingly kind " (having read it). "It is nothing, I believe, Mr. Lowe, that you would be ashamed of." "Certainly not ! " "Why, then, my dear sir, if you would do me another favour, you would make the obligation eternal. If you would but step to Peele's coffee-house with me, and just suffer me to take a copy of it, I would do anything in my power to oblige you." "I was overcome," said Lowe, " by this sudden familiarity and condescension, accompanied with bows and grimaces. I had no power to refuse; we went to the coffee-house, my letter was presently transcribed, and as soon as he had put his document in his pocket, Mr. Boswell walked away as erect and as proud as he was half an hour before suppliant, and I ever afterwards was unnoticed." Lowe added that he was left to pay for the coffee he had ordered to give Boswell opportunity of copying his letter.

A countryman of Boswell's, one of the habitual critics of the Galleries, knew me well, and would come to me in the most desultory way, with cordial greetings and incidental inquiries as to " what paper I wrote for," " why was I there," and " whom did I represent." I then wrote for three papers, but not upon art subjects. " Did I write art notices for them ? " he would inquire. " Merritt writes for the *Standard*, does he not ? Is he here ? " Beguiled by cordial familiarity, I incautiously said " my friend was unwell, and I was looking round for him." Immediately he mentioned in the paper for which he wrote—the *Reader*—that Mr. Merritt's criticisms in the *Standard* were done by another hand. This would have given great pain to Merritt, whom my questioner knew and for whom he always expressed the greatest regard. Had the treacherous information come under the eyes of the *Standard*, it might have cost my friend his appointment. When the inquisitive critic next put his familiar question to me, I said " his solicitude was very interesting, but I observed he never prefaced his inquiries by informing me what he was doing and for what paper he was writing." His curiosity there and then ceased. I suspected him of seeking Merritt's place. Of course I kept the incident from Merritt, and kept the *Reader* out of his sight.

Mr. Merritt remained art critic of the *Standard* until the time of his death. His criticisms were written on a theory we had often discussed ; it was that of subordinating merely technical criticism, giving mainly an animated description of the character of the pictures and design of the painter, with his characteristics as an artist. By limiting technical criticism to such points as were necessary for the connoisseur and picture buyer, and describing in what respect the pictures were additions to the scenic glory of art, his notices were always, and are still, readable, and they sent more persons to

the Galleries to see the pictures for themselves than any other
art criticisms of his time. Art critics mostly wrote not to
interest the public in art, but to show off their skill as critics ;
just as most books on education are written, not to explain
difficulties to uninformed students, but to show how much the
author is better informed than his rival teachers. Always
distrustful of his own work, Mr. Merritt cast aside his criticisms
after they appeared. I kept copies of them all, and made them
up into four volumes, which he afterwards was glad to refer
to and show.

"Robert Dalby and his World of Troubles," Merritt's best
work, I copied out several times for him. The "Oxford
Professor," which he never finished, I was to re-write for
him, just so far as to show him my idea how it should be
treated. In everything I did for him, I did but polish the
diamond : the diamond was his, not mine. Merritt had no
inside life. In description of outside life he had genius.
Separate passages were perfect and inimitable. He attained
a spontaneous grace which change could only mar. This
needs no testimony, since Mr. Ruskin wrote to him :—

"You have given great pleasure to Carlyle by your report,
and you always give much to *me* whenever you write to me.
I have no other friend who says such pretty things to me, in a
way that reminds me of the little courtesies of old days, when
people were graceful by kind act in a letter as much as in a
quadrille, and when flattery was the naughtiest of one's faults
to one's friends—never carelessness."

In later years, when we were still home companions, Merritt's
health became precarious. For two years his life was a daily
uncertainty. The whole household was absorbed in attending
upon him. Often I rose once or twice in the night, and went
to his room to see if he were alive, or needed aid. After he had
left me, he was again in danger, and when he became delirious
I sat up all night with him. When his death occurred I wrote
a solicitous letter to the editor of the *Standard* to procure the
art criticship for one to whom he had left his fortune, as I was
always willing to serve any one whom a friend of mine befriended.

Merritt never married until within a few weeks of his death.

Though a Bohemian in freedom and precariousness, he was Bohemian in nothing else ; yet all his life his most amusing satire had been upon the peril and subjection of marriage, and he could not bear to tell me or any one that he had married. On his death I made it known in the papers, that she whom he had married might not be exposed to incredulity, for none of his friends would have otherwise believed in his marriage. The last time I saw him, scarcely a fortnight before he died, he besought me to come to him soon, as he had many things to tell me. He said that in his will he had left small bequests of £50 each to two of my children, but he should arrange to fulfil another promise he had often made. I received a telegram from a common friend summoning me from the country, as he was in great danger. I at once returned, but he was in other hands, and no opportunity occurred to me of seeing him again. He had no idea that his days would be so short, and thought he had time to do everything he meditated. He bequeathed shortly before his death several thousand pounds which he had honourably earned, and never doubted that he should earn more for his own use.

After his death, what purported to be a " Memoir " of him appeared by persons who had not known him long, and were unacquainted with the circumstances of his life, in which it was said that " the persons with whom he lived shared the benefits of his increased earnings." Again, " It was touching to see how often he supplied one family especially who depended upon him for every comfort with the means of that enjoyment in the country or by the sea-shore, while he remained at home literally to work for them." A reference to Merritt's friend and townsman, George Hooper, was still worse. Mr. Basil Champneys, the editor of the book, vouches that these things " are done with perfect tact and graphic fidelity." I attempted to obtain some correction of these statements from the editor and the publisher, but found I had no resources to obtain it legally, and expectation of its being done from a sense of justice there was none. Besides my family, some eminent friends in London and many friends elsewhere who would see the book, knew of Merritt's long residence with me, and that these references related to me. After fourteen years there comes to me this opportunity of correcting them.

Merritt had all the irascibility of the artist, but he was honourable and truthful at heart, and would have been very wild had he lived to see these statements made in his name. All the years he resided with me we seldom went to the country or seaside but we took him with us, increasing our expenses to which for many years he was unable to contribute his share. His querulousness with our friends always embittered our days, and made us glad when the unpleasantness ended. To do him justice, he regretted this, but could not help it, and he strove to make amends in his way. I used to say to him he was like Dr. Johnson's good-natured, angry man—"he spent his time in injury and reparation." When he came to acquire means of his own he became more insupportable, and, as his income was good, I besought him to take apartments elsewhere. He wrote to me saying "I was killing him, as I had given him nineteen notices to leave my house." Were I "living upon him," it was very injudicious in me to beseech him "nineteen times" to do me the favour of going away. To mitigate the tone of my request, I used to repeat the lines of Martial—

> " In all thy humours, whether grave or mellow,
> Thou'rt such a touchy, testy, pleasant fellow,
> Hast so much wit and mirth and spleen about thee,
> That there's no living with thee nor without thee."

But I could "live without him," and I had ceaseless relief when I recovered the control of my house.

He did leave at length, but my personal regard for him never changed, nor his for me. Not long before his death he wrote to my friend Major Bell, saying, "It is nearly thirty years since my friendship for Holyoake commenced, and it is not likely to terminate till death."

When a person has arrived at years of discretion (some arrive very late, I am afraid : I have not reached that period yet), he sees many things which were always palpable, but which he did not observe until experience opened his eyes. Then he sees irritating things dispassionately. Many times I have tried to analyse the complex character of my artist friend. I often say of the inhabitants of a famous town which I know well, that God has given to them more humility and more pride than He has vouchsafed to any other collection of His creatures. Merritt was not born on the Tyne, but he had these qualities. He had an insatiable expectancy of the recognition by others of qualities he disclaimed having. Charles Lamb excelled all English humourists in the American wit of exaggeration. When, he said, Coleridge met him on his way to the India House and took him by the button to discourse to him, he, with his penknife, deftly released himself, and on returning in the evening found Coleridge still holding the button, preaching to it. No one misunderstood Lamb, who merely put a halo round a fact which he left palpable. Merritt, with less than Lamb's art and genial restraint, had the bright gift of enlargement, and misled, without meaning it, those who did not know him.

We say of some men that they are nervous, meaning all the while that they have no nerves. Merritt had none. But, in lieu of them, he had a set of organised electric filaments, which, the moment you touched him with a harmless phrase, gave you a shock. He was the first person in whom I observed supernatural sensitiveness, who, starting at the slightest reflection upon himself, would say habitually things which it exceeded mortal self-respect to tolerate. In those moods you avoided him, and forgave him because it was his nature, to which he had never taught restraint. When he became eminent he kindly undertook to teach my eldest son his art. It was a distinction to be his pupil. But, with frequent kindness, there were outbursts of imputation which imperilled manliness itself to submit to. I have seen his best physician refuse further to attend him in consequence of his porcupine episodes. Yet, being just at heart, he would, like Carlyle, speak generously of the same persons, and, if others disparaged them, would defend them with many a bright and graceful phrase. Merritt thought that no one would remember what he never meant. Had I not known what heredity and circumstances do for all of us, I should have had sharp and permanent contempt, where I had only compassion and forbearance. Pained as an honourable man is that his nature should so betray him against those whom he regards, Merritt made, when he had means, what reparation he could by gifts. These he made to persons in whom I was interested, which was his way of giving me (as he thought) pleasure. In vain I besought him not to do it. For myself, I never had any gift from him, nor did I seek one, and he knew it. Thus in some instances he destroyed my natural authority by attracting expectation to himself, and left me a legacy of mischief which made me say on one occasion that Merritt with the best intention brought great misery on others and requited some one else. His friendship was a pleasure to me and a misfortune. Merritt had the elements of a noble character in him, and, counting the disadvantages which he surmounted and the eminence he attained in art and in literature, owing everything to his honesty and skill, he deserves a place in the annals of remarkable men. A wise ancient said, "Know thyself." Merritt did not know himself. Of all knowledge possible to him he lacked this alone.

CHAPTER CIII.

ERNEST JONES, THE CHARTIST ADVOCATE.

(1848–1867.)

I own I have the sympathies of Old Mortality. In my time I have perpetuated the memory of many unregarded heroes, who gave their strength, and in some cases their lives, in defence of the people who had forgotten, or who had never inquired, to whom they owed their advantages.

Ernest Charles Jones will, however, be long remembered by Chartist generations. He was the son of a Major Jones, of high connections, who had served in the wars of Wellington, and was at Waterloo. He was subsequently equerry to the Duke of Cumberland, afterwards Ernest I. of Hanover, and uncle of Queen Victoria. Major Jones's mother was an Annesley, daughter of a squire of Kent. His only son, Ernest, was born in Vienna, in January, 1819. His father having an estate in Holstein, on the border of the Black Forest, Ernest Jones passed his boyhood there, and in 1830, when eleven years old, he set out across the Black Forest, with a bundle under his arm, to "help the Poles." With a similar precarious equipment, he in after years set out to help the Chartists. He was educated at St. Michael's College in Luneburg, where only high-caste students were admitted, and where he won distinction by delivering an oration in German. In 1838, he became a regular attendant at the English Court, where he was presented by the Duke of Beaufort. He married into the aristocratic family of Gibson Atherley, of Barfield, Cumberland, the name being borne by his son Atherley Jones, now member of Parliament. We of the Chartist times all knew the gentle lady who lived in Brompton during the dreary days of her husband's frightful imprisonment.

In 1844, Ernest Jones was called to the Bar of the Inner Temple. All along he had high tastes and high prospects. Thus he was reared under circumstances which did not render it necessary that he should have any sympathy with the people. But the inspiration of poetry came to him. The influence of Byron may be seen in his verse. He had no mean capacity of song. With better fortune than befell him when he had cast his lot with Chartism, and with more leisure, he would have been a poet of mark ; but he threw fortune away. His family did not like the idea of his being a Chartist rhymer. His uncle, Holton Annesley, offered to leave him £2,000 a year if he would abandon Chartist advocacy. If not, he would leave the fortune to another—and he did. Mr. Jones must have had in him elements of a valorous integrity to refuse that splendid prospect. He knew well what he was about, and that the service of the people would not keep him in bread. They whom he served were not able to do it—they had too many needs of their own. He had declined his uncle's wealthy offer in terms of noble but disastrous pride, and the fortune he relinquished was given to his uncle's gardener. Though he had chosen penury, he retained the patrician taste natural to him, and made a point of not taking payment for his speeches and addresses. There was more pride than sense in this. Those who consumed his days in travelling and his strength in speaking could and would have made him some remuneration. Without it his home must be unprovided. Making a speech has as fair a claim to payment as writing an article. Honest oratory is as much entitled to costs as honest literature. Mr. Jones often walked from town to town without means of procuring adequate refreshment by day or accommodation by night. On some occasions an observant Chartist would buy him a pair of shoes, seeing his need of them. Ernest Jones published the *People's Paper*—the sale of which did not pay expenses. The sense of debt was a new burden to him. On one occasion when I printed for him, and he was considerably in arrears, he said, "I must go to my friend Disraeli." An hour later he returned, and handed my brother Austin three of several £5 notes. He had others in his hand. That politic Minister inspired many Chartists with hatred of the Whigs, whom he himself disliked, because they did not favour his

circuitous pretensions ; and when he found Chartists of genius
having the same hatred, he would supply them with money,
the better to give effect to it.   I never knew any Chartist in
the habit of taking money, who took it for the abandonment of
his principles ; nor do I believe Disraeli ever gave it them for
that purpose.   Their undiscerning hatred answered Tory ends.

It was July, 1843, when Mr. Jones was sentenced to two
years' solitary imprisonment, and to find two sureties of £100
each and himself £200 for three years after his release—for
saying, " Only organise, and you will see the green flag floating
over Downing Street ; let that be accomplished, and John
Mitchell shall be brought back again to his native country, and
Sir G. Grey and Lord John Russell shall be sent out to
exchange places with him."   This was simply amusing, and
there was no more danger of this happening than of a flock of
pigeons stopping a railway train.   In the same speech for which
he was condemned, he gave the same advice to the meeting
that I had given to the delegates to the Convention in the
John Street Hall, on the night before the 10th of April, 1848.

When Jones was imprisoned, it was sought to humiliate him.
The Whigs did it, but the Tories would have done the same—
yet the Whigs were more bound to respect the advocates of the
people.   Jones was required to pick oakum.   Being a gentleman, he refused to be degraded as a criminal.   Politics was not
a crime.   In the case of Colonel Valentine Baker, the Government had just respect for a gentlemen ; but not when the
gentlemen was the political advocate of the poor, though Jones
was socially superior to Baker.

Mr. Jones was kept in solitary confinement on the silent
system—enforced with the utmost rigour for nineteen months.
He complied with all the prison regulations, excepting oakum
picking.   That he steadfastly refused, as he would never bend
himself to voluntary degradation.   To break his firmness on this
point he was again and again confined in a dark cell and fed on
bread and water.

When suffering from dysentery, he was put into a cell in an
indescribable state from which a prisoner who died from
cholera had been carried.   It may be reasonably assumed that
it was intended to kill him.   The cholera was then raging in
London, and, had Jones died, no question would have been

asked. Still the authorities never succeeded in making him pick oakum.

In the second year of his imprisonment he was so broken in health that he could no longer stand upright, and was found lying on the floor of his cell. Only then was he taken to the hospital. He was told, if he would petition for his release and abjure politics, the remainder of his sentence would be remitted. This he refused, and he was sent back to his cell. Let any one consider what those two dreary years of indignity, brutality, peril, and solitude must have been to a man like Ernest Jones— nervous, sanguine, ambitious, with his fiery spirit, fine taste, and consciousness of great powers—and restrain if he can admiration of that splendid courage and steadfastness. Unregarded, uncared for, he maintained his self-respect. Thomas Carlyle went to look at the caged Chartist through the bars of his prison, and increased, by his heartless and contemptuous remarks, public indifference to the fate of the friendless prisoner. Carlyle wrote :—" The world and its cares quite excluded for some months to come, master of his own time, and spiritual resources to, as I supposed, a really enviable extent." This shows that, like meaner men, Carlyle could write without facts, or even inquiring for them. Ernest Jones, "master of his own time," had to pick oakum, or spend his days in a dark cell. Thus his "spiritual resources" were limited. He was refused a Bible even, and had to write with his blood. His "really enviable" condition was that of knowing that his wife was ignorant whether he was dead or alive, and he was denied the knowledge what fate in the cholera season had befallen her or his children, for whom no provision existed.

In his savage imprisonment he did write poems, but it had to be done with his own blood—not from sensationalism, but from necessity, pen and ink being denied him. Undaunted, he returned on his liberation to his old advocacy of the people. Mr. Benjamin Wilson, of Salterhebble, Halifax, who knew Jones well, has given many facts not before known of his career in the " Struggles of Old Chartists."

Ernest Jones and I were associated in Chartist agitation while it lasted. I was a visitor at his fireside at Brompton. Mrs. Ernest Jones, a lady of great refinement, shared the vicissitudes of his Chartist days, which shortened her own.

Mr. Jones left London in 1859, and went to Manchester with a sad heart.   Practice at the Bar had to be won.   One night, after attending the court at Leeds, he was met by Mr. Moses Clayton, who found he had no home to go to.   A home was found him at Dr. Skelton's, and a brief also next day.   He had come to the resolution that night that he would see no morning. Afterwards better fortune came to him.   He had the chance of being member for Dewsbury.   He was nearly elected member for Manchester, and the reversion of the seat to him was likely when he suddenly died.   His grand energy, fatigue, and exposure killed him.   Had he reached Parliament, he had all the qualities which promised a great career there.   Shortly before his death he spent some hours with me in my chambers in Cockspur Street, overlooking Trafalgar Square, discussing a favourite theory of his—the manner in which an actor on the stage of the world should quit it.[1]

In every workshop in Great Britain, in mine and mill, and in other lands where his name was familiar, there was sadness when his death was known.   His friend in many a conflict, George Julian Harney, sent from America to the *Newcastle Daily Chronicle* an impassioned account of the effect of the news on him as he read it in a telegram in Boston.

Mr. Jones had a strong musical voice, energy and fire, and a more classic style of expression than any of his compeers in agitation.   When he spoke at the grave of Benjamin Rushton of Ovenden, he began :—" We meet to-day at a burial and a birth—the burial of a noble patriot is the resurrection of a glorious principle.   The foundation stones of liberty are the graves of the just ; the lives of the departed are the landmarks of the living ; the memories of the past are the beacons of the future."

Despite his popular sympathies and generous sacrifices for the people, the patrician distrust of them, now and then, broke out, as when he wrote :—

> " Ill fare the men who, flushed with sudden power,
> Would uproot centuries in a single hour.

---

[1] After his death an " Ernest Jones Fund " was proposed. Lord Armstrong, then Sir William, sent two guineas to the *Punch* office, which was sent to me for the Fund.

Gaze on those crowds—is theirs the force that saves?
What were they yesterday?—a horde of slaves!
What are they now but slaves without their chains?
The badge is cancelled, but the man remains."

There is some truth in these lines. The abatements I take
to be these:—1. You can't "uproot centuries" if you try.
2. The "crowds" are always better than they look. 3. The
"slaves" are always free in spirit long before they get rid of
"their chains." 4. When the "badge is cancelled," the "man"
who "remains" generally turns out a gladsome, practical
creature.

In the nobler vein which so well became him, he vindicated
with a poet's insight his own career :—

" Men counted him a dreamer? Dreams
Are but the light of clearer skies—
Too dazzling for our naked eyes.
And when we catch their flashing beams
We turn aside and call them *dreams*.
Oh! trust me every thought that yet
In greatness rose and sorrow set,
That time to ripening glory nurst,
Was called an 'idle dream' at first."

Mr. Morrison Davidson has published the most comprehensive
sketch of the career of Ernest Jones which has appeared, and a
noble volume might be made of his poems, speeches and
political writings. Because he opposed middle-class projects
and broke up their meetings, little attention was paid to his
views by those who would have been most impressed by them.
Before their day he was as well informed as Karl Marx or
Henry George on questions of capital and land, and held
eventually wider views of co-operation than were advocated in
his time. It would have been economy to mankind to have
pensioned Ernest Jones, that he might have devoted his genius
to oratory, literature, and liberty.

Those of this generation who have not in their memory any
instance of Ernest Jones's eloquence, may see it in the following
passage from his Lecture on the Middle Ages and the Papacy.

" You have been told that the Church in the Dark Ages was
the preserver of learning, the patron of science, and the friend
of freedom. The preserver of learning in the Dark Ages! It
was the Church that made these ages dark. The preserver of
learning! Yes, as the worm-eaten oak chest preserves a manu-

script.   No more thanks to them than to the rats for not
devouring its pages.   It was the Republics of Italy and the
Saracens of Spain that preserved learning—and it was the
Church that trod out the light of those Italian Republics.   The
patron of science !   What ?   When they burned Savonarola
and Bruno, imprisoned Galileo, persecuted Columbus, and
mutilated Abelard ?   The friend of freedom !   What ?   When
they crushed the Republics of the South, pressed the Nether-
lands like the vintage in a wine-kelter, girdled Switzerland
with a belt of fire and steel, banded the crowned tyrants of
Europe against the Reformers of Germany, and launched
Claverhouse against the Covenanters of Scotland ?   The friend of
freedom !   When they hedged kings with a divinity !   Their
superstitions alone upheld the rotten fabric of oppression.
Their superstitions alone turned the indignant freeman into a
willing slave and made men bow to the Hell they created here
by a hope of the Heaven *they* could not insure hereafter.   There
is nothing so corrupt that the Papacy has not befriended, and
but one gleam of sunshine flashes across the black picture, in
the architecture of its churches, the painting of its aisles, and
the music of its choirs."

CHAPTER CIV.

PARLIAMENTARY CANDIDATURE IN LEICESTER.

(1884.)

THE Liberals of Leicester had sent deputations to London in support of Mr. Bradlaugh, who was excluded from his seat in Parliament on the ground of atheistical opinions, which were held to disqualify him from taking the oath. The appearance at the bar of another member equally disqualified to make oath would have strengthened the argument for affirmation. A vacancy occurring at that time in the representation of the borough, I offered myself as a candidate. My primary qualification consisted in my being the only public man in England—not a Quaker—who on no occasion and for no private or public advantage had ever taken an oath. I made it clear that, if chosen as member for Leicester, I should take no oath either by speech or pantomime, nor profane the oath in the opinion of men of Christian conviction, by solemnly repeating words which indicated no corresponding belief in my mind. But if any tribunal, exacting the oath and knowing my opinions, treated the oath as a mere secular undertaking of good faith, there would be neither profanity nor deceit in taking it, though there would be repugnance in using a form of words otherwise disingenuous, ambiguous, and misleading.

Apart from this question, the chances were against me, as I had been long known as one having decided views on public questions ; whereas the most presentable candidates are men who have spoken no word of principle—written no books—made no effort—taken no side—professed no principle—helped in no contest—shared in no sacrifice—served in no forlorn hope. Men who have done nothing, who are uncommitted to anything, and upon whom no one has any reason to depend, are the candidates mostly chosen. The cowards who kept on the outskirts of the field while the fight was going on—all the supine and superfine, who sat before the cosy fire with their feet upon the fender, while the combatants were out in the tempest—find laid at their feet the spoils of progress which others have won.

As to my professions, I said I was no Tory Radical, professing to be more "advanced" than anybody else, and helping the enemy on every occasion. I was no Social Democrat, offering the people comfort as a charity instead of putting in their hands the right and means of commanding it by honest effort. I was no reformer by confiscation. I was not a Liberal who would trust, without conditions, the wise with the fortunes of the many, nor the many with the fortunes of the wise, nor set one against the other—but would charge both equally with responsibility for the honour and welfare of the State. I followed the path of the great Minister who brought in our new Franchise Bill. All other Ministers bringing in Reform Bills have studied how many they could exclude from it. Mr. Gladstone has been the first Minister who has studied how many he could include in it. I am for trusting the Minister who trusts the people, and for supporting with my vote that foreign policy which is just without sentimentality—brave without swagger—which keeps faith with treaties adversaries have made—fights with English courage for English honour, and does not knowingly murder for prestige.

Mr. Herbert Spencer's opinions on Parliament were published at the Leicester election. He, being a thinker and an opinion maker, was well fitted for Parliamentary service. He, however, declined, as he was for individuality and for independence of the views of constituencies. On Mr. Spencer's principle every man would have his will and nobody have his way. He thought "the influence possessed by members of Parliament" was rated too high—the representative being too "subject to his constituents." Mr. Spencer held that "laws were practically made out of doors and simply registered by Parliament." He, like Lord Sherbrooke, regarded the duties of the delegate as merely mechanical. Yet could there be a nobler function discharged or nobler office filled than that of explaining the opinions of those who had no other way of being heard save by the mouth of their member? Is a member a machine because he is a delegate? Where is there such a delegate as a judge upon the bench? His instructions are not merely given by word of mouth, or at a poll, but discussed in Parliament, fixed with strictness and printed in books ; so that the instructions of a judge are so defined that, when perfect, he can neither misunderstand nor misinterpret them. And yet is there not scope on the Bench for the greatest forensic genius? If a delegate to Parliament was confined as a judge is, he would have ample scope for his independence and individuality. But there is a much wider margin in Parliament. Many who were prominent in smaller circles, as in the Vestry or Town Council, found themselves powerless in Parliament, because there was required more art and persuasiveness—there a man has to see farther, to hear more, to understand better, to master all the points pertaining to a question, to accord regard to the convictions of others, and present a question in a light so clear, and with arguments so conclusive, that he can create conviction on the side of public justice. There is no assembly in the world where there is greater room for the display of the highest powers in representing a constituency, interpreting its views, maintaining them when assailed, and, when need demands, storming the fortresses of the enemy.

There were in Parliament several members disqualified like myself by conviction from taking the oath, and Leicester was the one town most likely to be desirous of opening a door through which an honest man might enter the House of Commons without humiliation. It proved not to be so, and thus my candidature ended.

CHAPTER CV.

THREE REMARKABLE EXILES.

(1884.)

ENGLAND has often been enriched by the inventive genius of industrial exiles who have sought our shores for religious liberty. Not less has it been indebted to political exiles, who, seeking freedom here, extended it by their teaching and exalted it by their example.

Kossuth was the chief of the few foreigners who took at once a high place as a public speaker in a new tongue. No sooner had he landed than he appeared as an English orator, displaying not only mastery but imposing force. Neither Bright nor Gladstone had then attained like ascendency on the platform, and Joseph Rayner Stephens, who might be compared with Kossuth for his mastery of tongues, was silent. Since Kossuth's day only one orator has with the same suddenness engaged public imagination—Joseph Cowen. But Kossuth's distinction was the greater because he spoke in a tongue foreign to him. And what was not less striking, his reputation was as much owing to what he said as to his manner of saying it. In his speech on Poland he said : " In the public life of nations, never is anything accidental. There everything is cause and effect. An act of political morality can never be neglected with impunity. Every such neglect is fraught with the necessity of atoning it with sacrifices, increasing step by step, which, however, never will remedy the evil, unless the wrong occasioned by that neglect be redressed. In politics a fault is equivalent to a crime, and no false political step can ever escape punishment."

In speaking in the House of Legislation, Ohio, Kossuth said : " The spirit of our age is democratic. All *for* the people and all *by* the people. Nothing *about* the people *without* the people. That is Democracy." The conception of the popular aspiration and the idiomatic expression of it are alike remarkable. He instructed as well as declaimed. In Kossuth's speeches you found definition as in Paine or John Stuart Mill, which is rare in popular orators and writers.

I published Kossuth's oration on the " Independence of Poland," delivered in Sheffield, June, 1854 ; but his speeches on the " War in the East " and " The Alliance with Austria," delivered in Sheffield and Nottingham the same year, were " published by himself." They were printed by Tucker, Perry Place, Oxford Street, and sold by him. As Kossuth had no place of business, he could not " publish by himself." Probably, by saying so, he merely meant to indicate that they appeared by his authority.

Louis Blanc was long resident in this country. He spent twenty years of exile among us, and understood men and things in England, our politics and prejudices, and more faithfully interpreted them to the French people than any other exile who ever dwelt in England save Mazzini. Mr. G. W. Smalley, an American, not an exile, has excelled in the same art. Kossuth, on the other hand, sometimes entertained suspicions which fuller information would have made impossible. An attempt to serve him would seem to him, as it did to Weitling, something very different. Foreigners as a rule are liable to suspicion, but Kossuth was so distinguished for cosmopolitan attainments that anything ordinary became noticeable in him.

In another respect, not of contrast, but of similarity, Kossuth may be compared with Louis Blanc. Kossuth was regarded as a man of flexible principles, yet, like Blanc, he proved to have inflexibility to a degree unforeseen. Kossuth lacked the penetration of Mazzini, and put such trust in Louis Napoleon as to enter into negotiation with him when he was Emperor ; yet he preferred to live an exile rather than acknowledge an order of things in his own country he disapproved.

Louis Blanc was distrusted because the policy of French Republicanism which he espoused was deemed materialistic. I published the manifesto of Kossuth, Ledru Rollin, and Mazzini, and also Louis Blanc's "Reply" thereto. Yet Louis Blanc possessed an inflexibility on questions of principle as austere as Mazzini himself. He was many times besought to return to Paris, and offers of a Parliamentary seat were made, to which he answered—

"Duty could only call me to Paris to take part in Parliamentary struggles, if the electors should assign me a post. But this post no power on earth can make me occupy, so long as I must needs, in order to do so, take an oath which is not in my heart.

"Do the people really wish to be the sovereign? Let them elect those who refuse to take the oath ; let them elect them, not in spite of, but because of their refusal."

These sentiments are all the more remarkable since few public men in England have expressed them or acted upon them.

This resolution was as noble as the warning was wise, and Louis Blanc remained an exile until Sedan swept the false Emperor away. His exile lasted twenty years. I knew him from the beginning to the end, during his residence in London and Brighton. It was said of him, and of his distinguished but more demonstrative brother Charles, that Charles was a reed painted like iron, while Louis was iron painted like a reed. This was true. Beneath Louis Blanc's passionless cordiality lay impassable determination, which neither profit, nor applause, nor obscurity, nor neglect could divert from honest principle. Though a small man, smaller than the First Napoleon, he had none of the self-assertion by which little people often seek to conceal their diminutiveness. Louis Blanc was a self-possessed man, and, alike when he conversed or spoke on the platform, you never thought of his stature under the boldness of his tones and his commanding gesture.

He ranked among the great political historians of France. Like M. Thiers, he made history a stepping-stone to power. The "History of the Consulate and the Empire" led to Thiers becoming a statesman ; and the "History of Ten Years" mainly inspired the Revolution of 1848, and made

Louis Blanc a member of the Provisional Government. Unlike Ledru Rollin, whom he resembled in a noble irreconcilability, Louis Blanc had literary genius and capacity for statesmanship, which consists in understanding what measures are best conducive to the greatest happiness of the greatest number, and acting with large toleration. Blanc continued to maintain his influence as a commanding force in French politics until his death. It seemed as though all Paris followed him to the tomb. Since the burial of Thiers so great a concourse had not marched to a tomb until Hugo died. I was proud to be one of his English friends invited by Louis Blanc's family to follow him to his grave.

Ledru Rollin was another exile of note who had a singular career. When he did return to France, another generation had grown up, to whom he was unknown. Exile is a fatal power in the hands of tyranny : since it not only kills influence, it kills reputation. Louis Blanc having literary powers, his pen kept his name before his countrymen. Rollin's power was in the courts, on the platform, and in the Senate. Exile destroyed it. Mazzini said of him that he was the only Frenchman who gave up a public position and sacrificed himself for the welfare of a country not France, and for a cause not French. He incurred exile by his generous championship of the cause of Italy. He was what he appeared in Madame Venturi's painting of him—of manly bearing, of conscious power, yet withal unobtrusive in manner. That Barthélémy—a duellist whom some regarded as a murderer, and who was eventually hanged at Newgate for an undoubted murder—was hostile to the famous tribune is proof that he was less extreme than he was taken to be. Some politicians speak better than they act : Rollin acted more wisely than he spoke. The Royalist press of England decried him because of the title of a book he published some time after his arrival in England—" The Decadence of England." That work contained nothing but what we knew —nothing but what we had said ourselves. Had the great Republican lawyer entitled his volume, " Extracts from the *Morning Chronicle*," or " England drawn by Horace Mayhew," or the " Fall of the English Foretold by Themselves," any one of these titles would have expressed the character of the work. But because the author employed another title, the public were incited to take offence at the book. Six out of every seven titles of books have no relation to their contents.

The sagacious French jurist, no doubt, saw signs of decadence in England, in aristocratic incumbrance. With the millstone of noble incompetence hanging round the neck of the nation, he might well think Britain was going to sink "ten thousand fathoms deep." What Ledru Rollin could not see was that England has the power of renewing its youth. The Sindbad of Britain will not carry the Old Man of Privilege on its back for ever. Soaring, it will drop the aristocratic tortoise on some well-chosen rock, and smash it. Rollin thought he saw the old English lion stuffed with cotton. The noble brute who, in the days of Cromwell, could roar until he made the isles resound and Europe reverberate, seemed turned into a puff-bellied, flaxen-hearted old beast, whose lungs were a pair of steam-boilers, his breath condensed vapour, his molars spinning-jennies, and his royal old tail a horizontal factory chimney. With these signs before him, Ledru Rollin might conclude the English nation was declining.

When the recruiting sergeant went to Manchester and Preston, did he not find the men too stunted to reach the standard and too weak to wield a sword ? The race had been spun up in Jacquard looms. Many who condemned Ledru Rollin's book hastened to abolish these signs of the decline of manhood in our manufacturing towns. We needed a foreigner to tell us this fact which our own statesmen did not see, or did not own, and did not alter, and have not done it wholly yet.

CHAPTER CVI.

REMARKABLE WORKING-CLASS POLITICIANS.

(1884.)

BEFORE mentioning those who are the chief subjects of this chapter, I cite two who will have no other biographer. One is Allan Davenport, known at the beginning of this century as an enthusiastic advocate of the Spencerian system—not the new one of Herbert Spencer, but his of agrarian repute. Davenport wrote verse. His last publication he dedicated to me. I remember it, because it was the first time that distinction came to me. The poet was thin, and pale, and poor. He lived about the East End, was known at every workman's political meeting, and any surplus over his personal needs arising from his daily labour, was spent in publications giving information to men of his order, whom he sought to serve.

The other was John Weston—the thinnest, wiriest, gentlest, yet most ardent, prompt, and demonstrative of working-class politicians. There was nothing of him save his voice and his ceaseless energy. He was a workman who owed everything to himself. He was a cow-boy and a page-boy in his youth, and at last hand-rail maker—a trade he learned himself. And no man knew it better, or so well, for he wrote a book upon it, which is an authority in the trade. He lived to be seventy-two, working ten to twelve hours a day at the bench, and making speeches when evening came. With the independence which only a good workman can afford to show, he carried his principles into every house, high or low, where he went, and gave his opinions upon public questions to the noblest employer who fell into conversation with him. He stood none of the Imperialistic Communism and State Socialism of Carl Marx, but confronted that master of agitation, and carried resolutions against him. Whatever good movement was on foot anywhere in the metropolis, Weston was soon in it, if, indeed, he were not there first ; and yet there were more home difficulties in his way, of the Zantippe type, than any man save Socrates had to encounter. But no discomfort deterred him. Of all men of gentle spirit I have known he was the fiercest worker : a jelly-fish in speech, he was dynamite in action. He had the genuine passion of progress which brings good to others, but only grati-tude and poverty to those who have it.

Those who look back fifty years usually remember a few persons among working-class politicians of whom they find no parallel at the present day. In diplomacy, in oratory, indeed in every department of human professions or trades, some observe the same thing. Fifty years hence, people will look back upon these days and distinguish a few men in every class who surpassed all others in conspicuousness of service, manifest-ing qualities unlike any of their compeers. The reason is that there is excellence in every generation, but not of the same kind. The Quintin Matzys and Benvenuto Cellinis have been superseded by machinery ; but the genius which conceives the wonderful machines that now do the work of the world is but another form of genius, and surpasses in its way anything which preceded it. Henry Hetherington, Richard Moore, and James Watson, three working-class politicians, had remarkable qualities not common now, though no doubt there are men of this day as remarkable in relation to their time and the new work now requiring to be done.

Henry Hetherington was a Londoner, being born in Compton Street, Soho, 1792. He was apprenticed to the father o. Luke Hansard, the Parliamentary printer. For some time he worked in Belgium. In London he was the most energetic working man who assisted Dr. Birkbeck in establishing Mechanics' Institutions. Though then a Radical politician, he was de-sirous that working men should have knowledge—the better to use the increase of freedom they were then seeking. In 1830 he was chosen by his Radical colleagues to draw up the " Circular for the Formation of Trades Unions," out of which arose the National Union of the Working Classes ; and out of that union arose Char tism.

In 1831, Hetherington commenced to print and publish his famous unstamped paper, the *Poor Man's Guardian,* at one penny, when newspapers were sixpence and ninepence each. This was the first messenger of popular and political intelligence which reached the working classes. Three convictions were soon obtained against him. He was imprisoned for six months and again imprisoned for six months. The names of " Hetherington, Watson, and Cleave " were in the mouths of every newsvendor and mechanic in the three kingdoms, Hetherington's name being always mentioned first. On the title-page of the *Poor Man's Guardian* appeared the candid but perilous words, " Published in defiance of the law, to try the power of right against might." This was not a profitable business. He had to leave his shop disguised, and return to it disguised—sometimes as a Quaker, a waggoner, or a costermonger. After one of his flights he returned to London to see his dying mother, when a Bow Street runner seized him as he was knocking at the door. To distribute his paper, dummy parcels were sent off by persons instructed to make all resistance they could to constables who seized them, and in the meantime real parcels were sent by another road. His shop-men were imprisoned, his premises entered, his property taken, and men were brought into the house by constables who broke up, with blacksmith's hammers, his press and his type ; as the reader has seen recounted in the chapter, " The Trouble with Queen Anne."

In 1840 he was sentenced to four months' imprisonment for publishing " Haslam's Letters to the Clergy "—a performance which would not disquiet General Booth, and which Mr. Spurgeon would dismiss with the feeble censure of being a " down grade " book. Hetherington defended himself, Lord Denman saying he had " listened to him with sentiments of respect." Acting on the militant advice of Francis Place, Hetherington indicted Moxon for publishing Shelley's works, when Serjeant Talfourd discovered that the power of indicting gentlemen for publishing the works of gentlemen " was a fearful engine of oppression," which led eventually to restriction being put upon that " right of action " dear to the clerical mind. He died in London, 1849, of cholera, through trusting to his habitual temperance and distrust of medical aid   At his /

burial at Kensal Green, 2,000 persons assembled, and I made
the first funeral oration it fell to me to deliver. I spoke from
the tomb of " Publicola " of the *Weekly Dispatch*, who had oft
defended Hetherington in the dark days of conflict. Hetherington had a strong, honest voice and genial manners. He
was the first trade unionist who told his colleagues that the
co-operative workshop was the bulwark of the strike, and that
they were not to rob any class, but take care no class robbed
them—or, as Carlyle put it later, " Thou shalt not steal ; thou
shalt not be stolen from."

James Watson was a Malton man (Yorkshire), distinguished
as a Radical and Liberal publisher by integrity, courage, and a
Puritan inflexibility of character. He came up to London to
act as shopman to Richard Carlile, and underwent successive
imprisonments when judges were insulting and their sentences
merciless. A magistrate being ostentatiously Christian was no
guarantee of justice or civility in his time. Becoming familiar
with Mr. Owen's views, Hetherington undertook in 1828 the
agency of the Co-Operative Store at 36, Red Lion Square,
and in 1829 he went through Northern towns promoting the
formation of co-operative, political, and free inquiry societies.
When he came to London, in 1823, it was to defend Carlile,
whom he had never seen, and who was then in Dorchester
Gaol. Mrs. Carlile had just been liberated after two years'
imprisonment. Carlile's house was then 201, Strand. For
selling a copy of Palmer's " Principles of Nature," which nobody cared for then and nobody understands now, Watson
was sentenced to twelve months' imprisonment. This was in
1823. Three of his fellow-shopmen were sentenced in 1824 to
three years' imprisonment. For ten years the Government
did business chiefly in sentences. In 1825, Watson was attacked by cholera, followed by typhus and brain fever. Julian
Hibbert took him to his house at Kentish Town and nursed
him eight weeks. Watson had learned printing, and Hibbert
employed him to set up a Greek work he was writing at that
time. Afterwards Hibbert gave Watson press and types, and
left him 450 guineas in his will, which Watson spent in bringing out editions of forbidden books. In 1832, when gentlemen
went abroad to escape the cholera, and left a Fast Day at home
for the poor, Watson was arrested for organising a public

procession of protest against a Fast, when the people needed less labour and more food. Watson and his friends Lovell and Benbow completed their "fast" in the lockup at Bow Street, which was the way to give them cholera. In 1833 he received six months' imprisonment for selling the *Poor Man's Guardian*. In 1834, within a month of his marriage, he was again subjected to six months' imprisonment. But nothing moved him from his purpose. To disparage these sacrifices, it was said in the hostile press that those who incurred imprisonment were tools and were unable to defend themselves. Then they did defend themselves ; when the judges made it worse for them. Watson, Hetherington, Carlile, all who defended the right of the free publicity of Radical or unorthodox opinion, were straightforward and defiant. Whether they fought against the Crown or the Church, they denied nothing they had done, they explained nothing away, they evaded nothing, and they never asked for mercy. Watson published Bronterre O'Brien's "Life of Robespierre," and Babœuf's "Conspiracy," and Thomas Cooper's "Purgatory of Suicides." I was his successor in business.

Hetherington and Watson were friends. Neither would accept any business which one thought the other ought to have, or would like to have. Of the same pursuits, they engaged in the same contests, were inspired with the same ideas, worked for the same public objects. Both suffered in the same way, for the same cause. Both regarded the cause they represented as sacred ; both had pride ; both exalted their principles by their character.

Another who did this was Richard Moore (born in London, 1810), a wood-carver in Hart Street, Bloomsbury. He took an active part in Westminster and Finsbury politics. He was one of the Radicals who acted under the inspiration of Francis Place. He and James Watson married two sisters, who shared their interest in public affairs. The People's Charter was signed by six members of Parliament and six working men. Moore was one of the six, and was one of the Council of the National Political Union of 1830, and of the Chartist Convention of 1839. For twelve years he was chairman of the Association for Repealing the Taxes on Knowledge. Though interested mainly in politics, he was, like Watson and Lovett, active in the Socialist movement of Robert Owen, in which he acquired, as others did, placability of character. He rendered Mr. Owen aid at Gray's Inn Rooms, when Mr. Owen gave the use of his large apartment on Sundays for his friend Edward Irving to preach in, when he had been expelled from the Scotch Church, Regent's Square, for heresy. Moore, as member of the council of the National Union, took part in opening a political news-room on Sunday, the first time working men had the indepen-dence to do it. Mr. C. D. Collett, in his life of Moore, relates that W. J. Fox approved of it, saying working men had as much right as gentlemen had to enter their newsroom on a Sunday. All his life Moore worked at his trade, never seeking anything for himself. He was unnoticed, because he had no speciality save disinterestedness, energy, and good sense. He had no arrogance, or egotism, or bluster, which destroy political associations among the middle as well as among the working class, where enthusiasm in adherents has often been dissipated by personal ambition in leaders. Moore was the reverse of all this. Never swerving from well-considered principle, abating no demand which was ascertained to be just, never imperilling a claim by putting it forward in an offensive way, he persisted in it to the end. On the way to the end, concession of some portion of the demand became oft imperative. These he would accept, and in due time proceed with the advo-cacy of the remainder.

When the Lodger Franchise Association of Finsbury closed, Moore himself discharged the balance of its expenses remaining unpaid (£20). As he left little at his death, a presentation was made to Mrs. Moore. Mr. Milner Gibson sent £25, Mr. Stansfeld, M.P., Mr. Cowen, Mr. Novello, and others joined. In these days, when newspapers fill columns with notices of the known who have done nothing, it is but justice to devote a little to the unknown who have done much.

The Rev. Mr. White, the Speaker's chaplain, as was befitting the end of the old Parliamentary Reformer, read the service at his grave in Highgate Cemetery, at which Mr. Joseph Cowen was present, which would have given gratification to Moore could he have known it.

William Lovett, with Watson, Moore, and Hetherington, made a quadrilateral of remarkable working-men politicians. Lovett was a Cornish man. In 1828 he was the first manager of the Greville Street Co-operative Store, where men afterwards famous, as J. A. Roebuck, J. S. Mill, and others, oft attended meetings for promoting social progress. It was Lovett's hand which drew the People's Charter, which Roebuck revised. Lovett was the first person who drew up and sent to Parliament a petition for opening museums and art galleries on Sunday. In 1839 he was imprisoned two years with John Collins in Warwick Gaol for having issued a protest against the violence of the Government in putting down public meetings in the Bull Ring, Birmingham, by London policemen. Lovett published a scheme, devised in Warwick Gaol, of political education for the people, for he was always for intelligent liberty. Lovett was an excellent political secretary. He observed everything, made notes of everything, and kept everything relating to important conference. His fault was that he had too much suspicion of the motives of others not taking his view of things. Later in life he was teacher and superintendent of the only secular schools we had in London, established and supported by William Ellis, an early colleague of Mr. Mill. Lovett died in 1877, and I spoke at his grave at Highgate, quoting as relating to him the words of W. R. Greg :—" It is not by the monk in his cell, or the saint in his closet, but by the valiant worker in humble sphere and in dangerous days, that the landmarks of liberty are pushed forward "—a sentiment which applies to all of whom I have here written.

QUITE A NEW VIEW OF JOHN BRIGHT.

(1850–1889.)

MR. BRIGHT resembled a Company Limited. Compared with average men he was a company in himself, but, not being registered under the Companies Act, few noticed that his trading capital of convictions (if his noble qualities may be so spoken of) was limited. No other simile I can think of so well describes what was not understood about him.

In politics there is more eagerness than observation. Public men are not adequately regarded for what they do, and are often praised for what they do not intend to do. Champions of a popular question are taken to be champions of all that the people desire. Those who have long observed public men know where and on what questions they will fail the people. Hardly ten leaders in a hundred are thorough and can be trusted all round—not so much because they are base, as because they are limited in knowledge or sympathy, and are for a question without knowing or caring for the principle of it. The safe rule is to accord leaders full credit for the service they do render, and not count on more, unless they give reason for such expectation.

The Tory hatred of Mr. Bright which long prevailed was without foundation, and the eulogies passed upon him since his death for merits but lately discerned, have given the public no consistent or complete idea what manner of man he was politically. Not being under youthful illusions as to public men is an advantage. I may do them more justice for the service they do render, and not defame them, nor feel disappointment at their not doing what is not and never was, in their nature to do.

Mr. Bright was not a political tribune of the people, though his fame was political. He was a social tribune—though he was against Socialism. Working men distrusted Mr. Bright when he first became known to them, because he was against the Factory Acts, which he regarded as opposed to free trade between employer and workman, and did not see that where humanity comes in, humanity is to be respected, and is not to be subjected to laws of barter. Mr. Bright was for Free Trade before everything, and the Chartists were of the same mind, being for political freedom before everything. We have lived to see men of higher position than Chartists persist in their own views to the peril of every other interest. Mr. Bright professed no sympathy with Chartist aims, and they knew he was not with them ; but when Free Trade brought them better wages and fuller employment they respected Mr. Bright for his defence of it, and when he advocated the suffrage they thought he was with them in their political theories, not seeing that Mr. Bright was still Conservative, and moving in a plane apart from them. He never expressed sympathy for struggling nationalities. The patriots of Poland—of Hungary, of Italy, of France—never had help from his voice. He was silent on Neapolitan and Austrian oppression which moved the heart of Mr. Gladstone. He was incapable of approving the perjury and usurpation of Louis Napoleon, but no protest came from him. He was for the extension of the suffrage, because it was a necessity—not because it was a right. With him the franchise was a means to an end, and that end was the creation of a popular force for the maintenance of Free Trade, international peace, and public economy. Politically, he regarded the voter not as a man, but as an elector—nor did he think it necessary that all men should be electors. He was content if the majority of the people had a determining power, and whatever franchise gave this was sufficient in his eyes. He had no sympathy with manhood suffrage, and less for womanhood suffrage. He believed in the aristocracy of sex, and thought the political equality of women unnecessary, a perplexing and disturbing element in electoral calculations. That manhood suffrage gave dignity to the individual, by investing him with power and responsibility, was not much in his mind. Womanhood suffrage, enabling half the human race to bring their quicker, gentler, and juster influence to bear on public affairs in which their welfare and that of their children are concerned, was outside Mr. Bright's sympathies.

There are two sorts of Tories—those who seek power for ends of personal supremacy ; and the better sort, who seek to retain power in order to do good, but the good is to be good they give the people—the Tory belief being that the people cannot be trusted to determine what is good for themselves. Mr. Bright was better than the better sort of Tories. He believed a majority of the people were to be trusted. So far he was for Liberalism—but he was for Liberalism Limited. The Whigs of 1832 put down boroughmongering and entrusted the franchise to a " worshipful company of ten-pound householders." Mr. Bright was for enlarging that company by the admission of six-pound householders. When the Duke of Wellington heard new prayers read which were not to be found in the old, crude prayer book of the Established Church, he refused to join in them, as being " fancy prayers." Following in the Duke's steps Mr. Bright contemptuously called any new scheme of enfranchisement, which increased the number of electors indefinitely, "fancy franchises." [1] The Duke was for addressing Heaven by regulation prayers, and in the same spirit Mr. Bright was for "standing on the old lines." He was against working-class representation just as the Tories were against middle-class representation. Those in possession always think they sufficiently represent those excluded. Mr. Bright was of this way of thinking. He had this defence : he meant to be just to all outsiders, and did not deem it necessary that they should be able to enforce their own claim in person. Later he applied this doctrine to the whole Irish nation.

He was against the ascendency of the Church as allied to the State, not because its ascendency was an offence against equality, but because it was contrary to the simplicity of Christ's teaching as he read it, and because a State Church gave religious sanction to State war. As a man Mr. Bright put Christianity in the

---

[1] He applied this phrase to my proposal, that proof of intelligence, such as a workman could give and which I defined, should be a certificate of enfranchisement.

first place as a personal influence—as a politician he regarded it chiefly as a public force to be appealed to on behalf of social welfare. What he hated was injustice ; what he abhorred was cruelty, whether of war or slavery ; what he cared for was the comfort and prosperity of common people. Whatever stood in the way of these things he would withstand, whether the opposing forces were spiritual principalities, or peers, or thrones. If they fell, it would be their own fault—the forces of humanity must triumph. He would not set up privilege, nor would he put it down—provided it behaved itself. He was no leveller, he envied no rank, he coveted no distinction ; but he was for the honest, industrious people, whether manufacturers or work-men, having control over their own interests—come what would.

It was to this end that he opposed the Corn Laws and advocated Free Trade and the repeal of the taxes on knowledge. He desired that the people might learn what their social interests were. He was for the extension of the suffrage, that those who came to understand their commercial and industrial interests should be able to insist upon attention, and not have to supplicate for it. If the governing classes had given heed to social interests, Mr. Bright would never have invoked the power of the people. Like Canning, he was for calling in a " new world " [of power] to redress the persistent injustice of " the old." He would no more have sought the suffrage than Robert Owen would the support of the people, if his aims could have been realised without them. Owen went from court to court ; he waited in the ante-chamber of Sidmouth and Liverpool in vain ; and when courts and Ministers gave no heed he appealed to the people. Because he did so, Liberals and Radicals thought he was with them, but all the while he was a Tory. Bright, like Owen, cared for the people'more than for theories ; and the people, whose principles were opposed to thrones, thought the great social tribune was with them all through. This was the mistake which they, and wiser men than they, have made. Bright aided the extinction of slavery because it shocked his sense of justice and humanity ; but had the slave been well treated, and not bought and sold and flogged, he might, like Owen, have seen no such harm in it as to warrant the disturbance of States to put it down. But when its immorality and cruelty became authentically known to Bright, his noble sense of humanity was outraged, and his splendid eloquence, like O'Connell's, was exerted on behalf of the slave.

He was friendly to co-operators—he spoke for their protection, but never in favour of their principle. Like Bastiat, he believed in the divinity of competition. He was at once the advocate of Peace and Competition — the principle of sleepless and pitiless resistance to the interests of others. With him adulteration was but a form of competition. This is true. But if adulteration be its concomitant, that is the condemnation of both. Mr. Bright thought this reasoning Utopian.

Mr. Bright, like Mr. Disraeli, had little respect for philosophers. He did not dread them like Lord Beaconsfield, but he mistrusted them in politics. The region of the philosopher is the region of the possible. Bright's mind ran always in the region of the practical. His tendency was to regard new rights as "fads." The philosophers laid down new lines—he was content with the old. He, as I have said, ridiculed a franchise founded upon intelligence, as a "fancy franchise." Yet he sat in the House himself under a "fancy franchise." The concession which enabled the Quaker to affirm was a "fancy franchise ;" the Jews were brought into the House by a "fanciful" alteration of the oath to meet their tribal but honourable fastidiousness. It was not well that he should have contempt for new paths discovered by thought ; but he was not without merit in his preference for established roads, since many men give all their time to searching for new precepts who would be the better for practising the good ones they already have.

If, however, the great Tribune had the characteristics herein described, the reader will ask, "How is it that he was so widely mistaken for an aggressive and uncompromising Liberal ?" Most men think that because a man goes down the same street with them he is going to the same place. Bright accepted the aid of the men of right, without sympathy with the passion for right, beyond the helpfulness of its advocates in the attainment of the public ends he cared for. Cobden did the same, but he owned it, and sought such aid. Bright did neither, but did not decline alien aid when it came. He was the terror of the Tories, and they never discerned that he was their friend. He opposed them for what they did, not for what they were.

When riotous Radicals of 1832 had became fat and contented
middle-class manufacturers, and were shrieking as dismally as
Conservatives against a transfer of power to workmen, Mr.
Bright, deserted by his compeers in Parliament, appeared alone
on provincial platforms, pleading for larger enfranchisement.
Members of Parliament, themselves Liberals, thought the
question of the suffrage hopeless for years to come, and said to
me, "Why does Bright go about flogging a dead horse?"
Tories expressed contemptuous scorn for his enthusiasm. Had
he been silent or supine, working men would be without substantial enfranchisement now. What Ebenezer Elliott wrote
of Cobbett they may, with a change of name, say of Bright :—

> "Our friend when other friend we'd none,
> Our champion when we had but one ;
> Cursed by all knaves, beneath this sod
> Brave John Bright lies—a man by God."

Yet he had limits in his mind beyond which he would not,
and did not, go. In 1870, he deprecated the admission of
working men in Parliament as likely to increase the evils of
class legislation, yet all the while the House of Commons is,
and always has been, full of class interests. Mr. Bright and his
friend Cobden were the great representatives of the middle
class, yet he did not propose that middle-class representation
should cease so that the evils of class representation
might cease or diminish. If any class at all ought to be
represented in the House of Commons, surely it is the working
class, who exceed all other classes in numbers and usefulness
in the State. But the idea of democracy was not in his mind,
and women, as part of the human race, having political
interests was simply abhorrent to him. He was always for the
Crown, the Bible, and the Constitution as much as any Conservative. He was against the Tories—when they put passion in
the place of principle and their interests in the place of duty—
but not otherwise.

It is quite a vulgar error to suppose that the democracy are
more undiscerning than patricians. They made as many mistakes about Mr. Bright as the people did. An illustrious poet
could write of him as :—

> " This broad-brimmed brawler of holy things,
> Whose ear is cramm'd with his cotton, and rings
> Even in dreams, to the chink of his pence."

True, this was said long ago. But no one who personally knew Bright, at his advent in public affairs, could think this. Bright was no "brawler of holy things." Sincerity and reverence were always deep in his heart. There was no "cotton in his ears." He knew Free Trade and peace would benefit the manufacturer, but would benefit the people more. No politician of his day was less influenced by the "chink of his pence" than John Bright. Carlyle, with all his clamorous philosophy, made the same mistake as the poet, in his contemptuous remark upon the "cock-nosed Rochdale Radical," who had as fair a nose as the scornful "Sage of Chelsea."

All the while Mr. Bright's eloquence was directed to the maintenance of an honest garrison in the fortress of authority. He was the one platform warder of the constitution, but it must minister to freedom and justice. He spoke no word against the throne from his first speech until his last. Quakers ask protection from power ; they never seek to subvert power. Their doctrine of non-resistance makes them the natural allies of monarchs. Penn had the ear of Charles II. Edmundson had ready audience of King James. Shillitoe prayed with the Emperor of Russia, who knelt by Shillitoe's side. Quakers were not spies against freedom, but honest reporters of wrong done, whose honest impartial word kings could trust. Mr. Bright was always of the Quaker mind. He regarded authority as of God, but he held that authority was responsible for righteous rule. He was a courtier with an honest conscience. He was for the perpetuity of the Crown, and also, and more so, for the welfare of the people. In one of his great speeches he avowed :—

> " There is a yet auguster thing,
> Veiled though it be, than Parliament or King."

Mr. Bright was always for freedom of conscience, and equally for freedom of action, at the dictate of conscience. "Are mankind to stand still ?" he asked in one of his earlier speeches. He was for order, but with order there must be progress. It was this conviction which made him insurgent against the policy of doing nothing. Now he is gone, there is no great popular Conservative force left, save Mr. Gladstone.

CHAPTER CVIII.

PERSONAL CHARACTERISTICS OF MR. BRIGHT.

(1850–1889.)

Or Mr. Bright's political appreciation of orthodoxy, an instance occurred in connection with the Repeal of the Taxes on Knowledge. It was proposed that I should move, and Mr. C. D. Collet second, an amendment at the London Tavern, at a public meeting convened by Mr. Peter Borthwick, M.P., for the purpose of founding a separate association for repealing the Paper duty, leaving out the repeal of the Stamp duty, which he did not desire—the Tories being opposed to it, and being also against the abolition of the newspaper stamp, which prevented the people having newspapers in their interests. Mr. C. D. Collet, the secretary, defended my being appointed to make the anti-Borthwick speech, on the ground that I was the most likely person to perform a disagreeable duty in the least disagreeable manner. Mr. Bright, when told of the appointment, objected on the score of policy—it not being advisable that the society should be represented on so conspicuous an occasion by a person of my known opinions on other subjects. " We might be described by the enemy as a society of atheists." Mr. Cobden, who was always for carrying a point by whatever force was at hand, said, when the arrangement was mentioned to him, that "for his part he saw no objection to my moving the amendment in question, as he would accept the assistance of the devil in a justifiable enterprise, provided he observed such regard to personal appearances as might preclude his identity at an untimely moment." As I was considered a person who would fulfil these conditions, I was appointed. There was no doubt in any mind as to my identity with the sable agitator who had been named. I and Mr. Collet made our speeches, and our resolution was carried. Mr. Milner Gibson, who had remained in an ante-room until the success of the motion was clear, came forward and took part in the meeting, it being thought best that he should not appear at all, unless Mr. Borthwick's proposal was doomed to defeat. Thus it came to pass that the resolution against Mr. Borthwick's separatist project was carried (January 2, 1851), and the Advertisement Duty, the Newspaper Stamp, and the Paper Tax were kept unitedly before Parliament until they were all repealed. Mr. Bright's objection to me was on grounds of policy alone. Personally he was always friendly to me.

As I have said, he possessed a strong sense of personal religion ; there was no narrowness in his judgments. He cared more for the conduct of men than for their professions. A Cabinet colleague of Mr. Bright has related that one day objection was made by some one as to the opinions he supposed me to hold, when Mr. Bright, who was present, stopped him by saying, " Holyoake is a very good Christian, and does not know it."

At the burial of Samuel Lucas, the editor of the *Morning Star*, I accompanied Mr. Bright to the grave of his sister, who died soon after her marriage. She was considered beautiful, as most of the Bright family are. Afterwards, speaking of many things, I asked him if he remembered a Moslem said to have been in his father's employ who was considered a famous manipulator of colours.[1] The man was unable, even for reward, to communicate his secret. His sense of the quality of colour was an instinct, and he decided the proportions by feeling (by feelth as the Saxons would say more expressively) on passing the colour through his fingers. On my early visits to Rochdale I often heard him spoken of by workmen, he being a foreigner and a Mohammedan. He attended church and passed as a Christian during his lifetime. When, however, his end came, it was found that he had the Koran under his pillow, and that he turned his face to Mecca to die. Christianity did very well for him to live by, but he could not trust it to

[1] Mr. Bright did not remember him. Mr. J. A. Bright tells me there is no tradition of him in the family, and he must have worked elsewhere in Rochdale.

die by. In the most unoriental of towns—Rochdale—he preserved his trust in his Oriental faith. Mr. Bright was much interested in the story of the man. He might, had he been in Mr. Bright's employ, have lived openly as a Moslem, and no disadvantage would have accrued to him on the part of his employer. Mr. Bright had in his works men of all political, religious, speculative, and socialistic convictions, who never had reason to conceal their opinions from him.

The last time I saw Mr. Bright was at One Ash, his residence in Rochdale, a few months before his death. He showed me the political presents in his rooms, especially those from America, and pointed out portraits of members of his family known to me. We conversed on many things. He was the same to me as ever, although he knew that with his later opinions I could never be brought to agree—even by the aid of machinery.

He was the friend of his workpeople ; respecting their views, he asked no questions, but they might ask him any, and he was often stopped in the mill yard when his advice was wished in some personal trouble. A visitor might at times see Mr. Bright, while walking home, overtake one of his waggoners, and converse with him as they went along, side by side.

At Lord Palmerston's desire, conveyed to me by Mr. Thornton Hunt, I undertook to ascertain whether Mr. Bright would take office, being of opinion myself that it was not advantageous for a great leader to remain outside the Cabinet, to criticise it for not doing more, and not to go in when it was open to him and attempt to do what he could, where his presence would at least be a deterrent influence against evil measures to some extent. Mr. Bright thought differently, and he was more competent than myself to form an opinion upon that proposal, which concerned himself alone. Years later, when, in obedience to what he was assured was the public interest, and under the influence of Mr. Gladstone's friendship, Mr. Bright took office, he had to present himself to the Queen as one of her Ministers. The Queen, with that personal consideration by which she was often distinguished, remembering that Mr. Bright was a Quaker and might have scruples at kneeling to a monarch, who refused to uncover his head in the presence of God—therefore caused it to be made known to Mr.

Bright that he might, if he pleased, omit the ceremony of kneeling *on* kissing hands.   A friend of Mr. Bright's, thinking this act of fine consideration for the feelings of others ought to be made public, asked me to state it.   When I had ascertained that there was no objection to the fact being mentioned in print, I communicated it to the *Newcastle Chronicle ;* but either from misreading or from the printer having no letter " n " in his case, it was printed " or " instead of " on " ; and it went forth that Mr. Bright was at liberty to dispense with kneeling *or* kissing hands on his presentation to the Queen, which was quite a superfluous concession, as a Quaker is never wanting in ceremonial courtesy to a lady, and Mr. Bright—himself a Monarchist by conviction—would never demur to kissing the Queen's hands.   The paragraph was copied into *The Times* with the same error in it ; it went through the press in the same way.   Mr. Camden Hotten, in his edition of the " Speeches of John Bright," repeated it.   I wrote to the *New York Tribune* correcting the error in America.   Nevertheless, owing to the error of a single letter, it has passed into English history that Mr. Bright neither knelt nor kissed hands when he became Minister of the Crown.

Mr. Paulton, who knew as much as most men of the early history of the Anti-Corn Law League, told me that both " Mr. Bright and Mr. Cobden were taught and confirmed " in the principles of commercial freedom they espoused by Mr. Thomas Thomasson.   Mr. Thomasson was a manufacturer of Bolton, who understood the political economy of trade better than any other manufacturer of his day.   Mr. Thomasson being a Quaker, it was natural that Mr. Bright should be impressed by him.   The first time Mr. Bright went out to deliver a lecture, he was doubtful of his success.   He had well considered what he would say, but on his way to the hall he called upon Mr. Thomasson to take his advice as to the quality of his arguments. Mr. Paulton said Mr. Cobden had often consulted Mr. Thomasson in a similar way.

CHAPTER CIX.

MR. BRIGHT'S ORATORICAL METHOD AND MANNER OF MIND.

(1850-1889.)

THOUGH engaged in business, with little time to spare for study, Mr. Bright became a great orator—on the principle explained by the Irishman, who said " a short sleep did for him, because when he slept he paid attention to it." Force of expression was natural to Mr. Bright. His fine voice and public applause made him conscious that excellence in public speaking was possible to him. But force and finish of expression came slowly. The great speeches of Sheridan and Fox do not—from such accounts as we have of them—justify their great reputation. That is owing probably to their not being adequately reported. When a speaker is master of his subject and sure of his terms, an exact report will give him fame. But if his speech be summarised, his reputation may suffer—unless he who makes the summary is capable of making the speech. Dr. Johnson was a man of this capacity, and his summaries made the fame of the orators of whose speeches he condescended to give an account. Porson said : " Pitt carefully considered his sentences before he uttered them, but Fox threw himself into the middle of his, and left it to God Almighty to get him out again." Fox got himself out before his auditors, by his overmastering energy, but his reader needed aid. Pitt's later speeches, fully reported (as I judge from reading some of them), had captivating fluency. When Bright's speeches are read, they justify the reputation assigned to them. He moved the hearers as Danton and Mirabeau did the audiences they addressed. Mr. Beresford

Hope's description of Mr. Bright—when he was advanced in years—as "the white lion of Birmingham" could best be understood by those who heard him. One night, at Birmingham, when he had delivered a long, forcible, but not brilliant speech, on Ireland, a vote of thanks was accorded to him late in the evening. In acknowledging the vote, there came a storm of oratory from him awakening a fury of enthusiasm in the somewhat languid meeting. "If you, my countrymen," he exclaimed, "are unanimous that justice should be done to Ireland, it shall be done." He spoke the words as though he were the tribune of the kingdom, and his resolute and commanding tone gave the impression that he was able to cause it to come to pass.

In the earlier elections in which Mr. Bright was concerned in Birmingham, he spoke at various ward meetings, when his language was often disjointed, and sometimes incomplete. It might be owing to the work of inferior or wearied reporters to some extent, but the language was that of an ordinary and excited speaker. Mr. Bright himself might be exhausted, but the defects of style were such as exhaustion would not occasion. It was the original manner, which cultivation had not then effaced.

At a Covent Garden meeting, October, 1843, Mr. Bright, in the course of his speech in defence of Free Trade, exclaimed :—

> "Oh! then, innocently brave,
> We will wrestle with the wave
> Where commerce spreads her daring sail,
> And yokes her naval chariots to the gale."

The loud and long-continued cheering evoked was owing to the orator's manner rather than his matter. Twenty-five years later Mr. Bright showed far greater taste in selecting quotations from the poets. Speaking in Birmingham on January 13, 1868, he said—

> "Religion, freedom, vengeance, what you will,
> A word's enough to rouse mankind to kill,
> Some cunning phrase by faction caught and spread
> That guilt may reign, and wolves and worms be fed."

There was instruction as well as honest rage in these lines.

At the Anti-Corn Law meeting of 1843, as may be read in

the *League* newspaper reports and elsewhere at that period, Mr. Bright told us, in various terms, that the cost of the army and navy was maintained in the interest of the upper class. Twenty-five years later I heard him recur to this idea at a banquet in the Birmingham Town Hall, but no longer in the crude form of earlier days. The flint-headed hatchet was exchanged for a flashing scimitar. He said that "the army and navy were but a gigantic system of out-door relief for the aristocracy." The effect upon the audience was notable. The satire of the expression was caught at first only by the quicker part of the audience, who cheered—when immediately a larger number saw the point and the cheering was doubled—then everybody saw it, and the hall resounded with cheering and laughter and striking the plates with knife and fork. The next day Lord Lyttelton wrote a letter denying that the words were cheered : but the banquet committee had to pay a considerable sum for breakages which occurred at that particular time.

Some years later Mr. Bright was speaking at St Martin's Hall. Mr. Ayrton came in. It was on the day of, or the day after, the great Reform procession which had passed through the Mall. Complaints had been made by the Tories that the procession should have been allowed so near Buckingham Palace. Mr. Ayrton uttered reproaches of the Queen that she had not condescended to witness it Then Mr. Bright arose and made his famous defence of the Queen. He could not foresee that Mr. Ayrton would come in, nor foreknow what he would .say—yet his language was as perfect as though premeditated. I sat by him as he spoke, and concluded from that night that a style of dignity and grace had become habitual to him. In earlier years he had spoken of the Queen at Covent Garden meetings with studied respectfulness, but never with the felicity of phrase which he had now acquired. He had the voice of an organ, at once strong and harmonious, which swelled but never screeched. A resolute face and a resolute tone gave him a commanding manner, which, united to a stately way of thinking, gave him ascendency in oratory. Disregarding details, he put the relevance of a question so strongly that it is difficult to express in other words the same idea with equal force. This is the mark of the style we call Shakespearean,

Miltonic, or Tennysonian—noble thought put in unchangeable terms. A single passage in one of his orations makes clear his method of speech. " I believe, he said, " there is no permanent greatness to a nation, except it be based on morality. I do not care for military greatness or military renown ; I care for the condition of the people among whom I live. There is no man in England less likely to speak irreverently of the Crown and Monarchy of England than I am ; but crown, coronets, mitres, military displays, pomp of war, wide colonies, and a huge empire are, in my view, all trifles light as air, and not worth considering, unless with them you can have a fair share of comfort, contentment, and happiness among the great body of the people. Palaces, baronial castles, great halls, and stately mansions do not make a nation. The nation in every country dwells in the cottage." Here is the Homeric, realistic tread of simplicity and power—not among metaphysical abstractions which flit before the mind like shadows, but among men and things palpable to every mind and touching living interests.

The Quaker gets from his self-chosen faith self-sufficiency, concentration, and force, and to this Bright owed his simplicity, directness and massiveness of speech.

In his earlier speeches he made furious personal imputations upon the landlords of the aristocracy who stood in the way of the Repeal of the Corn Laws. They thought he hated them. That was their mistake. On the contrary, he said that, if they would take the part of the people, he should welcome them in council and would " defer to their opinions."

Mr. Bright's invective was owing to his Quaker belief, and he was never free from invective. An everyday man will think his adversary has some common sense, and that if facts could be put before him his opinion would change. But a Quaker says, "I have an inner light which tells me what the truth is, and what is more, you have the same inner light which tells you the truth, and you are sinning against it." The true Quaker regards the "inner light" as the very voice of God, and is more wroth in terms than other men, and has more difficulty in forgiving dissent from his views.

Though a peace-lover from humanity as well as from faith, I once heard Mr. Bright express interest in ·battle. It was the third year of the American war, and the House of Commons

derided his predictions of the success of the Union, because it
had obtained no signal advantages in the field. An eminent
American came down to the House and spoke with Mr. Bright
on their prospects. Mr. Bright said to me, " If they would give
us a victory, we should soon put things right here "—meaning
in the House of Commons.

There hung, some years ago, in the National Portrait Gallery,
a portrait of George Fox in leathern garments, with a face of
great sensual beauty. No wonder the women of fifty towns
were in love with him. The portrait inspired me with respect
for a man of his nature, who gave up the worship of women for
his life in gaols. Seeing Mr. Bright in one of the rooms, I said,
" Go and see George Fox's portrait," which he had not noticed ;
" you will understand why he came to wear a leather dress and
attain his strange ascendency." He went to see it, and took
Mrs. Bright with him, who was then in town.

Mr. Bright never distinguished that sentimentality is the
sense of what ought to be, and practicality is the sense of what
can be. He had both senses, though he denied it. One night,
in the Smoke Room of the House of Commons, I asked him to
present a petition for me upon a question he thought unattainable. Seeing a Minister near, he said, " Take it to him. He
parts his hair down the middle. He is a man of sentiment—
just the man for you." He forgot that he came from the
Puritan stock who all parted their hair. He was himself a
shareholder in the *Morning Star*. All London was amazed
when the hard-headed Manchester school elected to be represented by the sentimental title of old Utopian journals.

Mr. Bright had moral imagination beyond any political orator
of my time. The ethical passion glowed in his speeches. It
was that which won for him popular trust. One night he had
quoted in Parliament George Fox—whom he did not name—
a fine passage to the effect—When death shall divest the soul
of its human garments of passions and prejudices, and we come
to know ourselves as we are, we shall wonder to find how much
our intentions have been the same. Speaking to Mr. Bright as
he came out of the House, I said : " That peroration was a
sermon which only you would have the courage to preach
there, and from you only would they listen to it." He
answered, " This is a House where sermons are more needed
than any place I know."

It may be said of Mr. Bright as Ben Jonson said of Lord Bacon, " There happened in my time one noble speaker, who was full of gravity in his speaking. His language, where he could spare, or pass by a jest, was nobly censorious. No man ever spoke more neatly, more pressingly, more weightily, or suffered less emptiness, less idleness in what he uttered. He commanded where he spoke. The fear of every man who heard him was lest he should make an end."

One morning, at a breakfast at Mr. Gladstone's, he said, " I want to speak to you about your book," meaning the " History of Co-operation in England," which he had permitted me to dedicate to him. " There is only one thing in which I think you wrong. You speak of capital as injurious in itself." I said that was not in my mind. He answered quickly, putting his hand on my shoulder, " But it is in your book." This was true. I had not distinguished that it was certain acts of capitalists which I deprecated.

In 1882, I took to America the fine, almost life-size photograph of Mr. Bright, by Mayall, which I presented to my friend James Charlton, of Chicago. That represents Bright as he appeared when he took the floor in Parliament, with fire and defiance in his face. The *Century* gave an engraving of it. Mr. G. W. Smalley, of the *Tribune*, was to write a paper on Bright. Not being able to do it at the time, it was given to Mr. Escott, a coadjutor of Captain Hamber on the *Hour*. I was indignant at seeing Mr. Bright depicted before the American nation by dashes of Tory disparagement, and resented it wherever I wrote.

One orator whom Mr. Bright would never admit that he equalled, was Wendell Phillips, whom he regarded, he said, " as the greatest orator who spoke the English tongue." In 1879, as Mr. Phillips was showing me the memorable buildings in State Street, Boston, Mr. Bright's son came up. He was visiting America at the time, and I introduced Mr. Phillips to him. Mr. Phillips took off his hat and stood uncovered all the time of the interview, after the Indian manner of doing honour to the father by treating his son with distinction. I wrote Mr. Bright of this fine act of courtesy on the part of Mr. Wendell Phillips. On my return to England he passed me on the platform of the Birmingham Town Hall as he was about to address his constituents. Not expecting to meet me so soon he turned back and said, " Why, Holyoake, you are always *somewhere*."

During several years I heard all the principal debates in the House of Commons. For two sessions he was continually assailed for his Franchise speeches. So constantly was this done, that every measure he was supposed to favour was condemned, until it seemed that his sympathy with a Liberal bill was dangerous to it. All the while the Tory party had come to see that he was right and had made up their minds to further enfranchisement, and this was the way in which they disguised the concession which had become inevitable. It was exactly the case described by the American poet at the collapse of the Slaveholder's Confederacy :—

> "Not all at once did the skunk curl up ;
> We saw it bounce and heard it lie—
> But all the while it was looking about
> For a hole in which to die."

Shortly after, Mr. Bright became the most popular man in the House and the country, and his approval valuable to politicians in difficulties.

The views of Mr. Bright's character I have described are such as impressed me who knew him in movements he liked and in those he disliked. Despite his avowed contempt for sentiment, he was the most sentimental member of the House of Commons. He had the same aversion to philosophers as Lord Beaconsfield, but for different reasons. He had great humility, as Mr. Gladstone has ; but in Mr. Bright it was the humility of genius falling below its own ideal—in Mr. Gladstone it is the humility of duty falling short of the obligation of service due to the Giver of his great powers. Mr. Bright was no friend of democracy ; he had no sympathy for it. With political principles, as thinkers define them, he little troubled. His great passions were for justice, public prosperity, the comfort and contentment of the people. To these ends he devoted his great powers. Of these he was the foremost champion of our time. All else was to him as though it were not. As far as he was concerned, thrones might stand. To him intellectual rights were impracticable ideals. But within the limits in which his mind ranged he commanded the admiration and gratitude of the English people.

This is why the people had honour for Mr. Bright, and put trust in him. He was a Liberal who strove for progress, vindicated it, pleaded for it, urged it forward, attacked all who withstood it. A Tory studies how he can stop it—defames it, obstructs it, and denounces all who are friendly to it : and when, despite of him, it comes to pass, he claims to have originated it.

When Mr. Bright's last illness came, bulletins went out which led the press to make remarks that his end was near. Mr. Bright might not see the papers, but they could not but affect his attendants, and he was too quick an observer not to divine foreboding in their faces ; so it came to pass by a friendly suggestion to the bulletin maker that they were less frequent and more placid. Mr. Bright was always cheered by friendly remembrances by his townsmen, and, having to address a great meeting of co-operators in Rochdale, representing twelve thousand of his neighbours, I moved that we sent a message (not a condolence) to him, saying—

" That this assembly, celebrating the forty-fourth anniversary of the Rochdale Equitable Pioneers' Society, desires to send to Mr. Bright a message of regard for acts of neighbourly friendship and counsel to the early Pioneers, and for his aid in Parliament in procuring legal protection for societies of self-help in their unfriended days. The Rochdale members send him their grateful wishes. They know he is sustained by a simple and noble faith, and by a conscience rich in a thousand memories of services to those who dwell in cottages or labour in our towns. The days of one who gave his strength for the benefit of the people ought to be " long in the land," and they who send him this message are glad to believe that his days will be yet long extended."

It gave Mr. Bright pleasure. It was the only resolution of sympathy made public having no dash of the undertaker in it.

He was the friend of industrious working people everywhere ; what is more, he had personal friendliness towards them, and sympathy with them, and helped them in difficulty, in old age, and need, as his own work-people knew. His choice was to dwell among his own people. He lived among them, he died among them ; he elected to be buried among them, and he left the lustre of his name to their town.

What Lord Tennyson said of the Duke of Wellington may be written on the tomb of Mr. Bright :—

> " His voice is silent in your council hall
> For ever ; . . . yet remember all
> He spoke among you, and the man who spoke
> Who never sold the truth to serve the hour."

A new fact concerning Mr. Bright, which illustrates his noble passion for justice beyond all instances I have known, has just been published in the Rochdale Congress Handbook. There is in that town, works known as the Mitchell Hey Mill, started by workmen on co-operative principles, giving the right of profit to all concerned in making it. As soon as the shareholders were numerous enough, they took the workmen's shares of profit from them. " Mr. Bright expressed disapproval of the decision," and meeting one of the co-operative leaders (Mr. A. Greenwood) "inquired if it could not be reversed. A large number of Members of Parliament had taken great interest in the experiment, and he also knew," he said, " manufacturers who would have been quite willing to allow workmen to share in a certain amount of the profits." Mr. Bright accepted the principle that a share in profit was included in equity to labour ; and had Mitchell Hey Mill been permitted to prove that equity could succeed in manufacture, he would have put his own mills on the same plan.

CHAPTER CX.

ORIGIN OF SECULARISM.

(1850–1890.)

As my name has been associated with Secularism for forty years, and as I have no intention of disconnecting myself from it, nor evading any responsibility for having originated it, I give some account of it before ending the present autobiographical series.

Not seeing in my youth what better I could do in a world where no one seemed infallible than to think for myself, led to my acquiring opinions different from other people. For a time it distressed me very much to find that I differed from the world, until it occurred to me that the world differed from me ; then I had no more anxiety. Those who believe because others believe the same, are without claim to authority ; while those who hold opinions because they have thought them out for themselves, have used the same liberty I had taken, and I was guilty neither of presumption nor singularity. If the world differed from me, it was doubtless in self-defence, and if I differed from the world, it was in self-protection. And, as the world did not make any arrangement to answer for my opinions, it was but common sense that I should myself select the principles for which I was to be responsible.

At Carlile's lecture, to which he invited me,[1] he took the line he adopted in his *Christian Warrior*, in which he taught that a scientific and mythologic explanation could be given of the main facts of the Bible. When I spoke, I explained the ideas from which I never departed—namely, that mythologic and astronomic modes of accounting for scriptural doctrine could

[1] See "Carlile the Publisher," vol. i. chap. xxxv. p. 87.

never be made intelligible and convincing except to students of
very considerable research. Such theories, I contended, must
rest, more or less, on conjectural interpretation, which could
never command the popular mind nor enable a working man
to dare the understanding of others in argument. Scientific
interpretation, I maintained, lay entirely outside Christian
acquirements, and seemed to them as disingenuous evasions
of what they take to be obvious truths. My contention was
—" The people have no historic or critical knowledge enabling
them to judge of the authenticity or genuineness of the
Scriptures—their astronomic or mythologic origin. That
controversy must always be confined to scholars. On the
platform he who has most knowledge of Hebrew, Greek, or
Latin will always be able to silence any dissentient who has
not equal information and reputation for learning and research.
If by accident a controversialist happened to have this knowledge, it goes for nothing as authority, unless he has credit for
classical competency. In matters of controversy it is not
enough for a man to know ; he must be known to know, before
his conclusions can have acceptance. To myself it was not of
moment whether the Scriptures were authentic or inspired.
My sole inquiry was—Do they contain clear moral guidance
which would increase our certainty of aid from God ? If they
do, I accept that guidance with implicitness and gratitude. If
I find maxims obviously useful and true, judged by human
experience, I adopt them, whether given by inspiration or not.
If precepts did not answer to this test, they were not acceptable,
though all the apostles in committee had signed them. To
miracles I did not object, nor did I see any sense in endeavouring to explain them way. We all have reason to regret that no
one performs them now. It was our misfortune that the power
delegated with so much pomp of promise to the saints had not
descended to these days. If any preacher or deacon could, in
this day, feed five thousand men on a few loaves and a few small
fishes, and leave as many baskets of fragments as would run a
workhouse for a week, the Poor Law Commissioners would
make a king of that saint. But if a precept enjoined me to
believe what was not true, it would be a base precept, and all
the miracles in the Scriptures could not alter its character :
while, if a precept be honest and just, no miracle is wanted to

attest it—indeed, a miracle, to allure credence in it, would only cast suspicion on its genuineness. The moral test of the Scriptures was sufficient, and the only one that had popular education in it, and needed neither ridicule, nor scorn, nor bitterness to enforce it, since it had the commanding advantage of appealing to the common sense and best sense of all sorts and conditions of men, of Christian or of Pagan persuasion. Ethical criticism has this further merit, that on the platform of discussion the miner, the weaver, or farm labourer, are on the same level as the priest. A man goes to Heaven upon his own judgment : whereas, if his belief is based on the learning of others, he goes to Heaven second hand."

My mind being given to open thought, I came to consider whether a simple theory of ethical duty was possible, which would save from indifference the increasing class of thinkers who regarded the theology then in vogue as *vague*, uncertain, irrelevant, or untrue. It seemed to me that doing good was being good—that it was good to do good, and that if a God of Goodness existed he would count goodness as merit ; and if no such God did exist, goodness was the best thing men could do in this world. It was best for ourselves for its satisfaction and its example, and it was best for others as they would profit by it. It was not less plain that there was no mode of doing good open to us so certain as by *material* means. What were called spiritual means could not be depended on ; the preacher who put his trust in aid from above still found it necessary to take up a collection. Looking to Providence for protection against epidemics or famine, still left a good deal for physicians and Poor Law Guardians to do. Those who, like Mr. Spurgeon, could fill their meal barrels by prayer, had no unfailing formula they could patent, of which the public could purchase the royalty. Clearly science is the only Providence which can be depended upon. Therefore, the morality of duty and material effort were the practical precepts of Life, yielding preservation in this world, and furnishing the best credentials to present in any other.

These principles being few, practical, and demonstrable to any capable of observation and reflection, they constituted an independent code of conduct which, owing nothing to ancient revelations, adherents of such views were under no obligation to waste time in reconciling the truth of to-day with error of the past. Distinct from received opinion, the form here described is at least equal to it, for, in the words of the Oriental motto before cited, "There is no religion higher than Truth." Secularism, it was hoped, would aid the "coming of the kingdom of man," to which Professor Clifford looked forward.

In my youth I had borne the burden of theologic hopes and fears until my mind ached, and if I could lead others into a simpler, surer, and brighter way, I was wishful to do so. The " Principles of Secularism," which I published, were submitted to the better judgment of others. Not being a fanatic, insisting on opinions without reason or relevance ; nor a prophet claiming authority for his word ; nor having a "mission" for which there was no necessity ; but being one of the few persons extant who had no impression of his own infallibility, I sought confirmation from better instructed minds. One was Mr. John Stuart Mill, who approved my proposal as a useful departure from the theologic thought of the day, ever obstructive of secular improvement. The reader may see the nature of these principles in " Chambers's Encyclopædia " in an article which I wrote at the request of the editor, who " wished an account of Secularism by one responsible for it, and not one by a dissentient, which might be a caricature." Professor Francis William Newman, to whom I was indebted for the better expression of some points than was possible to me, regarded all who believed that duty to man is prior in time and importance to duty to God, as Secularists—and in this sense he might be so classed himself, though he maintains Theism with a noble earnestness like that of Theodore Parker.

That this secular form of opinion implies Atheism is an error into which many fall. Secularism, like mathematics, is independent of theistical or other doctrine. Euclid did not ignore the gods of his day ; he did not recognise them in geometry. They were not included in it. But if pagan theology undertook to contradict mathematical principle, Euclid might have joined issue thereupon. But his province was geometry. At one time the only two men of note in England who maintained that the Secular was Atheistic, were Dr. Magee, the late Archbishop of York, and Mr. Bradlaugh. Twice I discussed this point with Mr. Bradlaugh—first about 1856, and again in 1870.

The reader may see the report of the last debate in " A Little Book About Great Britain," by Azimat Batuk, an agent of the Napoleonic dynasty, who wrote under a Turkish name. My argument was that a man could judge a house as to its suitability of situation, structure, surroundings, and general desirableness, without ever knowing who was the architect or landlord ; and if as occupant he received no application for rent, he ought in gratitude to keep the place in good repair. So it is with this world. It is our dwelling place. We know the laws of sanitation, economy, and equity, upon which health, wealth. and security depend. All these things are quite independent of any knowledge of the *origin* of the universe or the *owner* of it. And as no demands are made upon us in consideration of our tenancy, the least we can do is to improve the estate as our acknowledgment of the advantage we enjoy. This is Secularism.

When I first knew the party of independent opinion, it had no policy. Its sole occupation was the confutation of error, or what it took to be error, and went no further. Anything more was not then to be expected. The confutation of theologic error was a forbidden right, and they who exercised it did it at their peril, and they did much who maintained that right. But the time came when those who had succeeded in proving certain received principles to be wrong, were called upon to show what independent and self-dependent principles, in accordance with reason and conscience, could take their places and guarantee the continuance of public and private morality, and not only continue them but improve their quality. It was to this new theory of secular life, the sequel and complement of free criticism, that the name of Secularism was given.[1] Some societies, simply anti-theological, have taken the secular name, which leads many unobservant persons to consider the term Secularism as synonymous with atheism and general church-fighting ; whereas Secularism is a new name implying a new principle and a new policy. It would be an impostor term were it merely a new name intended to diguise an old thing.

[1] In Chambers's "Encyclopædia," in Molesworth's "History of England," in Cassell's "Encyclopædic Dictionary," in Dr. Murray's Oxford Dictionary, the reader will see definitions of it. In theological literature readers may meet with fair estimates of it. "Mr. Holyoake taught us many years ago those truths of Secularism which are happily no longer neglected by Christian teachers."—Rev. Hugh Price Hughes, in *New Review.*

CHAPTER CXI.

THE KNIGHT WHO UPLIFTED THE DEAD HAND.

THE "dead hand" has destroyed the grace of many gifts, as when a man endows a church on the condition that certain doctrines are to be for ever preached in it. This precludes progress in thought and furnishes a premium to the gentleman in the pulpit to go on preaching what is no longer true, and if true no longer useful to the hearers. The doctrine is dead, but the dead hand cannot be lifted. Though the object of the endower was no doubt that truth should be preached, yet the spirit of his provision cannot be acted upon owing to the terms of his gift not providing for this. In the case of charity schools it is different. The dead hand gets uplifted by cupidity. Schools founded for the education of poor scholars or poor children are perverted to the uses of children of the rich. The intent of the founder, his spirit and letter are alike set aside.

I knew one great donor who left no dead hand on his gifts, though they amounted to half a million. In Birmingham there lived, until lately, one Josiah Mason, who, when I and others were advocates of Social views in Lawrence Street Chapel, used to be one of the hearers. Josiah Mason had an inquiring, an observant, and ambitious mind, but his ambition was the wholesome ambition of usefulness. He had risen from the humblest occupation. When a young man he held a situation as manager of a business in which his master promised him a partnership. Under the inspiration of this promise he had put into his service the zeal and sagacity of a partner. At length he found that the promise was not to be fulfilled ; he left, and no inducement, not that of a salary higher than he had any prospect of obtaining elsewhere, could induce him to stay. He had self-reliance and self-help in him. No honest duty was beneath him, and industry and probity did the rest. He knew that thrift was fortune. He became a manufacturer eventually, and when the day of prosperity came, he built a great orphanage at Erdington, open to children of any sect and of any race. Neither opinion nor colour was a bar to admission. He had acquired Robert Owen's passion for the formation of character, and concluded that wholesome conditions and good practical education would go a good way towards it in the young. One day he explained to me himself his arrangements, which showed that he was a kindly student of child nature. He had their baths made of wood, and the spaces around on which they stepped into the bath also of wood, so that no cold or discomfort should be associated with a healthy habit, rendering it distasteful and repugnant. He had all the doors in the buildings made so that they would open in or out by a child pushing them, that the little ones might not be impeded nor kept in or out by knobs difficult to turn. He had the beams of the roof left visible, that a child who could not understand why the ceiling was kept up might see it was supported and would not fall down. The gas and water pipes he had left visible, so that they might understand everything that was liable to instruct them or excite their curiosity. In the chapel in which they were assembled on Sundays he prescribed that a preacher of any denomination might conduct the service, providing he was willing to discourse a wise and kindly morality, omitting the awful tenet of eternal punishment, which he thought a fearful terror to the young mind and a barbaric conception of God.

Adopting a wise provision, suggested by a philosophical lawyer he consulted (Mr. G. J. Johnson), he gave the whole property in trust to persons half chosen by himself and half by municipal authority ; and at his decease the trust was to be entirely controlled by the town. A further wise provision was that, at the end of every thirty years, the trust should be open for two years for suggestions of improvement in its objects needed to meet new requirements which time and experience might develop. Thus was substituted the authority of the public interests for the dead hand of the donor. I do not

remember any like instance of tolerant and sagacious thought-
fulness enabling a great public gift to be kept in line with
public progress.

The trustees chosen by Mr. Josiah Mason for the administration of the orphanage were nearly all personal friends of mine.
Meeting some of them shortly after the endowment (which
amounted to nearly a quarter of a million of money) was placed
in their hands, I asked " Under what circumstances they received
it and by what ceremony it was accompanied. Did they assemble
the citizens in the Town Hall and receive from his hands the
splendid gift with circumstances of public honour ? " It transpired that they had met him at luncheon at the Orphanage,
received the transfer of the building and its opulent endowments, and wished him good morning. Considering that the
giver of so unusual a gift was entitled to public honour, I
inquired why did they not ask a knighthood for him ? Honour
was the wine of old age, and such a recognition would be
creditable to the town. The answer was they did not see how
it was to be done, but if I thought it possible I might take any
steps to that end with their concurrence. Then I mentioned
the matter to such members of Parliament as I thought might
take an interest in municipal equity. I wrote upon the subject
in the papers, and asked Mr. Walker, the then editor of the
Daily News, who was always ready to promote any project for
local or public good, to mention the matter in his columns.
Public honour conferred upon mere worth is hard to be
obtained until the public take interest in it, and to do this it is
necessary that they have information. It was also necessary
that the knighthood I suggested should be concurred in by the
members of Parliament for the borough in which Mr. Mason
dwelt. Mr. George Dixon readily assented, and supported
the proposal ; but Mr. Bright saw objections to it, and asked
me, " Whether I thought it a good principle that a man should
be made a knight because he had given £200,000 to a town ? "
I answered, " If the question was whether an order of knighthood or other social distinctions should be created, its usefulness
was open to contention ; but, knowing as he did how knights
were made, how men who never rendered any public service
received that distinction, and many because they had become
possessed by ways unknown of £100,000—it did seem to me

not an unprofitable principle to establish that any one who *had given £200,000* to the community should be eligible for a knighthood." Mr. Bright admitted there was some reason in that view, and when he learned that Mr. Mason had not proposed to leave this money at his death liable to dispute and doubtfulness of application—but had actually divested himself of it while living, and placed its administration in the hands of the municipality—he concurred in the proposal.

In the deed of trust which Mr. Mason executed, he stated that when he first entered Birmingham as a youth he sold muffins in the streets. No bell had a purer tinkle than his. No muffins were warmer or cosier than his in the clean green baize which covered them. From that humble beginning he had risen by industry and integrity to the possession of great wealth, which he had devoted to a well-considered public purpose. I asked a member of the Government, Mr. Stansfeld, whose friendliness to unrecognised service I knew, to put Mr. Mason's candid and manly story into the hands of the Queen, who I believe would be interested in it. She was interested, and considerately ordered that Mr. Mason's knighthood should be gazetted that he might be saved the necessity of appearing at Court to receive the distinction, at his age, which was then 78. Thus the benefactor who made a great gift and attached no dead hand to it became Sir Josiah Mason. When I received intimation of the Queen's decision, Mr. George Dixon, M.P., said it was for me to communicate it to Mr. Mason because I had caused it to occur. I had pride in it, because it added well-earned dignity to one who was the providence of little children, and had done a generous thing in an unexampled way, and who would otherwise have remained unrecognised by any public distinction. Sir Josiah Mason afterwards gave a quarter of a million more to found and endow the Mason College in which no creed or want of one is any disqualification for entering it.

CHAPTER CXII.

APOLOGY TO THE READER.

MANY books at their close need this : and he who has perused these chapters has probably thought some apology was due long ago. The story of many persons and many events remain untold in them ; should I ever tell them, as in those I have related, one characteristic will be found—that of depicting the manners, prejudices, and progress of my time, so far as, judging from my own experience, may be of use to others. In any manifesto of a committee, of which I have been one, I have asked, in mercy to others, for brevity and clearness. Having myself a full share both of perversity and dulness, the statement which compelled my assent might be intelligible to the public ; for I never put myself forward as representing other than the average stupidity of mankind. In this way I have been of service to men wiser than myself. Only in this way I may have been of service to the reader, who, being better informed than the writer, has been saved time in making out his meaning.

Forty of my colleagues of former years, all counted, have died by my side, and I should be dead also had I been as strong as they. Being otherwise, I had to keep both work and pleasure within the limits of my strength, whereas they, being like Dr. Wendell Holmes's "one-horse shay," equally strong in every part, went down, without suspicion or foreboding, altogether.

In my life one constant source of pleasure has been—that of laughing at the absurdity of the things I like. Seeing principles as objects apart from me, I could not but notice the grotesque way in which unconsciously they were sometimes carried out. A friend of mine who had progress in his heart and was bent upon the redemption of the world, which has been the ambition of noble men in all ages, founded a " Redemption Society "—a big business surely—and we began to acknowledge the weekly receipts in the *Leader*, which ran—Leeds, 7d. ; London, 10½d. ; Glasgow, 1s. 3d.   These small sums for a vast end made it look absurd.   I suggested that the contributions should be allowed to accumulate before inserting them, which caused me to be counted unsympathetic.   In speech, in conduct, as in judgments, I am for proportion.   In social and political aims credence depends upon proportion between progression and possibility.   Far be it from me to pretend to be without points of amusement in the judgment of others.   The only apology for absurdity lies in admitting it when you have committed it.   There is no safeguard against ridiculousness, save by looking outside yourself, and observing the reflection which conduct makes in the mirror of circumambient eyes.

Many who enter on the path of public service are repelled, as I have seen, by the prevalence there of aspirants for the position of pontiffs, chiefs, and lesser popes and potentates. Yet it is a good sign that this ambition exists.   When, however, these persons are found decrying the thing another is doing, which you therefore conclude to be wrong and extol them for their wiser perception—you are discouraged on finding that they did not consider the thing wrong, but sought to prevent another doing it in order to have the credit of doing it themselves. Carlyle, proclaiming the doctrine of silence in order that his own voice might be alone heard, is an instance of the same thing in literature.   Surprise on the first discovery of this artifice is one of the instructive shocks of experience.

The ambition of distinction is wholesome so long as it permits equal opportunity to others.   In democracy there is no chieftainship to which others must submit their judgment against their reason.   There is no legitimate leadership, save the leadership of ideas, no allegiance save that of conviction, no loyalty save loyalty to principle.   The passion of personal ascendency—the more than impatience, the dislike such persons have of submitting their conduct to the judgment of others—their belief that they are superior persons and all others inferior—the desire to keep others separate and apart — the reluctance to consult them except when applause or suffrages are necessary to the success of their aims

—lies deep in the hearts of those who seek personal ascendency. When the genius of democracy enters the mind and teaches a leader to aim at the elevation of his cause or his country, rather than the elevation of himself, then he says with Byron—

> " I wish men to be free
> As much from mobs as kings—from you as me."

Those who look back on life disappointed because it has not been what they wished it to be, should be put back again into the kingdom of the unborn—they do not understand the world into which they have come. Those who look on their days with regret because they have not been what they might have been had they availed themselves of the opportunities they have had, have not adequately observed what has gone on around them. No one does avail himself of all his opportunities. Every one has to regret fatal or irreparable omissions. The dice of life are loaded by unseen agents before we throw them, and we may be glad if we win anything, not discontented because we do not win all.

My information, all told, does not amount to much ; but the best and surest part of it has been gained in discussion, and in listening to criticisms. It is wise to believe in the Arabic proverb :—

" Men are four.
" He who knows not, and knows not he knows not. He is a fool ; shun him.
" He who knows not, and knows he knows not. He is simple ; teach him.
" He who knows, and knows not he knows. He is asleep ; wake him.
" He who knows, and knows he knows. He is wise ; follow him."

Sayings are like glowworms. It is only in the night of experience that we discern the light in them. One reads the saying of Pascal : " What an enigma is man ! What a strange, chaotic, and contradictory being. Judge of all things, feeble earthworm, depository of the Truth, mass of uncertainty, glory and butt of the universe ! " It was a long time before it became evident to me that these contradictions which Pascal discerned of men in the aggregate are true of every man.   Each individual has within himself, latent or operant, all the characteristics of the race, which opportunity or circumstance (more enduring than opportunity), brings out.   Byron saw that man was " half dust, half deity."   Like Carlyle, a man may be at once brutal, contemptuous, and tender—unjust, yet loving justice—reverencing right in man, yet exhorting them to despotism.   Seeing that every person possesses all the qualities of mankind in proportion, what remains but to look with unexpectant eyes upon all, waiting to see what baser elements have been repressed or transmuted by wise education and noble conditions of life, or what lofty principles have been exalted and confirmed.   Only on such considerations can a man protect himself from mistaken judgments and irreparable disappointment.

It is less difficult to inspire persons with the passion for knowledge than to induce them to extend the advantage of it to others.   Too many despise those in the condition from which they have escaped ; their contemptible philosophy is that of the Coptic song which tells us that everywhere

> " This, and but this, was the gospel alway :
> Fools from their folly 'tis hopeless to stay,
> Mules will be mules by the law of their mulishness ;
> Then be advised and leave fools to foolishness—
> What from an ass can be got but a bray ? "

But mankind are not asses, though he is who thinks them so. Certainly there are men of mulish minds, and their muline judgments have to be tolerated on grounds of heredity.   But none knew better than Goethe, who wrote the Coptic song, that the average man could be exalted.   To this he contributed by his splendid genius.   He who alleges the unimprovability of others as an excuse for his doing nothing for them—and thinks only of himself—forfeits his right to exist.   There is no place or need for him in another life ; and were he raised from the dead, it would bring resurrection itself into contempt.

Once I had opportunity of aid unforeseen by me.   A valued friend (Mr. W. H. Dingnan), whom the Government of the day desired to requite for public service, generously proposed that I should be requited in his stead.   It being intended, I wrote to

Mr. Gladstone " not to give heed to it as I could not accept anything. I had spent many years in teaching working men the lesson of self-help, and that it was the duty of the people to support the State, and not the State the people. Should blindness come again or age render me incapable of my accustomed work, I might think differently." Age, with noiseless and unnoticed steps has arrived, and friends with it, who have mitigated its disablement. In 1876 Mr. John Stephens Storr, and in 1888 Mr. Thomas Allsop, were the cause of it. On each occasion a Committee, whose names will always be in my mind,[1] enabled all future work by me to depend on choice and pleasure.

A curious feature was this: Some whom I had served, not without cost and peril to myself when I might rightly have served myself instead, were as the Levite and passed by on the other side ; while others I had never known, even by name, whom I had never seen, upon whom I had no claim, whom I never had opportunity of serving, with others whose thoughts were alien to mine, showed me a disinterested friendliness. The world is a field sprinkled with generous seed which springs up in unexpected and unknown places. Whatever I have done since, I owe to these diversified friends. They gave me length of days and pleasure greater than they can know.

Every one who has taste in ideas, and is above adopting second-hand opinions—because they can be had cheap—incurs trouble in selecting those of the best quality and testing them himself. He who does this has trouble, but his pleasure and pride in true thinking is greater than the slovenly and shabby minded ever know. If a man could believe in everybody's creed, it would make things pleasanter in this world, and perhaps safer for the next ; since surely some of them must be the right ones. But he thinks meanly of the arbiters of Heaven if he supposes its doors are open to applicants of indolence, calcu-

---

[1] Among them were George Anderson, Robert Applegarth, Major Evans Bell, Lord Brassey, Rev. Stopford A. Brooke, Thomas Burt, M.P., Right Hon. Joseph Chamberlain, M.P., Right Hon. Sir Charles Dilke, Bart., Rev. J. R. Green, Judge Hughes, Walter Morrison, M.P., E. Vansittart Neale, Rev. Joseph Parker, D.D. To Drs. George Bird and Hugh Campbell I owed the recovery of my health, and to Mr. Brudenell Carter the restoration of my sight. Nor can I be unmindful that Professors Bain, Huxley, Newman, and Tyndall, that Harriet Martineau, Herbert Spencer, and many others, were among those to whose friendship I was indebted.

lation and low taste. The " land of the leal " belongs to those
who, like Savonarola, judge not authors according to their fame,
nor accept opinions because they are in vogue, but always keep
their eyes fixed on truth and reason ; not to those who, in
Diderot's words, think it more prudent to be mad with the
mad than be wise by themselves. This is my apology to the
reader for that wilfulness of opinion which I fear has often
perplexed or perturbed him in these pages.

THE END.

INDEX.

UNWIN BROTHERS, LIMITED, THE GRESHAM PRESS, WOKING AND LONDON.